TIMES THE FEAR

Lions
An Imprint of HarperCollinsPublishers

More heart-stopping Nightmares...

Horrorscope *Nicholas Adams*
I.O.U. *Nicholas Adams*
The Curse *Cynthia Blair*
The Trap *Cynthia Blair*
The Dark Room *Janice Harrell*
Bloodlines *Janice Harrell*
No Way Out *Beverley Hastings*
Class Trip *Bebe Faas Rice*
The Teacher *Joseph Locke*
Nightmare Inn *T.S. Rue*
The Pool *T.S. Rue*
The Attic *T.S. Rue*
Tales from Nightmare Inn *T.S. Rue*
Three Tales of Terror
Bebe Faas Rice/Nicholas Adams
Three Books of Blood *M.C. Sumner*

NIGHTMARES

3

TIMES THE FEAR

BLOOD BROTHERS
Nicholas Adams

LOVE YOU TO DEATH
Bebe Faas Rice

DEADLY STRANGER
M.C. Sumner

Lions
An Imprint of HarperCollinsPublishers

Blood Brothers, Love You to Death and *Deadly Stranger*
first published in the USA in l994, 1994 and 1993 by
HarperCollins Publishers Inc.
First published in Great Britain in Lions in 1994,1994 and
1993
This three in one edition first published in 1995
1 3 5 7 9 10 8 6 4 2

Lions is an imprint of
HarperCollins Publishers Ltd.,
77-85 Fulham Palace Road,
Hammersmith, London W6 8JB

Text copyright © 1994,1994 and 1993
Susan Albert and Daniel Weiss Associates Inc.,
Bebe Faas Rice and Daniel Weiss Associates Inc. and
Daniel Weiss Associates Inc.

The authors assert their moral right to be
identified as the authors of the works.

Printed and bound in Great Britain
by HarperCollins Manufacturing Ltd., Glasgow

NIGHTMARES

Blood Brothers

"*I have to deliver a message to somebody named Susan. I can't see you or hear you, Susan, but I have the feeling that you're out there, watching.*" He stopped and rubbed the stubble on his chin. "*I really hope you're watching,*" he said wearily. "*Susan, wherever you are, whoever you are, you're in danger, you and your friends. You guys are next.*"

NIGHTMARES

BLOOD BROTHER

Nicholas Adams

For Susan and Bill Albert—
thanks for all your help.

One

―――――――

"We'll be back in a moment with our wrap-up story for this Tuesday night. This is KGTX-TV, Channel Five, Galveston, Texas. Stay with us." The pretty blond anchorwoman smiled into the television camera as a commercial came on.

Susan Scott frowned as she got off the sofa and went into the kitchen. She'd meant to turn on the television at ten to catch the local news, but she'd been so busy moving furniture and hanging curtains in her new apartment that she'd forgotten. Now it was almost ten thirty, and she'd missed most of the report. Oh well. It was summer in Galveston, and nothing much was going on.

Susan opened the refrigerator and took out a soft drink. Her frown changed to a smile as she sat

1

down at the small table where she would eat most of her meals. She pushed her long brown hair out of her eyes and tried to stuff it back into her bandanna. Sure, the kitchen was small, with barely enough room to turn around between the sink and the refrigerator, but the room's size made it efficient—there was only a step between the stove and the refrigerator—and the yellow-checked curtains and framed sunflower print over the table gave it a cheerful sunshiny glow, even at night.

Carrying her drink, Susan went back into the other room. This one was just as cozy as the kitchen. There was the sofa bed, one of those foldaway things, that she'd bought at a flea market. Her sister-in-law had given her the battered coffee table. Her friend Angela had found the pole lamp and the stuffed chair with the saggy cushion at a garage sale. Susan had already covered the back of the sofa with a pretty pink-and-white quilt, and the coffee table would look fine once she refinished it; a little extra stuffing would do wonders for the chair cushion.

Susan sat down on the sofa and leaned back with a tired, happy sigh. She knew she was going to have to devote most of her off-work hours for the next couple of weeks to cleaning and painting, but it was all hers, and that made the wonderful difference.

Not that living with her brother Mack, his wife

Betty, and their two kids, Pete and Randy, had been bad. She really was grateful that they'd been willing and able to give her a home after her parents had been killed in a car accident during her freshman year of high school. Now Susan was seventeen, a grown up, and living alone meant that she was able to take care of herself.

The phone rang and she picked it up. "Hi," Mack said. "Everything okay out there?"

Susan grinned. Mack was a cop and took his vow to serve and protect rather seriously, especially when it came to his kid sister. "Are you checking up on me all the way from El Paso?" she asked.

Mack chuckled. "You bet. Just because I'm on vacation from the force doesn't mean I can't still take care of you, you know. I'm still your big brother, and you're not too big for me to check up on. Even if you have moved out."

"I haven't moved very far," Susan reminded him. "I'm right here over your garage."

"Well, I just wanted to make sure you were settling in okay," Mack said. "Betty and the boys send hugs, and me too. Lock up before you go to bed. Okay?"

"Sure. Thanks, Mack," Susan said. "Good night."

"Good night, Susan. We'll see you in a couple of days."

She was smiling when she put down the phone. She was happiest when she was on top of things and in control. And at that moment she was *very* happy. Everything in her life seemed to be falling into place exactly the way she'd planned.

"And now," the anchorwoman announced brightly, "we take you live to a late-breaking story."

Susan turned back to the television. As she did, the screen flickered and the lights in the apartment dimmed momentarily. Susan frowned. When Mack got back, she'd ask him to show her where the circuit breakers were. She probably ought to lay in a supply of candles, too. Now that she was on her own, it was a good idea to prepare for emergencies. Like blackouts and hurricanes.

The lights were burning brightly again, and she was relieved she wouldn't have to worry about the circuit breaker tonight. Or the weather. The TV meteorologist had predicted warm, sunny weather for the next few days. The tourists would love it. They'd ride their rented pedal-powered surreys up and down the busy sidewalks and crowd the beaches with their beach umbrellas and line up by the hundreds to ride the water slide and the bumper cars at Stewart Beach.

Not all the beaches were crowded, though. On the television the scene had shifted to a deserted, windswept stretch of sand. Susan thought how odd that was, considering how beautiful the day had been. A reporter in a jacket and tie stood somberly in the glare of the TV lights. His pale gray-green eyes narrowed as he looked straight into the camera. Behind him, Susan could make out the glimmer of waves and hear the wind in the microphone.

"This is Drew Morris, live from the southeastern end of Galveston Island." The reporter turned slightly and gestured at a group of uniformed men digging into the sand under the glare of floodlights. "We're just off East Beach Drive, behind the SeaWall Condominiums. Earlier this evening two local residents found a shallow grave on the beach here. A few minutes ago police uncovered a body."

Susan stared at Drew Morris's face. The reporter must be new—she couldn't remember seeing him before. And she would *definitely* have remembered him, she told herself. He was dark-haired and good-looking, and he had a deeply resonant voice. It was a description that could fit a half-dozen TV journalists, Susan thought. She leaned forward. What made Drew Morris different was his eyes. There was nothing casual about those eyes. They were probing, powerfully intent—perhaps even a little sad, Susan thought, as if the story he was reporting had some sort of personal significance for him. He turned back to face the camera, and those eyes seemed to fix on hers, to demand her attention.

"The body," he said, "was that of a young man."

Susan shivered a little and turned away from the TV. East Beach Drive? That was only a little way from the motel where her friend Frederica Gardner lived with her mother. Freddie always jogged on the beach at night, that is, when she wasn't singing with one of the local rock groups. Because Freddie had recently auditioned for a new job, she wasn't singing this week. She was probably out there now. She'd be sure to see the cops and the TV cameras. Maybe she was watching Drew Morris doing his live spot right this minute. Susan wondered if his eyes were as deep and mysterious in real life as they were on TV.

The reporter spoke again. "The police haven't yet released the man's identity or the cause of death," he said. There was a tone of deep sadness in his voice. "However, a police spokeswoman said that there were no obvious signs of foul play. But I find this whole case rather suspicious."

Susan couldn't turn away from the screen. Those eyes, those pale gray-green eyes, were fixed on hers with a commanding authority. She sucked in her breath, unaccountably sure that he was speaking directly to *her*. The skin on her arms prickled up into little goose bumps. Of course, that was a silly idea—he was just talking to the camera, the way TV journalists always did. Still, she couldn't

6

escape the conviction that his message was aimed at her, and her alone.

"There are many unknowns in this bizarre case," Drew Morris was saying. "Why would someone bury a young man's body on this windswept beach? Was that person hoping that the secret in this grave would be safe for all eternity?"

He paused for the space of a breath, and then went on, more slowly. "What kind of person would commit another human being to an unmarked grave? And why? These are important questions that demand to be answered." His eyes, steady and unwavering, bored into Susan's, as if he could really see her, as if he could see *through* her. His voice was urgent, pleading. "Please, join me tomorrow night for further details. Maybe together we can solve this mystery."

Another commercial came on. Susan leaned forward and shut the set off. Drew Morris, whoever he was, certainly had a talent for dramatization. It wasn't completely unheard of to find a body on Galveston beach. It didn't happen every day, but careless people sometimes fell off the jetty or off a party boat, and it certainly wouldn't take much of a storm to drift beach sand over a drowning victim. In fact, there had been a storm last week. It could have happened then.

But this new reporter had made this gruesome discovery seem like the strangest, most important thing that had ever happened in Galveston. What's more, he'd made it seem important to *Susan*, as if she were the only person in his audience. He had ordered *her* to listen to his follow-up tomorrow night, as if only she could help him make sense of it all.

Susan stood up and started for the kitchen. She felt chilly, and she shivered. She'd warm herself up with a cup of hot chocolate before she went to bed. Then she stopped. Hot chocolate? In June? That was silly.

Drew Morris had certainly made his point with her. She'd tune in tomorrow night. But whether it was to learn more about the mysterious grave on the beach or to see Drew Morris again, she couldn't be sure. There was one thing she was sure of, she decided, as she checked the lock on the back door and shut off the kitchen light. Drew Morris had the most compelling eyes she had ever seen. Eyes that seemed to look right through her. Eyes that held some deep and impenetrable sadness.

She saw those eyes again that night.

She saw those eyes in her dreams.

Two

Frederica Gardner—Freddie to her friends—thrust her pencil into her curly, copper-red hair, tied her ruffled red-and-white apron around her waist, and touched up her eyeshadow with her little finger. It was Wednesday morning, and her eight-hour shift at the Pizzeria was about to begin. Freddie let out an explosive sigh and shook her head, making a face at the mirror that hung on the wall in the small storage room behind the kitchen. Eleven to nine, with two hours off in the middle of the afternoon. What a drag. Pushing pizzas for the better part of the day. It was too bad that somebody hadn't invented a way you could make honest money without working. There wasn't much to look forward to on her shift except flirting with a few cute

9

customers, like that cool-looking new guy with the dark glasses and the slow, moody smile who'd been in twice last week.

She grinned at the green-eyed girl in the mirror, her copper hair like a curly halo around her freckled face. Yeah. If she could make a living doing vocals with Lenny's rock group, that would almost be like not working. Singing was fun. She considered, sobering a little. No, singing was more than fun. Singing was her life. When she sang, she poured all her feelings, her entire soul, into her music. As far as Freddie was concerned, all music was soul music.

"Hey, Freddie," Angela Sanchez said, coming into the storage room. She hung up her sweater and began twisting her long black hair into a knot at the back of her neck, securing it with a comb.

Angela always looked super with her hair done up that way, Freddie thought with a stab of envy. She shoved a stubborn red curl behind her ear. It didn't hurt that Angie had a great body, either. She wore clothes that hid it, but when you had a figure like that, it was hard to keep it a secret.

"Did you hear from Lenny last night?" Angie asked.

Freddie couldn't help smiling back, even though it wasn't a subject she particularly wanted to talk about. Angie was one of those rare people who make the day seem sunnier just by being there. Maybe it was because she always managed to look on the bright side of things, or because she somehow understood what was on your mind before you unloaded it.

Still, Freddie wasn't sure there was a bright side where Lenny was concerned, and her smile faded. "No, I haven't heard from him yet. What a jerk. I'm beginning to think he's not even going to call. He's probably going to pick that other girl—the one who doubles on guitar." *And who worships the ground he walks on*, she added silently to herself.

She had to admit it, she hadn't knocked them dead at the audition. She frowned at herself in the mirror. She'd looked good, and she'd picked her very strongest songs, the ones she practiced at home with a tape, but when the big moment arrived, she'd been thrown by the band's tempo. And by Lenny's ego. She'd flubbed the first number big time, and things sort of fell apart after that. She'd blown it. She hadn't heard from Lenny since.

Angie turned and put her arms around Freddie. "Hey, listen," she said softly, "don't worry so much about it, okay? I'm sure things will turn out. Maybe Lenny and his band aren't right for you. Maybe that's why the audition didn't go the way you wanted."

"You mean, like we weren't in sync or something?"

Angie nodded. "It's very important for people to fit together. Brad says bands can't make good music if they aren't on the same wavelength. If they don't have the same style, the same ideas. I guess musicians are sensitive to stuff like that."

"Yeah, maybe," Freddie said slowly. She wasn't exactly sure what made Brad—Angie's new boyfriend—an authority on harmony. He didn't strike Freddie as being terribly in tune to Angie and her feelings.

But in this case, Freddie told herself, the theory clicked. Lenny was such a jerk, she probably wouldn't ever have gotten in harmony with him, at least not in the way *he'd* want her to. It made her feel better to think that it wasn't lack of talent that had made her bomb the audition. Or her appearance. She gave herself another critical look in the mirror. She didn't exactly look like a rock star. Stupid red hair and a hard, athletic look earned on the tennis court and the track. Not exactly a sex symbol. Unfortunately, that was what Lenny was looking for. Sexy and older. Maybe she should hide out for a year.

"The more I think about it, the more I think you may be right. I didn't fit with Lenny's group," she asserted, leaning against the wall and watching while Angie put on her apron. "They're a pretty tough bunch of guys. If it came right down to it, I'm not sure I'd like to sing in some of the joints where they play. Or wear the kind of clothes they wear." *Or have to stay with them in a darkened basement late at night for rehearsal.* She looked questioningly at Angie. "Know what I mean?"

Angie nodded. "I know." She laughed and straightened her collar. "It's too bad Susan and I don't have your talent for music, Freddie. The three of us would make a great group. *We're* in tune. And we all have the same great fashion sense." Angie dramatically modeled her checked apron as she runway-walked across the room.

"In tune with what?" Susan Scott asked, coming through the door and narrowly missing Angie's kick and turn. Susan was already wearing her apron, and her long brown hair was weaved into a French braid that made her look older than she was. She glanced at her watch. "You certainly don't mean in tune with the clock. If we don't start loading that salad table, we're all in deep trouble."

Freddie grinned. "If we put a group together," she told Angie, "I vote for Susan for drummer."

"Drummer?" Angie asked.

"Yeah," Susan said. "Why the drummer?" She climbed up on a step stool and took a package of napkins off a shelf.

"Because she's got a good sense of timing," Freddie told them. "She keeps us moving." With a giggle she ducked the package of paper napkins Susan tossed at her.

13

"You better believe it," Susan said. "If I didn't keep you moving, who would? You two are so laid-back, you'd be fired tomorrow." Susan thought for a moment. "No. Make that yesterday."

Freddie grinned and picked up the napkins. "You're right," she conceded. "Laid-back and loving it."

"Come on," Angie said, putting her arms around both of them. "Time for the salad squad. Spinach, here we come."

Laughing, the three girls went into the kitchen, where a couple of other people were already at work mixing pizza dough. Susan opened the walk-in cooler and pulled out bowls of chopped veggies. The girls began to load the bowls onto a cart for the salad bar.

A few minutes later, Susan paused beside Freddie. "Did you run on the beach last night, Freddie?"

Freddie added a bowl of cold pasta to the cart. "Yeah, sure." In her otherwise haphazard life, running was the most disciplined thing she did. It helped her keep her weight down—weight could be a problem, working at the Pizzeria. Whoever saw a fat rock star? Opera and jazz, maybe, but not rock.

"I went out about nine thirty," she added. "I got back in time for the late show."

Susan pushed the cart into the dining room

where Angela was stacking plates at one end of the salad bar. "Then you must have seen the police digging on the beach behind the SeaWall Condos. Did you stop for a look?"

Freddie started unloading the cart, helping herself to a small pickle. "Police? Digging? I didn't see any digging."

Susan paused and turned. "You didn't see a bunch of cops and a TV crew? Off East Beach Drive?"

Freddie shook her red curls emphatically. "Nope. No cops, no crew." She put down a bowl of radishes, sticking a couple in her pocket. She couldn't get fat on radishes if she tried. "I'm pretty sure I would have noticed something like that," she added. "The beach was totally deserted all the way up to Apffel Park. Three miles of me and the moon and a few drowsy gulls. My favorite kind of night."

Susan stared at her. "No TV crew? But he *said*—" She stopped, looking puzzled. "Are you sure?"

Freddie frowned. "Susan, believe me. There was no TV crew. Unless they were shooting with hidden cameras. You know, like they were buried in the sand or something. Or maybe they were shooting with a periscope! Or hiding in the dunes, disguised as beach grass. Or maybe a creature from—"

Susan smiled. "Okay, okay. I guess I made a mistake," she said slowly. "But I could have sworn—"

"No swearing on the job," Angie said with a laugh.

"Right," Freddie said. "Maybe you just need a good night's sleep." She turned away to push the empty cart back into the kitchen, so she couldn't see the look of fear that had come into Susan's usually calm hazel eyes.

Three

Angela Sanchez put one pizza down in front of her aunt Carlota and handed the other to her younger sister Juanita. She liked it when her family came into the Pizzeria to eat. Nita was her favorite sister, and Aunt Carlota, who lived next door to Angie, was her favorite aunt. In fact, the three of them looked a great deal alike, with long black hair and big brown eyes.

"Would you two like to come over tonight?" Aunt Carlota asked. She leaned forward with a conspiratorial smile. "Don't tell your father, but I'm having a few friends over for an evening of fortune-telling. Maybe you'd like to have a glimpse into your futures, no?"

Angie laughed. "Are you kidding? I wouldn't

tell Dad that—not if I wanted to come, anyway."
Her father accused Aunt Carlota, who was Angie's
mother's sister, of being a witch. Actually, Aunt
Carlota saw herself as a *curandera*, a woman who
practices white magic. She was able to use the tra-
ditional healing herbs, potions, and amulets that
had been a way of life in Old Mexico. Friends and
family came to Aunt Carlota for all kinds of mysti-
cal and magical help—from casting spells to healing illnesses to taking a look into the future. It
made Angie's father furious. It was a lot of superstitious nonsense, he said. Educated people
shouldn't have anything to do with those old
ways. And he wanted his children to be educated.
But Aunt Carlota was a kind and gentle person,
and Angie liked her. If she was a *curandera* as well,
that was fine with Angie.

"Will you come?" Aunt Carlota asked.

"I can't. I've got a date," Nita said, digging into
her pizza. "Sorry."

Angie shook her head. "I can't make it tonight,
either," she said. She leaned forward with the
same conspiratorial smile. "Don't tell Dad, but I'm
seeing Brad tonight."

She glanced at the clock. It was almost seven.
Brad would be along pretty soon. He always ate
dinner at the Pizzeria, and he always got plenty of
extra pizza if he wanted it, no charge, as long as
Gwen, her boss, wasn't looking.

Angie and Brad Rayburn hadn't been dating long, and she'd been happy since the beginning. Brad was so low-key and easygoing. He treated her well and always told her how beautiful she was and how much he cared for her.

"Your secret's safe with me," Aunt Carlota said with a smile. She knew about Angie and Brad, and if she disapproved, she didn't say so—unlike Angie's father, who had a fit when he found out his daughter was getting involved with an unemployed musician.

Juanita smiled at her. "So what do you want me to tell Dad tonight?"

Angie sighed. "I guess you can tell him I'm at Susan's, helping with her new apartment." She didn't like lying to her father, but if that was the only way she could see Brad, well, she had to do it. Angie wasn't a rebel, but she figured that people ought to be able to do what they wanted to do. And that went for Brad and his music, too. She wasn't that into Brad's sound, but if he was, and he didn't make her hang out with his strange musician friends, that was fine with her.

"Well, I hope you have a nice time. Stop by and see me when you can," Aunt Carlota said.

"I'll come by in the morning," Angie said. She glanced over her shoulder toward the kitchen. Gwen always managed to show up at the worst times and give her waitresses that I-know-you've-

19

been-goofing-off-and-I-don't-like-it look. "I guess I'd better get back to work before I get in trouble." She said good-bye and went back into the kitchen, where a rack of pizzas was coming out of the oven. As she began slicing one, Susan came up behind her.

"Angie, did you watch the Channel Five late news last night?"

Angie turned around. "No," she said. "The TV was on, but Dad was watching the Astros game. Why?"

"I still don't get that report I saw about that grave on the beach."

"Sorry, Susan." Angela shook her head. "I don't know any more about it than Freddie did. I know I didn't see anything in the paper about it this morning."

"Oh," Susan said absently. She looked around. "Where is Freddie, anyway?"

Angela started slicing another pizza. "I saw her go into the dining room a minute ago." She smiled a little. "That guy's back."

Susan brushed back an escaped strand of brown hair and tried to tuck it into her braid. "What guy?" she asked, slightly distracted.

"Don't you remember? It's all she talked about last week. The guy with the dark glasses who's been flirting with her." Once Angie and Brad had gotten serious, she'd stopped noticing the cute customers. But this one had caught her attention, mainly because he'd never taken his sunglasses off. Which was a little strange, she thought. The dining room was pretty dark, even in the afternoon. She guessed he thought sunglasses made him look cool.

"Oh, yeah, *that* one." Susan raised an eyebrow. "Are you sure that it wasn't Freddie who was flirting with him, instead of the other way around?"

"She probably was," Angie said with a grin. "So what else is new, huh?"

At that moment Freddie came into the kitchen. She was smiling a strange half smile, and her eyes were glazed over, as if she were sleepwalking. She bumped into a table, and a pitcher of water rocked and nearly tumbled over.

"Hey, watch where you're going, Freddie," Susan said, grabbing the pitcher.

"Huh?" Freddie asked. Her eyes focused, and she looked around as if she'd just woken up. "Oh, wow, you guys," she breathed. "I'm in love! He's wonderful! We're going on a date. Tomorrow night. After the audition. I have an audition. And a date."

Angie stared at her. "Love? How can you be in love? You haven't even gone out with him yet."

"Are you sure it isn't heartburn instead of love?" Susan asked skeptically. "After all, you have been chowing on those jalapeños all day.

And what's this about an audition?"

Freddie wrinkled her nose. "Just because you're both too self-controlled ever to fall in love at first sight doesn't mean that *I* can't." She leaned forward eagerly. "Not only is this guy super-sexy and *extremely* cool, but he's got his own band! And guess what! His group's opening a club right here in Galveston!"

"His group?" Susan inquired. She scratched her head, pretending to be puzzled. "What kind of group? Social group? Study group?" She grinned. "A group of groupies? A group of guppies? A group—"

"Ha ha," Freddie cut in sarcastically. "You are *so* funny." She turned to Angie. "They call themselves Blood Brothers." She clapped her hands excitedly. "*And* they're looking for a lead vocalist! I'm going to audition tomorrow night. Before the beach party he's giving." She trilled a little tune. "He thinks I've got a great voice."

"How does he know?" Susan asked. "Did you hum a few bars of the menu?"

"Oh, Freddie," Angie exclaimed, feeling Freddie's excitement. "It's your big chance! See? I *told* you it was a good thing you didn't hit it off with Lenny."

"And not only a vocalist," Freddie rushed on, her eyes sparkling. "The Brothers are looking for a guitarist, too. I told him about Brad."

"You did?" Angie asked. She clapped her hands. "That's terrific!"

"Yeah. And he says he's eager to meet him," Freddie says. "He'd like him to audition right away. Like tomorrow night." She grabbed Angie's hand. "Hey, maybe we can combine the auditions and the date. Want to double?"

"I wish I could," Angie said. "But tomorrow night is my sister's sixteenth birthday party. Maybe after we—"

"Hang on a minute," Susan broke in. "Isn't it a little weird that a rock group is opening a club?"

"Maybe they've made a lot of money," Angie suggested, thinking how great it would be for Brad to get steady work. "Maybe they're tired of being on the road and they're ready to settle down." A job in an established club, right here in Galveston, would be a hundred times better than pickup work. Maybe her father wouldn't object so much if Brad had a job like that.

"But if they made a lot of money," Susan said, "we'd know about it. I mean, we'd have heard of them." She frowned. "Blood Brothers? Doesn't ring a bell."

"So since when have you been an expert on rock groups?" Freddie demanded. She leaned against the wall and fanned herself with her hand, closing her eyes dramatically. "Wow. I tell you guys, he is totally amazing!"

Susan stepped to the door and peered into the dining room. "So that's Santa Claus, huh? The guy with the black hair?"

Freddie came up behind her. "Yeah, that's him. Isn't he cute?"

"I don't know about this guy, Freddie," she said doubtfully. "Are you sure you want to get involved with somebody you're working for?"

Freddie bristled. "So what's wrong with that?"

"Do you really think getting involved with a Blood Brother is a good idea?"

"Just because you don't go for the name of his group—"

"It's not that," Susan said, looking troubled. "It doesn't feel . . . it doesn't feel right, somehow. He's spooky-looking."

Freddie grinned. "Yeah, he's spooky, all right," she said. "Gives me goose bumps. Even makes me feel dizzy when I get close to him, like in the movies." She closed her eyes with a dreamy sigh. "This guy is so sexy. I can't believe he's for real."

Angie stepped to the door to see for herself. The guy was sitting at table twenty-two, in the farthest, darkest corner. The dining room was gloomy, as usual, and she could barely make out his face. She leaned forward. He looked younger than she would have thought, for somebody who had made enough money to buy a club. Late teens, probably. His face was lean and high-cheekboned, and his jaw was cut in a firm, sharp line. His black hair was swept back, and his eyebrows were a straight, dark slash across his face. He was wearing dark glasses and a black T-shirt. As she watched, his head swiveled in her direction, as if he was aware that she was studying him.

Angie swallowed. No wonder Freddie had gone overboard. Once you started looking at this guy, it was hard to look away. At the same time, there was something else. Something that made you *want* to look away. She shivered. Of course, she hadn't had a lot of experience with guys. Her father had seen to that. Maybe that was it. Maybe this guy was totally ordinary, and she was overreacting. She turned away from the door.

"So, Freddie," Angie said, "what's this guy's name?"

"His name?" Freddie asked dreamily.

"His *name*," Susan said. She snapped her fingers in front of Freddie's face. "You know, what people call him when they want to get his attention. Or when they say yes after he's asked them for a date."

"Oh, yeah." Freddie sighed. She straightened up. "It's Flint."

"Flint?" Angie asked.

"I think it fits," Susan said with a shrug.

25

"Well," Freddie said, "at least I've got an audition and a date. What have you got?"

Susan looked at her watch. "I've got seven o'clock," she said. "Time for us to get on the register, Angie." She grinned at Freddie, who was still too distracted to notice. "Hang in there, Juliet."

Four

―――――――――

Brad Rayburn leaned across the counter at the cash register as Angie took his order. In a couple of minutes she'd bring him a large pizza, double cheese and everything but anchovies, just the way he liked it. Not bad for two bucks.

Brad grinned. He knew that in the beginning Angie had felt uneasy about their little arrangement. She didn't like stealing, even if it was from a witch like Gwen. But when he'd pointed out that she got an all-you-want-to-eat lunch for free and that she never ate anything more than a little salad, she'd agreed that it was okay. He was taking her lunch, that was all. Angie was so crazy about him that if he could justify things, he could usually get Angie to go along with anything.

Well, almost anything.

Angie was saying something to him, half whispering as she handed him the change from his five. Brad wasn't listening. His grin had changed into a small frown. He took the coins, letting his eyes linger on Angie's pretty throat, where the gold chain of her crucifix disappeared under her blouse. You'd think, when a girl had a body like Angie's, she'd show it a little more. Not that he was after only one thing with Angie. She had a lot going for her, like those terrific big brown eyes, and her graceful, hip-swaying walk, and the soft, sweet way she had of letting him know that he was somebody special. And she was fun to hang around with.

Angie was still talking when Brad tuned her back in. "Sorry," he said, smiling. "Guess I wasn't paying attention. At least not to what you were saying."

Angie got his point and blushed. "I said," she whispered breathlessly, "that the guy over in the corner is opening a club here in Galveston. He's got a band called Blood Brothers. He told Freddie they're looking for a guitarist. He wants to talk to you about an audition."

That got his attention. He stared at her. "An audition?" he asked incredulously. "No kidding! How'd he find out about me?"

"Freddie told him," Angie said. Gwen was

coming out of the kitchen, and she stepped back hurriedly, raising her voice. "Your pizza will be out in a minute, sir. Please have a seat and I'll bring you your drink."

Brad turned around, squinting in the dim light. The guy at the back table smiled at him and raised his hand in a lazy, beckoning gesture. He wore dark glasses, which wasn't too odd, considering he was a rocker. Not only did musicians tend to be a bit eccentric, but they could be hard to get along with, too. That was why he'd been out of a job for the past couple of months—because the leader of the last band he'd worked with had been such a jerk that nobody could get along with him. Brad had given Angie some story about his style not matching the band's. Musical integrity, he'd called it. But the truth, plain and simple, was that they had fired him for missing too many rehearsals.

"Hello, Bradley," the guy with the dark glasses said as Brad reached his table. His voice was mellow—smooth and deep. A baritone. Probably lead vocalist as well as head honcho. "I believe you're the man I've been waiting for."

"Oh, yeah?" Brad asked carelessly. He sat down, careful not to betray any eagerness. In this business you played it close to the heart. You didn't give away any advantage. "Brad," he said. He hated being called Bradley. "My name's Brad."

The guy smiled slightly, as if he were amused at something. "Flint," he said.

Brad stirred uneasily as Angie set a glass down in front of him, smiled, and disappeared again. "Okay," he said. "Flint." It was those glasses. Brad couldn't see the guy's eyes. He liked to be able to see the person he was talking to, see whether his eyes and his mouth were telling the same story. He shifted again. "So what makes you think we can do business?" he asked. "What kind of music are you into?"

Flint didn't answer his question. "I understand," he said softly, "that you play guitar." His voice was oddly accented. Maybe he was some kind of foreigner. European, maybe. They had some hot groups in Germany. England, too. "I understand that you are a very good guitar player."

Brad turned the cold glass in his fingers. "Yeah," he said. "*Lead* guitar." No point in letting this guy Flint get the idea that he'd do backup work—although he probably would, if it meant steady work. But that wasn't the way you started negotiating. You started at the top. That way you were in control.

"That's good," Flint said approvingly. "I would be interested in hearing you play, Bradley. My group is called Blood Brothers."

Brad shrugged. "Original name," he said. The last group had called themselves Bad News. And that's exactly what they turned out to be. He leaned forward. "What kind of music do you do?" If they weren't in the same groove, this was a waste of time.

"Our name is unique," Flint replied, "as is our music." He smiled then. Or rather, he stretched his lips across his teeth. Brad wasn't sure if it was a smile or not, since he couldn't see the eyes. "I can guarantee," he added, "that you will find working with us far more rewarding than your last employment. Infinitely more rewarding." The smile again, if that's what it was. "I can almost guarantee, Bradley, that you will not be forced to leave us."

Brad scowled, forgetting his question about the music. "Did Freddie tell you that?" he asked. His scowl deepened. He didn't think Freddie even knew about his getting fired, but the music scene in Galveston was pretty small, and word could have gotten around.

"No. Frederica didn't tell me. Nobody had to tell me," Flint said. He leaned back in his chair and gracefully stroked his black hair. His fingers were long and thin, the nails carefully manicured and sharply pointed.

Brad wiped the palms of his hands on his jeans. This entire exchange was making him more than a little nervous.

Not raising his voice, Flint went on. "Furthermore, Bradley, I am quite certain that

31

should you decide to join our group, you will find yourself anxious to practice with us. I do not foresee the regularity and quality of your participation being an issue for concern."

Brad blinked. Definitely a foreigner. People around Galveston didn't talk like that. Who was this guy? And how did he know so much about Brad? He was beginning to feel very uncomfortable. Maybe he'd better—

"Don't bother yourself about it, Bradley," Flint said. He leaned forward and touched Brad's hand with one long finger. "It is of no consequence."

Suddenly Brad found himself agreeing. Whatever had been on his mind—bad news, good news—it wasn't important. What was important now was that this guy Flint was offering him the possibility of work. Real work. That would make Angie happy. Maybe, if the job turned out to be steady, she'd agree to get an apartment with him. Of course, she'd probably want to be engaged first, but he could handle that. If he had a regular gig, he could handle just about anything, no sweat.

"Sure, Flint," he said easily. "Yeah, you're right. A hundred percent right. Say, what about that audition, huh? And what's this about a club you're buying? Here in Galveston?" It was the right place, that was for sure. Lots of teens with nothing to do came down from Houston every weekend, looking for action. Big-money teens. You could tell by the sports cars, dune buggies, and big-wheel pickups that jammed the beach. Brad smiled. If he had a regular gig, maybe he'd get a sports car too.

Flint nodded. "Yes, Bradley. That is correct. In Galveston. Our new club will be called Dark of the Moon." He smiled. "We are, shall we say, targeting the teenage audience. Particularly the tourists. You will be available for an audition tomorrow night?"

It was more of a statement than a question. Brad seemed to remember that Angie had been planning something, but he couldn't quite think what it was. "That's cool," he said. He figured he could reschedule whatever it was that Angie had been planning.

"Perhaps," Flint said, spreading his hands on the table in front of him, "we could arrange a small party before the audition. A beach party, say, for some of your friends and some of mine."

"Hey, yeah," Brad said. "A beach party."

"Fine," Flint said. "Around eight? There is a nice spot on East Beach Drive. I will arrange for the food and drink. After the party we will hold your audition at the house my group has rented."

Brad frowned, still trying to remember what it was that he and Angie had been planning. Whatever it was, it probably wasn't too important, or he wouldn't have forgotten it. Anyway, he couldn't very well say no to a party before his big chance, could he? Of course not. That would be just plain stupid.

"Frederica has already agreed to come," Flint said. "Would you please see to it that Susan is there as well? I have a friend who would very much like to meet her. And, of course, you will bring Angela. Even though she doesn't swim, I'm sure she will enjoy the evening."

The skin prickled on the back of Brad's neck. Angie hated that she couldn't swim. It wasn't something she bragged about. "Hey, how do you know so much about us?" he demanded. "I mean, if you're new in town, how'd you find out about—"

Flint touched Brad's hand again. "These questions are not important," he admonished in a soft, reassuring voice. "Just be sure Angela comes with you."

Brad found that he had no more questions.

"But, Brad," Angie objected, feeling frustrated, "we *can't* go to the beach tomorrow night!" She leaned back against the car seat and looked out at the silvery glaze of moonlight on the water of the bay. She and Brad were parked at their favorite spot, where they could see a long stretch of quiet beach, deserted now in the moonlight. "It's Juanita's sixteenth birthday party. I don't see how you could have forgotten. I'm even getting off work early so I can help out."

A look of surprise crossed Brad's face, and Angie knew that he really had forgotten about the party. But he didn't like to admit that he'd made a mistake.

"Yeah, but this guy's offering me an audition. This is the break I've been waiting for."

"That's another thing we need to talk about," Angie said. She bit her lip. She really wanted Brad to find a job that he liked. But there was something about Flint that made her feel terribly uncomfortable. The more she thought about it, the more she felt . . . well, afraid. She knew that was pretty silly, and it certainly wasn't something she could say to Brad. "Are you sure about playing with him? I mean, do you even know what he and his band are really about?" she asked. She wished she could think of a good reason to ask him to look for a different gig.

"Am I sure?" Brad laughed. "You've got to be kidding, Angie. The Brothers and me—we're going to make sweet music together." He leaned toward her and ran his finger tenderly down her neck. "Like you and me, huh? We make sweet music together."

Angie closed her eyes, pushing Flint out of her mind. She loved it when Brad touched her softly like that. Now, as he pulled her gently toward him, she went willingly into his arms, lifting her lips to his.

After a moment Brad nuzzled her neck. "About tomorrow night," he said softly.

Angie sighed. "I can't," she said. "My folks expect me to help. It would mean a lot to Juanita for me to be there. And it would mean a lot to me for you to be there."

"We don't have to stay all evening, do we?" Brad asked, punctuating each word with a gentle kiss on Angie's face. "Listen, couldn't we slip out around eight? By that time everyone else will be there, and we can leave without hurting your sister's feelings."

Angie frowned doubtfully. "I don't know if that's a good idea, Brad. I promised. And I have to help clean up after—"

"You'll never be missed, I guarantee," Brad interrupted. "There'll be so many guys there, Nita won't even know you're gone. And I'll have you back by nine thirty. How's that, huh? You'll be back for cleanup time." He bent down to kiss her again.

"Well," Angie said slowly after their lips parted, "I guess, if it's only for a little while—"

Brad gave her a sly grin. "You can wear your new red bikini."

Angie felt alarmed. "I told you I could never wear that bikini for anybody else but you," she protested. Just thinking about the way she looked in the skimpy swimsuit made her blush.

"For anybody but me and a few friends," Brad said soothingly. He pulled her close again. "Listen, I just want to show you off a little. I want them to see what a wonderful girlfriend I've got. You don't mind if I feel that way about you, do you? That I'm so happy you're mine?"

Angie minded. What she and Brad had together was very precious to her. But it was also very private, and she wanted to keep it that way. She didn't like the idea of wearing her bikini in front of Flint—or the rest of the Blood Brothers, for that matter. She didn't want these people to get the wrong idea about her. "Anyway," Brad added confidently, "it'll be a good time. Freddie's going to be there, and Susan, too."

"Susan?" Angie asked, surprised. She'd known about Freddie, who'd had a date with Flint, plus the audition. But Susan hadn't mentioned anything about coming to the party.

"Yeah," Brad replied. "Flint said he had a friend who wanted to meet her, so I stopped off in the kitchen tonight while I was waiting for you and asked her. She wasn't exactly thrilled, but she said she'd come when I told her you'd be there too."

"I wonder," Angie said thoughtfully, "how Flint's friend even knew about Susan. I mean, when did he see her?"

Brad shrugged. "Who knows? Maybe he stopped in at the Pizzeria, took a look, and liked what he saw." He grinned. "Or maybe he staked out her house." He trailed his finger down Angie's cheek to her neck, then bent toward her and kissed the hollow of her throat, where her blouse opened. "Who cares?" he whispered.

Angie took a deep breath and tensed herself to pull away. She knew where this was leading. But before she could move, Brad reached up and pulled the comb out of her hair. It tumbled down over her shoulders.

"All I care about is you, Angie," he said in a husky voice. "You drive me crazy, you know that? Your body, your skin, your hair—" He kissed her again, his fingers reaching for the buttons of her blouse.

Angie shivered, loving his lips, the touch of his fingers. But at the same time she knew that the feeling was dangerous. She shouldn't be doing this. It might be old-fashioned, but that's the way she'd been raised.

"No, Brad," she whispered urgently. She pushed his hands away and pulled back from him. "Please don't."

"But, Angie," Brad said, reaching for her again. "It would be so wonderful, you and me together."

Angie shook her head. They'd been through this over and over again. Why couldn't he understand?

She glanced at her watch. "I've got to get home, Brad. It's nearly ten, and Mom worries if

38

I'm not back at the end of my shift."

Brad leaned back in the seat, heaving an audible, frustrated sigh.

Angie twisted her hair up and thrust the comb through the knot at the back of her neck. "Maybe," she said, changing the subject, "the job with the Brothers will work out."

Brad nodded. "Yeah," he said. "With a few paychecks under my belt, things are gonna be different. Hey, maybe then we can get a place together. Makes sense, doesn't it? Going halves on the rent? That way we'd be able to afford something close to the beach."

Angela's mouth tightened. She really cared about Brad, but how could she reject everything her parents had taught her and move in with him, without any real commitment—a guarantee that he wouldn't move out on her a few months later? For her it was too big a risk, too important a decision. Before she dared to do such a thing, she had to be sure that Brad was as serious about their relationship as she was. She wasn't sure about that at all—at least not yet.

"You know how I feel, Brad," she said quietly. "Love isn't something to be taken lightly. For two people to do that, they have to know for certain—"

Brad turned the key in the ignition. "Yeah, I know," he broke in. He grinned at her. "We'll see how things turn out, okay?"

Angie sighed as they drove off. If she was waiting for a commitment, she'd have to wait a while longer.

Five

"Well, here it is," Susan said. "Home sweet home." She turned the key in the lock and stepped into her darkened apartment with Freddie a pace behind her.

"Hey, nice," Freddie said, looking around. "I'm impressed."

Susan laughed. "And you haven't even seen it with the lights on yet."

For a moment she stood by the door in the half dark, admiring the way the moonlight fell through the open window and across the floor. Now that she had the furniture arranged the way she wanted it, the room looked good, especially with the moonlight turning the gauzy curtains to silver and etching a silver puddle on the floor.

Freddie went to the window. "Hey, look, a view," she said, laughing. "A formal garden and a beach." The window looked out on Betty's small vegetable plot and the kids' sandbox.

Susan flicked on the light switch, and the room sprang to life. "What I like best about it," she said, "is that it's mine. My own private place. It isn't very big, but I love coming in and closing the door behind me, knowing I can be all alone." She grinned at Freddie. "Or invite a friend over," she added. Freddie had followed her home to borrow a cover-up for tomorrow night's beach party.

Freddie lowered herself into the chair with the saggy cushion. "Yeah. I wish I could have my own place too. Maybe I will next year, if I can make enough money. And if I can talk Mom into it."

Freddie's mother ran the Holiday Plaza, a motel over on Holiday Drive. She and Freddie had a large suite of rooms on the second floor. Susan sometimes felt sorry for Freddie. Her mother was always so busy with the motel that she didn't have much time for her daughter.

"Of course," Freddie added, "if this singing job with Flint and the Brothers comes through, maybe I'll make *lots* of money." She held up both hands. Her fingers were crossed. "I could even get my own suite at my mom's place," Freddie joked.

"Maybe," Susan said, trying to sound enthusiastic. For some reason Flint made her feel uneasy, which was kind of odd, because she hadn't even met him. Flint was certainly good-looking, in a dark, brooding sort of way. She could see that when he sat in the back of the Pizzeria. But there was something else, something she couldn't quite put her finger on. Maybe he looked too smooth. Maybe Freddie was already too infatuated with him. Whatever it was, she felt uncomfortable.

Freddie gave a dreamy sigh and swung her legs over the arm of the chair. "How lucky can a girl get?" she asked. "An audition—*and* a date."

"Yeah, how lucky," Susan said dryly. She wasn't looking forward to tomorrow night's party. At least Freddie and Angie would be there, and Brad was all right. And it *was* time she got out and had a little fun. With the job and moving she'd been so busy lately that she hadn't had time even to think about partying.

She looked down at her watch, seeing with some surprise that it was already ten o'clock.

"Mind if I turn on the television?" she asked. "I want to catch the follow-up on last night's story about that grave on the beach." Was that it, or did she really just want to see Drew Morris again? She'd thought about him several times that day, in a strange, anticipatory way. If she didn't know better, she'd almost think she was falling in love with him. But that was ridiculous. You didn't fall in love with somebody you saw on television—at least, not if you were practical, down-to-earth Susan Scott.

"Oh, you mean that story that nobody else knows anything about? Be my guest," Freddie replied. She ruffled her coppery hair and settled back into the couch. "Wake me up when they show the invisible blood," she added, closing her eyes.

"I'm having a sandwich. Want one?" Susan asked. "I have lemonade too."

Freddie's eyes didn't open. "Sure," she said. "Sounds great. In the meantime I think I'll catch a few z's."

Susan flicked on the TV. The Channel Five anchorwoman was already on, doing a story about the annual Muscle Beach Extravaganza. Susan went into the kitchen, where the sound of the newscast was a background to her thoughts. She wasn't really listening, though. She was thinking about Drew Morris. When she realized what she was doing, she forced herself to stop. She had to admit that if it wasn't love, at least it was a pretty heavy crush.

The weatherman was finishing his report as Susan returned to the living room. She got out her new place mats and napkins, thinking about Drew Morris's story from the evening before. She frowned a little as she went back into the kitchen for the sandwiches and lemonade. She wondered if the story would be on again tonight, or if she really had imagined it all. If the TV news crew had been out there on the beach, you'd think Freddie would have run into them. It wasn't easy to miss a sound truck and a camera crew and all those lights.

In fact, the whole thing had been on Susan's mind all day—so much so that at three in the afternoon, when she got her lunch break, she'd hopped in the car and driven over to the beach. She parked on East Beach Drive, in front of the SeaWall Condos, and walked along the beach for a hundred yards or so. She hadn't seen anything. And when she got back to the Pizzeria, the evening paper was on the newsstand, without a word about the police digging up the grave. It was really weird; it was as if it had never happened. But Susan knew it had. She could never have dreamed up Drew Morris's compelling eyes or his urgent voice. No, what she had seen on the television the night before had been real. The strange thing was that it didn't seem to connect with anything else.

"Here's your sandwich," Susan said, and Freddie's eyes popped open.

"Great," she said enthusiastically as she swung her legs down. "Thanks." She looked at the TV, where the sportscaster was wrapping up his baseball report. "Did I miss anything important?"

"Not unless you were betting on the Astros," Susan replied with a laugh. "They lost to the Braves in the bottom of the ninth." She sat down on the sofa as the anchorwoman came back on the screen. "Now for our final report of the evening—" she began.

The lights suddenly dimmed. "Hey! What's going on?" Freddie asked.

"That happened last night, too," Susan said, frowning.

"Maybe you ought to ask Mack about it," Freddie said.

"I plan to, once he gets back from El Paso. I also want to get some candles, in case Mack doesn't get back soon enough," Susan added.

"Yeah, candles." Freddie munched her sandwich. "It's hurricane season, you know. Mom bought a bunch last week. And canned food, too. You ought to stock plenty of canned stuff." She grinned. "Hey, now that you've got your own place, we could have a hurricane party here. What do you think about that?"

But Susan wasn't listening. She was leaning forward, watching the television, her sandwich forgotten in her hand. Drew Morris was standing in front of a motel, speaking into a microphone. His handsome face was pale and more drawn than it had been the night before, and it seemed lined with sadness. His pale gray-green eyes were fastened on

Susan's with an intensity that made her tremble.

"Our live report tonight," he said slowly, "is from a motel, in southeast Galveston, on Holiday Drive."

"Hey!" Freddie exclaimed. She thumped her glass down on the table. "That's our motel!"

"A body has been found," Drew Morris went on soberly. "That makes the second body in two days in this seaside town. Not in a sandy grave this time, but in a bed on the second floor of the motel behind me. The victim here is a young woman in her early twenties. The coroner has not yet determined a cause of death, and police are withholding her identity. Last night, if you recall, the body of a young man was found in a shallow grave on the beach not far from here." His voice deepened, and Susan thought it was filled with an inexpressible sadness. "The question we now have to ask is *why*. Why did these two young people lose their lives? Is there a connection between these two seemingly unrelated tragedies? Will other deaths follow? And who will be next?"

Susan dropped her sandwich onto her plate and twisted her fingers together, her mouth suddenly bone-dry. Those gray-green eyes held hers, connecting the two of them in some sort of inexplicable bond. A powerful force, coming from him, seemed to surge through her. She once again was sure that the reporter was speaking directly to her, as if he wanted to—*had* to—have an answer. An answer from Susan, as if Susan somehow held the key to the mystery he was reporting. The urgency of his questions pulsed through her.

"These are the questions that must be answered," Drew Morris repeated, his voice emphatic, low, taut. His eyes looked tormented, as if he were searching some bleak horizon for the truth, but finding only clouds and darkness. "Why? And who? Who will be next?"

"Whoa," Freddie muttered, shaking her head. "This is *weird*. I mean, this is *really* weird." She rose from her chair. "Where's your phone? I'm going to call my mom and see if she's okay."

"In the kitchen," Susan said, her eyes still on the screen. But Drew Morris's face had faded away, and she got up and turned off the television set. Then she went to the window and looked out. But with the light behind her, all she could see was her own pale face reflected in the dark glass.

She closed her eyes. Even though she knew it wasn't rational, she still couldn't shake the feeling that the reporter had been speaking to her, and to her alone, as if his story were a report that *she*, of all the tens of thousands of viewers, had to hear. She bit her lip. Maybe she should call the station and ask for Drew Morris. Maybe she should talk to him and find out why—

Then she caught herself, and her eyes flew

open. This was ridiculous. It was crazy! Drew Morris was only a good-looking reporter—with eyes she happened to find attractive—doing a job. It happened that he'd drawn two tough assignments, one after the other, and maybe he'd gotten too deeply involved with the stories. That happened sometimes. It would account for the tormented intensity of his gaze. Sure, that was it. Any reporter would be likely to feel an interest in two cases like these. And the connection she felt with him? Well, that was her imagination working overtime, that's all it was. Fantasy. A fiction.

In the window, as in a mirror, she saw Freddie come out of the kitchen wearing a puzzled expression.

"Crazy," she muttered. "Weird. Wacko."

"What?" Susan asked, turning around.

"Didn't that reporter say he was doing a live spot?" Freddie demanded.

Susan nodded. "Yeah. So?"

"So Mom swears there's no TV crew," Freddie said. "Not earlier, not now. I made her go out and look." She scowled. "I *know* it was our motel. They didn't show the sign, but I saw that stupid tilted palm tree out front that leans like the Tower of Pisa. I keep telling Mom to get it cut before it falls on some tourist."

Susan felt the skin prickling on the back of her neck. "There wasn't any sign of the TV cameras on the beach last night, either," she said quietly. It was as if Drew Morris were a figure from an unknown dimension, suddenly visible on her television set.

Freddie shook her head. "Listen, would you mind if I borrowed that beach cover-up and drove on home?" she asked. "I mean, I hate to eat and run, but this thing has me curious. I'd like to know what's going on."

Susan headed for the closet. "So would I." If Mack were here, instead of on vacation in El Paso, she could ask him. He was a cop—he'd know. But he and the family wouldn't be back until tomorrow.

"I'll call you if I find anything out," Freddie promised, taking the cover-up from Susan. "Anyway, I'll see you at work in the morning." She grinned. "And don't forget our triple date tomorrow night."

Susan wrinkled her nose. "I don't know about this, Freddie. I think I might change my mind. I'm not exactly crazy about the whole idea."

"Don't you dare," Freddie said. "I need you for moral support. Tomorrow night's a big night for me."

Susan grinned. "Oh, yeah? And are you worried about your morals?"

"Some friend you are," Freddie said affectionately. "You'll be there? Please?"

"I guess," Susan said. She smiled. "For you."

"Hey, aren't you even curious about this guy who wants to meet you?"

"Maybe," Susan admitted. "Yeah, a little. But not enough to make me want to spend an evening with"—she was going to say "with Flint" but thought better of it—"with a bunch of people I don't know," she amended.

"It'll do you good," Freddie said breezily. "You don't go out often enough."

Susan sighed. This was an argument they had at least once a week. "Thanks for the advice," she said. "I'll keep it in mind the next time two or three guys ask me out." It was what she always said.

"The reason they don't," Freddie said, "is that you're too serious. You've got to lighten up."

"Yeah," Susan said. "I'll work on it."

Freddie gave her a hug. "See you tomorrow," she said, and banged the door shut behind her.

Feeling restless, Susan turned on the TV for a few minutes and watched a sitcom. Then she turned the set off and went into the kitchen to put away the dishes and check the lock on the back door. In the living room again, she turned off the light and sat on the sofa, watching the moonlight stream through the window. Thinking of Drew Morris, and of his eyes still fastened relentlessly on hers, Susan could feel him gaze at her from the silvery shadows. Again she felt the sense of urgency that had pulsed through her when he spoke. She heard his voice, his questions, echoing in her head.

Why?

Who?

And who would be next?

Six

Freddie trudged through the warm sand, shaking the water out of her hair. She glanced up and down the beach. In one direction, toward Galveston, she could see the expensive condominiums rising like tall glass towers. In the other was the concession stand at Apffel Park. Ahead lay the dunes, shadowy in the deepening twilight, and the fire the guys had built. Behind her was the ocean, flat and calm, growing dark. Down at Stewart Park, on the other side of the condos, there was plenty of noise and bright light, and the beach was crowded, even at night. But here the beach was secluded and quiet, nothing but sand and sky and water.

Susan sat up and tossed her a towel. "How was the water?"

"Great!" Freddie said. She toweled herself off and flopped down on the blanket beside Susan. She sighed again. "The whole evening has been terrific. The audition was wonderful, the Brothers are out of this world, Flint is . . ." She looked out into the water, where Flint was swimming around like a dolphin, flashing in and out of the surf.

"You seem to have run out of adjectives," Susan said quietly.

"Well, you might too," Freddie replied, "if you could bring yourself to spend some time with him. You know, talk to him, get to know him." She knew that Susan wasn't wild about Flint, but she didn't have to ignore him completely, did she?

"You may be right," Susan said. "I really haven't given him—or any of the other guys either, for that matter—a fair chance. I'm sorry if I'm ruining your good time."

"That's okay," Freddie said. "You're not."

Susan didn't reply. Freddie saw that her eyes were on Bishop, the guy who had asked to meet her. He was out in the deep water with Brad, beyond the surf. Freddie grinned a little. Bishop was blond and good-looking. If she hadn't seen Flint first, she might have fallen for Bishop. Or even Russel or Sid, the other two Brothers, neither of whom had come to the beach party. They were both super-cute too. The Brothers probably found themselves surrounded by love-struck groupies all the time. That was okay, she thought, chuckling to herself, as long as *she* held the inside track.

On the other side of Susan, Angie sat up, adjusting the top of her skimpy red swimsuit. Freddie had to smile at that, too. Angie was obviously nervous about that bikini. Bishop's low, admiring whistle hadn't helped the situation.

"So they hired you?" Angie asked.

"Yeah," Freddie said happily. "Of course, it's only week to week for a while, until they see how I do. But it's a chance."

"How did you like it?" Susan asked. "The music, I mean."

Freddie frowned a little. "Well, it's going to take some getting used to," she said. "I'll have to adjust my style a little. But I guess that happens with any new group."

She hadn't known what to expect when she went into the audition earlier that evening. For one thing, she'd thought Brad was going to be there, but as it turned out, they were auditioning separately. His would come later that evening. But the big news was the Brothers' music. Technically, it was very unusual, based on the synthesizers Flint and Bishop played. There was a heavy, deep rhythm of bass and drums. They worked in minor keys, too, which gave the music an eerie quality. And then there were the lyrics.

"Adjust how?" Susan wanted to know.

"That's hard to say." Freddie really couldn't explain. Singing with the Brothers, she had done things with her voice that she hadn't known she could do. She'd felt the music's energy in a new way. But it was a scary energy, dark, so powerful . . . She frowned. She didn't want to try to explain. They'd think she'd gone totally flaky. But Susan and Angie were waiting for an explanation. "I guess it's the kind of music you feel in your gut," she said finally. "It's kind of, well, mesmerizing. The lyrics especially. They're sort of . . ." She paused, searching for the right word. "I don't know, seductive."

Susan began folding the beach towels. "Seductive, huh?" She laughed a little. "Sounds dangerous."

Seductive, yes, Freddie thought, poking her toes into the sand. When she sang with the Brothers, it was as if all her own energy, her own soul, somehow drained from her, so that she was charged entirely by the music. In fact, she'd been surprised—and a little scared—at the way it had pushed her to go beyond her limits. Beyond her range, which ordinarily wasn't anything spectacular. The power even took her beyond her technical ability.

"Sing something for us," Angie said.

"I can't," Freddie said.

"How come?" Susan asked. "Did you have to sign a pledge? No singing outside the club?"

"No. I can't remember any of the songs," Freddie said simply. That was weird, too. She had a good memory. She always remembered lyrics, especially when they were powerful, as the Brothers' were.

"Too bad," Angie said.

"Yeah," Freddie said, making her tone lighter. "Well, I guess you'll just have to come to the club and listen." She squared her shoulders. When she really got going with the Brothers, when she knew the lyrics better, she'd like it a lot more. Right now it was probably just a matter of not being familiar with the mood, the rhythm. And not being quite sure what the Brothers wanted from her.

Susan nodded. "We'll be there," she said. "In the front row." She changed the subject. "What did you find out last night when you got home? About the girl they found dead in the motel, I mean."

"A dead girl in the motel?" Angie asked, startled. "What happened? Who was she?"

"There wasn't any dead girl," Freddie said.

Susan straightened up. "But we saw—"

"I know what we saw," Freddie said, "or at least what we thought we saw. But I'm telling you what I saw. There were no TV crews, no cops, no dead girl—" She shrugged. "I guess we made a mistake. The only explanation is that there's some other motel on Holiday Drive with a leaning palm tree out front. I guess I've never noticed it. Either that or there was something funny about that lemonade you gave me."

Susan was looking troubled, but she only said, "Yeah, I guess you're right. About another motel, that is. I'm still curious about the grave on the beach, though."

Freddie saw her looking down the beach, toward the condos. That's where she had said the grave was supposed to have been. Freddie couldn't quite put it all together. The grave on the beach and the dead girl in the motel—

"What time is it?" Angie asked Susan.

"Nine fifteen," Susan said, looking at her watch.

"Oops," Angie said. She scrambled to her feet and waved at Brad. "I've got to get back to Nita's party. It'll be time to clean up the mess."

"I'm ready to go," Susan said. "Want me to take you home? It'll give Brad a little time to get ready for his audition."

"Thanks," Angie said, and began to pull her jeans and shirt on over her dry suit. Freddie suspected that her parents, who were on the strict side, didn't know that she even owned a bikini.

Susan stood up. "Are you going over to Flint's for Brad's audition?" she asked Freddie.

"I wasn't invited," Freddie said. She looked up. The three guys were coming toward them from the water, bodies sleek and shiny. Flint and Bishop were wearing their dark glasses. That struck her as funny, and she giggled. Boy, how cool could you get? She turned to Susan. "I heard Bishop asked you out."

Susan nodded.

"Well, what did you say?"

"I said no thank you," Susan replied evenly. She glanced toward the guys. "Bishop isn't exactly my type" she added, in a lower voice.

"The trouble with you, Susan," Freddie said, "is that you're just too picky. What's wrong with Bishop?"

Susan shrugged. "I'll let you know when I've figured it out myself," she said. "In the meantime let's just say that I'm not likely to be the Brothers' greatest fan." She grinned at Freddie. "Although I can't wait to hear *you* sing, after they've opened the club."

For once he hadn't been upset that Angie had to leave early. The beach party had been fun, Brad thought, taking his electric guitar out of the case, but he'd been glad when it was time to break it up. Angie had seemed on edge all evening. She was probably upset about missing her sister's party and couldn't let go and enjoy herself. Susan had been kind of a wet blanket, too, and Brad had no idea what her problem was. But Flint and Bishop were great. He grinned. In fact, he hadn't come across such friendly, interesting guys in a long time. And that was good. It was important to like the guys you worked with.

He'd also managed to find out quite a bit about the Blood Brothers while they'd been partying. They'd been playing up in Dallas for a while, apparently. That's where they lost both their lead vocalist and their guitarist. Then Flint had come into some money—an inheritance of some kind—and they'd decided to relocate and start up their own club. They were calling it the Dark of the Moon. But before they could open, they had to find replacements for the band members who had left. That's where he came in.

Lucky for the Brothers he was available, Brad thought confidently. He carried his guitar into the house. He reminded himself that it probably wasn't cool to act too cocky. He didn't want them to think that he thought he had the job sewn up, even if it was true.

The house the Brothers had rented was a huge old Victorian, with high ceilings and big rooms, lots of them. It was a good house for a group like this, Brad decided. The guys lived upstairs, and downstairs there was plenty of room to store equipment and to practice. It was in the middle of town, but there weren't many houses on the block. The lots on both sides of the house were vacant, and there was a big cemetery across the street. No band could afford to have the neighbors calling the cops all the time because of loud music. In this business the dead made good neighbors. He grinned at his own joke.

The four Brothers, in black jeans, black tees, and dark glasses were already waiting for him in the practice room. Flint smiled and nodded at an empty stool, handing Brad a tall, cool glass. Brad took his place, beginning to feel a little nervous. But that was okay. A few nerves would pump up his adrenaline. He plugged in his instrument, gulped at the glass, and flexed his fingers. A lot was hanging on tonight. He had to be good.

He *was* good. After a few technical preliminaries about tempo, key, and so on, the group swung into the first number, pulling him with them. Brad had a good ear for melody and rhythm, and he picked the first song up easily. The group's sound was original. Actually, though, it wasn't really a sound. It was more like an effect, something he felt more than he heard. He felt it in his bones, in his blood, in some almost subliminal way.

All through that first number, Brad tried to stay on top of the music, to figure it out, the way he usually did when he sat in with a new group. He tried counting out the drum tempo, picking out the chord structure, and anticipating the melody—what there was of it. But that didn't work with these guys. The sound drifted and twisted, snakelike. It wasn't anything you could analyze. Anyway, his mind wasn't working too well. His brain kept disconnecting.

Sometime during the second number, though, he stopped worrying about contolling the sound. He found himself falling into the music, letting it flow through him and out of his fingers. That was when he got good. Very good. He got deep into the music. He stopped caring about being good or landing a job with the Brothers or even impressing Flint. He cared only about being part of the music, having it inside him, flowing in his veins like sweet, hot blood.

After the third or fourth number—who was counting?—Flint looked up from the synthesizer. He moved his head, and the rest of the Brothers stopped playing. They all looked at Brad.

"Yes," Flint said appreciatively. He reached out and touched Brad's arm with a smile. "Yes, indeed," he said. "I believe we have found our man." The other Brothers nodded in turn as Flint looked pointedly at each one.

Flint then took off his glasses, and Brad could see that his eyes were very dark, very deep, very expressive. His eyes had the music in them. He moved from behind the synthesizer and came closer.

After that the evening got really hazy. Brad

never could remember it, even when he tried.

"You've been staying out this late on a regular basis?"

Susan turned around, the key to her apartment in her hand. Mack was coming up the stairs behind her. He was still wearing his uniform, so he'd probably just gotten off duty. She smiled affectionately. Even if he was putting on his big-brother act in a major way, she was glad to see him—probably because he'd been away for two weeks.

"It's not even ten," Susan said defensively, opening the door. "How was El Paso?"

"Hot." Mack tossed his cap onto the coffee table and sat down heavily. "And dry. Like the desert." He glanced around. "Hey, not bad. You've got this place looking like home."

Susan was already in the kitchen. "Iced tea?" she called out.

"Please. Heavy on the ice."

In a moment Susan was back with the drinks. She switched on the TV. "I hope you don't mind," she said. "I've been following a news story." She sat down, intent on the television.

"Oh, yeah?" Mack asked lazily, sipping his tea. He kicked off his shoes. "Well, the newsroom's going to be busy tonight. They dug up some guy's body on the beach a few hours ago. And some girl turned up dead in a motel just as I was clocking out."

"What?" Susan asked. "But the girl in the motel—that was *last* night! And what did you say about a body on the beach?"

Her brother gestured at the set. "If you'll listen, you can hear all about it. Probably be the lead story."

The anchorwoman was looking at the camera, somber-faced. "Our top story tonight," she said, "is the discovery of a shallow grave on the beach, near the SeaWall Condominium. Police have uncovered the body of a young man. He has been identified as a Dallas television newsman named Drew Morris, who disappeared four days ago." On the screen flashed the face of a smiling young man, dark-haired, handsome. He had pale gray-green eyes.

Susan sucked in her breath, not believing. Her heart was thumping so loudly that she knew Mack must be able to hear it.

"Drew . . . Morris?" she whispered. She felt stunned, as if she had lost a friend. But behind that loss there was a deeper, darker fear. If Drew Morris was buried on the beach, who was the man on the TV screen the last two nights?

"Yeah, Morris, that's the guy," Mack said, leaning forward, his elbows on his knees. "Some guy from the condo was walking his dog on the beach about seven tonight. The dog dug up the grave."

The anchorwoman's sober face filled the screen

again. "Police have not yet identified the cause of Mr. Morris's death. Channel Seven in Dallas reports that he was in Galveston following a story involving the daughter of a prominent North Texas physician. Police conjecture that his death may be somehow connected to the story he was investigating. Meanwhile, in a second-floor room of the Holiday Plaza, a motel on Holiday Drive, police have found the body of a young woman. Reporter Roger Morgan is live on the scene. Roger?"

Onto the screen flashed Freddie's mother's motel with the leaning palm tree out front. A blond reporter stood in the glare of the TV lights, looking straight into the camera.

But Susan didn't get to hear what Roger had to say because her phone started ringing just as he opened his mouth. When she picked it up, she heard Freddie's breathless voice on the other end of the line.

"Susan? Susan, you'll never guess what—"

"There's a body," Susan said. "Right?"

"Right," Freddie replied. She started to say something, swallowed loudly, and tried again. "Some girl in 2E. They're taking her out on a stretcher." She paused. "I mean, they're taking her out *now*. Not last night. Tonight. Right this minute. The cop in the hall says she was found just a little while ago."

65

Susan cleared her throat. "If you'll turn on the TV, you can see the whole story."

"Yeah, but we've already seen the whole story. Only we saw it *last* night."

"I know," Susan said, shaking her head to clear it. "It's crazy. I don't get it either."

There was noise on the other end of the line, then Freddie's voice. "I'll talk to you later," she said hurriedly. "Some guy wants to interview me."

Susan put down the phone and turned back to the television.

"The name of the young woman is being withheld until the family has been notified," Roger Morgan was saying. "We'll have more on both these stories as the details come in. We'll be right back after this commercial break." The camera pulled back and a soft-drink commercial came on. Susan turned down the sound.

"I guess they're not going to put in the stuff about the throat," Mack said. "Probably a good idea. People might start looking over their shoulders."

"Throat?" Susan asked. Her voice felt strangled.

"Yeah." Mack frowned. "Like she'd been bit by a snake or something." He looked at her, half-teasing. "Down at the station we've been joking that it looked suspiciously like a vampire bite. You sure you want to stay here by yourself tonight, with vampires on the loose?" Mack asked, his voice sounding like Dracula's.

"I think I'll risk it," Susan said. "But thanks for your concern."

She thought for a moment, then turned to face her brother. "The grave on the beach. Drew Morris's grave. You're sure it was found *today*?"

Mack gave her a puzzled look. "Yeah. That's what I said. Earlier this evening. I was in the station when the call came in. Why do you ask?"

"I think it's just a case of déjà vu," Susan replied. "And it's freaking me out a little."

Mack looked around. "You sure you're not going to be lonesome out here by yourself, Susan? How about if I lend you a couple of kids? I can guarantee the vampires or whatever it is that goes bump in the night won't come around with those boys here. Better than garlic or holy water."

Susan managed a smile. "I think I can handle a few vampires," she said, turning the set off. "But give the boys a hug for me, will you? Tell Betty I'll take them to the beach next week."

Mack drained the last of his iced tea, put his hat back on his head, pushed his feet back into his shoes, and stood up. "Yeah, sure," he said, stretching wearily. "Boy, do I hate the first day back after vacation."

Susan got up too. "Mack," she said, "this Drew Morris guy—do you know anything about him?"

"Nothing that wasn't on TV."

"If you find out anything else, will you please tell me?" Susan asked urgently.

"Yeah, I guess." Mack gave her a look. "Any particular reason?"

For a minute Susan was tempted to tell him. Then she stopped herself. Mack was a hardheaded, practical cop who believed in what you could see, taste, touch, hear, and smell. "Just the facts, ma'am," he liked to say, "just the facts." He'd never believe her. He'd think she was going nuts. Susan pulled in her breath. She had a hard time believing, herself. If Freddie hadn't been here with her last night and seen Drew Morris, Susan would have thought she must have dreamed the whole thing.

"No," she said with a little sigh. "No reason. I'm curious, I guess."

"I'll see what I can dig up," Mack said. "Oops. Sorry about the pun." He was on his way to the door when the lights suddenly flickered.

"That happened last night, too," Susan said. "And the night before."

"Guess I need to check the breaker box," Mack said.

"I'd appreciate that," Susan said. "Thanks for stopping by."

"Don't forget," Mack said, one hand on the knob. "You can have the kids anytime you want them."

"Thanks for the generous offer," Susan said, smiling a little. "Good night."

While Mack clomped noisily down the stairs, Susan closed the door behind him and leaned heavily against it. For a minute she closed her eyes. The whole thing was absolutely preposterous. Crazy. Unbelievable. Drew Morris, reporting on the finding of his own body. Drew Morris, standing beside his own grave, fixing her with the compelling gaze that seemed to speak to her alone.

Susan opened her eyes. The lights flickered again, then went off. As Susan stood wondering whether Mack had shut off the power, the television screen began to glow, as if it had its own independent energy source. As she watched, a face filled the screen.

It was the face of Drew Morris.

Seven

Susan dropped limply into the chair and closed her eyes. There had to be some rational explanation. Maybe she hadn't turned the set off. Maybe the station was making a tribute to the dead newsman. Maybe his picture was on the screen as a memorial. Yes, that was it. That's what had happened. She hadn't actually turned the set off, and when she opened her eyes, the memorial tribute would be over. They'd be showing a sports clip or a commercial or something.

But when Susan opened her eyes, Drew Morris's picture was still there. It obviously wasn't part of a news story. Drew Morris didn't have the combed, collected, in-charge look of a TV journalist. He looked gaunt and disheveled, and the dark shadow of a beard crossed his face. Under the shadow his skin was deathly pale, his gray-green eyes were wide and had an oddly fixed look. Then his lips began to move. Susan had the inescapable feeling that he was saying something to *her*.

She reached for the volume control, and as she did, she saw the power was still off. Her mouth suddenly went dry. Her hand was shaking so badly she could hardly control it.

"—know this sounds idiotic," Drew Morris was saying as Susan turned up the volume. "If I were watching my face on the screen, I'd think the whole thing was crazy too. Or I was crazy. Or both." He stopped for a moment as if he were struggling with the words. "I have to deliver a message to somebody named Susan. I can't see you or hear you, Susan, but I have the feeling that you're out there, watching. I hope you're watching." He stopped and rubbed the stubble on his chin. "I really hope you're watching," he said wearily. "Susan, wherever you are, whoever you are, you're in danger. You and your friends. You guys are next."

Susan found herself on her hands and knees, her face inches from the screen. Her breath caught in her throat. "What?" she cried. "What are you talking about?" Then she bit off the words and pulled back. "What am I doing?" Susan said out loud to herself. "This is dumb. I'm talking to a TV set! A TV set that isn't even turned on!"

Drew Morris turned his head, almost as if he were listening. "I know you're out there, Susan. I have the feeling that you believe, even though you don't want to. But you have to listen to me. If you're going to get through this, I mean get through this *alive*, you've got to believe." He closed his eyes for a moment and the screen flickered.

"Believe?" Susan asked hoarsely. "Believe what? That you're dead? That you're alive? That you're talking to me this way?" She reached for the power switch and punched it. "I'll show you how much I believe," she said viciously.

Drew Morris's face remained on the screen, unchanged, even though the power indicator was glowing. "There's a force in your life, Susan," he said, "and you can't control it."

"A force?" Susan cried, feeling half-hysterical. "What I've got is a *television* I can't control!" She hit the power switch again, turning it off.

"—dangerous force," he continued. "A powerful energy that can destroy you completely. I don't fully understand this, either. If I did, I'd tell you more. I want to help you."

"Help me what?" Susan cried.

He didn't hear her. He was smiling grimly, a tortured twist to his mouth. His chuckle had a harsh, grating sound.

"Here I am, a newsman with the biggest story of the century, and I can't seem to get the facts straight. I can't . . . *remember*. Everything that's happened to me in the last few weeks is fuzzy, like I'm seeing it through a fog. There was a girl. A girl named Sara. Sara Robertson, I think. She's important, but I can't remember how. And there's other important stuff, things I can't remember at all. I just know they happened. Me dying, for instance."

His hand went to his throat as if he were feeling for something. Then his voice dropped to a gritty, breaking whisper, filled with pain.

"I know I must sound like a lunatic to you, Susan. I'm dead, and I don't know how I died. I've tried to remember, but I can't. All I know is that I died, and somebody stuck my body in a grave on a beach. But if I can't remember anything about the past, I can see a little way into the future. I can see enough to know that you're in danger, you and Freddie and—"

"Freddie?" Susan whispered, the cold fear washing over her. "How do you know—"

But the image of Drew Morris's face had distorted, and the television screen was filled with white snow. An instant later, it went dark. Susan was staring at the dead screen, listening to her heart pound, when the phone rang.

For a moment Susan thought she wouldn't answer it. She'd just let it ring. But then she felt herself getting up, saw her hand reaching for it, heard the tiny sound coming from her throat. She cleared it, and her voice, apprehensive and shaky, said hello.

"The cops just left," Freddie said excitedly.

"What?" Susan asked, not quite connecting.

"The police," Freddie replied. "The TV crews too. They took a bunch of pictures of the building and the motel room and stuff, and they all left. But this reporter was hanging around and I talked to him and—"

Susan's heart thumped heavily in her chest. "What reporter?" she broke in harshly. "What was his name?"

"His name?" Freddie asked. "Oh. Roger something. Morgan, I think. Roger Morgan. A real cute blond. He's the one who did the live report tonight. I watched him do it."

"Oh," Susan said tonelessly. Her fingers were clutching the receiver so hard they hurt.

"Yeah. And listen to this, Suz. Roger says there wasn't anything about a girl's body on last night's news. He says we were dreaming. Or nuts. He says they didn't run any story about a grave on the beach, either. Until tonight, that is." She paused. "That's what you were asking me about the other day, isn't it?"

"Yes," Susan said. She took a breath. She wanted to laugh, but she didn't dare let herself. If she did, she wouldn't be able to stop. The whole thing was crazy, insane. They'd both seen Drew Morris on TV last night. She'd seen his first story, about the grave. She'd seen him tonight, too, with the TV set turned *off*.

"There's something more," Freddie was saying. "This guy, Roger, he says there's something weird about the girl's body. Her throat's got some kind of funny marks on it. Like puncture wounds or something. I wonder if she was on drugs. In the neck, though? Ugh."

Susan thought for a minute. "Freddie, did the reporter tell you the girl's name?"

Freddie paused. "Yeah, he did. Now, let's see, it was . . . I'm not sure I—"

"Sara?" Susan asked.

Freddie sounded surprised. "Yeah, that's it. Sara. Sara Roberts or Robertson or something like that. How'd you know?"

"Lucky guess."

Freddie gave a skeptical laugh. "You picked it out of the air, right? Roger said she was from somewhere up in North Texas. She came down here a couple of weeks ago. She'd only been in the motel for the last three days, Mom said. But apparently they're not putting any of that stuff out until they notify the family, since she was so young." She paused. "So are you going to tell me how you knew?"

Susan tried to swallow the knot of fear that was tightening in her throat. *Sara Robertson. A girl named Sara. She's important, but I don't remember how.*

"I can't tell you right now, Fred," Susan said. "Listen, I'll see you at work tomorrow. Okay?"

Freddie's voice was urgent. "Susan, are you all right? You sound kind of funny. Do you want me to come over?"

"No," Susan said. "Thanks. See you tomorrow." She put the receiver down and turned to stare at the silent television screen. After a while she checked the lock on the back door, pulled out the sleeper-couch, and went to bed. A half hour later she got up and pulled the plug on the television set.

It was after three before she finally fell asleep.

After she hung up the phone, Freddie puzzled for a few minutes over the strange case of the girl in 2E. But she couldn't really concentrate on anything but Flint and the Brothers, and whether she was actually going to be able to sing with them. Oh, she had the job—somehow she'd managed to impress Flint enough to get hired. And she'd done some things with her voice under the spell of the music that had surprised her. Amazed her, really. But she still wasn't sure that she could actually sing the kind of music they played, and she was really worried about the lyrics. If she couldn't remember them long enough to practice them, how would she ever remember them onstage? When her mom turned the office over to the night clerk and came upstairs at midnight, Freddie was sitting at the piano, anxiously one-fingering her way through a piece of music Flint had handed her after the audition—*minus* the lyrics.

Freddie felt better when she went over to the Brothers' house the next night after work. It was her first practice session with the group. The guys, including Brad, were already into a number when she got there. She walked quietly into the old front parlor and sat cross-legged on the floor in the corner, her back to the wall.

She felt better because she had decided something important. The trouble the last time was that she got too deep into the music. The secret was in staying detached. Tonight she'd think while she sang, rather than simply feel her way through. If she could concentrate on technique, she'd be able to figure out what it was that gave the music its vitality.

But as she sat there, thinking became harder and harder. How could she concentrate on technique when there didn't seem to be anything to concentrate on? These guys had mastered their instruments and their sound. They worked together perfectly, as if they were reading each other's minds. All five Brothers, including Brad, stood there with their instruments, wearing dark glasses and playing calmly, easily, *perfectly*, the instruments blending together in a rich, full sound that surged with power and energy. She felt herself being swept up by the sound, pulled by it into some dark place that was far away and somehow not quite . . . safe.

For a while she struggled to stay outside the music. But it was no use. It was like the time she got caught in the undertow at the beach, trying to fight the water and knowing in her heart she couldn't win. Resisting had taken all her energy, had exhausted her. If it hadn't been for Susan, who had seen that she was in trouble and come to her rescue, she would have drowned. But no one was here to rescue her this time. Freddie would have to surrender.

The number ended. Flint smiled at her. "Ah," he said, in his accented English, "I am glad to see you are *listening*. Perhaps now you will struggle less against the music?" He gestured with a commanding motion toward an empty stool beside him. "Come now and sing with us, Frederica."

Without knowing exactly how she got there, Freddie found herself sitting on the stool. Flint leaned toward her, the single light in the room glinting off his dark glasses. He dropped a soft kiss on her cheek.

"Now," he said, "let us do the song Frederica sang with us last night, at the audition."

"I need a lyric sheet," Freddie said. "I don't remember the words."

Flint put his hand on her arm. "The lyrics will come to you when you give yourself to the music," he said softly. "Do not try to learn it with your mind—feel it with your heart."

"But how can I sing it without learning it?"

Flint smiled slightly. "Let the music teach you," he said.

Freddie found herself too tired to argue with him, almost too tired to sing. As the Brothers began to play, she tried to think where she was supposed to come in, tried to remember the words. But it was too hard. She missed her first cue. Then she missed her second. Then, when she'd given up completely, it all suddenly came together: the cue, the lyrics, the power. Her voice was deep and full—majestic, even. As the rhythms and sounds filled her soul, she welcomed them. The music was as cool and sweet as the spring tides, as profound as the farthest depths of the ocean, and as inviting as the softest whisper. And the words made sense. They made perfect sense.

The group practiced for what seemed like hours, but might have been only a few moments. Freddie didn't know and didn't care. Her anxiety had gone, and she was left feeling calm, soft, open.

She could have sung all night. She actually hoped she would. Then with a slight hand movement, Flint stopped the band.

"I think," he said, "we will be ready to open on Saturday. Do you agree?" The Brothers all nodded. They put down their instruments, as if on a signal, and left the room.

Flint took off his glasses and looked intently at Freddie. His dark eyes were warm, appreciative, full of admiration for the work she had done tonight. Freddie smiled at him.

"You are beginning to feel the music," he said. "You are now inviting it inside of you. It is so?"

"Yes," Freddie said.

"And you are enjoying it?"

"Yes," Freddie repeated dreamily. "It feels good. It feels right." She rested her head on Flint's shoulder.

It was late, and she was tired. Which was entirely too bad, because the Brothers had conveniently left them alone. And Flint was so attractive, so powerfully, irresistibly attractive. The room seemed to fill with a darkening haze. The guys must be playing somewhere at the back of the house, she thought dimly. She could hear the music, faint and sweet and alluring, as Flint leaned toward her and kissed her softly.

Freddie wasn't sure what time it was when she got home. The next morning she slept through the alarm. She was nearly an hour late getting to work.

Angie sat down angrily across the table from Brad. She hadn't seen him since he'd started playing with the Blood Brothers. When she took him his pizza ten minutes ago, he'd surprised her with some startling news—news that made her go numb. Unfortunately, the place had been so busy, she couldn't talk to him then. Now she was breaking all kinds of rules by sitting down, even though she was on her break. Gwen didn't like her employees to sit with the customers, especially when the dining room was full. But tonight Angie didn't care. She was mad and had to find out what was going on.

"What exactly are you trying to tell me?" she asked, trying to keep her voice level. She wished Brad would take off those sunglasses he was wearing. She couldn't see his eyes. She couldn't see what he was thinking.

Brad pushed his pizza away, even though he'd barely touched it. "Like I said," he said flatly. "I've moved in with the Brothers. I just finished hauling my stuff over there. It's a big old house. Plenty of room for everybody. And this way we can practice at any time."

Angie stared at him. "But I thought . . ." There was a hard lump in her throat, and she had to blink to keep the tears back. Before he started playing with the band, Angela thought that he might be ready to make a commitment sometime soon. And he had. But the commitment he made was to the band, not to her.

Brad leaned across the table. "Angie, this doesn't mean I don't want to live with you. You mean a lot to me. I still love you. I want you near me always. Forever." He looked deep into her eyes and kissed her softly on her lips. "That's why I want you to move in with me."

Angie's eyes widened. "But you already moved in with someone else. Four someone elses."

"Yeah. So? As I say, it's a big house. Flint would let us have our own private room. There's a bathroom at the end of the hall, and a huge kitchen. If we live there, we can save a lot of money and be together all the time. And you can have people over to visit—Nita can stay with us whenever you want. There really is a lot of room."

Angie looked down at her hands. "Do you think you're ready for something like this?" she whispered. "I mean . . ."

"You mean, am I ready for a commitment?" Brad's lips curled up in a smile. "You know me, babe. I'm not into commitments in a major way. But if it'll make you happy . . . I mean, there's nobody else, I swear. I'm not interested in girls, plural. Just you." He took her hands in his. "Just us."

"But I can't move in with . . . a bunch of guys," Angie replied, flustered. "It wouldn't be . . . my folks would be really upset." She shuddered, imagining how strange it would be. To move in with Brad, whom she loved, would be a big enough deal. But to move in with the whole band?

Brad scowled. "When are you going to stop thinking about your parents and start thinking about us? You're not a kid anymore, Angie. You're a woman. It's time you grew up and stopped taking orders from home." He leaned back. "It would be good for you to live with my music for a while, too. That way you'll know how you really feel about me."

"Live with your music?" Angie asked. She searched Brad's face. There was something different about him. It wasn't just that he hadn't even touched his food. She couldn't be sure what it was, especially because she couldn't see his eyes. He seemed tired and impatient, not his usual easygoing self.

"Yeah, live with the music," Brad repeated. "You're interested in what I'm doing, aren't you?"

Angie nodded wordlessly.

"Well, then, you ought to get into the music with me. You can't love me if you can't love my music." Brad pouted a little when he said it.

Brad had played with other groups since they'd been going together, and he'd never insisted that she get involved with his music. As a matter of fact, he used to like it that the music was separate. It was a kind of private place that belonged only to him. And she had always been more than happy to stay out of this part of his life.

As if he had read her mind, Brad said, "Yeah, I know. You don't like the stuff I'm into. And I've always kind of kept it apart from what was ours together. But I see now that that was wrong. If we're going to be together—I mean, *really* together—there can't be anything between us. We've got to share everything. The music, especially."

Angie got a warm feeling inside her for the first time since they started this argument. *We've got to share everything.* Yes, that was right. Two people who loved one another ought to share. But she still didn't see how she could compromise her own values and upset her father.

Before Angie could even respond, Brad pushed back abruptly from the table. "Come on," he said, jerking his head. "Walk me to the car." He held out his hand to her.

Angie looked at her watch, then looked back toward Gwen's office. "I've only got five minutes left on my break," she said.

"Come on, then," Brad said roughly, thrusting his hand into his pocket. "We're wasting time."

Angie got up and followed him outside into the early-evening dark. They walked around the corner to a quiet street where the car was parked. He opened the door and motioned her in with a quick, impatient gesture. He got in too and pulled her against him.

"Hey," he said, when she pushed away. "What's the matter? We haven't seen one another for three days, remember?" He kissed her, hard.

Angie shivered. When she looked up at him, she saw only herself, reflected in the dark glasses. "What is it, Brad?" she whispered.

"What's what?"

"You. You're different. What is it? Is it the guys you're playing with?"

"I don't know what you're talking about," Brad said. He put his fingers under her chin and tilted it up. "I'm me," he said softly, "the guy who's crazy for you. You're the one who's acting funny." His mouth was on hers again, then on her face, her throat.

Angie pulled in her breath. The way he was kissing her, it *was* different. More urgent, more demanding. It was a little scary, but also pretty exciting. "Not now, Brad," she managed breathlessly, at last. "How about later tonight, huh? After I get off work. I've got to get back now, or Gwen will have my head."

Brad sat back against the seat. "I can't later," he said. "We're practicing tonight. The opening's on Saturday. You're coming, right?" It wasn't so much a question as a command.

Angie nodded slowly. She wasn't exactly looking forward to an entire evening of loud rock in some dark club. But she had to show Brad she supported him. And, of course, it was Freddie's opening night too. She wanted to hear Freddie sing.

"Susan and I are coming together," she said. "Juanita's coming too."

Brad grinned. "Nita? Great! I'll introduce her to Russel, our drummer. I bet he'd go for her."

Angie frowned. She wasn't sure she wanted her sister to start hanging around with Russel. She was only sixteen.

But she didn't say that to Brad. She just said, "We'll see," and kissed him quickly.

"About moving in—?"

"Let's talk about it later," Angie said, and got out of the car. As she walked back to the Pizzeria, though, she was sorry she'd said that. Brad might think she was actually considering it as a real option.

Still, the thought wouldn't leave her. It would be wonderful to be able to spend all their free time together. And her insides went soft at the thought that he loved her enough to want her to share his music. He was different from the last time they'd been together, there was no denying that. There was a new kind of energy in him, in his kisses, that made her pulse race.

Yes, it was scary.

At the same time, it was wildly exciting.

Eight

It was nearly nine on Saturday night, and the hot, humid darkness of a Galveston summer night blanketed the city. Susan stopped her car—the secondhand blue Honda she'd bought with last summer's paychecks—in front of the small frame house where Angie lived. They were headed to Dark of the Moon, where Freddie and Brad were having their big debut with the Blood Brothers.

Susan tapped the horn twice. As she waited for Angie and Nita to come out of the house, she wondered how Freddie was feeling. Susan had called the motel earlier to wish her luck, but Mrs. Gardner reported that Freddie had already gone over to the Brothers' house. She sounded irritated.

"I've hardly seen Freddie since she got involved with that new band," she said. She had never been very enthusiastic about her daughter's singing, and she seemed even less so now. "And from what I've seen," she added with a motherly sniff, "I don't like it very much at all. Whatever that group is doing to her, it's not good."

Talking about Freddie behind her back made Susan uncomfortable, but she had to admit that she agreed with Freddie's mom. Since Freddie had started practicing with the Brothers, she'd become remote and out of touch with the people around her, almost as if she weren't there at all. She'd made dozens of mistakes at work, and Susan had done a lot of covering up. Thinking about it, she wondered whether it was the late nights or Freddie's romance with Flint that was making the difference in her. Whatever it was, Freddie was certainly acting dopey and confused. When she'd shortchanged the second customer in a row, Susan had mentioned it to her. Freddie just shrugged and smiled in a lazy way that accused *Susan* of acting strange.

Susan made a grim face. Freddie might be right about that—Susan *had* been acting strange lately. But Susan didn't have to look farther than her own living room for the cause. She hadn't reconnected her television set. That had been a gesture that said, plain as day, I don't want to hear from you, Drew Morris. She hadn't been bothered by his voice or his face since.

But that didn't mean she hadn't thought about him and his bizarre message. And the eerie mystery that continued to surround the grave on the beach. And the death of Sara Robertson, the girl from Dallas. It frightened her to think about it, but the image of Drew Morris—his intense face, his commanding eyes—stayed with her, even when she tried to shut him out of her mind.

As much as Susan tried to escape the reality of these horrors, she couldn't escape Mack, who apparently thought it was his duty to keep her up-to-date on the developments in both murder cases. He especially seemed to get a kick out of giving her the coroner's reports. Drew Morris had died of a heart attack. That seemed strange in somebody so young, but apparently there was a history of heart disease in his family. So the cause of death was pretty straightforward. The only mystery now was how his body had come to lie in a shallow grave on the beach behind the SeaWall Condominium.

Sara Robertson had died of something called pernicious anemia, something about a low red blood cell count—although there hadn't been any indication that she'd been suffering from any illness. The coroner's office couldn't account for the strange puncture marks on her neck, but they'd ruled out drug use. Neither case was high priority with the cops, according to Mack, since both victims had died of natural causes. They weren't murdered.

"You mean, it's okay for somebody to bury a body on the beach?" Susan had asked.

Mack shrugged. "Not exactly. But whoever did it didn't leave a card. Besides, we've run out of leads."

So there it was. Two deaths, two mysteries. And a television set with a mind of its own telling her that she and her friends were in danger. It was no wonder she'd been acting as if she'd had something on her mind lately.

"Hi," Angie said brightly. She plopped down in the front seat as Nita got into the back. Both sisters looked pretty in crisp, summery dresses and strappy sandals, their long hair loose and flowing. Susan had opted for something more casual, a short denim skirt, simple yellow top, yellow sandals.

Angie's Aunt Carlota had come out of the house with the girls to see them off. She paused by the car. "You know," she added a little uneasily, "I don't think I like the idea of you girls going to a place called Dark of the Moon. All kinds of strange things can happen in the dark of the moon. It is the witching hour of the night: a time for evil."

"Oh, don't be silly, Aunt Carlota." Nita giggled. "You think of things like that because you're a witch. It's a theme club for teens. It's completely innocent. The name doesn't mean anything."

"A name like that means *something*," Aunt Carlota said. "You girls should be careful."

"We will," Susan promised. She liked Angie's aunt, even though she didn't quite believe the superstitions and the old magic she practiced. But Aunt Carlota did have a great many believers around Galveston. For a moment Susan wondered if Aunt Carlota could maybe use her magic to find out who had dug the grave on the beach, or how the weird marks had come to be on Sara Robertson's neck. Perhaps she could even explain the face on Susan's TV screen.

But this wasn't the time to ask. Besides, if she told her about Drew Morris's face on the television screen, Aunt Carlota would probably insist on coming over to exorcise the evil spirits from her apartment. Susan wasn't ready for that. She said good-bye and backed out of the driveway.

Susan was beginning to feel better about the night ahead of her. At the very least it would help her to forget about Drew Morris.

Dark of the Moon was packed by the time Susan, Angie, and Juanita showed up. The band wasn't on yet, but some people were dancing to the jukebox. Susan was afraid they wouldn't be able to find seats, until Angie found the table Brad had reserved for her. Looking around, Susan was amazed at the number of people who had shown up. They'd probably been drawn to the theme, Susan decided, since they probably never heard of the band.

Dark of the Moon. The club certainly lived up to its name, Susan thought. Angie's aunt would probably have dragged them out of there in an instant. Ghoulish caped figures with dead-white faces and staring eyes took money at the door. Bats hung from the ceiling, and skeletons glowed purple under black lights. Open coffins stood in the corners, covered with cobwebs. The waiters wore black T-shirts and black jeans, white face makeup, and blood-red lipstick.

But Susan didn't think the theme was hip or cool. The bats made her shudder, and she had the feeling that the ghouls were watching her with their red-rimmed eyes. The whole atmosphere was entirely too creepy for her liking, and it was making her uncomfortable.

At nine thirty someone switched off the jukebox, and the band came out wearing all black, with dark sunglasses, as usual. Flint gave a brief welcome to the club and introduced the members of the band. Susan had to admit that his low, accented voice had an intriguing quality. She glanced over at Nita and Angie. Nita was almost hypnotized by Flint and by what he was saying. Angie, of course, was staring at Brad. Susan glanced at Freddie, standing behind Flint. She was wearing a short, tight, sleeveless black dress, cut very low in the back. Freddie's attention, like that of practically every other girl in the club, was riveted on Flint.

When the band began their first number, and Freddie began to sing, Susan understood immediately why she had called the music seductive. Susan found it captivating, mesmerizing. It was as eerily hypnotic as Flint's voice had been. But it wasn't just the music—it was the lyrics, too. They were slippery and hard to catch. The few phrases she did understand made her feel unaccountably uneasy. She was glad that they vanished from her head as soon as she heard them, like words heard in a dream.

With an effort Susan pulled herself away from the music and looked around at the rapt faces. Nobody was moving. The few people who had been on the dance floor were now sitting down and listening. Almost everybody seemed to be captivated by the music. Those who weren't, like her, were glancing around uncomfortably. A few were leaving.

By the end of the set, Susan was distressed and fidgety. She would have left, but her friends showed no sign of moving, and she couldn't leave them there. As the houselights brightened, the Brothers came over to their table and sat down.

Susan tried to make conversation with Freddie, telling her how well she sang and how great she looked and how much fun the club was, but she might as well have been talking to a wall. Freddie was moody and silent. She didn't even look at Susan as she spoke—all her attention was focused on Flint. In fact, nobody seemed to want to talk very much. Angie and Brad were dancing, but the others just seemed to want to sit and listen to the jukebox play the Brothers' music.

After a little while Bishop asked Susan to dance with him. Feeling bored and sleepy and hoping that some physical movement might break the spell, Susan agreed.

On the floor Susan felt heavy and languid, as if she were half-asleep. The lights were dizzying. Mirrored balls hung from the ceiling, catching the colored lights and sprinkling them onto the dance floor. The fingers of color reached into her, making her feel light-headed and giddy, and she stumbled.

"You're fighting it," Bishop whispered in her ear, tightening his arms around her. "Go with the music. Let it take you."

Susan knew that Bishop was right. That's what you did when you danced, you went with the music, you let it take you. But she didn't *want* this music to take her. It was totally irrational, she knew, but she felt somehow threatened by the group's music. It was almost as if the music itself wanted something from her, something she was unwilling to give.

She felt threatened by Bishop in the same way, Susan realized. He had a strange effect on her. Susan had dated before, and she'd even thought she was in love once or twice. This was different. She was breathless, and her pulse was beating fast and hot in her throat. In Bishop's arms her body felt fluid, wanting to move in a different way. The feeling frightened her. She was trembling and she held herself tightly, making an effort to conceal how she felt.

"You don't have to be so stiff, you know," Bishop said, looking down at her. His glance was unreadable behind his glasses, but his lips were curved in a slight smile. "Loosen up, Susan. I'm not going to hurt you. I want you to have fun, that's all." He held her closer then, forcing her body to move with his.

And then, suddenly, she was dancing, easily and lightly, without intention, without thought. It was as if she were in a trance, in a dream. Everything else disappeared, too, the lights, the room—it was just she and Bishop and the sweet music that wrapped them up and pulled them in.

The next thing she knew, she was sitting at the table again, breathless, flushed, her pulse racing.

"Did you and Bishop have a good dance?" Angie asked.

"What?" Susan asked. Her head felt thick and fuzzy, and somewhere deep inside her there was an unmistakable cold fear.

Nita giggled. "You were really *gone*," she said. "Russel and I danced by and said hi, and you didn't even notice. Gee, I wonder what they're putting into those drinks."

Angie leaned closer. "Are you okay, Susan?" she asked. "You look kind of . . . strange."

"I have a headache," Susan said, closing her eyes. The fear and apprehension in her middle grew tighter, like a knot. "I guess it's the music."

It was the music, and more. It was Bishop, and the way he had held her, and the club, and . . .

Susan's headache began to pound.

The second set had ended, and Angie was waiting for Brad to come back to the table. She couldn't believe how much she was enjoying the music, the club, the people. There had been a wonderful misty quality to the evening, as if she'd been wrapped in a silvery, dreamlike fog filled with soft sparkles of pastel light that exploded like Roman candles in the velvety darkness. She couldn't remember ever feeling this wonderful before.

It was funny, too. She hadn't looked forward to the music, yet that was what she had loved most tonight. She had been fascinated by its strange, eerie sound, the way it reached out for her and pulled her into its deep rhythms, making her want to relax and let it flow through her, like a warm, honey-sweet river. The music and the lyrics opened a part of her that she hadn't known existed. She loved listening to the words Freddie sang, words that seemed to speak to her inner being. She just wished she could remember them when the song was over.

Most of all, she loved watching Brad play. For her he was the star of the entire show. Several times during the set he'd looked up and smiled at her—a slow, sexy smile that made her heart pound. Yes, they *could* share the music, Angie decided, the way he wanted them to. She could come to the club every night and listen. Maybe she could even—

She pushed the thought away. No, she couldn't

move in with him. It was out of the question. But watching Brad, she felt the temptation. Swaying dreamily to the music, she couldn't help thinking how wonderful it would be if . . .

When the set was over, Susan leaned across the table. "Angie, I've got a ferocious headache. Are you ready to go?"

"What did you say?" Angie asked. The melody of the last song was still echoing in her head, and she felt so dreamy that it required an effort of will to focus her attention on what Susan was saying. If she didn't know better, she'd almost think she was drunk. But that was silly. This was a teen club and there was no alcohol. No, if she was feeling hazy, it was the wonderful effect of the music.

"I said," Susan repeated, "that I have a headache. Are you and Nita ready to go?"

Angie looked across the floor. Brad would be here in a moment, and they were going to dance again. The jukebox was playing one of the Brothers' songs, and Nita was dancing with Russel. They really seemed to be hitting it off. When Brad had mentioned that he wanted to introduce them, Angie hadn't thought it was a good idea. Now, though, it seemed perfect. It seemed to round everything out: she and Brad, Nita and Russel, Freddie and Flint. Now, if only Susan would stop being such a spoilsport and give Bishop a chance—

"Where's Bishop?" she asked. It was hard to make her mouth form the words.

"I don't know," Susan replied. "My head hurts. I can't think about anything right now, including Bishop." She reached for her purse. *Especially Bishop*, she added silently to herself. "I've got to get out of here, Angie. Are you coming with me, or are you going to wait for Brad?"

Angie smiled. "Brad will take me home," she said. "We'll go to the Brothers' house first so I can see the place. Freddie will come too." She put her hand on Susan's arm. "Why don't you come with us, Susan? We can have a party." She pointed across the crowded room. "Look, there's Bishop. I'm sure he'll ask you to dance with him again. Why don't you stay?"

Susan didn't look at Bishop. She leaned toward Angie. "Are you all right, Angie? You're not acting like yourself."

Angie tossed her hair back over her shoulder with a wicked laugh. Oh, Susan, always so smart, always thinking she had the right answer. But tonight she was wrong. Tonight, for the first time in her life, Angie felt she was being her real, true self. Ever since they'd started going together, Brad had accused her of being prudish and old-fashioned. But the real Angie wasn't like that at all, and the Brothers' music had helped her to escape.

She was the Angie who understood that whatever feels good is good. The Angie who knew how to let herself go, knew how to have fun. And tonight she was going to show Brad how much fun the *real* Angie could be.

"I'm fine," Angie said. The Brothers' music on the jukebox grew louder, and she smiled.

Susan got up. "How about Nita?"

"She's fine too."

"Well, good night," Susan said. She stood for a moment, as if she were hoping that Angie would change her mind. Then, abruptly, she was gone.

Brad came over. "What's the matter with Susan?" he asked gruffly. "Doesn't she like the music?"

Angie kept smiling. "She just thinks too much. She'll be okay."

Brad pulled her up and she went into his arms. "Let's not worry about Susan," he said into her ear. "Bishop will take care of her."

"That's good," Angie said, pressing herself against him. "Susan needs somebody to take care of her. The way you take care of me."

"Yeah," Brad said. He laughed a little. "That's exactly what she needs."

Angie didn't answer. She wasn't worried about Susan. She wasn't worried about Nita, either. She wasn't thinking of anyone but Brad. And the music. The music that pulsed softly through her

102

with the rhythm of her own blood. The music that was letting her be herself, for the first time in her life.

It was after midnight when Susan got back to her apartment and let herself into the dark living room. She didn't turn the light on. She just sat down on the sofa, across from the silent television screen, and stared into the darkness. The moon, full and round, made a silvery lagoon on the floor.

The fear that she'd felt back at the club was still with her, though it was heavier now, and more real. She hadn't wanted to leave Angie and Nita behind, or Freddie either. A part of her had wanted to insist that they all leave together, that it wasn't safe to stay. That there was some kind of dangerous force that threatened to pull them in, pull them under.

But another part of her, the rational part, knew that she was overreacting. Dark of the Moon was a club with a trendy theme. There was nothing to be afraid of. Besides, Angie and Freddie—even Nita—were old enough to know what they were doing.

Susan looked down at her hands. If there was nothing to be afraid of, why were her palms sweaty and slick? Why was this terrible feeling of foreboding making her stomach feel queasy? And worst of all, why did she feel, with an absolute, desolate certainty, that she had said good-bye to Freddie and Angie and Brad and Nita for the last time?

You're in danger, you and your friends. You're next.

The voice, uninvited, came from the back of her mind. It came with a loud clarity that made her sit up straight and pull in her breath.

I want to help.

"Then help," Susan whispered out loud. "What is this thing I'm so afraid of?"

You believe—but you don't want to believe. If you're going to get through to me, you've got to believe.

For a minute Susan sat still. Then, moving deliberately, she got up and plugged in the television set. She sat down again and folded her hands in her lap, waiting.

Feeling sillier and sillier by the minute.

You goose, the rational part of herself said in a dry, sarcastic tone. *What do you think you're doing? Waiting for someone to commune with you through the TV? Have you totally lost your mind?*

There was a soft knock on the door. Susan started violently, cold fear lancing through her. Who could it be at this hour of the night?

She swallowed. It wasn't that late, really. The knock was probably Mack or Betty. They'd heard her drive up and wanted her to baby-sit tomorrow. Or maybe it was Angie, or Freddie. Maybe they'd changed their minds about going to the Brothers' house and decided to stop by.

Without turning on the light, Susan got up and went to the door. There wasn't anything to be afraid of, but there wasn't any point in taking risks, either. She left the chain on and opened the door cautiously, just a crack.

"Who is it?" she asked.

"Hey, Susan," a soft voice said. "Why don't you invite me in?"

Nine

Susan's breath caught in her throat. "Bishop?"

"Yeah. You left without saying good night."

Susan leaned against the wall next to the door, her knees suddenly weak. She was feeling the way she had felt when she and Bishop danced. "I . . . I had a headache," she whispered.

"That's too bad," Bishop said. "It was probably the lights. They kind of get to me, too. That's why I wear dark glasses when I play." He paused. "Listen, would you mind asking me in for a minute or two? I promise not to stay too long. I want to talk, that's all. We didn't really get to talk tonight, and there's so much to say."

He was right, Susan thought dimly. There *was* so much to say, so much—She saw her hand on the chain, felt her shoulder muscles tense to open the door. Then she stopped and summoned her strength to resist. "I don't think so, Bishop," she heard herself say. "It's late, and I need to—"

"It's not that late," Bishop said. He put his mouth to the crack in the door. "I really liked dancing with you, Susan. I brought a tape. I thought maybe we could dance together, just the two of us. Would you like that?"

Yes, Susan thought, remembering how it had felt to let herself go with the music. *I would like that*.

"Then invite me in," he said, as if he had read her thoughts. His voice was soft and gentle, a whisper. But the command was imperative. "Invite me in, Susan."

Susan felt herself weakening. There was no harm in inviting Bishop to come in for a little while. They could talk and dance. . . .

"Please," he said softly, forcefully.

Susan lifted the chain on the door and opened it. "Come in," she said, stepping back.

Bishop smiled lazily and stepped through the door. He was still wearing his black outfit, but he'd taken off the dark glasses. He looked around the apartment. "Very nice," he said approvingly. "I like it."

"I'll turn on the light," Susan offered, moving toward the lamp. In the corner she noticed that the television screen was glowing softly, as if it were on. She'd probably forgotten to turn the power switch off before she unplugged it. When she'd plugged it in again, it had come on by itself.

Bishop moved swiftly between her and the lamp. "No," he said. He gestured toward the open window, where the moonlight was streaming in, soft and silvery. "It's perfect like this, don't you think?"

Susan was about to object. But suddenly it didn't seem important. Bishop was right—the room was perfect with just the moonlight, her, and him. She smiled to herself, glad he had come. It would be nice to have a talk and to dance a little.

Bishop looked around. "Do you have a tape player?" he asked.

Susan pointed to the bookshelf. Bishop walked over and put the tape on, turning the volume down low. The music—soft and sensual—began to fill the room.

Susan's breath caught, her eyes widened. There was that feeling again, that cold apprehension, deep inside. It made her want to resist, struggle—to put her fingers in her ears and shut out the invasive sounds of the words.

Bishop moved toward her, his arms out. "Dance?" he asked. He was smiling. In the moonlit shadows his eyes were pools of deep, lovely darkness, with tiny dancing lights.

Susan found herself growing breathless. In the

next instant, without meaning to, she was moving toward him, lifting her arms. There was nothing to be afraid of, nothing to struggle against. Looking into his eyes, she could forget her apprehensions, her childish need to resist. Looking into his eyes, she knew she need never be afraid again. She would be one with Bishop and the music and—

Danger.

The single word was so clear and emphatic that Susan was sure it had been spoken out loud. But there were only the two of them in the room. She pulled her eyes away from Bishop's and glanced at the TV. The screen was blank.

"Look at me, Susan," Bishop whispered. He put his fingers on her cheek and gently turned her face toward him.

Suddenly Susan was frightened. No, it was greater than that. A cold terror sliced through her like a knife. If she gave in to Bishop, to the music, *to the dream*, she would be lost. Forever. And she knew it with the utmost certainty.

She closed her eyes. "Help me," she whispered out loud, her words a plea. "Oh, please, *help* me!"

The television set crackled.

"It's okay," Bishop said in a low, crooning voice. His eyes were still fixed on hers. He put his hand on her shoulder. "Let's turn the set off. We don't want to watch TV, anyway, do we?"

"I'll turn the set off," Susan heard herself saying mechanically. "We don't want to watch TV."

But as she moved slowly toward the set, the screen began to brighten, and a picture came on.

The face on the screen was that of Drew Morris.

Angie and Nita got out of Brad's car in front of the Brothers' house.

"This is it," Brad said.

Russel climbed out and shut the car door behind him. "Great place, huh?"

Nita glanced across the street. "You've got to be kidding," she said. She wrinkled her nose. "A cemetery?"

Brad laughed. "Hey, dead people are perfect neighbors. They don't call the cops because of a little noise late at night." He reached for Angie's hand. "Come on. I want to show you something."

Angie cast a look back at her sister. "I can't stay too long," she said. "I don't want to get in trouble for keeping Nita out too late."

"That's fine," Brad said. "But if you ask me, Nita doesn't seem to care if she ever goes home again." Angie looked over and saw Nita was saying something to Russel with a giggle, and he had his arm around her shoulders.

"Where are we going?" Angie asked, as Brad led her into the house and down the front hall, past stacks of big instrument cases. It was a huge old house, dark and shadowy. No wonder the Brothers had come up with such a spooky theme for their club. They'd probably thought of it right here, in this very hall.

"Let's go upstairs," Brad said. "I want to show you my room."

"Really, Brad," Angie said, holding back. "I—" She stopped. *Wait*, she told herself. *That's the old Angie talking.* The *real* Angie wouldn't be afraid to let Brad show her his room, sit down, and talk for a while. Then she'd collect Nita, and Brad could take them both home, long before her father began wondering where they were.

Brad's room was at the end of the upstairs hall. He opened the door and Angie followed him in. He lit a candle.

"Don't you have any lights?" Angie asked.

Brad chuckled. "Sure. But I like the candle. It's more romantic, don't you think?" He gestured around the room. "What do you think of the posters?"

In the flickering light of the candle, the posters had a dark, powerful effect. They were full-size pictures of the Brothers with their instruments.

"Nice, huh?" Brad asked.

Angie nodded.

He followed Angie's gaze as she looked around the room. "See how big this place is? More than enough space for both of us."

"I don't think—" Angie began automatically. Then she stopped.

Brad looked down at her. He'd taken off his dark glasses, and his eyes were a pale blue, glittering in the darkness. "Don't say no," he instructed her. "Say, 'I'll think about it.'"

"I . . . I'll think about it," Angie whispered.

"That's my girl," Brad said. He kissed the dimple in her chin. The hollow of her throat. Her mouth.

Angie clung to him dizzily, trusting his strong, powerful arms to hold her, to keep her from falling. She loved the way Brad was kissing her, the way he was holding her. It was almost perfect. There was only one thing that would make everything even better.

"Brad," she said dreamily, when he had lifted his lips from hers, "could we listen to some of the Brothers' music?"

Brad chuckled. "Yeah," he said. "If that's what you want."

"That's what I want," Angie said softly. "More than anything." She pulled his head down to hers and kissed him again. "Almost anything."

Freddie sat at the table, her chin in her hands. She felt absolutely wrung out, as if she'd just finished running a marathon. It was long after midnight, and the club was empty except for her and Flint. They were alone. At last.

Flint stepped out of the office, locking the door behind him. He came over to the table. Standing behind her, he put his hands on the back of her neck and began to massage gently.

"Are you tired, Frederica?" he asked.

"Yes," Freddie said. "Very. It was a big night. We were a hit, don't you think?"

The truth was, though, that she couldn't remember most of the evening. It was the same way when they practiced. Once she invited the music inside her, she could never recall what happened. It was a very strange sensation. But each time it was easier to give in, to let the music take over. If only she weren't so tired afterward, it would be wonderful.

Flint sat down across from Freddie and took off his glasses. "You were very good, Frederica." He stroked her arm. "You bring a new life to the lyrics."

"Do you think so?" Freddie's arm tingled where he was stroking it.

"I know so," Flint said. He picked up her arm and kissed the inside of her wrist, very gently. "You are one of us. Isn't it so?" He looked at her.

"Yes," Freddie whispered. "Yes, it is so." She shivered as his lips came down on her wrist.

Susan stood staring at Drew's image on the

television screen, feeling the blood drain from her face, the roaring in her ears almost drowning out the music.

"Susan," Bishop said sternly, stepping forward, "we don't want to watch television. We have better things—" He stopped when he saw the face on the screen.

"Hello, Bishop," Drew said.

"*You!*" Bishop hollered. He stepped back, his mouth twisted, ugly. "What are you doing here?"

Susan reached for a chair to steady herself. "You know him?" she whispered incredulously.

Bishop didn't answer. But he didn't need to. Susan could read his feelings in his face. Bishop knew Drew Morris. And he was afraid of him. Mortally afraid.

"Turn off the music, Susan," Drew Morris said gently. "You'll be able to think better with the music off. And Bishop and I can have a little talk."

Susan took a step toward the tape player. Bishop glared at her. "Leave it on," he said.

"No," Susan whispered. She groped her way to the tape player and switched it off. It was like stepping out of a fog bank into clear air.

Bishop thrust her aside roughly and strode to the door. Hand on the knob, he turned. His face was white, his eyes glittered like black diamonds, his jaw clenched.

"Don't think you're going to get away with this," he growled. "Give it up, Morris. You've already lost. You're a dead man."

"Then why are you leaving?" Drew Morris asked. "We need to talk, you know. There's an old misunderstanding we have to clear up."

Bishop's only answer was another savage growl. He walked back to the center of the room to confront the image on the screen. "We don't *need* to talk about anything," Bishop said. "And even if we did, I don't take orders from mortals. Especially dead ones."

"Ah, Bishop," Drew said. "Now I remember your stubbornness. But I, too, plan to stick around. I may be dead, but I am not gone."

With that Bishop turned and strode back to the door. He jerked it open and flew down the stairs. A minute later Susan heard Bishop's car tires spinning on the gravel; then he was gone.

Susan turned back to the television set, half expecting Drew Morris to be gone too. But he was still there. She dropped down on the sofa, her knees so weak she could no longer stand. Her mouth was dry. Her hands were trembling. "Drew?" she whispered. She knew it was crazy to be talking to the television, but no less crazy than what had just happened. Anyway, she had to talk to him. Insane as it was, she *had* to.

"I need to know what's going on," she said in a

low voice. She knotted her fingers together. "You said before that you couldn't remember everything, but I need to know what you know. I need to know what the danger is."

Drew Morris's pale gray-green eyes regarded her seriously. "I was doing a story on runaways," he said slowly. "A girl named Sara"—he paused for a moment, then his face brightened—"Robertson. She was my lead." He closed his eyes for a moment. When he opened them again, he spoke slowly, as if his memories were coming back bit by bit. "When I got onto her, she was a groupie, hanging around with this band in Dallas. Yes, that's how it was. She came down here, and I followed her, hoping to find out why—" He broke off.

"Tell me," Susan urged. "Tell me, Drew."

"Look," he said flatly. "This isn't the kind of thing any rational person would believe. But you *have* to. If you don't believe me, Susan, I can't help you. And you won't be able to help your friends. So before I go any further with this crazy, twisted tale, I need to know that your heart is in the fight. There's a lot of work ahead of you, and I need to be sure of your commitment."

"Tell me," Susan repeated urgently. "*Please.*"

"Sara Robertson came here with the Blood Brothers, the band your friend Bishop plays in. And they got her. I suspect they got other groupies, too—several teens in the Dallas area disappeared while the Brothers were there. But I know they got Sara, because I saw it." He managed a thin chuckle. "They tried to get me too, but I outfoxed them."

Susan stared at him. "What do you mean they tried to get you? And how'd you outfox them?"

"I died first."

"You died first," Susan repeated automatically. Then the true meaning of the words sank in. Her eyes opened wide. "Do you mean they *killed* people? And they tried to kill *you?*" she asked in a shocked whisper.

"Yes. But there's a law, you see, that they can't take what you won't give them. And I'd known about the bad heart for a long while. I knew they were onto me, that I was beginning to know too much. I didn't have much time left, so I checked out before they could get me." Drew chuckled again, wryly. "I'll bet the Brothers don't have many of their victims just up and *die* on them. . . ."

"Wait a minute," Susan said, confused. "What law? *Whose* law?"

"Whoever's running this show. I'm finding out that there's a lot I don't know about the way these things work. I'm learning quickly, though." He was beginning to sound excited. "I'm telling you, Susan, if I could only file a story from here—" He glanced around. "Wherever here is."

118

Susan cleared her throat. "Sara Robertson," she said, trying to gain control of her voice. "How did she die?"

Drew's mouth twisted. "The Brothers were out for blood."

"You mean they wanted revenge? Why? What did she do to them?"

"Sara? She didn't do anything. It was completely random. I'm telling you, they were simply out for blood."

"Then why—?" She clenched her hands. "Drew, will you please stop talking in circles? What is it about the Brothers that makes them want to kill people?"

"Do you believe?"

"How can I know if I believe," she countered, "if you won't *tell* me!"

Drew looked at her, his pale eyes grim. "Haven't you figured it out yet, Susan? The Blood Brothers are vampires."

Ten

Susan's laugh felt dry in her throat. It turned into a cough. "Of *course* they're vampires," she said. "That's why they call themselves Blood Brothers and wear those stupid dark glasses, pretending that the light hurts their eyes. It's all part of the act, like the name of their club. The Brothers are nothing but hype."

Drew shook his head, his eyes somber. "I'd give anything if that were so," he said, "but it's not. You're wrong, Susan. Dead wrong. I told you you'd have to believe. The Brothers are vampires. *Real* vampires."

Susan stared at him. "But that's not possible," she breathed. "I mean, vampires are superstition— folklore. Vampires are what they make movies out of, not rock bands."

Drew's voice was cynical. "Since when is it possible to be talking to a dead man on television?" he asked. "It doesn't make sense that Sara Robertson is dead, either—with a puncture wound on her throat."

A *puncture wound.* Susan's hands felt clammy, and she wiped them on her denim skirt. *The coroner never did explain the puncture wound.*

Drew's voice became gritty. "Bishop's errand here tonight was a vampire errand. How much sense does that make?"

"A vampire errand?" Susan repeated, her voice rising. She put her hand to her throat. "Are you saying he came for *me?* That's crazy!"

Drew's chuckle was bitter. "Of course it's crazy. That's why you have to throw out everything your mind is telling you about what can and cannot be. You have to *believe* in the irrational and in what you've always thought impossible."

"I can't," she said, beginning to cry. "I'm sorry, but I just can't."

"Then I can't help you," Drew said flatly. "Or Freddie, or Angela, or . . . wait, there's somebody else." He stopped, frowning. "I'm not getting her name. She's somebody's sister."

"Nita?"

"Yes, Juanita. I can't help her either."

Susan closed her eyes. The cold inside of her congealed into a hard, metallic-tasting fear, and

122

she remembered the dread she'd felt at the club—the feeling that she'd said good-bye to Freddie and Angie and Brad and Nita for the last time.

Drew was speaking again, and Susan opened her eyes. "Your friend Brad is already gone," he said. "I don't think there's anything you can do about him. But the others—" He hesitated. "I can't say for sure, but if you act quickly, you might be able to save them. In order to help, though, you must not let yourself be taken."

Susan nodded solemnly. "Go on," she urged.

"The Brothers don't possess their victims all at once," Drew explained. "They take them little by little, over a period of several days. And their victims have to consent—that's one of the rules they operate under. As I said, they can't take what they aren't given."

With a shiver Susan thought of Freddie standing behind Flint earlier that night, her eyes fixed on him. Had she already consented? And if the Brothers could take all her friends, how would Susan be strong enough to resist?

Drew smiled crookedly. "Their methods can be pretty persuasive," he said, as if he were plugged into Susan's thoughts. "The music, for instance. Some people find it irresistible. The lyrics tell them anything they want to hear. The music promises them the freedom to do whatever they *feel* like doing."

Susan could feel herself trembling. Drew was right about the music. That was what had frightened her earlier at the club and then again when Bishop had come over. You could do anything you wanted and forget about paying the consequences.

Drew's mouth tightened. "If you move fast, Susan, if you get to your friends right away and tell them what you know about the Brothers, they might still be able to respond to you. Some of them, anyway."

Susan recoiled as if he'd hit her. "You mean, I'd have to tell them . . . what you told me?" How could she? How could she tell them that she'd gotten this urgent message about vampires from a dead man who appeared to her on television? "They'd think I've lost my mind," she whispered. "They'd never believe me."

"They might," Drew said quietly.

Susan shook her head. "This is idiotic. People in their right minds don't—"

Drew snorted. "There you go, being rational again. I tell you, the Brothers don't operate under the laws of reason." He paused. His tone got serious once again. "There's something else you have to do, Susan."

A half-hysterical giggle rose in Susan's throat. "I hope it's easier than believing."

"It's harder," Drew said grimly. "You have to keep yourself safe. If you're taken, your friends won't stand a chance."

"Taken?" The giggle came up again.

Drew's voice was hard-edged, grating. "You invited Bishop in, didn't you? That gives a vampire a carte blanche. It's one of the rules."

The giggle died. "Do you mean he can come in—anytime?"

"Whenever he wants."

Susan stared at him.

"This isn't a game, Susan." His face was stern, but sympathetic. "There are a lot of superstitions about vampires, as you know, and many of them are rooted in the truth. Garlic and roses and wild thyme, for instance. It's true. They'll ward off vampires. A cross works too, if you believe, and it's easier to find a cross than to happen on some wild thyme. If you don't already own a cross, get one. Put it on. And for heaven's sake, *never take it off.*"

"I guess I could get one from Angie tomorrow. She has a lot of them."

"No, you can't wait that long. Bishop might be back tonight, and you need to be prepared. Make one out of a couple of matches. Better yet, make two or three. Put one by your bed. Hang one around your neck."

"But I—"

There was a loud, commanding knock at the door.

"Is it . . . him?" Susan asked.

"How should I know?" Drew asked. "I can't see through the door any more than you can."

Susan got up. "Excuse me," she said. She giggled again, at the idea of saying "excuse me" to a television set. Then she stopped giggling. She suddenly felt cold. If it was Bishop, she wouldn't let him in. She didn't have to tell him that she'd learned the truth about him. She could just say it was too late for company.

The knock came again. "Susan?" a harsh voice asked. "Susan? Open the door." It was Mack.

With a feeling of relief Susan went to the door and opened it. Mack was standing there in his uniform with his arms folded across his chest.

"What I want to know," he demanded abruptly, "is what you're doing entertaining company at this time of night."

"Mack," Susan said tiredly, "don't you have anything better to do than worry about me?"

"The car woke Betty up," Mack replied. "Spinning tires in the gravel, she said. Woke the kids up, too. She didn't want to come out here herself, but she told me about it when I got home just now." He scowled darkly. "It's one o'clock in the morning. And you're only seventeen, remember? I don't care if you have graduated from high school—you're still my little sister, and I'm still responsible for you."

"I'm sorry, Mack." Susan knew he was only doing what he thought was right. "I didn't invite him to come over. He just showed up. And he stayed only a few minutes. I asked him to leave." It was *almost* the truth.

"Yeah, well . . . ," Mack growled. He managed to give the impression that he was taking her explanation under consideration and he might—just *might*—accept it.

Susan sat down hard on the sofa. "It's late, Mack. And my friend's gone. Can we all go to bed now?"

Mack harrumphed. "All right." He headed toward the door. Then he paused and turned to face Susan again. "Oh, one more thing," he said as if he just remembered something. "Pete Dupree asked Betty and me to go fishing tomorrow on his boat. Can you keep the kids?"

Susan smiled. So Mack had an ulterior motive for coming up here at one in the morning. "Sure," she said. "I'd be glad to baby-sit."

"So you know, there's a tropical storm coming up the Gulf from the Yucatan. If it hits around here, it'll churn up the bottom and ruin the fishing for a couple of weeks. This may be our last chance for a while, so we'll probably take advantage of the situation and might not be back until dark."

"Stay as late as you like. I don't have any plans."

"Thanks." Mack was gruff, but placated. "And listen," he added, as a parting shot, "tell your friends that you don't have company after midnight. If they want to know why, tell them your brother says so, and he's a cop." He looked at her. "You got that?"

"I got it," Susan said with a small smile. She wondered what he'd say if she told him that the guy who'd spun his tires was a vampire. Maybe he'd get out his gun and threaten to shoot. Susan wondered if it would do any good if he did. Could a vampire be killed by an ordinary bullet? She seemed to remember something about silver bullets—but where did you get a silver bullet?

She caught herself, feeling trapped in the absurdity of her questions. She was acting as if what Drew had told her was real. She was acting as if *Drew* was real. But still—

Mack was halfway down the stairs when she called to him. "Uh, Mack, what ever happened with Sara Robertson?"

Mack turned around. "Who?"

"The girl they found in the motel last week. The girl who followed the rock band down here from Dallas."

Mack frowned. "How'd you know about that?

I thought her family was keeping the whole thing a secret. They didn't want it getting out that their daughter turned into a groupie, so they've been keeping it out of the papers."

Drew Morris, the dead guy on the beach, told me, Susan wanted to say. But she only shrugged, making her voice sound casual. "I don't know. I must have heard it at work. News gets around." She swallowed. "What . . . was the name of the band?"

"Blood something. Yeah, Blood Brothers. That was it. Pete is handling the investigation, and he brought the bandleader in for questioning. He turned out clean. Anyway, the girl died of natural causes. There wasn't any crime."

Susan stood still, feeling the blood pound in her temples. "Oh," she said.

"Betty will send the kids out about nine," Mack said. "You got stuff for breakfast?"

"Yes," Susan replied absently. When Mack got to the foot of the stairs, she shut the door and put the chain on, moving slowly and deliberately. Then she turned around.

"Drew?" she asked.

The television screen was blank. Drew was gone.

Before she went to bed, Susan stood by the phone a few minutes, debating whether she should

129

call Angie and Freddie. But the thought that the phone would wake up their parents kept her from doing it. Anyway, what would she ask them once she managed to get them on the line? *You haven't been bitten by a vampire lately, have you, Freddie?* Or *Remember, Angie—to keep a vampire away, just say no.* The thought made her smile, but the smile faded immediately.

Susan slept very little that night. She dreamed once of Drew. He was standing on the beach, holding his arms out to her. She ran toward him, laughing, happy to be with him, eager for his arms around her. But just as she reached him, he began to fade into transparency, only to reappear at the top of a dune, beckoning to her with an enigmatic smile. She started toward him, but the way was suddenly blocked by Flint and Brad and the other Brothers. Flint gestured toward a white sheet-covered mound at his feet. Fearfully, she lifted a corner of the sheet. Under it were the bodies of Freddie, Angela, and Nita, still and waxy-white, each with a puncture wound in her throat.

As she opened her mouth to scream, Drew was standing beside her, touching her. "To save them," he said, "you have to believe."

Susan's scream was a whimper. "I believe in you. *You* save them."

"I wish I could," Drew said sadly, "but I can't.

You're the only one who can save them. To do it, you have to trust yourself, believe in the Brothers, and control the power."

With that, he was gone.

Eleven

When Susan got up the next morning and looked at herself in the bathroom mirror, she saw dark circles under her eyes. She put on some extra cover-up. Even if nobody was going to be around but the kids, she didn't want to be reminded of how little she had slept.

"I'll have pancakes for breakfast," seven-year-old Pete announced.

"French toast," Randy asserted. He scowled at Pete. "I'm older. You have to eat what I say." Randy was nine.

"I say we're going to have fried-egg sandwiches," Susan said, getting out the skillet, "and I'm older than both of you put together." The boys couldn't quarrel with that logic and played quietly while Susan cooked. After breakfast she sent them out in the yard to play pirates with the toy swords and daggers they'd brought from El Paso, with the promise that later they would go to the video store and rent a movie.

Susan was glad for the day off from work, more so than on any other Sunday when the Pizzeria was closed. And since the kids pretty much took care of themselves, she had plenty of time to herself—to tidy up, do some laundry, and *think*.

Of course she'd heard stories about the supernatural, she thought, as she rinsed out her red blouse and hung it on the line across the back porch. She smiled at Randy, who waved to her from the swing set where he was hanging upside down by his knees, his dagger in his hand. She'd read about vampires and evil demons in *Dracula* and *Dr. Jekyll and Mr. Hyde*. She'd seen vampire movies, too. But all that stuff was fiction. Some interesting, some boring, but all of it the product of somebody's imagination.

But she couldn't see how Drew's appearance on the television set could be a product of her imagination. Freddie had seen him, and so had Bishop. Bishop had even recognized him, a fact that came as close to confirming Drew's story as anything else. And Mack had verified the rest of it—the part about Sara Robertson being a groupie of the Blood Brothers. And if that was true, wasn't it log-

134

ical that the *whole thing* was true?

Wasn't it logical that the Blood Brothers were vampires?

Susan could admit the possibility of a reality beyond the one she knew, and she could admit—because she had *felt* it—that the Blood Brothers and their music were dangerous, but she still couldn't believe in vampires. It was too ridiculous.

After giving Randy and Pete a snack that they claimed was for the crocodiles in the moat, and sending them back outside, Susan picked up the phone and called Angie's house.

"Angie and Nita are still asleep," her mother said. "They got in very late last night, you know. So late, in fact, that neither of them could get up for Mass this morning." She sounded angry, and it seemed that she blamed Susan.

At Freddie's the phone rang and rang. She finally answered, sounding very groggy. Too groggy to talk, really. She'd had a late night, and she was planning to sleep all day. "I'll see you tomorrow," she said, yawning, and clumsily hung up the phone.

So much for being in danger, Susan told herself, putting down the phone. *So much for vampires.* She couldn't decide whether she felt foolish or just plain relieved.

The kitchen door opened. "Hey, Susan," Randy yelled as he and Pete burst into the room, "we need some more peanut butter and crackers."

"More?" Susan asked, laughing. "Those crocodiles must be very hungry today."

"It's not for them," Pete said happily. He climbed on a chair to get the box of crackers. "It's for our new friend. He's a pirate, too."

Susan frowned. "What friend?"

"Me," a voice said.

Susan whirled, startled. "Who—? Oh, you."

Brad grinned lazily at her, the light glinting off his dark glasses. "Yeah, me," he said, leaning his shoulder against the doorjamb, looking relaxed in his black turtleneck and black jeans. "I was driving by and thought I'd stop and say hi. The boys invited me in."

"Invited you in?" Susan swallowed. *That gives a vampire carte blanche. It's one of the rules.*

"Yeah," Brad said. He tousled Randy's hair. "Randy and me, we're buddies, right?"

"He's Jean Lafitte the pirate," Randy shouted, brandishing his red plastic dagger. "And I'm his loyal mate. Come on, Pete, hurry up with the crackers. The ship's about to leave."

Pete turned to Susan and said, "Brad's going up in the tree house with us. We're going to have a picnic."

Susan frowned. Drew had said that Brad was already one of them, and in her dream he had been with the other Brothers, standing over the bodies of her friends. But now that he was here, leaning against her door, all that seemed pretty silly. Brad was a real, live person, not a vampire. But somehow she still didn't trust him.

"Wait a minute, guys," Susan told the boys. "Your ship's not going anywhere—except to the video store."

"The video store?" Pete climbed down from the chair. "Super! Can we have popcorn too? Come on, Randy. Race you to the car!"

"Hey, I'm a video freak," Brad said. "What are you going to get?"

"*Captain Hook*," Randy shouted. "Want to watch it with us, Brad?" Before waiting for an answer, Randy dropped his dagger and dashed out of the room and down the back stairs after Pete.

"Uh, you can't," Susan said quickly. She gave the first excuse she could think of. "I mean, I can't ask you to stay. I'm not supposed to have company when I'm baby-sitting."

Brad grinned. "You're old enough to live by yourself, but you're not old enough to have company while you're baby-sitting? Come off it, Suzie."

Susan reached for her purse. "No," she said. "And my name is Susan. Now, if you'll excuse me, I need to lock up." She went through the living room to bolt the front door. Brad was still there when she came back into the kitchen, leaning against the door.

"Bishop said to tell you hi," he said carelessly.

Susan took a deep breath. "Tell him hi back for me," she said in the most casual tone she could manage. She frowned a little. It was hot outside today, and humid—good tropical-storm weather. Why was Brad wearing a turtleneck?

"I will," Brad said. "He was a little bummed by what happened last night, you know."

Susan went past Brad through the door and stood waiting for him to follow her out. "He was?" she asked. She wondered about just how much Brad knew about what had happened the night before. Would Bishop have told the others about Drew Morris?

"Yeah," Brad said. The corners of his mouth tightened. "So was Flint, when he heard about it. He asked me to give you a message, Suzie."

Susan reached past him to close the door, but he put his hand on her arm. "I said, I have a message from Flint," he repeated. There was a clear threat in his voice.

"What kind of message?" Susan asked quietly.

"He said to tell you to stay away from Angie and Freddie and Nita," he said. "He thinks you're a bad influence on them."

Susan's eyes widened in disbelief. "What? Who does he think he is, telling me to—"

"Hey, cool it, Suzie." Brad's voice was smooth, soft. "I'm trying to make this easy for you. I don't

138

want you to get hurt, so I'm telling you this for your own good, okay? Nobody's going to involve you in anything if you don't want to be involved. We're not going to force you to hang out with us, or even to come to the club. Everybody's got free will, you know? All you have to do is stay out of the picture and you're home free. It's that simple."

From the driveway Susan could hear her nephews honking the horn. "Hey, Susan! Let's go!" Randy yelled. "Pete and me are tired of waiting."

"I've got to go," Susan said, trying to free herself from Brad's grasp.

Brad's fingers tightened on Susan's arm. "You do know," he said softly, "that you can always get in the picture yourself." He released her arm, and stepped back. "There's always room for another fan. Sometimes people don't like our music at first and change their minds later, after they've really listened to it. You know what I mean?"

Susan looked at him. What was he saying? Was he really talking about the music or—

"I'm not sure," she said.

Brad nodded. "Well, hey, that's a start," he said encouragingly. "If you're not sure, maybe you ought to try listening to the music again sometime." He turned and went down the stairs ahead of her, and stopped at the car.

"Hey, guys," he said, "thanks for the invitation.

I can't stay for the movie, but maybe I'll be back to see you. What do you think? Do you want me to come?"

Susan stepped forward, but before she could say anything, the boys had chorused a loud "Yeah!" and Randy had added, generously, "You can come *anytime*, Brad."

Twelve

Susan had already finished putting out the stuff for the salad bar when Freddie finally made it into work on Monday. Angie, who was usually very punctual, hadn't shown up yet, and Susan was really starting to get worried.

"How are you?" Susan asked Freddie. It wasn't a casual question.

Freddie rubbed her eyes. "Sleepy," she said. Her cap was crooked, and she was putting on her apron wrong side out. "Tired. Worn out. Pooped. How are you?"

"You've got your apron on backward," Susan said gently. "Were you out late last night?"

"No." With an effort Freddie reversed her apron. "The club isn't open on Sunday night. We practiced for a couple of hours in the evening, and I got to bed early for a change." She gave Susan a wry smile. "Mom saw to that. She's put her foot down about the late hours. I guess I'm going to have to tell the guys that we've got to start practicing earlier." She took a pair of sunglasses out of her apron pocket and put them on.

"What's the matter with your eyes?" Susan asked, a small buzz of alarm sounding inside her.

Freddie shrugged. "Nothing serious," she said. "They just feel a little gritty, that's all. These glasses aren't really dark enough, but they're all I figure I can get by with on the job. Knowing Gwen, she'll probably have something to say about them." With a sigh she picked up a stack of plates and started out of the kitchen. "All I know is I could really use a day off. I've got an incredible headache."

Susan was slicing mushrooms when Angie arrived. She was walking slowly, shoulders slumped, feet dragging. Her face was pale and her eyes shadowed.

"I'm sorry I'm late," she said listlessly. "I slept right through the alarm." She looked around. "Has Gwen hit the roof yet?"

"She's not even here," Susan replied. She cleared her throat. "Uh, did you and Nita go over to the Brothers' house on Saturday night after the show?"

Angie brightened. "Yeah. You should have come too, Susan. They've got a great house. We had a terrific time."

"What did you do?" Susan asked. She began slicing peppers, watching Angie out of the corner of her eye.

Angie smiled vaguely. "Oh, danced, that's all. And listened to music." She sighed, eyes half-closed. "Brad gave me a tape of the Brothers' music. Nita and I have been listening to it all weekend."

Susan frowned. "But I thought you didn't like rock."

"I thought I didn't either. I like the Brothers' music, though," Angie said, picking up a knife. "It makes me feel . . ." Her voice trailed off.

"Makes you feel how?" Susan persisted.

Angie began to slice onions for the pizza topping. "I don't know." She shrugged. "Like it lets me be myself, maybe."

Susan pushed the peppers into a bowl. "I don't understand," she said.

Angie turned. "That's because you didn't really listen to the music the other night," she said angrily. "If you did, you'd know what I'm talking about. But you won't listen. You're afraid the music might *do* something to you." Her voice was almost a sneer. "You're afraid the music might make you drop that phony I'm-so-good, I'm-totally-in-charge act and find out what you're really all about down deep inside. You'll find out you've got the freedom to do what you feel like doing, and that it's good for you." She eyed Susan. "Yeah, that really freaks you out, doesn't it?"

Susan stared at her friend. In all the time she'd known Angie, she'd never heard that ugly tone of voice. And what Angie was saying about the music was exactly what Drew had said.

Angie turned away again, as if she were struggling with herself. She dragged the back of her hand across her eyes. "I'm sorry, Susan," she muttered. "I didn't mean any of that—I don't even know where it came from. Forget it, will you?"

"That's okay," Susan replied. She frowned. "What's wrong with your eyes, Angie?"

"It's the onions," Angie said tonelessly. But her eyes stayed red-rimmed and bloodshot for the rest of their shift, and Susan never saw her smile.

Mack came in on his lunch hour for a pizza. "Hey, thanks for baby-sitting yesterday," he said. "The kids had a great time."

"I enjoyed it too," Susan said, ringing his sale on the register, "although I have to admit that I started getting a little seasick the third time through *Captain Hook*. How was your day? Did you guys catch anything yesterday?"

Mack handed her a ten. "Not much. Probably the storm. They named it today—Clarissa." He frowned. "Hey, listen, if it blows in along the coast here, I want you to close up that apartment and stay with us in the house. You hear?"

Susan laughed. "What makes you think," she asked teasingly, "that your house is any safer than the garage apartment?"

"Nice try," Mack said. His mouth was set stubbornly. "I don't care if it makes sense. I want you with us. If they order an evacuation to the mainland, I don't want to waste time looking for you."

"Okay," Susan said. She went to get Mack's iced tea. Her brother could be a pain, but it was good to know that he was looking out for her. It made her feel connected to something. Suddenly she wondered whether Freddie and Angie still felt that way about their families. She thought maybe they didn't. She handed Mack the glass.

"You got any lemon?"

Susan found it for him.

"And did you tell your friend about the no-company-after-midnight rule?"

"I haven't seen him," Susan replied. "But I'll tell him when I do."

Mack shifted his big bulk, looking uncomfortable. "Sorry for giving you such a hard time Saturday night," he said gruffly.

"It's okay," Susan said softly. If she could have reached him, she would have hugged him.

Later on that evening Nita came in. Susan was

surprised when she saw her. Nita's olive-toned skin looked sallow, and her face was drawn and tired looking. She was wearing a sleeveless top with a high collar.

"Angie," Susan said in the kitchen, "is Nita okay?"

"What do you mean 'okay'?" Angie asked defensively. She grabbed a plate off the stack. It slipped through her fingers, and she muttered something under her breath as she bent to pick up the pieces.

Susan was startled. She had never heard Angie curse before. She reached for the broom. "I mean," she said carefully, "is Nita feeling all right? She looks like she's got the flu or something."

"Yeah, she's got the flu," Angie said, ignoring the broom. "So butt out, okay?" She flung the pieces of the broken plate into the trash.

Susan leaned the broom against the wall and put both hands on Angie's shoulders. "I'm not going to butt out," she said quietly. "Something's going on with you guys, and I want to know what it is. I want to help you." She touched Angie's face. "I'm not telling you what to do or anything. I just care, that's all."

Angie's face softened. "I'm sorry," she whispered. "I don't know what's gotten into me today. I guess maybe I'm coming down with Nita's flu, too." Then something seemed to happen inside her, and the tenderness went out of her face and voice. She stepped back. "I said, *butt out*, Susan," she said flatly. "We don't need your help."

Susan was exhausted when she got home. Tourist season had started with a bang, and the Pizzeria had been packed all day. Freddie had left at four because of her headache, and even though Angie had stuck it out for the entire shift, she hadn't done anything right. Covering for Freddie and Angie, Susan had done three times the work she normally did, and when she climbed the stairs to her apartment, she was so tired she could hardly move.

Once inside, Susan went into the living room and sat down heavily. She was trying not to think of Freddie's pained face and the flat, ugly sound of Angie's voice when she'd told her to butt out. She was trying not to think of Drew, either, or of the things he had said. She had always prided herself on being reasonable and logical. How could she believe him?

But she couldn't stop thinking. She kept remembering Angie's accusation that she hadn't really listened to the music, that she'd been afraid of what the lyrics might tell her. It was true. She *was* afraid of the Brothers' music. She'd been afraid of it at the club on Saturday night, and later, when Bishop came over and put a tape on the player.

But there was something in it that made Angie and Freddie act the way they were acting, and she had to find out what it was. Listening to the music, Susan decided, really concentrating on the words, was the only way to find out.

Susan smiled a little, thinking of Mack and his worries. If he knew about this, he'd tell her not to listen—he hated rock, anyway. If Drew were here, he'd certainly tell her not to listen. But she wasn't responsible to them, she was responsible to herself. And her heart told her that if the music was exerting some strange influence over her friends, she had to find out what it was.

What are you up to tonight, Susan?

Oh, nothing much. Listening to a little vampire music, that's all.

Still, it was something she had to do. Moving very deliberately, she went into the other room and turned all the lights off except the desk lamp. She stood for a moment looking down at the television set. She unplugged it and walked over to the tape player. Standing there, she remembered how frightened she had felt when Bishop played the tape before. She remembered that she'd wanted to put her fingers in her ears and shut the music out. This time she had a reason to listen to it. She switched on the player and turned the volume up high. Then she forced herself to pull up the chair in front of the speaker. She sat down in

148

it, closed her eyes, and began to listen. For the first time she really *heard* the words.

Yes, they promised freedom, freedom from everything she'd ever thought or learned. They promised that you could do what you wanted to do, that you didn't have to follow anybody's rules but your own. They made sense. They made perfect sense. And they made you feel powerful, so powerful that you knew you could conquer the world. All you had to do was—

The tape had stopped playing when Susan realized, dimly, that someone was knocking at the door. With difficulty she roused herself, forcing her eyes open. It was late, after eleven, and she didn't feel like answering the door, no matter who it was. Anyway, why should she? It was her house, and she could do things *her* way. Right now all she wanted to do was listen to the music. She got up to turn the tape over.

But the knock came again, louder and more commanding. Maybe she'd better. The room seemed foggy, and she stumbled as she went toward the door. Sleepiness, that's what it was. Pushing pizzas all day had worn her out. She'd listen to the tape once more and then go to bed.

Susan saw that the chain was on. She smiled a little, holding on to the doorknob. That was good. It was good that she'd remembered to put on the chain. She was safe when the chain was on. She leaned her forehead against the door.

"Who is it?" she asked groggily.

The voice was soft. "Don't you know?"

Susan closed her eyes. "I . . . don't want to see you right now, Bishop." Her tongue felt thick. It was hard to speak.

"I know," Bishop said sympathetically. "It's been a long day, hasn't it? We don't have to talk, Susan. We can just sit quietly if you like." He paused. "We can do anything, you know. We can listen to some more music, if that's what you want."

Listen to music, Susan thought blurrily. Yes, that was a good idea, a very good idea. Listening to music would make her feel good. She fumbled the chain off and opened the door.

"Come in," she invited him.

"Thank you," Bishop said. He took off his dark glasses and smiled at her.

Thirteen

Bishop closed the door behind him and put the chain on. He turned around to face Susan.

"Not expecting big brother tonight?" he remarked casually.

Susan licked her lips. They were very dry. "I don't . . . maybe," she said.

Bishop glanced at the television, saw that it was unplugged. "Ah," he said. He nodded knowingly. His smile grew.

Suddenly Susan was afraid, and the fear cleared away some of the fog. She caught her lower lip between her teeth, feeling cold, feeling her hands grow clammy.

"Go away," she said. "It's getting late. I have to—"

"But you played the music," Bishop said softly. He took a step toward her. His eyes were dark and deep, his voice rich and compelling. "You invited me. You must want me here, or you wouldn't have invited me in."

Don't invite any of them into your house. It was Drew's warning. She should have remembered! She should have made the crosses he told her to make, too. Susan stepped back, away from the hypnotic darkness in Bishop's eyes. But she couldn't back up any farther. She was against the wall, beside the open window.

"I want you to go away," she repeated. She raised her voice, hearing it thin and reedy, close to hysteria. "I take back my invitation. Go away!"

"Let me kiss you," Bishop said gently, taking another step toward her. "You'll see, Susan—it's not so bad. You'll like it. Your friends do. They want you to be with them, Susan. They want us all to be together. He wants it too. He commands it."

"He?" Susan whispered, the fear washing over her in a numbingly icy wave.

"The One who commands us." Bishop's eyes gleamed. He smiled. "A kiss, Susan. One kiss." He took another step toward her.

Susan stood still, captured by Bishop's eyes. She felt herself waver, wanting to take a step forward, wanting to feel his arms around her. Perhaps, if he held her, she wouldn't feel so afraid.

She could join Freddie and Angie. And then, with a shudder, she remembered the sheet-covered mound in her dream, the waxy-white bodies under, and Drew standing beside her.

"*Don't move.*" The command was firm, sharp. The voice came out of the empty air beside her. Susan wrenched her eyes away from Bishop's to her right. The figure beside her was dim and shadowy, nearly transparent. Drew!

A grimace twisted Bishop's face. His eyes blazed. "What are you doing here?" he hissed.

Drew raised his voice. "In the name of everything that's good and loving, I command you to leave."

Bishop laughed, a mocking cackle that raised goose bumps on Susan's arms. "You're too late with your mumbo jumbo, Morris. The lady's already asked me in, not just once, but twice. You know the rules." He stepped forward and raised his arms protectively over Susan. "She's mine, and you can't do anything about it. You're only a ghost, Morris. I can see right through you." His lips stretched across white teeth in a triumphant smile, his voice became richly gloating. "I am the Undead, and this one is mine!"

Susan's eyes widened. On the floor under the lamp table she could see one of her nephews' toys—the red plastic dagger Randy had been playing with while he watched *Captain Hook*. The

153

blade and the handle came together in the form of a cross.

Without thinking what she was doing, she swept the dagger from the floor. Seizing it by the blade, she held it out in front of her.

"Go!" she cried. She lunged forward and thrust the plastic dagger into Bishop's face.

There was a flash of blue fire, and then Bishop's agonized scream filled the room with a horrible sound. He fell backward against a chair, knocking it to the floor with a crash. His flesh was seared where the cross had touched his cheek. Then he launched himself forward in a writhing, twisting dive through the window. In the darkness outside Susan could see a sudden flash; then there was nothing but a dying scream.

Susan shut her eyes. When she opened them, she saw the cross in her hands pulsing with a powerful blue light. Then it died away, and she was holding a red plastic dagger.

"Hey," the voice beside her said, "not bad for a beginner."

Susan turned. She could see the outline of Drew's figure in the dimness. It had bulk, solidity. It looked almost real.

"I . . . I—" She stopped, swallowed, tried again. "Did that really happen? Is he gone?"

"Yes, it happened. And yes, he's gone." He smiled. "You've killed one of the Undead, Susan.

You probably won't get a medal of honor, but it's quite an achievement anyway."

"Thanks," Susan managed. She swallowed again, her mouth dry as dust. She looked at him. The outlines of his body were firm, sharp, clear. She couldn't see through him anymore. "Are you really . . . ?" She couldn't finish her question.

"Really a ghost?" Drew looked down at his hand, flexed his fingers. "Well, I thought so. But now I'm not so sure." Wonderingly, he raised his hand and touched her face, very gently. "I can feel your skin, Susan. Can you feel my fingers?"

Susan shut her eyes. "Yes," she whispered. "I can feel your fingers." Her skin tingled where Drew was touching it. "Does that mean you're not a . . ."

"Don't ask me," Drew said. "I'm not writing the script for this show."

Susan opened her eyes again. Drew was leaning toward her, his eyes on her mouth, as if he were going to kiss her. Then he straightened up.

"I think," he said softly, "I'd better not press my luck."

Susan shivered. "How did you get here?"

"Beats me." Drew sounded wryly amused. "Didn't you invite *me*, too?"

Susan remembered her thought of the sheet-covered mound she had dreamed, with Drew standing beside her. "Did you materialize when I

155

thought about you? Just like that?"

Drew looked down at her, smiling. "That's what it looks like," he said. "But I don't know how. I'm not in charge here." His voice was getting fainter, the outline of his figure blurry.

"Drew," Susan whispered urgently, "don't go away! I need you. I need to know what to do next! I've got to help Freddie and Angie."

"I said, I'm not in charge here," Drew's voice said, sounding faint and tinny. She could almost see through him again, see the outline of the sofa and the chair behind him. "I'll get back to you."

"But when?"

"When I can. From now on I guess it depends on you."

"Wait a minute, Drew," Susan said desperately, reaching out for him. "*What* depends on me?"

"Whether I get back to you," he said in a soft voice. "You have the power. You have to learn how to use it." He seemed to make an effort, and the outlines of his image grew sharper. "Talk to Angie's aunt," he added more clearly. "She can help."

And then he was gone.

The next morning Susan was awakened at nine by the shrill ringing of her telephone.

"Did you watch the weather report last night?" Mack asked, not even saying hello.

"No," Susan replied groggily. After Drew had disappeared, she had made a rude cross out of two ice-cream sticks. Then she'd gone to bed, with Randy's plastic dagger under her pillow. Sleep was slow in coming, though, because her mind was searching for ways to help Freddie and Angie break free of the Brothers. But all her searching ended in murky blackness. She couldn't see any way out.

Mack's voice was brisk, businesslike. "Hurricane Clarissa is heading inland. They're forecasting landfall on the Texas coast, somewhere between Freeport and Port Arthur. That puts us in the middle. It'll be here by three o'clock this afternoon."

Susan sat up.

"They're calling it a Class Three," Mack said, "so we don't have to evacuate here in the city. But the entire police force is being called in, so I've got to work. I want you in the house with Betty and the kids, so I know where you are. Call the Pizzeria and tell them you won't be in. They may not even open today, anyway."

Susan shook her head to clear it. "I've got some things to do before the storm hits," she said.

"Fine. Do them and get back here by one. Okay?"

"Okay," Susan said slowly. She got up and pulled on jeans and a T-shirt. She was thinking of Drew, and the way he'd looked last night when he'd seemed about to kiss her. How did it feel to be kissed by a ghost? When he'd touched her, his fingers had seemed so *real*, and there'd been a wondering look in his eyes, as if he could actually feel the softness and warmth of her skin.

She shook her head, pushing the memory away. She couldn't think of Drew now. She had work to do. As she fastened her long brown hair into a ponytail, a vague plan began to form in her mind. She called work and told Gwen she wouldn't be in. As she got ready to leave, she stuck Randy's red plastic dagger into the belt on her jeans, under her T-shirt.

Outside, the air was still and heavy with the weight of the oncoming storm. The sky overhead was metallic, filled with gray clouds, and the sun wore a silvery halo. As Susan drove past the supermarket on the corner, she saw people scurrying around in prehurricane excitement, buying emergency supplies—extra food, candles, water. But Susan had a different emergency on her mind. She couldn't even think about the hurricane.

It was after ten by the time she got to Angie's house. Mrs. Sanchez was outside, fastening the hurricane shutters over the windows. At the house next door Aunt Carlota was doing the same thing. The two women were talking over the hedge about the storm.

When Aunt Carlota saw Susan, she waved.

"Good morning," she said, climbing down from the ladder. "Ready for the big storm?"

"If you're here to see Angela," Mrs. Sanchez said, "she's still in bed." She scowled. "She called in sick to work this morning."

Aunt Carlota came over to the hedge. "I saw her yesterday afternoon at the Pizzeria. She looked awfully tired."

"Is she all right?" Susan asked.

Mrs. Sanchez fastened the last shutter. "She's just worn out. She and Juanita were over at that club again last night. When they got home, their father told them they can't go back. I don't think it's good for girls to be out so late, either."

"We were young once, too," Aunt Carlota said knowingly. "I'm sure it's nothing to worry about."

Mrs. Sanchez shook her head apprehensively. "I tell you, 'Lota, I don't understand it. Angela's always been so good. I could always count on her to do what's right. But the last three days—it's like she's a different person. Juanita, too."

"Would it be all right if I went in to see her?" Susan asked Mrs. Sanchez.

"Go right ahead. Maybe you'll be able to figure out what's wrong."

Susan went into the house and down the hall to Angela's room. She could hear the Brothers' music through the door. She opened it. "It's me, Angie," she said. "Susan."

"I don't want to see you," Angie replied. "Get out of here. Go away."

With a quick step Susan went to the tape player and jabbed the off button savagely. Then she reached for the cord and snapped up the blind. What she saw on the bed made her gasp.

Angie was haggard, her face white, her eyes red-rimmed and circled with dark flesh. When the light struck her eyes, she shielded them with her hand.

"Pull the blind down!" she said hoarsely, groping for a pair of dark glasses on her bedside table. "And turn the tape back on!"

Susan dropped the blind down and sat on the side of Angie's bed. "Do you know what's happening to you?" she asked quietly.

Angie leaned back against her pillow. "Happening?" she asked, putting on her sunglasses. "Nothing's happening. I'm finding out who I really am for the first time in my life, that's all. Brad and the Brothers . . ." She smiled slyly. "Really, Susan, you're totally missing out. I don't see why you won't—"

Susan grabbed her by the shoulders. "Don't you know what they are?" she cried desperately. "Don't you know what they're doing to you?" She shook Angie's shoulders, hard. Her head flopped back loosely, like the head of a rag doll. There were two faint red marks—*puncture marks*—on her throat.

Susan dropped her hands, feeling sick.

"But I *like* it," Angie whispered. Her mouth was trembling. A muscle in her cheek twitched. "I like listening to the music. I like going to the club. I want to be with Brad and the Brothers always." She smiled a strange, slow smile. "Brad says it'll be only another night or two before I'm one of them. Then I'll feel better, he says. I won't be so sick and draggy all the time. This is a phase I'm going through. After tonight I'm sure I'll feel better."

Susan caught her breath. "But what about your parents? Your mother said your father's forbidden you to go back to the club."

Angie's laugh was shrill. "You think I'm going to let that old man order me around?" She stopped laughing, and her face took on a crafty, cunning look. "I'm leaving, anyway. I'm going to move in with Brad tomorrow. That way I'll be able to spend all my time with the Brothers. I'll be able to listen to their music whenever I feel like it." Her mouth twisted. "Without people barging in and turning it off."

Susan took her hands and held them. "What about Nita?"

Behind the dark glasses Angie's eyes slid sideways. "What about her?" she mumbled. "Nita's okay."

"Where is she?"

"At the Brothers' house. She came in here this

161

morning and climbed out my window so Mom wouldn't see her leave."

"Does she look like you?" Susan asked bluntly.

Angie frowned. "What?"

Susan snatched off Angie's glasses. She dragged her out of bed and propelled her toward the dressing table beside the window, where she pushed her down on the bench in front of the mirror and jerked up the blind. Angie's bloodshot eyes stared into the mirror, her hair hanging in matted strings around her pale face. The muscle in her cheek twitched violently.

"Is this what you want for your sister?" Susan whispered.

Angie stared defiantly at her reflection. "What's wrong with the way I look?" she asked. "I'm a little tired, that's all. It's part of the process. Brad says I'll feel better soon. The same thing happened to him, when he became one of the Brothers." She grinned, showing white teeth. "After tonight I'll feel wonderful. Brad promised."

Susan shuddered. "You can't let this happen, Angie!" she cried. "If you don't care about yourself, you have to care about Nita!"

Angie swiveled to face Susan, her eyes narrowed, the pupils tiny slits of black. "If that's all you came for, Susan, to tell me what I can and can't do, you might as well leave. If I didn't listen to my father, what makes you think I'll listen to

162

you? I'm not going to give up Brad and the Brothers. Not for Nita, and certainly not for you."

Susan felt a deep, exhausting despair. She couldn't reach Angie. It was too late. And if it was too late for Angie, it was probably too late for Freddie and Nita, too.

And then she remembered Randy's plastic dagger. She pulled it out of the belt and held it up like a cross. The plastic began to glow an eerie blue, as if it were lit from the inside. Susan could feel a throbbing current of energy pulsing from the cross through her arms and across her back. She pulled herself up, feeling tall and strong. Was this what Drew had meant when he said *You have the power?*

Angela's eyes widened and she shrank back, her arm up to shield her face. "Don't," she whispered. "Please, don't!"

When she spoke, Susan's voice was not her own. It came from a force outside her, speaking through her, strong and commanding.

"In the name of everything that's good and loving," she said, "I command you to depart from evil!"

Angie's muscles tensed, her face twisted in pain. Her body convulsed with a terrible, racking shudder. Susan wanted to turn away, but her curiosity kept her eyes riveted on her friend. Finally Angie collapsed onto the dressing table, limp, breathing in shallow gasps. Susan dropped the dagger and held Angie's hand as tightly as she could. As she waited, a tiny spot of color came into Angie's cheeks. Susan could also see that the puncture marks in her friend's throat were beginning to fade.

Susan stood looking down at Angie. She felt a strange, heady exhilaration, as if she were still charged with the energy that had flowed through her. She gripped Angie's hand harder. "Angie?" she whispered. "Are you all right?"

Angie slowly sat up, her eyes unfocused. "I . . . I think so," she managed. "What did you do?"

"I'm not sure," Susan said. She picked up the plastic dagger from the floor, and then she stuck it back into her belt. "I guess this toy has something pretty powerful in it."

Angie stared at the dagger. "It's not a toy," she whispered. "It's a . . . cross." A sudden understanding came into her eyes. "Is . . . *that* what I became? One of . . . them?"

Susan looked at her. "Almost," she said quietly. Angie needed to hear the truth. The ugly, hideous truth. "You almost became a vampire. But you're safe now." At *least I hope so,* she thought. A new, cold thought sliced through her. But was Angie safe? Was she back to her normal state for good? Or would she return to the condition she was in when Susan found her?

Angie dropped her face into her hands. "Oh,

Susan," she whispered, anguished, "what have I done? Not just to myself, but to Nita! Have you seen her? Is she okay? How could I—"

Susan knelt down and put her arms around Angie. "It wasn't your fault," she whispered. "It was the Brothers. They are evil. They want to corrupt everyone who hears their music. They want everyone to be like them."

Angie began to cry, long, shuddering sobs that shook her shoulders. Susan held her close and let her cry. Finally she sat up and reached for a tissue and blew her nose. "I must have been out of my mind," she said. "I thought I loved Brad, but it wasn't love—it was an obsession. I couldn't see what was happening to me, or to him, or . . ." Her voice trailed off.

"Do you think," Susan asked softly, "that Brad can come back?"

Angie's mouth trembled, and her eyes filled with tears again. "I . . . I don't think so," she whispered. "He wouldn't want to come back, now that he's tasted that incredible power. I think he's . . . gone."

"I'm sorry, Angie," Susan said.

Angie's chin firmed and she straightened her shoulders. "But if you got me back, can't we get Nita back too?" she said. "And Freddie." She stopped, looking suddenly afraid. "But how, Susan? You have no idea how powerful they are! How can we do it?"

165

Suddenly Susan saw a movement outside the window. She turned and looked across the narrow yard between the houses. Aunt Carlota was standing on the ladder, a frozen statue. She must have seen everything.

Susan pulled Angie up. "Get dressed," she ordered. *Talk to Angie's aunt*, Drew had said. *She can help.*

"Where are we going?" Angie asked, climbing into her jeans.

"We're going next door," Susan said, "to talk to a white witch."

Fourteen

"Es milagro," Aunt Carlota said quietly, beckoning them into the kitchen. "It is a miracle." She kissed each girl once on each cheek and then on the forehead.

"You saw," Susan said.

"Yes," Aunt Carlota replied, "I saw." She poured them each a cup of hot herb tea. "Now you can tell me the whole story."

It took only a few minutes for Susan to tell her everything, beginning with Drew's first appearance on the television and ending with the scene in Angie's bedroom.

When Susan finished, Aunt Carlota took a deep breath. "I have heard of demonstrations of such power as the one you practiced this morning," she said, "but never have I seen one. It is truly a miracle."

Susan wrapped both hands around her cup, warming her cold fingers. "It wasn't much," she said, embarrassed by the awe and admiration in Aunt Carlota's voice.

"Yes, it was." Aunt Carlota gave Susan a respectful look. "You are a powerful *curandera*, my child. A strong healer."

Susan shook her head firmly. "No," she said. "I'm no *curandera*." She pulled the toy dagger out of her belt and laid it on the table. "It was this. This was what killed Bishop. And saved Angie."

Aunt Carlota smiled. "The power," she said firmly, "is not in the instrument of healing but in the heart of the one who heals." She pointed to the jars of herbs that lined her kitchen shelves. "The potions and charms and amulets that *curanderas* use are important. But these objects are vested with the power of the healer, not the other way around." She touched Susan's dagger. "This little piece of plastic has only the power *you* give it, Susan. You must have faith—not in this, but in yourself. And in your incredible power."

You have the power. It was Drew's voice Susan heard, as clearly as if he stood at her shoulder. At the recollection she felt a sudden sense of longing. It was his belief in her, his reassurance, that made her strong. If he were here, she could face anything, no matter how frightening. She could even face Flint and the Brothers. But Drew wasn't here. And without him she felt very small, very much afraid, and very vulnerable.

"But even if I do have the power," she said in a low voice, "I don't know how to use it. All I did with Angie was say a few words. It was nothing."

"Yes, a few words. A few simple words. But they were words from the heart. They were words of love. The strength of good over evil is powerful when one believes. And when one has love."

Susan nodded solemnly. Drew had given her the gift of belief by making her face the truth. And love? Had he given her that, as well? She looked at Aunt Carlota. "But I don't know what to do. I don't know how to save Nita and Freddie. You have to help us."

"I will help," Aunt Carlota agreed, and Susan felt a tremendous sense of relief. She and Angie wouldn't have to go to the Brothers' house alone. Aunt Carlota would be there with them, with her magic.

Aunt Carlota went into the other room. When she came back, she held three silver crosses in one hand and a large quartz crystal and a cloth bag in the other. She hung one cross around Angie's neck and gave the other two to Susan.

"These are for Nita and Freddie," she said. "They can wear these for protection. You do not need one, since your dagger should serve you quite well." Next she handed the crystal and the cloth pouch to Susan. "These are for you."

"Will we . . . will we have to destroy the vampires?" Susan asked faintly, not even looking at what she'd been given. "Will we have to use . . . stakes?" She swallowed, remembering a gory scene from a movie. "Through the heart?"

"Their evil must be destroyed," Aunt Carlota said. She smiled slightly. "Legends about stakes through the heart are a way of explaining something to people who need a picture in order to be able to see. The vampires must be destroyed, but you do not need to use stakes." She nodded at the small pouch in Susan's hand. "In that bag I've given you wild thyme and rose petals to sprinkle in the doorway of the house. That will help to purify it. But there are no magic words and no magic agents I can give you, Susan. It is only *your* power that can purify. And the words must come from you. The crystal is an amulet. It will help keep *you* pure in the presence of great evil."

"Hey, wait," Susan said, suddenly apprehensive. "You're coming with us, aren't you?"

Aunt Carlota shook her head. "This is *your* task," she said emphatically. "It has been given to you to do, not to me. I can give you advice, but I cannot do the work. If I interfere, I might upset the balance and work against you."

"But I don't know what to *do*!" Susan protested. "I need you to teach me!"

"You do not need a teacher," Aunt Carlota said gently. "No one taught you how to bring back Angela—you trusted your heart. That is what you must do now, Susan. That is your power." Her face relaxed into a smile, and she touched Angie's arm. "Angela will be there. And your friend Drew. They will be your helpers." She cocked her head, listening to the wind. "Now, go quickly. The storm is coming."

Susan's insides knotted. She could see the faces of the Brothers in front of her, their eyes filled with an unimaginable power. What if she failed? What if the evil that was in the Brothers swallowed *all* of them? Her hands felt cold and clammy. "Maybe we should . . . wait," she whispered, "until after the storm is over."

Angie moved closer to Susan. Her face was taut, her eyes dark. The silver cross gleamed against her throat. "We can't wait," she said, reaching for Susan's hand. "After the storm it may be too late. Nita and Freddie need you *now*, Susan."

Aunt Carlota nodded. "It is your time to do battle," she said. "And the storm will concentrate your power."

"Concentrate it?" Susan asked uncertainly. "What do you mean?"

"I can't explain it. It is something you will have to experience for yourself. But be careful, my dear. There is danger to you, too. A *curandera* is a conduit for tremendous energy. You must be strong enough to channel that destructive power without letting it destroy you." She looked at Susan, her eyes direct, compassionate. "Hate destroys, Susan. To purify, you must love. Love is the undoing of evil."

"But I don't understand," Susan began.

"You will," Aunt Carlotta said simply.

Angie stood up. "Come on, Susan," she said urgently. "Let's go."

Susan stood too. "I guess I'm ready." *Ready or not, here I come, vampires. Armed with my trusty toy dagger.* She almost laughed aloud at the utter absurdity of it.

Aunt Carlota reached into a small clay bowl on the table. "There's one last thing," she said. She pulled something out of the bowl. "Put these in your pockets."

She had given each of them a handful of garlic cloves.

As Susan and Angie drove along Sea Wall Boulevard in the direction of Freddie's mother's motel, Susan sensed a gray restlessness in the sea. Breakers were beginning to surge onto the almost-deserted beaches. The waves were slow, lethargic, but they contained enormous power. The threat of a hurricane had sent the tourists scurrying home. The only people in the water now were the surfers, taking advantage of the rolling breakers to get in a few hours of extra-good surfing. Everybody else was busy stowing anything that might blow away and nailing big sheets of plywood over glass windows to protect them against breakage. There was no panic. People who lived in Galveston were used to taking precautions against the tropical storms that blew in from the Gulf.

"There won't be a can of soup left in this whole town in another hour," Angie said as they drove by a grocery jammed with shoppers.

"You're probably right," Susan replied bleakly, remembering Freddie's cheerful advice to stock up with plenty of soup in case of a hurricane. *Freddie.* What would they find when they got to Freddie's? After all, she and Brad had been with the Brothers the same amount of time. Worse, Freddie was in love with Flint. Would they be able to bring her back? Or was she gone, too?

Angie put her hand in her pocket and pulled out the garlic. "I wonder how this works. Is it supposed to hurt them? Stop them? Make them disappear?"

"I wonder," Susan said grimly, "*if* it works." She thought somberly about their small arsenal of weapons. A toy dagger, a crystal, a bag of herbs, a silver cross, and a few cloves of garlic. Superstitious nonsense, she would have said two weeks ago, even a week ago. But that was before. Before Bishop had catapulted out of a second-story window and vanished in a burst of fire. Before she had met Drew. Before she had seen Angie come back.

The parking lot in front of the Holiday Plaza Motel was almost empty. Freddie's mother was directing two men who were boarding up windows. Sudden gusts of wind whipped up from the beach, blew in their faces, and tossed the palms in front of the motel.

"Freddie?" Mrs. Gardner asked. "She's got the flu or something. I told her to go back to bed." She raised her voice. "Hey, Charlie, when you've finished that window, take the diving board off and stow it, will you?" She turned back to the girls. "Last big storm, the wind ripped the diving board off and sent it through the office window."

"We need to see Freddie," Susan said. "We won't stay long."

"Go ahead." Mrs. Gardner shrugged. "If you catch what she's got, don't say I didn't warn you." She frowned. "Tell Freddie I'm going to the grocery store. If I don't get there pretty quick, there won't be anything left."

"We'll tell her," Angie said.

The girls went up to the second floor, where Freddie and her mother had a two-bedroom suite overlooking the swimming pool. They stood outside Freddie's door for a moment, listening. Inside, they could hear the sound of the Brothers' music, then Freddie's voice, singing the lyrics.

Angie's face went white, and she covered her ears with her hands. "You've got to shut off that music," she whispered. "I don't think I can stand to listen to it."

"Stay out here until it's off," Susan instructed. She raised her hand and knocked at the door.

The music stopped. There was a silence. Susan knocked again, louder this time.

A chair scraped. "Go away, Mom," Freddie's voice said. She sounded irritated. "I told you, I don't want anything to eat. I'm practicing."

"It's me and Angie," Susan said. "We have to talk to you."

Another silence. "So talk," Freddie said finally. "What do you want?"

"Not through the door," Susan said. "We need to see you, Freddie."

"Buzz off," Freddie said. The music came on again, louder this time.

Angie's face twisted with pain, and she put her fingers in her ears. Susan pushed the door open and stepped into the room, closing the door behind her.

Inside, it was almost totally dark, except for the glow of a flickering candle. Freddie was sitting on her bed wearing black jeans and a black T-shirt. On the table beside her was the candle and her tape player. Susan stepped to the bedside table and with a quick motion grabbed the cassette from the recorder and began to rip out the tape. In seconds there was a loose mound of plastic spaghetti at her feet.

"It's okay, Angie," she called. "You can come in now." The door opened.

Freddie was staring at her. "You ruined my tape!" she wailed. "How am I supposed to practice if I don't have a tape?"

Angie flicked on the light switch, and the room was flooded with a bright light. With an anguished cry Freddie rolled over and buried her face in the pillow.

"Let us look at you," Susan said quietly, putting a hand on the pillow.

"I've had the flu," Freddie said. Her voice was muffled by the pillow. "The light hurts my eyes. Turn it off." A cough rattled dryly in her throat. "*Turn it off!*" she screeched.

Susan pulled the pillow down. "Oh, no," Angie whispered.

Freddie's eyes were deep, shadowy pools in her hollowed face. Her freckles stood out in sandy splatters against her pale skin. She had put on lipstick, but it was smeared garishly red across her strong white teeth.

Her hands shaking, Freddie pulled the neck of her T-shirt up to her chin. "I've been sick for a couple of days," she muttered, her voice cracking. "What did you expect—Madonna?"

Susan yanked Freddie's hands down. There was a red mark on her throat.

Angie sank down beside the bed and took Freddie's hands in hers. "Hurry, Susan," she urged. "*Hurry!* Do it now!"

"Do what?" Freddie asked, struggling to get away. "What are you trying to do? Let go of me, Angie!" She struggled harder, swinging her legs over the side of the bed, and managed to pull free. "Angie, you were with us. You wanted to be one of us. What's happened to you?" She caught sight of the cross around Angie's neck, and her eyes narrowed to dark slits. "I might have known," she spat. "Traitor!"

Angie stood up and put her arms around Freddie. "Please, Freddie," she begged, "let us—"

Suddenly Freddie lunged forward, shoving Angie to the floor. "You're not going to try any fancy tricks with me," she snarled. She stood in the middle of the floor, arms raised, fists clenched. "I am one with the Brothers!" she cried in a strong, resonant voice. "I call on you! Come, Brothers! Come to me now!"

There was a moment of silence. Outside, a fierce gust of wind rattled the motel sign as if it had been hit by a giant's fist. Inside, the temperature in the room plummeted. The air was filled with an electrical tension that almost crackled.

Susan's mouth was dry. "Are we too late, Angie?" she whispered fearfully. If Freddie was already one of them, the power might destroy her completely, as it had Bishop. Or perhaps Freddie could summon a stronger power—a power that could destroy them!

"I don't know," Angie said, picking herself up off the floor. Her eyes were wide in her white face. "But we have to try. Do it now, Susan!"

Suddenly there was another gust of wind, and the lights went off. It was dark in the room, except for the candle burning beside the bed. In its flickering light Freddie's shadow on the wall, arms upraised, head back, was the shadow of a monster.

Susan had no choice. She pulled out the dagger and stepped toward Freddie. The dagger began to flash with a brilliant blue light. As Susan held it up, it become a kind of lightning rod, drawing life from the enormous energy of the storm, growing brighter and brighter until it was blazing. Susan could feel the fierce power coursing through her, charging her. The hairs on her arms and neck were raised, and her skin tingled. Before her, Freddie raised her hands in front of her face to shield her eyes from the brilliant blue light.

"In the name of love," Susan cried in a firm,

clear voice, "I command the evil in you to be gone."

Freddie shrieked, a high, whistling scream, furiously defiant. "No!" she cried. "No, no, *no*! I am one with the Brothers!"

One with the Brothers? How could Freddie say that? How could she *want* to be one with the evil force that had destroyed Drew and Sara Robertson and Brad—and countless others? A powerful anger ignited inside Susan, racing through her, hot and remorseless, a force far stronger than anything she had ever felt in her life. Susan felt herself grow taller, stronger, invincible. With such anger, such hatred, she could destroy the Brothers and the evil they stood for! She could purify the world, cleanse it forever from the horrible darkness of—

Hate destroys, Susan. To purify, you must love.

Susan stood still, staring at Freddie's contorted face, twisted with such ferocity that it was no longer recognizable. Love? Love *that*? If Freddie were herself, it would be easy to love her. But she was one of *them* now, and hate was the only possible—

To purify, you must love.

Slowly, reluctantly, Susan lowered the dagger. The blue light dimmed, the power and energy in her arms diminished. Her fingers numb, she dropped the dagger onto the floor. Without it she felt weak, vulnerable, powerless. Snarling, Freddie reached out with her foot and kicked it away. She

179

hunched over, ready to charge.

"Susan!" Angie screamed. "Pick up the dagger! Susan!"

Susan lifted her arms and put them around the hunched figure. "I love you, Freddie," she whispered.

Freddie's face twisted and she reeled, pulling away from Susan. There was a burst of yellow flame, a sudden scorched smell, and the candle went out as if it had been snuffed. The room was pitched into sudden and total blackness. Even the blue brilliance of the dagger had been extinguished. Outside, another squall rocked the building, and there was a loud, splintering crash.

"Susan?" Angie asked. Her voice rose hysterically. "Susan? Freddie? Are you all right?"

"I think so," Susan said limply. She felt as if she had suddenly been drained of all her life, just as the light had been drained from the dagger.

Freddie moaned.

There was the scratch of a match, and Angie relit the candle. Susan saw that Freddie was sitting in the middle of the floor, a dazed look on her white face. Her T-shirt was scorched across the shoulder. Her eyes looked almost normal again, though, and the red marks on her neck were beginning to fade.

"Will somebody please tell me," she said thickly, "what's going on?" She felt her jaw.

"Which one of you guys punched me out?"

Angie rushed over to her. "How do you feel, Freddie?"

Freddie made an impolite noise. "Lousy," she said. She struggled to her feet, leaning on Angie. "I feel like I've just gone three rounds with the current heavyweight champion."

Susan's legs felt rubbery. She sat down on the bed. "How much do you remember of the past few days?"

"Enough," Freddie said grimly. "So was I really a vampire? I mean, did I drink . . . *blood?*" she whispered in horror.

"No, you didn't," Angie hastened to reassure her. "Susan saved you before you were completely transformed."

Freddie looked at Susan. "Wow. Where'd you learn how to do that?"

"It's a long story, Fred," Susan said. "I don't think we've got time for it right now."

"Well, thanks anyway," Freddie said. "It was pretty awful while it lasted." There was a wry twist to her mouth. "I guess this means I've got to look for another singing job, huh?"

Susan managed a grin. "Next time check references first, huh?" She reached into her pocket and pulled out one of Aunt Carlota's silver crosses. "Here. This is for you. Wear it, and it will protect you."

Freddie looked at it. "I never thought of myself as the religious type," she said. "But after what I've been through—" She slipped it over her head.

"You'd better have these, too," Angie said, giving her a couple cloves of garlic.

Freddie wrinkled up her nose. "You've got to be kidding."

"I wish," Susan said grimly. She stood up. "Okay. Let's get going."

"Get going where?" Freddie asked, looking from one to the other. "I feel like I've been gone for the past week. I'm not going anywhere, except maybe back to bed for a couple of days. Anyway, haven't you heard? There's a hurricane happening out there."

"Forget the hurricane," Susan said. "And forget how you feel. We've got work to do." She picked the dagger off the floor and thrust it into her belt.

"What kind of work?" Freddie asked, confused. "You don't mean the Pizzeria, do you?"

"No, Freddie," Susan said gently. "There are others who need our help."

A look of sheer terror crossed Freddie's face. She held up both hands. "Wait a minute, you guys," she said, backing away from her friends. "We're not going *there*, are we? I can't. If I go to the Brothers' house, they'll get me again. They can, and they will."

"Juanita's there," Angie said starkly. "You don't have to go. But *I* do."

182

Freddie shut her eyes and stood silent for a minute. Then she blew out her breath and opened her eyes. "Well," she said, "I suppose it's only fair to hand in my resignation in person." She rubbed a hand through her red hair. "Too bad." She sighed. "It looked like a *very* steady job. Eternal, if you get what I mean."

Susan put her arm around Freddie's shoulders. "I'm sorry for the way things turned out," she said.

"Yeah, me too," Freddie replied. "But now I know what they mean when they talk about soul music."

Fifteen

Susan stopped her Honda in front of the cemetery, down the street from the Brothers' two-story Victorian, and turned off the ignition. It was early afternoon, but the blowing gray-green clouds cast an eerie, ominous twilight over the city. Gusting in off the Gulf, the wind filled the air with a fine salty mist and bent the palm trees like beach grass. Driving through the downtown area, Susan had seen that the streets were emptying fast, as people finished their storm preparations and headed for shelter away from the fury of the hurricane. With the sidewalks deserted, signs taken down, and windows boarded up, Galveston liked as if it were bracing for war.

That was how Susan felt, too. Braced for war.

It is your time to do battle, Aunt Carlota had said. Susan sighed wearily. The last struggle, with whatever evil power had filled Freddie, seemed to have taken all the strength out of her—and Freddie and Angie must feel even worse. None of them were ready to do battle with anybody, much less the darkest powers of the universe. She would far rather start the car again and go home to the everyday world of Mack and Betty and the boys. A world where vampires were something you laughed at in old TV sitcoms, and the hurricane would be the most powerful elemental force she would ever have to face. She would much rather go someplace quiet and think about Drew.

In the front seat next to Susan, Angie swallowed a sob. She was looking at the Brothers' house.

"Brad?" Susan asked softly.

Angie nodded. Her brown eyes were filled with tears. "He really thought he'd found a home here," she said bleakly. "He loved being a Brother. It gave him something to live for."

And something to die for, Susan thought to herself, *and to kill for*. But she couldn't say it out loud, so she just put a comforting hand on Angie's arm.

Angie brushed the tears from her eyes. "It's no use crying for Brad," she said fiercely, "when it's

Nita who needs us. Come on, let's go before the storm gets any worse." At that moment the wind ripped a large branch off a tree by the curb. It crashed to the pavement inches from the front of the car.

Freddie swallowed noisily. "Are you sure," she asked, "that this is the best thing to do? It's really blowing a gale. And what if we—I mean, what if the Brothers . . ." Her voice trailed away.

What if. Two words Susan didn't dare ask herself. "I guess there aren't any guarantees in the vampire extermination business," Susan said, trying to make a joke out of it. "But we're doing it anyway." She opened the door and got out.

Framed by shrubs and dark trees, the house loomed large on its narrow lot. Somebody had boarded up the big front window, and there were hurricane shutters over the other windows. Susan shivered. With the shutters closed the house looked like a huge gray mausoleum.

Bending into the lashing wind, they walked up the front sidewalk. Susan wasn't sure whether it was because she was extraordinarily sensitive now, after her encounters with the forces that had inhabited Freddie and Angie, or whether it was the house itself—but a feeling of chill foreboding seized her, and her stomach cramped.

"Do you think we ought to go around back?" Freddie whispered as they stood at the bottom of the porch steps. "Sort of sneak up on them?"

"No," Angie said firmly. "We have to go through the front door." She looked at Susan. "Do you have that bag of herbs Aunt Carlota gave us?"

Susan pulled the bag from her pocket and looked at it uncertainly. Aunt Carlota had said she should use it to purify the house, whatever that meant. But the bag felt nearly weightless in her hand. It contained less than an ounce of dried plants—not very potent medicine to cure the kind of evil the Brothers embodied. Suddenly there was a blast of wind that almost swept them away. Behind them they heard a sharp crack and a ripping noise, and the girls grabbed for one another and turned. The ancient pecan tree beside the walk was toppling over, as if it had been pushed by a giant hand. It lay now across the entire front yard, blocking the way to the street.

Freddie stared at it, white-faced. "I guess that means I can't go back and sit this one out in the car."

"Sit this one out?" Susan tried to laugh. "You'd miss all the action."

"Oh, yeah?" Freddie muttered. "Listen, this kind of action I can miss out on any day of the week. I'm basically chicken when it comes to blood."

Angie shuddered. "Do we have to talk about blood?"

"We have to talk about what we're going to do once we get in the house," Susan said.

"There's no time for talking," Angie said urgently. She grabbed Susan's hand and started up the steps. "Let's just do it."

"Even if we don't know what we're doing," Freddie said darkly, following them, "is anybody taking notes? This would make one heck of a made-for-TV movie."

The front door was open a crack. Inside was a chill, musty blackness, like the inside of a tomb. Angie pushed the door, and it gave a shrill creak.

Freddie jumped.

Not quite sure of what she was supposed to do, Susan opened the cloth bag and sprinkled the herbs on the threshold. As she looked down at the petals and dried leaves, they began to smoke. A clean, flowery fragrance filled the air, and the musty odor began to fade.

As the sweet-smelling smoke rose around her, Susan felt stronger and less afraid. Out on the street the winds seemed to have stopped, as if the herbs had some sort of magical power over the storm. It was almost as if time had frozen. She remembered that in the center of a hurricane was something called the eye, a space of intense

189

quiet around which the winds swirled furiously at maximum force. She felt for a moment as if *she* were the eye of the storm, surrounded by forces that raged out of control, while within her was calmness and strength. Then, with a decisive gesture, she pulled the plastic dagger out of her belt and held it up.

In her hand the dagger glowed like a neon tube and illuminated the hallway. Behind her Angie pulled in her breath, and Freddie whistled softly.

The dagger was a beacon in the darkness, pulling them forward into the chill blackness of the house. Susan felt guided by some invisible power. It coursed through her, lending her a strength she didn't know she possessed. All her fear was gone now. She felt invincible, ready to confront any power, no matter how dark or how evil. And she didn't have to think about what to say or do. The words were there in her heart, on her lips.

She turned and struck the dagger hard against the doorjamb. "In the name of all that's good," she said loudly, "I command the evil to be gone from this place."

Everything happened at once. A searing flash struck the door in front and framed it in brilliant blue fire, so bright they couldn't look at it. The door itself went flying outward, and all the air in the house rushed through the opening in a screaming blast, nearly pulling the girls with it. In the front parlor the boarded-up front window exploded outward, sheets of plywood sailing like playing cards and shards of glass flying everywhere. With the blast came a heavy, putrid odor of something long dead, and the smoldering smell of something burning. From somewhere deep inside the house, Susan heard a shrill squeak, then another and another, a chorus of earsplitting screeches. Soon they were surrounded by a raspy cloud of dark, leathery wings, beating and scratching at them.

"Bats!" Angie screamed, and cowered against the wall, frantically shielding her head with her arms. For a long moment the hallway was filled with hundreds of the huge red-eyed creatures. Then they swirled out into the storm and vanished. The door swung shut behind them, leaving the girls standing in total darkness, with only the blue light of Susan's dagger to see by.

Freddie brushed the hair from her eyes. "Wow, what an *effect*," she whispered with a laugh that sounded like a rusty hinge.

"Is it safe to go on?" Angie asked.

"Go on?" Freddie said, alarmed. She peered ahead at the end of the hall, where the stairs rose into the blackness. "How do we know all the bats are gone?"

"We don't," Susan replied. "Not for sure. And we don't know that they were bats."

"What else could they have been?" Angie asked, shuddering.

Freddie stared at Susan. Her voice dropped to a whisper. "Are you saying they might have been—?" Her eyes lit up. "You mean we've driven them out? We've won?"

Angie shook her head grimly. "If those were vampires flying out the door, we haven't won, we've lost. They've *escaped*! They're free to go anywhere!"

Susan's mouth felt dry. The batlike creatures—were they the spirits of the Brothers' old groupies? Or the Brothers themselves, flying out into the storm to search for a new home, a new base of operations? She felt her heart begin to pound, the fear return. Or were the Brothers still in the house, hidden in its nooks and crannies, waiting for the storm to end, darkness to fall?

Angie's hand dropped. "We're not going to find Nita, standing here chattering," she said. She grabbed Freddie's hand and gave Susan a push. "Let's go."

Susan raised the dagger in front of her, and the three girls walked toward the end of the entrance hall. By the vivid blue light of the dagger, Susan could make out a stairway slanting steeply on the left. Beyond that, darkness. The house was filled with an oppressive silence that weighed down on them like a heavy blanket. The burning odor got stronger with each step.

Angie clutched her arm. "Look!" she gasped, pointing up the stairs. "It's Nita!"

A faint golden light appeared at the top of the stairs, and Juanita stood in its glow. She was wearing a gauzy white dress that drifted around her softly rounded figure. Her black hair was pulled back with a narrow white ribbon, and she was smiling dreamily, her lips a deep rich red against pearly teeth, her skin creamy, translucent.

Susan's eyes widened in surprise. She remembered Juanita as a plump, pretty girl who always made the most of her natural good looks. But this girl was beautiful. Strikingly, incredibly, *unnaturally* beautiful.

"Hello, Angela," Nita said softly. Her voice was warm and melodious, welcoming. She held out her hand.

"Oh, Nita," Angie breathed thankfully. "I'm so glad you're all right! I've been so worried about you." She beckoned. "Come on—let's go home before the storm gets any worse. Mom and Dad are going to be frantic."

Nita laughed, a delicious, silvery laugh. "There's no need to worry," she said. "We're safe from the storm here." She leaned forward. "Come on up, Angie, and bring Freddie and Susan with you. We're having a hurricane party."

Angie put her foot on the stairs, but Susan pulled her back. "Something's wrong," she whispered. "I can feel it."

"But that's my sister," Angie said, pulling away from Susan. "I have to go to her."

"No," Susan said. The air had grown much colder, and there was a draft blowing down the stairs. Behind Nita, Susan could see a dark space, blacker even than the emptiness beyond the stairs.

Freddie frowned. "Susan's right, Angie. Nita looks too good to be true. Something strange is going on here."

At the top of the stairs Nita leaned forward. "Angela," she called in a singsong voice. "Please, Angela, come up. There's something I want to show you."

Angie wrenched her arm free. "I don't care what you guys say, I'm going up there. I'll get her and bring her down, and then we can all leave. The Brothers must have gone, anyway. Flown away with those . . . things."

The draft chilled the marrow of Susan's bones. "No," she whispered, reaching for Angie. "He's here. Flint's here. I know it."

But Angie wouldn't be held back. She was taking the stairs two at a time. At the top she threw her arms around Nita, who stood unmoving, still smiling her dreamy, unearthly smile.

"Oh, Juanita," Angie cried, "I'm so glad I found you." She put her arm around her sister's shoulders. "Come on, we're going home."

A looming black shadow stepped out of the darkness. A hand fell on Angie's shoulder. Angie gave a scream and clutched Nita. Susan tensed as the figure stepped forward, and her blood turned to ice. *Flint!*

A sudden blast of wind shook the house. Something hit the roof like a shower of stones. The bricks from the chimney, perhaps.

"The storm is worsening," Flint said in his accented English. "Surely you will remain with us for a small hurricane party." He chuckled dryly. "Even if our other guests have been forced, shall we say, to take rapid flight. What is it they say? We shall make beautiful music together."

Beside Susan, Freddie was staring upward, her face lit. "Flint!" she cried.

Flint turned, looking down at them. "Ah, Frederica, my love," he said in a velvety voice. "I am so glad that you have come, too. Without you our party would not be complete." He smiled warmly. "Come, my dear. Come and join your friends."

Susan put her hand on Freddie's arm. "Stay here, Freddie," she commanded. "I'll go up and bring Angie and Nita down."

But Freddie's eyes, dazed, were fixed on Flint. Moving like a sleepwalker, she took a step up the stairs.

"Freddie!" Susan cried. "Don't do it! Don't give in to him!"

Flint's laugh was like the grating scrape of a fingernail on a blackboard. "Ah, Susan. How refreshing your caution is. I must confess that your resistance intrigues me far more than your friend's too-easy responsiveness. You are strong, Susan, and powerful. What a joy it would be to join your power to my own. And what a marvelous gift our union could give to you, to immortalize that power you hold." His smile grew seductive and he paused, his dark eyes fixed on hers. "You would perhaps permit me to invite *you* to our little party, in Frederica's place?"

"Yes," Susan said boldly, meeting Flint's eyes. "I'm the one you want." She pushed Freddie aside and started up the stairs.

Freddie gave a desperate moan. Her knees buckled and she fell against the wall, stretching out her hand. "No, Flint! Not Susan," she cried. "I want to come! *I'm* the one who loves you, not her!"

Flint chuckled. "Your time will come, dear Frederica. For now you must wait there." He stepped in front of Angela and Nita. His voice was commanding. "Do you come to me of your own free will, Susan?"

"I do," Susan said. "I give my consent." Her heart was pounding, and her breath was coming in shallow gasps. The confidence, the invincibility she had felt when she struck the dagger against the door, was all gone. It had drained away, taking all her strength with it. But there was only one direction she could go—up. Into whatever horror awaited her there.

"Then come, my love," Flint said, and raised his hand. He smiled. "And bring your little toy, if it amuses you."

Her hand trembling, Susan raised the dagger. By now she was used to the sensation of energy surging through it as it began to pulse with blue fire. But she wasn't prepared for the enormous electrical jolt that nearly knocked her off her feet, nor for the blue light that enveloped her entire body. She remembered what Aunt Carlota had said about the storm concentrating the power. But if the force in the dagger was stronger, wouldn't Flint's power be stronger, too?

"Ah," Flint said, "a touch of theatrics. Is this the plaything that so unsettled our guests that they took wing and flew away?" He pulled himself up, looming over her at the top of the stairs, his eyes black and burning, his smile taunting. His voice was full of disdain, and Susan could see his long white teeth gleaming.

Susan didn't reply to his teasing question. She

put her right foot on the stairs, then her left, then her right, concentrating on taking one step at a time. Slowly she moved toward the blackness that was Flint. Somehow she had to get close enough to touch him with the dagger, and she could destroy him as she had Bishop.

But the thought of coming within arm's reach of that shadowy figure was almost paralyzing. If she was close enough to touch him, *he* could touch her, pull her against him, bare his teeth . . .

At the awful thought Susan's hand began to tremble so hard, she almost dropped the dagger. The blue light that had enveloped her began to fade, the power to seep away. Her knees and arms felt rubbery. Flint was right. It was only a toy, a plaything. How could she hope to destroy such unspeakable evil with a child's plastic dagger? As the doubt flooded through her, the blue light began to fade from the dagger itself, like the dying flame of a candle.

"You see?" Flint laughed. "You think to conquer me with a toy. If I were you, my dear, I would not press my luck." He raised his hand, beckoning her closer. "Come, Susan. I invite you. Drop the trinket—it means nothing. You see? It has lost its power."

Susan stopped still, almost at the top of the stairs. *I don't think I'd better press my luck.* It was Drew's line. At the thought of it she remembered Drew's fingers on her face, her question, *How did you get here?* And his answer, *Didn't you invite me?*

"Drew," she whispered urgently. "Drew, I invite you!"

Flint laughed. "He cannot help you now, my dear. You are mine."

Susan closed her eyes, trying to concentrate. Where was Drew? Was her power so weak she couldn't make him hear her? Or was Flint's power so strong that it drowned hers out? The moments stretched out endlessly as she waited for Drew to appear. Perhaps it was the energy of the storm that was keeping him away.

Behind her Freddie broke the silence with a whimper. "You see, Flint? She doesn't care about you. It's someone else she's inviting. She cares for another. *I'm* the one who cares about you, Flint."

Flint's laugh was hard, grating. "She will care."

Susan screwed her eyes shut and clenched her hands. "Drew!"

"Hey, you're doing fine," a conversational voice spoke at her shoulder. "Don't panic."

Susan turned. A shadowy form stood beside her. "But I'm so frightened."

"Of course you are," Flint said, sounding smug. "You should be frightened."

"He wants you to be afraid," Drew explained.

"He's counting on it. Fear drives out power." He chuckled. "But you don't have to be afraid of him. He can't take what you won't give him. Remember that."

"Susan," Flint commanded. "Give up the toy."

Angie stepped forward. "No, Susan!" she cried. "Don't give it up."

Susan held up the plastic dagger so Drew could see it. "The power's gone," she said. "The light's out."

"No, it isn't," Drew said calmly. He took Susan's hand and touched the tip of the dagger to her cheek. It began to glow blue again, and she could feel the pulse of its energy. "The power isn't in the dagger or the cross or the herbs. It's in you. That's what Aunt Carlota told you. All you have to do is believe in yourself."

Susan stared at him. "You heard what Aunt Carlota told us?"

His pale gray-green eyes were amused. "Ghosts get around. It's one of the privileges."

At the top of the stairs Flint was leaning forward, frowning. "Forget about Drew, Susan. Come to me, my dear."

"I do have the power," Susan said more to herself than to Drew, or even Flint. She squared her shoulders and summoned all her strength—*her* strength. She held up the dagger so Flint could see it. Then she opened her fingers and let it fall. Its light paled, then flickered for a moment, then went out. In the silence she could hear Angie's horrified gasp.

"What did you say?" Flint asked. "Speak to me, Susan."

Susan raised her voice. "I said, you're right, Flint. The toy has no power."

"Ah," Flint said, with a sigh of deep satisfaction. His eyes gleamed smoky red in the dimness. "Then you will join our party without further delay, will you not?"

Susan looked up at him, daring to meet his eyes. Her heart thumped in her chest. "I don't have any choice, do I?"

"No. You have no choice." Flint's voice deepened, took on a magnetic quality. "Come, my dear."

Susan forced her rubbery legs to advance one step; then another. Three more, and she would be within reach of him. Within *his* reach. At the thought she felt mortally afraid. Why hadn't she held on to the dagger? If she had kept it, she might have a better chance. But without it Flint might think she was powerless, vulnerable. Without it she might be able to catch him off guard.

Two more steps.

Flint laughed softly, expectantly. His eyes held hers. "So. You come to me at last, on my terms! You, the sweet, stubborn one. You, the powerful one."

One more step.

Flint rubbed his clawlike hands together. His face was dark, his eyes flashing red with triumph, his wolfish teeth gleaming. "We shall see who is stubborn now, shall we?"

And then Susan moved. Softly, swiftly, she stepped up to Flint and put her hand on his heart. As she did, she felt her arm throb, she saw it turn incandescent, saw her flesh become transparent, saw her very bones. She recalled Aunt Carlota's wisdom.

"Love," Susan said softly, "is the undoing of evil."

At the sound of the words, there came a flash of fire and the smell of scorched flesh. Flint screamed silently and spun away, gasping for breath. His hands clawed at his chest. Behind him Nita cried, a high, sobbing cry.

Susan reached for Flint's arm. As she touched him, there was another fiery flash, an explosion. A whirl of dark air, a howling tornado of evil, gathered itself and rushed past Susan, down the steps, and through the open door, to join the storm outside.

It was over.

Susan collapsed on the stairs, completely drained. The world spun around her, her mind was a gray fog. She was vaguely aware that Angie had pulled her sister down the stairs toward her. Nita was sobbing hysterically, calling Flint's name, and

Angie was shaking her shoulder, saying something in urgent Spanish. Somewhere downstairs Freddie was yelling. Suddenly Freddie's cry penetrated the fog.

"Fire! The house is on fire! We've got to get out!"

Sixteen

Susan found herself sitting on something hard. It was the low stone wall around the cemetery. She was soaked through, and the chill gale-force wind was lashing her shoulders, whipping her hair. She lifted her face and let the rain wash it clean. She didn't care that she was wet. Her three friends were beside her. They were safe. The Brothers were gone. That was all that mattered.

Freddie was shaking her. "Are you okay, Susan?"

"I . . . I think so," Susan said, feeling dizzy. She licked the rain off her lips. It tasted good.

"Boy, we got out of there just in the nick of time," Freddie said.

Susan shut her eyes. As if it had been a dream,

she remembered Nita crying, hysterical, and Angie talking excitedly. Each sister had taken her by an arm, lifted her up, and pulled her down the stairs and out the front door, with Freddie coming behind. For a moment Susan wondered what had happened to Drew. But of course nothing could happen to him, she reminded herself. He was a ghost. Nothing could hurt a ghost.

"Look!" Angie said excitedly, pointing across the street.

Susan looked. Heavy gray-black smoke poured out the front door and the blown-out front window of the Brothers' house. Along the side, furious flames licked up the wooden wall to the roof. Susan knew that in a moment the whole house would go up. Despite the coming storm, small knots of curious neighbors had gathered on the sidewalk in front of the burning house.

"We should call the fire department," Nita said.

"Somebody's already called them," Angie replied. "Here they come now." Susan could hear the wail of a siren heading their way.

A fire truck pulled up in front of the house. Firefighters dragged out their hoses while others raced with axes and extinguishers around to the back of the house. The onlookers moved back out of the way, and several went into their houses to escape the growing storm. One of the firefighters ran back to the truck and got on the radio to put out a second alarm. At that moment the wind sucked a sheet of orange-red flame through the broken window with a roar like a blast furnace. The whole front of the house was engulfed in flames.

"With this wind they'll never save the house," Freddie said, shaking her head. "In a way, I'm almost sorry to see it go. It was a really beautiful house, even if the owners were a little twisted."

Angie turned to Susan. "Did *you* do that?" she asked wonderingly. "I mean, when you lit up the doorway with that blue flame, was that what set the place on fire?"

Susan shook her head. "Your guess is as good as mine." She pushed her dripping hair out of her eyes.

"It was awesome," Freddie said. "You're like the bionic woman." She stared at Susan. "Hey, have you thought of doing stuff like that for a living? I'll bet those guys out in Hollywood would pay you a bundle."

Susan put her head down on her knees. She ought to feel triumphant, right? She had faced the darkest, most awful power in the universe, and had beaten it. Why didn't she feel as if she had achieved something?

It was a question she couldn't answer. Maybe because her victory was only temporary. Flint and the Brothers were gone; at least in the form she had known them, they were. But their power remained. They could create new forms, be it here or in a different place. What would happen then? Would there be another battle? Or, next time, would they win without opposition, without a fight?

Freddie nudged her. "Here comes a fireman," she said in a low voice. "What are we going to say to him?"

Susan looked up. A man in a yellow slicker and helmet was coming across the street. "Get Nita out of here," she told Angie urgently, handing her the car keys. "She's in no shape to answer any questions."

Angie grabbed Nita's arm. "Help me, Freddie."

Freddie took Juanita's other arm. "We'll wait in the car for you," she said to Susan. They walked off.

The fireman came up. "I'm Lieutenant Patterson," he said. "One of the bystanders here thinks you were in the house when the fire started. Is that true?"

"Yes, that's right," Susan said. "I came with my friend to pick up her sister. There was another girl with us. We were on our way out when we smelled the smoke."

The lieutenant scrutinized her face as if he were trying to decide whether she was hiding anything. "Were the residents at home?"

"No," Susan said. "They weren't there. And I don't know where they are now," she added truthfully, anticipating his next question.

"I'll need your name for my report," he said, taking out a notebook, "and the names of your friends." Across the street somebody shouted and waved, and he stuck the notebook back in his pocket. "Hang around for a few minutes, will you?" he said. "Looks like we're turning in another alarm." He turned and sprinted across the street.

Susan sat on the stone wall, shivering. The storm was worsening, and she knew she ought to call Mack and let him know she was safe. But a few more minutes wouldn't hurt. She sat quietly, watching the roaring mass of flames. The house, and everything it seemed to symbolize, was coming to an end. *The end?* she thought bitterly. *Is it really the end? Or is it only the end of the beginning?*

A few minutes later the second fire truck pulled up. Right behind it a white van rounded the corner and screeched to a halt directly in front of Susan. CHANNEL FIVE, KGTX-TV, was printed in big red letters on the side. Two men got out. One threw open the side door, swung a television camera onto his shoulder, and ran across the street, where he knelt down and started filming the blaze. The other man, obviously a reporter, walked toward Susan. He wore a green nylon windbreaker with the hood pulled up over his head.

"Hi," he said. He turned so that he had his back to the wind, and stuck his hands in the pockets of the windbreaker. "Looks like we got here a little late. Did you see what happened?"

"Sort of," Susan said guardedly. "I think it might have had something to do with the electricity. There was some blue fire around the front door, then a lot of smoke." It was the same story she planned to tell Lieutenant Patterson when he came back for his report. It was the truth—or part of it, anyway. She hoped it would stand up to scrutiny.

"Anybody live there?"

"Some rock musicians."

A squall rocked the truck. A power pole at the end of the street blew over with a crash, sending a shower of sparks into the dark.

The reporter looked apprehensive. "Maybe we should get out of this wind. You're soaking wet."

Susan stood up. "I'm waiting to make a report on the fire," she said. "Your first hurricane?"

"Yeah. We don't get weather like this up in Dallas. Up there all we get is tornadoes. And I've managed never to be on the scene when one of those babies came churning through."

Something inside her turned over. "You're from Dallas?"

"Yes," he said. "I came down here a couple of weeks ago, chasing a story for one of the Dallas stations. I decided to stay, and I was lucky enough to get a job filling in at KGTX."

Susan swallowed. The goose bumps that had risen on her arms had nothing to do with the rain and wind. "Welcome to Galveston," she managed at last. "I hope you'll like it here." She looked at him, but all she could see was the hood of his windbreaker. "What did you say your name was?"

He turned to face her. "I didn't say," he replied. "But I think I'm going to like it here." His pale gray-green eyes lingered on her face. "In fact, I'm *sure* of it."

"Drew?" she whispered incredulously.

The guy grinned. "Yeah. Hey, how did you know?"

Susan smiled back. "I think maybe I saw you on television," she said.

NIGHTMARES

Love You To Death

He chuckled. Julie was a prize worth winning. And when she was his, they would be together, and happy, forever. Just the two of them. They wouldn't need anyone else.

She would make him forget the terrible parts of his life. His father. Alison. The Place.

But what if her friends tried to interfere, like last time, the way Alison's had?

Let them try. They'd be sorry if they did. He was older and smarter now. He knew how to handle creeps like that.

Yes, he'd make them sorry if they did.

And this time he wouldn't get caught.

NIGHTMARES

LOVE YOU TO DEATH

Bebe Faas Rice

To Marie and John, with love.

CHAPTER ONE

Afterward—for the rest of her life, in fact—Julie Hagan would wonder at the suddenness of it.

One moment was all it took. One brief moment and her life was changed forever.

"Wow, check that out!" Shelley Molino said, her Bambi-brown eyes widening, as she stared over Julie's shoulder toward the entrance to the cafeteria.

Julie set her loaded tray on the table, the special table reserved by unspoken law for members of Jefferson High's elite "in" group.

Then she turned and followed Shelley's gaze.

And caught her breath as the boy in the doorway looked back at her.

Even at this distance, halfway across the

busy, noisy school cafeteria, Julie felt drawn to him. Felt the sudden, almost physical current that seemed to flow between them. Deep inside her, she felt everything—heart, stomach, whatever—give an odd little lurch. She pressed her hand to her mouth, almost frightened by her reaction to him.

What's happening to me? she thought. *And why? Is it his looks? Or is it the way he's staring at me?*

The boy had stepped to the side of the entrance now, away from the crowd of students that surged through the door behind him. He was leaning against the wall, his hands in the pockets of his faded jeans, a slight frown on his face. And he was staring at her.

Yes, staring. She was sure it was at her.

His eyes . . . so dark, so intense. Were they black? Blue-black, maybe? It was hard to tell from here.

He isn't exactly what you'd call handsome, Julie thought, trying to collect her wits. *Rugged? Yeah. Sexy? Definitely sexy, and there's something about the way he's standing that tells you he knows how to take care of himself.*

"Hey, Tara," Jessica Claggett said, her voice breaking through Julie's daze. "Has that guy over there got a thing for you, or what?"

Tara, Julie thought, dismayed. *He's been staring at Tara, not me!*

Julie hoped she didn't look as humiliated as she felt. What on earth made her think *she* was the one he'd been watching so intently? He probably hadn't even noticed her standing there, gawking at him with her mouth hanging open. At least she hoped he hadn't. She must have looked like a total jerk!

He had been staring at Tara Braxton, the resident Southern belle. Her ancestors had founded this small but classy little town and then modestly named it after themselves: Braxton Falls, Virginia. Braxton Falls on the Potomac. Tara's social credentials in this part of the country carried a lot of weight.

Yes, he was watching Tara, all right. Naturally. Who else rated that kind of attention? Tara and Jessica had come to the table right after Julie. They'd been standing behind her the whole time. And *he'd* been looking past her at Tara, while she'd mistakenly thought that . . .

And yet . . .

No. It was always Tara who got the cute ones. Gorgeous Tara with her thick, straight black hair and long-lashed gray eyes. She was the one boys looked at first.

3

Julie sat down at the table, taking care to turn her back on *him*. She'd show him she'd known all along just who it was he'd been staring at. And that she didn't care.

Tara sat down facing her and preened a little, stealing a quick glance across the room from under lowered lashes.

"Has *who* got a thing for me, Jess? If you mean that gorgeous six-foot hunk over by the door, I haven't noticed."

Jessica and Shelley laughed appreciatively. They had been friends with Tara since grade school, but they still acted a little too eager to please. They were constantly flattering Tara, trying desperately to keep on her good side.

"You were saying yesterday you hoped we'd get some new guys at school this year," Shelley said to Tara. "Well, this one is definitely new. We'd all remember *him* if he'd ever set foot in this place before."

"Shelley, don't keep looking at him!" Tara scolded. "I don't want him to know we're talking about him. I'm going to play hard to get with this one." She laughed and a dimple flashed briefly in one cheek. "This will definitely make things more interesting around here. He's mine, starting right now, so hands off, everybody."

4

"If you've set your sights on him, Tara, the poor guy doesn't stand a chance," Jessica said, smiling.

Tara flipped back her long hair and looked pleased.

She really likes this, Julie thought. *She likes having this power over people. That's what her looks and money and social status mean to her. Power over the rest of us.*

Julie wondered why she hung out with Tara and the others. She'd been wondering that a lot recently. Why, when she certainly knew better, had she tied herself up with this snobby little trio who didn't believe in associating with what they called "losers and dweebs"? Anyone outside their small circle of carefully selected class beauties, student-body leaders, and top-notch school athletes was considered beneath their notice.

Julie sighed, picked up her fork, and poked at her food. Mystery meat again, covered with some kind of runny-looking sauce.

"Don't look now—Shelley, don't turn around!—but Mr. Sexpot is going through the cafeteria line," Jessica reported in a stage whisper. "Maybe he'll come this way. Wait . . . no . . . he's going to the corner where the science nerds hang out—that ought to give creepy Norine Goldsmith the thrill of her life."

"I don't think Norine's all that interested in boys right now," Julie said.

"Why not?" Jessica asked. "'Cause she likes computers better?"

"No. Norine's trying to get a scholarship to Cal Tech, and that's the most important thing in her life right now. I wouldn't expect you to understand that, Jessica."

Julie hadn't meant to sound so cold and hostile. It had simply come out that way, and it was too late to change it now. Fortunately, it was hard to insult Jessica. Things seemed to bounce right off her.

"Well, pardon me, Miss Priss," Jessica responded, making a face. "Aren't we touchy today, defending the nerds and making life safe for democracy?"

"Girls! Girls!" said Tara. "All for one and one for all, remember? We're friends, okay?"

Julie suddenly felt tired. Tired and bored.

What's wrong with me? she wondered. *Must just be the back-to-school blues.*

She glanced off to the far corner, to the science nerds' table. *He* looked as good from the back as he did from the front.

Am I jealous of Tara? Is that it?

No. It wasn't just that. Julie wasn't surprised by Tara's going after the new guy. But she'd been feeling critical of Tara, Jessica, and Shelley for several months now. Before last summer, even. She'd been friends with them ever since she moved to Braxton Falls three years ago. She'd been a shy eighth-grader then, eager for acceptance. She'd been thrilled when the three prettiest, most popular girls in her class included her in their group.

"Three's a bad number," Tara had explained. "You know—two's company and three's a crowd and all that. Somebody always feels left out when there are only three of you. Four is much, much better."

But now that she was sixteen and a junior at Jefferson High, Julie didn't like being a member of Tara's foursome anymore. They acted so silly and shallow sometimes. But still, hanging out with them did mean she was always included in the band of popular kids that revolved around Tara.

And if she *did* stop hanging out with Tara and the others, her last two years at Jefferson High might be pretty miserable. Tara would probably see to it that she was snubbed as a pun-

7

ishment for her disloyalty. She'd done it before to a girl who'd made her mad, and Julie didn't think she was strong enough to cope with treatment like that.

And besides, she thought with a shrug, *why should I do something crazy like that, anyway? Who wouldn't want to be one of the movers and shakers of Jefferson High? They're the ones who make things happen and have all the fun. And it makes Mom happy that I'm friends with Tara.*

For Julie's mother, moving to prestigious Braxton Falls had been the realization of all her girlhood dreams.

When her husband parlayed a small restaurant into a modest chain of fast-food diners, Mrs. Hagan talked him into moving to Braxton Falls and buying a huge custom-built home in Hunter Valley, an area that had once belonged to Tara's aristocratic ancestors. And nothing thrilled her more than knowing that her daughter was considered good enough to be friends with one of the famous Braxtons.

The cafeteria table was filling up now, and Julie found herself squashed between Brad Stafford, junior-class playboy, and Nick Wells, the editor of the school paper.

"You're awfully quiet today, gorgeous," Brad

said, flashing his famous, even-toothed smile, the smile that could bring every girl at Jefferson High to her knees.

Well, almost every girl. Julie was the exception. Brad wasn't her type. For one thing, he was too good-looking, with that blond hair, and those blue eyes and white teeth. She didn't trust all that perfection. He was always pretending to come on to her lately, hamming it up as he grabbed her knee or played footsie with her. Julie found it all really embarrassing.

At this very minute she could feel his thigh jammed up against hers, from hip to knee. Of course, the table was crowded, but he was sitting a little closer than he had to. And when he started wriggling his eyebrows at her, Julie decided she'd had enough.

Furious, she planted an elbow in his side and shoved. Hard.

"Ouch!" he gasped, moving away from her. "Geez, Julie, take it easy, will you? Can't a guy get a little friendly around here without you laying on the ninja stuff?"

"Go get friendly with someone else, Romeo," she snapped.

"You're beautiful when you're angry," Brad said, rubbing his side gingerly.

9

Tara waved him to silence with a fluttering motion of her hand and leaned forward across the table, lowering her voice.

"Listen, guys, does anybody know anything about that new boy? The tall, good-looking one?"

This is her way of playing hard to get? Julie thought, amused. *By the time school lets out today, everyone within earshot will know that Tara Braxton's going after the new guy.*

"He's a senior, that's all I know," Nick Wells offered. "And he's from out of town. I don't know why he's a couple weeks late starting school, though."

"Isn't he great?" asked Lisa Doyle, sighing. "What a hunk!"

Lisa was one of the best cheerleaders at Jefferson High. A slim, compact little blonde, she combined top-quality gymnastics with her routines.

"I was over by the principal's office when he checked in this morning," she went on. "Naturally, I asked around about him, but all anyone knows is that his name's Quinn McNeal, and that he's eighteen and a senior. Karen Slack works part-time in the office. She promised to find out everything she can about him."

"There are a couple of rumors going around about him," said Colin King. As the captain of the football team, Colin had probably looked the newcomer over with an eye toward recruiting him, Julie figured. Quinn was certainly big enough.

"I don't know where they started," Colin said. "One kid told me he's a former dropout from another town who's come back to school to finish his education. But then someone else said he was orphaned in some kind of accident and that he's been in the hospital for a long time because of it."

"That explains why he looks older than other senior guys," Lisa said. "And Karen heard him tell the principal's secretary he lives alone in a basement apartment in town, so the orphan rumor must be true."

"Hmmm," Tara said, her eyes glowing. "He gets more interesting by the minute. He's a real mystery man, isn't he?"

When they got up to leave the cafeteria, Julie took a quick look around, hoping to get another glimpse of Quinn. She had to see if he would affect her the same way this time as he had before.

He wasn't there.

A terrible feeling of loneliness swept over Julie. She felt abandoned.

And then she saw him. It was almost as if he'd been waiting for her.

He was standing in a dark corner of the hall. And he was looking at *her*—she was sure of it—not at Tara.

Julie tried not to stare at him.

His hair was dark and thick, with an unruly lock that fell over his forehead. His cheekbones were prominent in his lean face, and his nose looked as if it had been broken at some time in the past—it was a little flattened across the bridge. Julie thought it only made his face more interesting, more masculine.

And his mouth, with that full, finely sculpted upper lip . . .

Julie turned away, her heart beating erratically, and took a deep breath. She wondered what it would be like to kiss that mouth.

CHAPTER TWO

I can't believe it, he thought. *That girl, that beautiful girl, with the crowd of giggling, silly cheerleader types . . .*

For a minute I thought she was Alison. Same long golden-brown hair. Same big amber-colored eyes. I could see their color, even from where I stood.

And the way she looked at me—almost as if she recognized me. I could swear she recognized me.

But she wasn't Alison. How could she be? Alison is . . . gone.

And then later, in the hall, when she'd drawn a breath and turned away. That faint flush on her cheeks, and the way her pulse fluttered in her throat. He'd seen it fluttering like a butterfly in the hollow of that beautiful, creamy-skinned little throat. Her skin was like silk. He could imagine the feel and scent of that warm, living silk. . . .

No, he cautioned himself. *I mustn't think of that now. Not yet. I rushed it last time . . . and look what happened. This time I'll take it slow and easy. I'll make her wonder, make her want me to make my move. But first she has to notice me, and I think she has.*

He smiled. A thin, faint scar, running downward, bisected his upper lip, giving him a slightly crooked, arrogant-looking smile. Like a pirate, someone had told him once.

Yes, she noticed me all right, he thought. *And I could tell she felt the same thing for me that I feel for her. She knows me. She's always known me, just as I've always known her.*

He liked slender girls, he liked the look of slender frailty, and she was as slim and willowy as a princess, just as Alison had been. And she had that same proud, graceful way of moving her pretty little body.

He frowned.

But she's not Alison, he told himself. *I've got to stop thinking of Alison and looking for her in every face I see. That part of my life is over. And didn't I pay a high enough price for it? Four years in*

14

The Place, and the terrible loneliness of knowing I must live a lifetime without Alison.

And yet . . . that girl. That girl with the amber-brown eyes.

Am I being given a second chance?

CHAPTER THREE

The big news at school the next day was that there was no news.

"Quinn McNeal's records aren't with any of the others," Karen Slack told Lisa Doyle, who promptly passed it along.

Julie, Tara, Shelley, and Jessica were at their lockers before third period when Lisa excitedly gave them the news.

". . . And Karen says she's sure Mr. Reed's got them locked up in his special file," Lisa concluded. "But why do you think he'd do something like that?"

Tara closed her locker carefully and shifted her books from one arm to the other. Her gray eyes narrowed.

"My, my," she murmured. "This Quinn McNeal

gets more mysterious all the time, doesn't he?"

"Maybe he's really some exiled prince or something, and we're not supposed to find out!" Shelley said breathlessly.

"That is so dumb, Shelley," Jessica said. "Why would he come down here? He could go to a fancy prep school up north, if he was so rich."

"Well, if he isn't a prince, he should be," Shelley insisted. "He looks like one, doesn't he, Julie?"

"He's . . . he's very . . . good-looking," Julie agreed. She felt a blush begin at the collar of her blouse and work its way upward, toward her hairline. Oh, why couldn't she grow out of this stupid, babyish habit she had of blushing?

Julie saw Tara eye her closely. Her scarlet lips were set in a thin line.

"Just to set the record straight," Tara said evenly, tapping a long fingernail on her notebook, "you all *did* hear me when I said that Quinn McNeal is on my list of things to do, didn't you? I'd hate to see somebody get in the way."

She made her point well. *She always does,* Julie thought rebelliously. *And what would she do, I wonder, if somebody actually dared to disobey her?*

*　　*　　*

Wild speculations about Quinn and his missing school records continued at lunchtime. But Julie wasn't paying attention to her friends. Without even looking up from her plate, she could feel Quinn's eyes on her.

Am I imagining this? Julie wondered. She knew she could look over and see for herself if he was watching. But somehow she couldn't make her eyes turn toward Quinn. *Anyway, if he is looking,* she thought, *what am I supposed to do about it?*

Quinn was at the far end of the cafeteria again, not at the table with the science nerds—at another one, even farther away. But this time he was facing Julie.

Or Tara.

It was obvious that Tara thought he was looking at her, Tara Braxton, the hottest thing in the South since Scarlett O'Hara. She was doing her animated, pink-cheeked, sparkling-eyed thing, the way she always did when she was out to let some guy know she was available.

Julie noticed how Tara made a point of not looking over at Quinn, while still managing to make it clear she was playing to him, teasing him into noticing her.

Nick Wells, sitting beside Tara, looked upset.

Julie saw the angry pulse that beat in his temple. His fingers tightened on the edge of his tray, knuckles whitening suddenly when Tara flung back her long hair and laughed her special there's-a-boy-watching laugh.

Nick was no fool. Julie had always respected his intelligence. It was obvious he knew what Tara was up to—hadn't she come onto him the same way last June when he'd been named editor of the school paper?

Tara only went for the important guys, the rich ones or the ones who wielded some kind of power on campus. Nick was well aware of that. He knew Tara was using him. He'd admitted it to Julie, who worked on the staff of the school newspaper with him.

"It doesn't matter, Julie," he'd said. "I'll take Tara on any terms. I'm crazy about her—always have been. But this is the first time I've ever gotten anywhere with her."

He and Tara had been a hot item all summer, and Nick obviously had been counting on it to continue.

And now Tara was making a play for the new guy.

"Anyway, Karen says there's no way she can get access to Quinn's records if—" Lisa was saying.

Nick cut in on her. "Isn't it about time we went on to some other subject around here? I'm sick of hearing about Quinn McNeal."

Lisa sniffed. "Just because we're *mildly* interested in the administrative handling of our records here at Jefferson High . . ."

"You're all trying to snoop into this guy McNeal's private business, that's what you're doing. And there's probably nothing mysterious about him at all," Nick said. "We all know that Mr. Reed's too old and absentminded to be a principal. I'll bet he lost those records and doesn't want to admit it."

"Nick's right," Brad agreed. "That poor old guy can't even find his own rear end with both hands."

"What a disgusting thing to say," Tara said.

Brad put on an injured, innocent expression, blue eyes opened wide. "I was only trying to be helpful"

Tara looked sideways at Nick, arching one perfectly plucked eyebrow, and smiled playfully.

She's being cute now, trying to charm Nick, Julie thought disgustedly. *Just in case things don't work out with the new guy.*

Tara's lips were soft and pouty as she leaned toward Nick. "I know somebody who got out of

20

bed on the wrong side this morning—"

"You mean you were there, you wild thing?" Brad asked with an exaggerated leer. "Does your mother know?"

Tara ignored him. "—and I think I'd better see if I can do something to sweeten him up."

She leaned over and kissed Nick on the tip of his nose.

A soft, dopey look immediately came over his face. *Like Silly Putty*, Julie thought. *I wish I knew how she does it.*

"Hey, Julie, how about sweetening *me* up? I'm feeling mean as a snake today," Brad said, reaching under the table and groping for her knee.

"No wonder. You *are* a snake!" Julie retorted, getting to her feet and gathering up her trash.

From the corner of her eye, she could see Quinn rise from his seat and head her way. No, not her way exactly. Toward the trash bin. The same one she was heading for. They were going to arrive there at exactly the same moment!

He's been waiting for me, Julie thought with dead certainty. *Watching me and waiting for me to get up so he can make his move. He's planned this "accidental" meeting so that he can . . .*

So that he could what? Talk to her? Introduce himself?

Or meet Tara?

But Julie knew that it definitely wasn't Tara. It was Julie.

But why?

I'm no competition for Tara, she thought. *I'm pretty enough, but Tara's a stunner. A guy like that deserves a stunner.*

And yet Julie had known all along that something was happening between Quinn McNeal and herself. It had started yesterday. That was the first step, today was the second.

Julie stood before the garbage bin, not looking up. She could see long legs in faded jeans beside hers. There was the beginning of a small, ragged hole in the knee of one pant leg.

Quinn reached out and took her tray, his hand brushing hers in passing.

A shock went through Julie. Startled, she looked up and met his gaze.

He felt it, too, she thought. *There's no way he couldn't have noticed that connection.*

Julie's cheeks felt warm. Her neck. Her ears. She was suddenly very aware of every cell in her body.

They stood looking at each other for what seemed an eternity. She realized later that it had only been several seconds. But in those seconds the noise of the room seemed to dim and she was aware of only him. The way he stood. That faint scar on his lip.

And then he smiled, just the beginning of a smile. Before Julie could respond, before she could snap out of her reverie, he upended her tray with one quick flick of the wrist, sending her uneaten pizza and milk carton into the bin. Then he laid the tray on the conveyor belt that trundled it off to the kitchen.

Julie realized her hand was outstretched, as if she were still holding her tray. Blushing, she dropped it to her side. He gave her another quick little sketch of a smile, turned on his heel, and was gone.

I still don't know what color his eyes are, Julie thought dazedly. *Black, or dark blue?*

"My, my, isn't our new student helpful?" said a voice in her ear. Tara wasn't cooing now. Her voice was rock-hard and edged with steel.

Julie turned and faced her.

Tara's eyes were a flat slate-gray and cold as a winter sky.

"It was *me* he wanted to meet, Julie, but you had to rush right over and make a fool of yourself, didn't you? Next time, butt out!"

CHAPTER FOUR

Julie waited until later, when Tara had cooled down, before attempting to talk to her.

"Look, Tara, about what happened between Quinn and me—"

"What *did* happen between you and Quinn, Julie?"

"Well, nothing, but—"

"Right. And that's why I got so upset." Tara opened her eyes wide, trying to look sincere and caring. "It was really pathetic. If only you could have seen the way you stared at him! Honestly, Julie, I was *so* embarrassed for you. I mean, I'm one of your very best friends, and it really hurt me to see you acting like such a dweeb."

"I didn't stare at him," Julie lied.

"Trust me, Julie. You were definitely *not*

cool." Tara threw an arm around Julie. "Look, I'm the one Quinn's coming on to, so don't make a fool of yourself over him, okay?"

With another fake smile, Tara turned her back and sauntered off down the hall. Julie sighed and headed into her classroom. She sat next to Jessica in biology. Usually, before class started, they'd talk and laugh together. Today it was different. Jessica opened her notebook and began to look through her notes from the previous day, studiously ignoring Julie.

Julie laid her hand on Jessica's arm. "Aren't you speaking to me today, Jess?"

Jessica raised her head in pretended surprise. "Oh, sure, Julie. What's up?"

I'm in love, that's what's up, Julie longed to say. *Talk to me about love at first sight, Jess. Does it really happen? Does it last? And what should I do about it?*

Instead she said, "Tara's really mad at me, isn't she?"

Jessica looked away. "Well, it really wasn't fair of you to make a move on Quinn McNeal, Julie. After all, Tara said she liked him, didn't she?"

"But I didn't make a move on him," Julie protested feebly.

"Tara says you did," Jessica said flatly.

And whatever Tara says, you believe. Aren't you my friend, too, Jess? Everybody thinks you are. They envy the four of us, they think we're the best of friends—close enough to tell each other everything.

"So you think I tried to beat Tara out, is that it?" Julie asked.

Jessica shifted in her chair. "Let's just say, Julie, that the four of us have to be loyal to each other. I mean, we've been together for a long time. And Tara's always been a good friend to you and Shelley and me, hasn't she?"

Maybe we've never really been friends, the four of us, Julie thought. *Maybe we've only been using each other all these years.*

"Sort of," she answered Jessica.

"Sort of?" Jessica's eyes, normally placid, shot off sparks. "What do you mean, *sort of?* Where would you be now if Tara hadn't taken you under her wing when you came to Braxton Falls three years ago? You were a nobody then, Julie!"

Maybe I'd be with the science nerds, Julie thought dreamily. *Or the literary crowd. And I might feel more comfortable and happier around them than I do around you and Tara.*

"So where would you be?" Jessica repeated angrily.

"Nowhere, I guess," Julie replied wearily, opening her biology book. "Nowhere at all."

For the first time in her life, Julie was in love. And with a boy she hadn't even spoken to yet. She longed to talk to somebody about him. To say his name aloud to a sympathetic ear: QuinnQuinnQuinnQuinnQuinn!

But who could she talk to about it?

Not Jess or Shelley, that was clear, now. Lisa Doyle, maybe? No, not her. Lisa would have it all over school by first period tomorrow.

Her mother? *Forget it!* Julie thought. *If Mom knew the kind of feelings I have for Quinn, she'd give me that outdated lecture about the birds and the bees again. Of course, there's always Mollie. . . .*

That night, after supper, Julie rapped on her sister's bedroom door.

"Come in!"

Julie smiled to herself as she turned the doorknob. How many girls her age would turn to a fourteen-year-old sister for advice? But Mollie was different. She was funny, incredibly intelligent, and could always be trusted to keep a secret.

27

Mollie was curled up on her bed, reading glasses perched on the end of her nose, a thick novel propped on her knees.

"Would you believe *War and Peace?*" she asked, making a face. "Ms. Landsburg is giving extra credit to anyone who finished it this semester. It's really not bad, though, once you get used to all those complicated Russian names."

Mollie's room looked more like an office than a teenage girl's bedroom. No ruffles and stuffed animals for her. Everything was spartan, pared down, intellectual looking. "Early bookworm," their mother called it.

Bur Mollie wasn't really a bookworm. Her "thing" was computers. She wasn't just a computer nut, she was a computer genius. So were her friends, especially her best friend, Tommy Tomagawa. Julie envied the fun they seemed to have together, their lack of pretense, and the way they talked to each other from the heart.

Julie sank down in the wing chair by the bed. "Look, Mollie, I need to talk."

Mollie immediately closed her book and took off her glasses. "Sure. Shoot."

"It's about this guy, Mollie. I need your advice."

Mollie hooted with laughter. "You've got to

be kidding! Me? Give you advice on your love life?"

She stopped laughing when she noticed her sister's serious expression.

"But you're the social wheeler and dealer in the family, Julie," she protested. "I thought *you* had all the answers. What on earth do I know about guys and dating?"

"Not much, I admit," Julie said. "But you're the only one I can talk to about it right now. You've got to keep it quiet, though. Just between the two of us, okay?"

"If you say so." Mollie drew a cross over her heart. "Hope to die."

"There's this guy—" Julie began.

"What's his name?"

"I don't think you know him. He's a new senior. His name's Quinn McNeal."

Mollie sat bolt upright. Her book slipped off her knees and to the floor.

"Quinn McNeal? *That* one? Are we really talking about *the* Quinn McNeal?"

"What do you know about him?"

"Only that as of nine A.M. yesterday, every freshman girl got a case of the mad hots for him, that's what I know about Quinn McNeal. Everyone but me, of course, because I happen to be incredibly cool and laid-back for my age. So what about him?"

"I know you're probably not going to believe this, Mollie, but I think Quinn's interested in me."

"You? Wow!"

Mollie put her head to one side and squinted at Julie thoughtfully. Then she nodded.

"Okay. I believe it. Why not? You're pretty. You could get just about any boy you wanted. Lots of guys like you. They always have."

Julie was touched by her little sister's praise. Mollie wasn't one to pass out empty compliments.

"It isn't just a question of like," she said. "It's a little more than that. . . . I mean, I *think* it's more than that. I hope so anyway, because I . . ."

"Julie, what are you talking about? What's happened here? The guy just checked in yesterday. What goes on in the junior-senior locker area, anyway?"

"I wish I knew what's going on," Julie said. "Please don't laugh, but I feel like someone in a movie or a book. I took one look at him yesterday and—I swear, Mollie—it happened. All those things you read about. It was like . . . like electricity . . . and . . ."

She stopped and looked down, blushing. "And now I can't get him out of my mind. It's like I'm obsessed with him or something."

Mollie thoughtfully chewed on a thumbnail, a habit she'd been trying to break.

"A *coup de foudre*," she said, almost reverently.

"A what?"

Mollie cleared her throat and repeated it. "It's what the French call a *coup de foudre*. A lightning bolt. Love. Freely translated, it means love's just knocked your socks off." Mollie thought for a minute. "But what about him? Are you sure he feels that same way?"

Julie nodded. "I think so. It's the way he looks at me, Mollie. He just stares at me. I can't even describe what it's like, and how it makes me feel. And today . . . he kept watching me and watching me all through lunch. I didn't even have to turn around and look. I could *feel* him looking at me. And then when I got up to dump my tray, he was there. He took my tray and his hand touched mine, and I felt it again. That electricity thing."

"Your magnetic force field," Mollie said. "We all have them surrounding us. The Russians or somebody invented a camera that can actually photograph it and—"

"Mollie! Can you give your scientific expertise a rest for a minute and talk about me?"

"Oh, sorry. So when this electric thing happened between you, what did he say?"

"Nothing. That's the strange thing. He didn't say anything. Just smiled a little and walked away. And I didn't say anything, either. It was like I was struck dumb or something."

Mollie snorted. "That's a first."

"Am I being silly? Can something like this *really* happen so fast? I only saw him for the first time yesterday, and we haven't even spoken to each other yet."

"*Romeo and Juliet* took place in only four days," Mollie said dreamily. "Four days from the eyes-across-the-room bit to the double suicide in the tomb."

"*This* is your way of cheering me up?"

"Well, Romeo and Juliet were a year or so younger than you, Julie, and obviously a little more impulsive."

"So what should I do . . . and why am I asking you about this, anyway?" Julie said.

"Because you're desperate," Mollie said with an unconcerned grin. "And because you want me to tell you to do exactly what you've been planning to do all along. So, okay, I'll say it."

She leaned forward, like a judge over a court-room desk. "Go for it, Julie, go for it. Follow your instincts."

"You mean it?"

"Yup. These things happen, so why worry because it seems a little unusual? Or because it isn't happening to any of your airhead friends?"

"Oh!" Julie put her hand to her mouth, remembering Tara. "That's the other problem, Mollie. Tara wants Quinn for herself. She really got on my case this afternoon about him."

"So what? She can't always be the belle of the ball."

"Yeah, but she really got mean about it. She could make my life miserable."

"I could never figure out why you're friends with her in the first place," Mollie said. "What kind of friend acts that way?"

"She's not that bad, really," Julie protested halfheartedly.

"Oh, yeah?"

"I mean, we've been friends since—"

Mollie rolled her eyes. "I know. You were a shy little eighth-grade nothing until Tara made you a star. And the old 'we've been friends for years' bit."

"Well, she did, Mollie. And we have been

friends for years. Doesn't that mean anything?"

"It might mean, sister dear, that it's high time you moved on to more enriching, fulfilling friendships. There are lots of interesting kids at Jefferson High—and most of them won't boss you around all the time the way old Bubblehead does."

"Boy, Mollie," Julie said, laughing in spite of herself. "When somebody asks you for advice, you really give it."

"I give full value for your nickel," Mollie said. Then she added, "But I wouldn't worry, Julie. If Quinn goes for you, not Tara, she won't want to lose face. She'll probably try to act as if nothing's wrong, don't you think?"

"Maybe. And maybe it's time I stopped trying to please Tara. I'm not a lonely little eighth-grader anymore."

"That's more like it!"

Julie got up from the wing chair, bent over her sister, and kissed the top of her head.

"Thanks, Mollie."

"For what?"

"For everything. For being here. And for listening. I just needed someone to talk to, I guess."

CHAPTER FIVE

She was beautiful, even more beautiful up close than he'd realized.

More beautiful than Alison? Yes, in a softer, sweeter, more vulnerable way.

There'd been something a little hard and uncaring about Alison. Those girls she'd hung out with had done it to her. It should have been *them*, not Alison . . .

No, he wasn't going to think about that anymore. Not now, when he had Julie to love.

Julie. He savored the taste of her name on his lips. Julie.

My Julie.

He stretched out on his narrow bed and put his hands beneath his head, seeing her face—Julie's face—on his ceiling, replaying every delicious, exciting moment of their meeting today.

Those eyes. That hair. The way she'd looked at him when he'd taken her tray and their fingers touched.

She'd felt it, too, he could tell. That sudden, warm little shock when flesh brushed against flesh.

She'd blushed. He loved the way it had tinted her face so delicately, calling attention to the fine bones of her cheeks and forehead.

I wonder what she's doing now, he thought. *Is she thinking of me?*

Yes, of course. She has to be. If I'm thinking of her, she's thinking of me. It's almost as if there's an invisible cord connecting us. She tugs and I feel the pull. I tug, and she feels it.

He'd tested that today, in the cafeteria. He'd looked at her, willing her to feel his eyes on her. And she had. He could tell. She wanted to turn around and look at him.

He smiled fondly.

She probably didn't think he noticed her looking at him out of the corner of her eyes. Well, she'd learn very soon that he was aware of everything she did. Every breath she took.

Soon. But not right away. He'd wait just a little longer. Build up the suspense, the anticipation, both for himself and for her. You always appreciated something more when you've had to think about it, hope for it, yearn for it.

He was sure she wouldn't spoil it by coming up and talking to him. She wasn't like that. She wasn't one of those loud, bold girls.

Her friend, now, that black-haired one with the blood-red lipstick, had done her best to make him notice her.

He frowned and uttered an expression of disgust, remembering the way she'd kept throwing her body around like an alley cat and laughing in that stupid, empty-headed way.

And *she* was Julie's friend? His Julie?

No, she wasn't right for Julie. Julie was perfect, but that friend of hers was a bad apple. A corrupter. Not fit to be around the girl he loved.

In fact, he didn't want Julie hanging out with any of them. That blue-eyed guy, for example, who kept looking at Julie, touching her, trying to make her laugh . . . It had taken all his willpower and self-control not to go over there and knock that guy flat on his rich, pampered little butt.

But that blue-eyed guy wasn't worth losing his cool over. Julie didn't even like him. Quinn could tell by the way she looked at him, her lips pressed together primly with disapproval.

He chuckled. She was a prize worth winning, all right. And when he did win her, they would be together, and happy, forever.

Just the two of them. They wouldn't need anyone else.

She would make him forget the terrible parts of his life. His father. Alison. The Place.

He rolled over and adjusted the pillow under his head.

But what if her friends tried to interfere, like last time, the way Alison's had?

Let them try. They'd be sorry if they did. He was older and smarter now. He knew how to handle creeps like that.

Yes, he'd make them sorry if they did.

And this time he wouldn't get caught.

CHAPTER SIX

"Hey, Julie! Wait up."

"I can't, Brad. I'll be late for English lit."

"This will only take a minute."

Julie turned and leaned against the wall, waiting as Brad shouldered his way through the stream of scurrying students.

"I didn't see you at lunch today. Where were you?" he asked.

"I had the car, so I went off campus."

"All by yourself?"

"I needed a little time alone."

Brad's blue eyes were worried. "Are you all right? Is everything okay with you?"

"Look, Brad, I can't talk now. I don't want to be late for class."

"Okay, so I'll walk with you. It's just down

the hall, and the first bell hasn't even rung yet."

Sighing, Julie gripped her books tightly and began walking again, Brad hovering anxiously at her shoulder.

"It's Tara, isn't it?" he asked.

"What do you mean?"

"Tara's been treating you like dirt the past couple of days. And it's all because of that new guy—Quinn what's-his-name. Isn't it?"

Julie stopped and looked at him in surprise. "What do you know about that?"

Brad shrugged. "I'm not as dumb as I look, Julie. I notice things. Particularly about you. In case you haven't noticed, everything about you interests me."

"Please, Brad—" Julie began.

Brad held up one hand and smiled wryly. "Don't worry, I'm not trying to come on to you or anything. At least not right now. It's just that I don't like to see anybody trying to hurt you, and Tara's been doing a real number on you lately."

The first bell rang.

"I really appreciate your worrying about me, Brad," Julie told him hurriedly. "But everything's okay. Tara's just miffed about . . . something. You know how she gets sometimes."

40

She glanced over at her classroom. Mr. Houghton was standing in the open doorway, one hand on the knob, beckoning to her. He liked to start class right on time, with everyone seated before the second bell.

"I've got to go," she said. "But thanks, Brad. Thanks for worrying. That was sweet of you."

"I'm a real sweet guy. See ya later." Brad tossed her a little two-fingered salute and was gone.

Julie found it hard to keep her mind on what Mr. Houghton was saying, even though he was one of her favorite teachers, and English lit one of her more enjoyable classes.

They were discussing Shakespeare's *Othello*, and the violent jealousy that caused Othello to murder his innocent wife.

I've sure had some firsthand experience of jealousy lately, Julie thought. *Tara knows there's something going on between Quinn and me, and she's burning up with jealousy about it.*

But what *was* going on between her and Quinn?

Nothing . . . and everything.

Julie had read somewhere that just before a tornado the earth gets still and heavily oppressive, as if the oxygen has been sucked out of the air.

That's how it was with her and Quinn. Something was coming. She could feel it.

And so could Tara.

Mentally Julie counted off the days she'd known Quinn: Thursday, that was the first. He'd come to school on Thursday. Then Friday, that was the day he'd touched her hand when he'd taken her tray. She'd thought about him all Saturday and Sunday, walking around in a daze, wondering what he would do on Monday.

Monday was Day Five. Long enough, surely, for him to make his move.

But he hadn't. And not yesterday, Tuesday, either.

It wasn't that he was ignoring her, though.

The term "stalking" came to Julie's mind, but she brushed it aside. And yet wasn't that what he was doing? Stalking her?

No, being stalked was a frightening thing and this wasn't frightening. It was exciting. Thrilling. She loved his looks, the way he moved, everything about him, and she was being consumed by her growing obsession with him. Like an addict, she lived only for her next "fix," her next sight of him.

These past two days, in the halls, she would turn around, feeling his presence, knowing he was there. And she would be right. He'd be behind her—at a short distance, but behind her. A couple of times he'd even accidentally bumped into her, disappearing before she could collect her wits.

It was almost as if there were some sort of extrasensory bond between them. Julie didn't even have to see him now to know when he was there, somewhere, watching her, brooding over her. She could feel his eyes on her . . . on her hair, her body.

How much longer would they drift like this, alone but together? Should she go up to him and speak? No, it wasn't the right time yet. She sensed that he wanted it like this. That it was his way of making himself known to her, courting her. That what was happening between them was too important to rush.

I think this is what I've been waiting for all my life, Julie thought dizzily.

The only thing that clouded her happiness was Tara. Julie didn't know what to do about Tara.

On Monday, Tara had come to school dressed for a manhunt: miniskirt to show off her

43

gorgeous legs, a short, tight sweater, and her hair in the flowing, careless, tousled look that, Julie knew, took Tara hours to achieve. She'd positioned herself by the front entrance to the school that morning, waiting for Quinn.

"Today's the day," she'd told Jessica and Shelley. "That McNeal hunk won't know what hit him."

The three of them laughed together, sharing the joke. Tara was deliberately ignoring Julie, still punishing her for what had happened in the cafeteria on Friday.

"I believe it. You look gorgeous, Tara," Jessica had said admiringly.

Julie had walked up to the trio earlier, trying to act as if nothing were wrong, but was unable to get a conversation going with them. None of them had called her over the weekend, either. They usually spent a lot of time together on the phone as well as at the mall on weekends, but whatever the three of them had done, Julie hadn't been included. And judging from the cold look Shelley gave her Monday morning, she felt the same way as Jessica—that Julie had been disloyal to Tara on Friday.

Julie finally shrugged and moved a short distance away to join a group from her homeroom

44

who were talking about current movies.

Out of the corner of her eye, she watched as Tara reached in her shoulder bag and pulled out a tube of lipstick. She smeared it on her lips without using a mirror. Julie had never figured out how she did it.

"Oooh, that's a sexy color," Shelley said approvingly.

"Crimson Passion," Tara said with a knowing wink. "Nick says it's a real turn-on."

"What about Nick?" Jessica asked. "If you drop him for Quinn, he's really going to be hurt."

"Well, those are the breaks of the game, aren't they?" Tara replied, running her hands through her hair and shaking it back, readying herself for her first encounter with her intended victim. "All's fair in love and war."

And then Quinn had treated her, the fabulously beautiful and desirable Tara Braxton, like a fly on the wall!

When Quinn walked up the stairs, she'd turned the full wattage of her cheerleader smile on him, but he didn't seem to notice.

Then she'd dropped her books right in his path.

Without saying a word Quinn had stooped,

picked up the books, and handed them to her.

"Thank you," she'd said in her most seductive voice. "I'm such a klutz!"

He'd smiled slightly, then started to move off, up the stairs and into the building.

Tara sidestepped toward him. Then, prettily, in pretended confusion, moved with him as he tried to go around her.

For a few seconds they seemed to be doing a bizarre little tango.

This was Quinn's chance to say something. A come-on line. Something—anything—that would be the start of that Something Big that Tara had in mind.

Instead, smiling politely, Quinn took hold of Tara's shoulders and moved around her and up the stairs.

Julie witnessed the entire performance. She saw Tara's jaw drop slightly and her cheeks flush with anger—saw Tara toss her head and try to laugh off what had happened, then turn and say something under her breath to Shelley and Jess.

They laughed dutifully, looking a little bewildered.

And then Quinn had turned and looked over at Julie. Looked at her long and hard, the kind of look that made her legs buckle slightly at the knees.

There was no mistaking that look.

Quinn was showing who he was interested in, making it clear that it definitely wasn't Tara.

Tara saw it, and her face turned an unbecoming mottled shade of red and white.

And Julie had known that she was the one who would have to pay the price for Tara's humiliation.

She'd been right. Her relationship with Tara had tobogganed madly downhill from that moment.

And as she'd expected, Shelley and Jessica took Tara's part.

Tara knew a hundred different ways of snubbing someone, and she used at least a dozen of them on Julie in the two days following the big meeting-Quinn-McNeal disaster.

She started right away, at lunch on Monday.

"Shelley, Jess," she'd said loudly, making sure Julie was listening. "Let's go to the mall after school. We can meet Nick and some of the guys later for pizza."

No mention of Julie. When Jessica looked over at Julie questioningly, Tara had said, "Oh, I'm sure Julie will be busy with homework. You know how hard she has to work to make the honor roll."

In a detached way Julie felt sorry for Tara. Most of the upperclassmen had been standing around watching when Quinn had walked past her, ignoring her charms. It must have been a major embarrassment for someone like Tara, not that she was going to admit it to anyone.

"Maybe he had something else on his mind," Julie heard Shelley tell Tara later that afternoon. "You know, like maybe he was depressed or worried or something."

Julie was in a back booth of the girls' room. Tara, Jess, and Shelley were at the sink. Otherwise, the room was empty. They evidently thought they were alone, judging from the frankness of their discussion.

"Yeah, he had something else on his mind, all right," Tara said grimly. "Sweet little Julie Hagan, from the looks of it. Who ever would have expected someone like *her* to make a play for a guy like that? Especially after I made it clear *I* wanted him."

"Maybe she wasn't making a play for him," Jessica said. "I mean, she was just standing there and . . ."

Tara laughed. It wasn't her usual tinkling,

48

melodious laugh. "She's making a play for him, trust me. I can tell. I knew she was interested in him that very first day. She was all blushes, remember? Besides, she's been acting kind of funny lately, anyway."

"She *has* been a little distant or something ever since school started," Shelley said. "But I don't think she's been trying to get to Quinn behind your back, Tara. I mean, she's one of *us!*"

"Maybe it's not her fault that Quinn is interested in her," suggested Jessica.

"Believe me," Tara said, "if Quinn is interested in her, she's been doing something underhanded to get his attention."

"That doesn't sound like Julie, though," Jessica said doubtfully.

"Oh, yeah?" retorted Tara.

"But what should we do about it?" Shelley asked. "Should we talk to her or what?"

"No. We'll just play it cool for now—we don't want the whole school gossiping about us. We won't be too obvious about how we feel about her, but we won't be too chummy, either. If Julie thinks she can steal Quinn McNeal from me, she's got another thing coming."

"What do you mean?" Shelley said.

"I mean I'm going to give him another

chance. I always get every guy I go after, and I will this time, too. I want Quinn McNeal and I intend to have him!"

Her voice was flat and hard.

"But how?" Jessica asked. "Quinn isn't like all the other guys here. He seems older. More sophisticated."

Julie, in her booth, could hear water running as Tara concentrated on a plan of attack.

Then the sound of the towel dispenser coughing up a couple of towels.

"I think it's time I threw a party," Tara said slowly. "When in doubt, throw a party."

"A party?" Jessica said. "You mean, at your house?"

"Where else? Listen, don't you think that if he sees me on my home turf, he'll forget all about Julie Hagan?"

"He ought to," Shelley said. "Your home turf is pretty impressive."

"I don't think he realizes just who you are, Tara," Jessica agreed. "I mean, you're not some little nobody from nowhere, you know. So when's the party?"

"As soon as possible. This weekend, if I can set it up."

"Are you going to invite Julie?"

Tara barked a laugh. "Do I have any choice? If I don't, people will talk. After all, we've been friends for years, haven't we? The last thing I want is anyone feeling sorry for Julie."

Julie, in her booth, didn't dare make a sound. If those three knew she'd overheard what they were saying, she'd be in bigger trouble than she was already. She hoped they'd leave soon. How much more could they possibly do to their faces and hair?

The class bell rang. Julie heard them leave. When she felt it was safe to follow, she slipped out of the room and ran down the hall to class.

The next couple of days were hard for Julie. She wasn't good at lying, yet she had to walk around looking happy and normal, in spite of Tara's little underhanded put-downs—the raised eyebrow and slight sneer whenever Julie said something, the shoulder turned to her, shutting her out of the group, the glances exchanged with Jess and Shelley that indicated they were sharing something that didn't include Julie.

She tried talking to Shelley about what was happening, but Shelley only said, "I really can't talk about it now, Julie. I need some distance from it, you know? Maybe we can go into this another time."

And Jessica was even worse. "You really let Tara down," she repeated stubbornly, in spite of Julie's protests that she had done nothing to make Quinn ignore Tara. "And after all Tara's done for you, too!"

And in the meantime Julie was being frozen out of the old foursome.

Mollie was the only person she was able to confide in.

Mollie was her usual optimistic self. "Hang in there, Julie. Tara will settle down after a while. You know her. When she sees that Quinn isn't interested in her—and he certainly doesn't seem to be—she'll find somebody else, or she'll decide Nick's the one she wants after all."

Quinn didn't come to school on Wednesday. He'd been out for half a day Tuesday, too. Julie wondered about him, hoping he wasn't sick, yet she was glad he wasn't there to see her being cold-shouldered by Tara. And she was glad she didn't have to watch Tara coming on to him again, either.

What if Tara's right? she asked herself. *What if she does succeed in getting Quinn interested in her?*

How will I be able to handle something like that?

The thought made her almost sick. Again, she was surprised at the intensity of her feelings for Quinn. And they hadn't even really met or spoken to each other yet!

Today, Wednesday, she'd borrowed her mother's car and driven off campus for lunch, glad to get away from Tara's pettiness.

Brad had noticed. Brad knew what was happening. How many others did?

And how much more of this can I take? she wondered.

Quinn was still absent on Thursday. Julie began to worry about him, but was relieved to see him turn up at school Friday morning.

So, obviously, was Tara. If he wasn't available for her party, all her plans would go down the tube.

She'd been running around all morning, inviting everybody on her list of "eligibles" to her house on Saturday night.

Julie wondered when Tara would get around to inviting her, and she'd been debating whether or not she should accept.

She knew that if she didn't, there would be a lot of gossip around school. If people were beginning to notice the big chill between her and Tara, this would confirm it. And she wasn't ready for that yet.

If she went and had a terrible time, so what? She'd go, put in a couple of hours, and leave. No big deal. At least Brad would be glad to see her.

When Tara finally came up to her and, pretending they were still good friends, told Julie about the party, Julie accepted.

"Yeah. Sounds good, Tara. What time?"

"Seven," Tara replied. "The usual."

"Great!" Julie said, trying to sound enthusiastic. "I'll be there."

And if Quinn's there, too, she wondered, will he finally talk to me? What can I say to make him think I'm as interesting as he seems to think I am?

And what will Tara do to me if I succeed?

CHAPTER SEVEN

He hadn't realized his absence from school would be that obvious.

No problem. He'd told his landlady, Mrs. Landon, he was sick, hadn't he? And she'd backed him up to the police. And she would again, in the highly unlikely event the police came around a second time, asking questions.

Yes, on Wednesday he told her he had one of those stomach bug things, said he'd come down with it on Tuesday afternoon, had to come home from school, even, and that it didn't seem to be going away. Right away she'd brought him down a big pot of chicken soup. Nice lady, but a lousy cook. Terrible soup. He'd thrown it down the garbage disposal after she left. But still, she'd be able to swear in court, if it ever came to that,

that he's been sick and she'd ministered to him.

And she was absentminded, too, and suggestible. When he asked her if he'd been playing his TV a little too loudly on Tuesday afternoon, she said yes, maybe he had . . . not that it bothered her, but he ought to have been sleeping, not watching TV, sick as he was.

He hadn't had his TV on at all. He'd just asked her that, planted the idea in her head, so that she'd say, "Yes, that nice Quinn McNeal was in his apartment on Tuesday afternoon. I heard him moving around, watching his TV."

He'd realized everyone knew he was missing from school when that black-haired witch, Tara, practically attacked him Friday morning, all smiles.

She was throwing a party, she said, and she wanted him to come. Wanted him to come to her charming old antebellum mansion—it even had a name, Maywood—for a party on Saturday night. Just her, him, and the cream of Braxton Falls society.

But Julie would be there. He knew she'd be there, so he'd accepted.

Tara had seemed relieved when he said he'd come. You'd almost think she'd planned the party around him. Maybe she had. She sure was trying to come on to him. Did she really think he'd be interested in a shallow flirt like her?

Well, that didn't matter. He was going anyway. What a laugh. He, Quinn McNeal, partying in a mansion with all those snobby little rich kids. Things sure had changed since Alison.

Alison's friends had thought he was scum. Treated him like scum.

So why wasn't he scum now? Maybe because his father, Daddy Dearest, was dead. They didn't know anything about Quinn's father, but his death was going to help Quinn anyway.

Funny, wasn't it? The only decent thing his father had ever done for him was tumble down those stairs so neatly and break his neck.

What a shame this hadn't happened four years ago; when Quinn had been so violently, passionately, in love with Alison. It would have made for one less enemy, one less abuser, at least.

But now his father was dead, and for the first time, he'd actually done something constructive for Quinn. All those years of abuse and drunkenness . . . and to think that now he, Quinn, was heir to a piece of fairly valuable property in Middledale, a small town nearly seventy miles west of Braxton Falls.

The town was spreading. There was talk of a mall. A real-estate developer had been quietly approaching the home owners in Dad's run-down neighborhood. Most of them had sold, and for a good price, but his fool of a father had turned the man down flat. Quinn couldn't understand why. Maybe his brain had turned to mush from all that drinking.

But now Quinn would be able to sell the house. Get a good hunk of cash for it, too.

When he'd met Julie, he knew right away he'd be needing some money. She was special. Classy.

At the present time he was working four, sometimes five evenings a week delivering pizzas, making only enough to meet his everyday expenses. The sale of the house, when it came through, would give him a decent income. He could quit his job at the pizza parlor.

A girl like Julie needed to be taken places, nice places. Expensive places. Besides, if he had to work nights, some other guy might move in on her. That blue-eyed guy in the cafeteria, for example. He didn't want her having anything more to do with that bunch of phonies. As soon as she was his, he was going to see to it she didn't run with that crowd anymore.

So far, everything was working out nicely for him.

At least he hoped so.

The Middledale police, though, had come snooping around.

That's where he'd been Thursday. The Middledale police station.

They'd called him Thursday morning and told him about his father's death and asked him to come in for questioning.

Neighbors had found his father's body Wednesday afternoon, all crumpled up at the bottom of the staircase in the front hall. The police said he'd been dead about twenty-four hours.

Accidental deaths, they told him, had to be investigated. Quinn's father was being held in the local morgue, with an identification tag hanging around one dirty big toe.

"Yes, that's my father," Quinn had told them.

Of course, they wanted to know when Quinn had seen him last. They hinted that it appeared his father had fallen down the stairs with a force not commensurate—that was the word they used—with a simple fall. That maybe he'd been violently pushed.

"Your father's neighbors say the two of you

never got along," said the fat-faced sergeant in charge of the investigation. "So can you tell us where you were on Tuesday afternoon?"

"I was sick in bed in the basement apartment I rent in Braxton Falls," he told them. "Ask my landlady. She can vouch for me.

Mrs. Landon had come through for him, the old sweetheart, just as he'd known she would. So he was in the clear, and the police seemed satisfied that the death was, in fact, accidental.

Well, no wonder. The death fit the conventional pattern, didn't it? Every town had its local drunk. And what could be more natural or predictable than this colorful character, the town drunk, falling to his death one day down a long, steep flight of stairs?

He'd made arrangements with a funeral director for his father's cremation.

"No, I don't want the ashes. And no service, please. My father didn't have any friends and often told me he didn't want any kind of burial ceremony."

That wasn't what his father had really wanted, but what difference did it make? He was gone forever, and what he wanted didn't matter now.

Quinn was free. Free of his father and the miserable past. And soon he'd have enough money to compete with those snobby rich guys who were always coming on to Julie.

He'd go to that party on Saturday night, and when the time was right, the moment absolutely perfect, he'd get Julie alone and tell her what she meant to him.

And then she'd tell him she loved him, too.

CHAPTER EIGHT

When Julie arrived at Maywood Saturday night, the party was in full swing, judging by the number of cars in the driveway. She had to park down by the tall wrought-iron gates at the entrance to the broad circular drive and make her way up a slight incline to the front door, careful of her heels in the crushed gravel.

The wide marble foyer was lit by a huge, glittering crystal chandelier that hung down from an upper floor. Wanda, the Braxtons' maid, directed Julie downstairs to the entertainment area.

As she went down the winding, carpeted stairs, Julie marveled at the enormous effort and expense that must have gone into restoring and redoing an old plantation house like this.

To her left was the games room. Julie wandered in and looked around. No sign of Tara . . . or Quinn.

A huge antique pool table with massive carved legs stood in the middle of the room with a triple-width Tiffany-style lamp suspended over it. A couple of guys from the football team were intent over a cutthroat game of pool and didn't look up as she passed them.

Over in a corner a small group, cheered on by Lisa Doyle and a couple of other pom-pom girls, were playing electronic games.

Brad's head surfaced and he grinned.

"Hey, Julie! Over here!"

Julie smiled and shook her head slightly. This was not the night to get clutched to the side of Brad Stafford.

French doors in the games room led out to a half-enclosed deck, but the doors were shut. Julie walked over and looked out.

A large, luxurious hot tub sat in the middle of the deck. It was cold. No steam was rising from its depths.

The Braxtons had been the first family in town to get a hot tub. In an uptight little burg like Braxton Falls, hot tubs were initially viewed with distrust and considered suspiciously decadent, although Mrs. Braxton went around telling people that it was doing wonderful things for her arthritis.

Tara had a few other tales about the uses of a hot tub, but Julie never stayed around to listen to them. Tara exaggerated a lot, anyway.

"Don't be such a prude, Julie," Tara had called once to Julie's rigid, retreating back. "What's wrong with skinny-dipping? You can't see anything. You're under all those bubbles!"

Across the hall from the games room was the family room, if you could call something that vast and luxurious a family room. Julie wandered into the dimly lit room and looked around.

Soft music, old-fashioned cheek-to-cheek dance music, was playing, and some of the Oriental throw rugs had been moved to the side of the room. Several couples were in the middle of the floor, heads together, swaying dreamily to the music. . . .

Jessica was there with Thad Turner, a freshman at college who was home for the weekend. They'd been an "item" since last summer. According to Jessica, it was the real thing.

Well, good luck, Jessica, Julie thought. *I hope you're right. Maybe dating a college guy will help get you out from under Tara's thumb.*

Shelley Molino was dancing with Colin King. The two of them seemed to be getting together more and more often these days. Shelley looked over at Julie but didn't wave and smile at her, the way she would have two weeks ago.

That hurt a little. Julie had to remind herself that Shelley wasn't mean, just weak, and was easily led around by Tara.

Shelley and everyone else I know, Julie thought.

She heard Tara before she saw her. Even over the music, Tara's wild soprano laugh stood out.

She was over in a corner, surrounded by a group of people, mostly guys. The turquoise silk outfit she was wearing—plunging vee-necked crop top and palazzo pants—lit up her part of the room.

Julie realized immediately that Tara was playing to an audience, and it wasn't those cute jocks and student-body leaders clustered around her, either.

Sure enough, there was Quinn.

He was sitting in a dark corner opposite Tara, but he wasn't looking at her. As far as Julie could see from the bored, slightly cynical expression on his face, Tara was playing to an empty house.

Then Quinn looked up and saw Julie. His eyes widened, and he leaned forward in his chair.

Julie felt the warm blood rise in her cheeks.

Get up. Come over here. Talk to me, she willed.

"Look, everybody, here's Julie," Tara called out. "And doesn't she look sweet!"

There was a chorus of "Hi, Julie" all around. Julie nodded back and then glanced over at Quinn.

The mood of the moment had been shattered. Quinn had sunk back in his chair, his face unreadable, nursing his cola. A sour, bitter anger replaced the aching tenderness Julie had felt for him just a brief moment ago.

I'm getting tired of this, she thought suddenly. *What's he up to, anyway? If he's as interested in me as he's pretending to be with those long, brooding looks, then why hasn't he done something about it?*

And suddenly Julie realized she'd had too much.

Too much of Tara and her nastiness. Too much of Quinn with his silent, eternal, devastating stare.

She'd been hoping tonight would be the night. That Quinn would finally do something to break the ice—talk to her, ask her out, something!

She turned on her heel and left the room. Brad was out in the hall. He tried to say something to her, tried to take hold of her arm, but she brushed him off and kept going.

Up the stairs, hitting every tread, wishing it were Tara. Or Quinn.

A minute to get Wanda to help find her purse, and then out into the night.

The wind had picked up a bit and was blowing fluttering rags of clouds across a fat yellow moon.

Julie walked quickly down the driveway to her car, not caring if the gravel chewed the suede off the heels of her shoes.

She was just opening her door when she heard a light, firm tread behind her.

She knew who it was.

She turned, not knowing what to say or do.

And then, smiling, Quinn McNeal came to her through the moonlight.

Up close, under the streetlight, Julie saw that Quinn's eyes weren't as dark as she'd thought. They'd appeared almost black from afar.

"Why, your eyes are blue . . . dark blue," she said softly, reaching out and gently touching his cheek with her fingertip.

It was an involuntary gesture that she regretted immediately.

Why on earth did I have to go and say that? she asked herself incredulously.

She dropped her hand and blushed furiously. *What a stupid thing to say . . . and do,* she thought.

But Quinn, still looking at her, reached down and took her hand, holding her palm against his warm, rough cheek.

Julie was surprised to feel his hand tremble.

A sudden gust of wind blew her long hair against his face.

And then he kissed her. He drew her close against him and kissed her again. And again.

He released her and ran his hands down her arms.

Julie was shocked at her physical response to his kiss, his touch.

He cleared his throat.

"Look . . . Julie," he began. He seemed to linger over her name. "This probably sounds crazy, but—"

Other footsteps on the gravel. Other shadows between them and the moon. Julie was suddenly aware that they were not alone.

CHAPTER NINE

Two figures materialized in the darkness beside them.

A prickle of fear ran down Julie's back. There was something menacing, threatening, about the way they stood, shoulder to shoulder.

Julie could see their faces in the moonlight. Strangers, both of them. No one she had ever seen at Jefferson High. They were older, too, and certainly not the type Tara would invite to one of her parties.

Maybe they're only harmless party crashers, she told herself as she waited for them to speak. But Julie knew they were more than that. There was nothing harmless about these two.

Quinn seemed to sense it, too.

"What do you guys want?" he asked. His

voice was mild, but Julie could feel his body grow tense, his muscles tighten. He took his arm from her shoulder and moved away from her, a step to the side, as he spoke.

"Now what do you think we want?" sneered the bigger of the two. "What would little rich kids who like to party have that some poor guy like me would want?"

"Please," Julie said. "If it's money you're after . . ." She held her handbag out to them.

"I'll take care of this, Julie," Quinn said.

"Oooh, so it's Julie," the other stranger said. Then, in a mocking falsetto, "Isn't that sweet, Norm? Her name is Julie. Can I have her when you're done with Mr. Wonderful here?"

"Sure, Frankie, she's just your type. I think she's got the hots for you already," Norm replied. "Isn't that right, Julie?" He made kissing noises at her.

Then, before Julie had time to realize what was happening, Quinn moved. His foot lashed out, catching Norm in the groin. As Norm doubled over, grunting and clutching at his stomach, Quinn, his fists joined, hit him hard on the back of his neck.

Norm fell to the ground, moaning, and Quinn turned to Frankie, who'd been watching, too startled to move.

"Now it's your turn," he said in a low, harsh voice.

He grabbed Frankie by the wrist, spinning him around to twist his arm up behind him at an unnatural angle. Then he kneed him sharply in the back, yanking his arm up even higher as Frankie's back arched in pain.

Julie heard a loud snap followed by a muffled scream from Frankie. Muffled because Quinn had thrown his other arm around Frankie's throat, throttling him.

That snap! Was it a bone breaking?

Julie gasped. Oh, God, this was terrible. Quinn was going to kill him!

"Please, Quinn! That's enough!" she whispered.

On the ground Norm began to move, to crawl sideways, like a crab.

Without releasing his hold on Frankie, Quinn pivoted slightly and kicked Norm in the ribs. Then he kicked him again, harder this time.

Norm sprawled out full length, sobbing.

Quinn laughed softly. He seemed to be enjoying what he was doing. Julie almost didn't recognize his face in the moonlight. It was twisted. Cruel.

He raised his foot to kick Norm again.

Terrified now, Julie lunged at Quinn and grabbed him. "Stop it! Stop it, Quinn! Please!" she sobbed.

Quinn turned and looked at her. The expression on his face cleared. He looked almost puzzled.

"And what do you think they would have done to you, Julie, if I hadn't been here?"

Frankie was crying now, silently. Tears of pain streamed down his cheeks. His nose ran, as if someone had turned on a spigot. He bent over, writhing in Quinn's grasp.

Quinn looked down at him in disgust. Then he released him, pushing him away with a quick, violent motion.

"You're not so tough now, are you, creep?" he snarled.

Frankie stumbled and nearly fell, but managed to catch himself before he did. His arm—even his shoulder—was hanging oddly.

"Quinn, I'm going to run back to the house and call the police."

"No!" he yelled. "No police."

"Please, girl, get the police," Norm moaned, clutching his ribs. "This guy is trying to kill us."

"Do you hear me, Julie? No police," Quinn told her. "I'd rather settle this myself."

Yanking the sobbing, trembling Norm to his feet, he demanded, "Where's your car?"

Norm didn't reply. He shrank away from him in terror, as if afraid Quinn would hit him again.

Quinn shook him. "Answer me. Where's your car?"

"Over there," Norm moaned, pointing. "Just outside the gates."

Quinn roughly dragged Norm and Frankie toward the battered Ford Escort they said was their car. Frankie was sagging, clearly almost fainting from the pain in his shoulder, and Quinn had to bear him up with one arm as he pulled him and Norm along.

Julie, following behind, marveled at his strength. Quinn was tall, but lean. *He must be all muscle*, she thought numbly.

Before thrusting Frankie and Norm into the car, Quinn shoved them against the hood and barked: "Hand over your wallets!"

"Sure, guy," Norm said. "Take them. There's not much money, but—"

"I don't want your money, just your driver's licenses."

Quinn had to reach into Frankie's pocket for

him—Frankie's shoulder was in pretty bad shape.

Quinn quickly removed the licenses and tossed the wallets onto the backseat. And then, in a voice that frightened Julie even more, he said, "I know who you are now."

He slapped their licenses against his open palm. "I know who you are now," he repeated. "And no matter where you go, I have ways of finding you if I need to. So I don't want you to give me any reason for tracking you down, okay?"

"Okay, okay, man!"

"What I'm saying is, I don't want to see either of you again, or hear of you, or have any reason to even suspect you're still alive, stinking up the world. Do you understand? Do you know what I'm saying?"

"We get you, man. Hey, we're out of here. For good. That's a promise, man!" said Norm.

"Yeah! That's right!" put in Frankie.

Quinn's voice became even more deadly. More menacing.

"And if either one of you ever comes near Julie again," he said between clenched teeth, "comes *anywhere* near her . . . *I'll kill you.*"

CHAPTER TEN

Julie was still trembling long after Norm and Frankie peeled off down the street, laying a strip of rubber in their haste to escape.

All she knew was that she had to get away from that place, away from what had just happened.

"Are you okay, Julie?"

"I'll be all right in a minute."

Wordlessly, Quinn put her in her car and slipped into the driver's seat beside her.

"But what about your car?" Julie protested. "You can't just leave it here overnight."

"I'll walk back later and get it, after I take you home. It's not that far."

"You . . . you know where I live?"

"I know a lot of things about you, Julie."

Quinn started the engine and drove out through Maywood's massive gates. Then he turned left and headed down the hill past the luxurious homes of Hunter Valley.

He drove quickly and directly to Julie's house and pulled into the driveway.

He's been here before, she told herself silently. *Did he come here at night, watching me the way he did at school?* The thought unsettled Julie for a moment. *He probably only came by to check out my address,* she decided.

Besides, that wasn't important now. All that mattered was that he was here, sitting next to her, his face only inches from hers. He kissed her gently, lingeringly, savoring her lips.

She loved the shape of his face, the sharp, clean line of his jaw and chin.

"I found out where you lived that very first day," Quinn confessed.

"You did? How?"

"That girl in the office, Karen Slack. She gave me your address."

"That's weird, Quinn. Karen's really boy crazy. I can't imagine her doing a Cupid act for someone else."

"Oh, it was definitely not a Cupid act," Quinn said, laughing. "I told her I found a dent in the side of my car and I was sure you were the one who did it. I said I wanted to come by your house and bring you to justice."

"But I didn't drive to school that day!"

"Well, she didn't know that," Quinn said. "But enough about Karen Slack." He moved closer to Julie, murmuring something about how beautiful she was and touching her hair—he seemed fascinated by her hair—twining a long strand around his finger and tenderly tucking a stray curl behind her ear.

"I love your hair," he said. "I've always loved your hair."

"Always?" Julie asked. "Like forever? Quinn, do you have the feeling we've known each other before . . . somewhere else . . . in another time? I'm beginning to think I do."

Quinn pulled away from her, his blue eyes darkening and his mouth tightening.

"No, Julie, don't say that," he commanded. "We're starting out new, you and I. It's like getting a second chance at life."

Julie was a little surprised at his reaction. And yet, there were so many surprising things about Quinn.

She was amazed by the depth of feeling he seemed to have for her. She'd never inspired such powerful feelings before in any of the boys she'd been involved with. Was it because he was more experienced and mature than other guys his age? And what made him that way?

There was so much she wanted to learn about him.

"We could go inside," she suggested.

"No," he said, reaching for her again. "I like it here. I like looking at you in the moonlight. But what will your folks think, you parked out here with a stranger?"

"They're at a country-club dance. They won't be home for hours."

Julie's voice quivered a bit at that last word. The thought of staying here for hours with Quinn, touching him, kissing him, took her breath away.

He smiled, as if he could guess what she was thinking.

To cover her embarrassment, she said as matter-of-factly as she could, "You know, Quinn, I don't know anything about you. Nobody does."

"There's not much to know," he said, turning slightly and laying his head back on the headrest.

"Your folks," Julie prompted. "Someone said you're an orphan."

"My mother left my father and me when I was a baby."

"Oh, Quinn, that's terrible!"

"I can't say I blame her, Julie. My father was a drunk and a bully. When I was little, though, and Dad was beating on me, I used to hate her for not loving me enough to stick around and protect me."

"My God, Quinn, your father used to beat you?"

Quinn nodded. His eyes seemed cold. Distant. "It happens all the time, child abuse. Now they're trying to do something about it. Telling kids what to do, who to tell about it. Nobody told me what to do when I was little, though. I thought I was supposed to take it and not say anything."

"What about your father now?" Julie asked. "Is he . . . is he sorry for what he did?"

"I hope he's paying for it this very minute," Quinn said fiercely.

Then, glancing at Julie's shocked expression, he said, "He died on Tuesday. Fell down a flight of stairs when he'd been drinking and broke his neck."

Quinn didn't seem at all sorry, and Julie didn't blame him. Still, she couldn't help being surprised.

"This past Tuesday?" she asked. "Then that was why you were absent from school?"

"Actually, no. I had the flu Tuesday and Wednesday. The police came and told me about Dad on Thursday. That's why I didn't come to school that day, although I was okay by then. It's a good thing, too. I had to go to Middledale—that's where my father lived—and . . . and claim his body."

"And you haven't said a word, not one word, about it to anyone?" Julie was aghast. So much had happened to Quinn, her own darling Quinn, and yet he didn't go around complaining or looking for pity. She couldn't understand him.

"Besides making arrangements for what they call the 'disposition of the remains,'" Quinn said, "I talked to a realtor about selling Dad's house. It's the only thing he left me. It's not much, but the land is being zoned for a mall. I think I can get enough out of it to live comfortably for a while. And now I can quit my pizza-delivery job. It's been a real drag."

"I didn't know you delivered pizza," Julie exclaimed. "I wish I'd known. I would have ordered one every night."

Quinn laughed. "I come by here all the time.

I've seen you through your front window a couple of times. I'd pull over and watch you."

He stopped, sat up, and pulled her to him.

"Julie, if you only knew how I'd sit there, looking at you, wanting to do this."

Julie felt groggy when she emerged from his embrace. That was the only word for it. Groggy.

Quinn released her guiltily, hastily, as if he'd gone too far.

There was an old-fashioned streak about him, Julie decided fondly from the depth of her daze. A cavalier, that's what he was. Or maybe a knight in shining armor?

She shook her head slightly, to fight off the delicious, sinking sensation she seemed to feel now that she was—at long last!—in Quinn's arms.

Quinn turned again, his hands on the steering wheel, his breathing calm.

"Well, anyway, I'd take Grady with me on my deliveries. Old Grady would paw at me when we parked too long, looking in your window."

"Grady? Who's he?"

"My cat."

There was an unmistakable tone of pride in Quinn's voice when he said that.

"You have a cat?" Julie asked.

81

Now *here* was a facet of Quinn's life Julie would never have guessed at. Quinn, a cat person?

"Yeah, he's kind of old and crotchety, but we belong together," Quinn said.

He went on to tell Julie how he'd found Grady wet, muddy, and furiously angry, in a ditch.

"He'd obviously been abandoned," Quinn said. "Probably thrown from a car. I couldn't help admiring Grady for the way he was taking it."

"Oh?" Julie said, amused by Quinn's obvious love for his pet.

"Yeah," Quinn said. "Grady was spitting mad. I got a few scratches and bites trying to get him out of the ditch. But now we're best friends." Quinn smiled at Julie.

"People say cats are independent and unfeeling," he continued. "But that's not true. They really get attached to you."

It had started to rain—a thin, cold drizzle that clouded the windows. Julie felt cut off, isolated from the rest of the world, and she wished they could stay that way forever.

Quinn reached out and drew two entwined hearts on the misty window. He added an arrow and their initials, and smiled sheepishly at her.

"I've been waiting to do that," he said. "That makes us official, okay?"

Julie ran her finger gently along the thin scar that bisected his upper lip. "Somebody said you were in an accident and lost a year of school. Is that where you got this?"

"It wasn't an accident exactly," he said brusquely. "But I *have* been away. And I did lose a year of school. My past three years were . . . well . . . kind of private tutoring, you might say."

There were so many things Julie wanted to ask Quinn about himself. So many questions.

But when he drew her to him again and their lips met, she forgot everything else.

CHAPTER ELEVEN

I kissed her, he thought joyfully. I held her and kissed her and I know, by the way she responded, the way she clung to me and kissed me back, that she loves me too.

She loves me as much as I love her. No . . . maybe not as much as that. Not yet. She couldn't possibly love me that much already. But she will. In time. I'll teach her to make me her whole world, just as she is mine.

He picked up Grady, who was rubbing against his ankles, nuzzled him lovingly, and carried him into the small alcove that served as a bedroom.

He tossed the cat onto the bed, threw off his clothes, and crawled between the sheets.

She loves me.

Alison loves me.

No . . . wait a minute. It's Julie, not Alison.

Alison is . . . gone. Gone forever. I saw her lying

there, white and bloodless. Mustn't think of Alison.

Julie's the one I love. And isn't she beautiful? That long, silken hair, just like Alison's. No! Not like Alison's! Forget Alison. Think only of Julie. I love Julie. Julie! Julie is sweet and lovely and good. She'd never try to trick me and make a fool of me the way . . .

No, Julie would never betray me. She loves me and I love her. It's different this time.

And tonight I saved her. I was there for her and I saved Julie from those two. I know what they wanted. It wasn't her purse, her money. No. They wanted to do terrible things to her, to throw her down on the ground and . . . but I was there. And I knew what to do.

Yes, I knew what to do. I learned how to fight in The Place. I was a dumb kid when I went in there, but I learned fast. I had to.

But those two. That Norm and Frankie. Yes, they said they wouldn't come back, but I know their type. They would never come back again for me, but they'll want revenge. Revenge for what I did to them. The shame I inflicted on them.

And so they'll get revenge on me by hurting Julie. They'll find her and trail her, and then . . . No. I will never allow that to happen.

Those two are scum.

They shouldn't be allowed to live.

CHAPTER TWELVE

❧

The next morning Julie resolved not to tell her parents, or anyone, about what had happened in the driveway of Tara's house.

"Don't, Julie," Quinn had warned her in the car the night before. "If we get involved, we'll have to fill out police reports and answer questions. And they'll be calling us down to the station every time there's a robbery or a purse snatching. Besides," he'd argued, "I took care of the problem, didn't I? We'll never see those two again."

Julie shuddered, remembering Frankie and what he might have done to her if Quinn hadn't been there.

"But what if they *do* come back?" she'd asked. "Those two were mean. Really mean,

Quinn. Maybe they'll think it over and decide to get revenge."

"No. No, they won't." Quinn's face was closed, unreadable. "Trust me."

But now Julie remembered another look on Quinn's face—the look he'd worn when he was beating up on the two muggers.

He'd looked almost as if he were enjoying it.

No, that can't be true, Julie thought. After all, she had been half out of her head with fear at the time. Surely she'd imagined it. Quinn was saving her, wasn't he? How many guys did she know who could have handled the situation the way he had?

Mollie obviously sensed, the minute Julie sat down at the Sunday breakfast table, that something big had happened to Julie the night before.

"How was Tara's party?" Mollie asked casually for the benefit of their parents, but flashing her sister a secret and urgent questioning look,

"Oh, that's right, Julie," her mother said, looking up from the stove where she was scrambling eggs. "How was the party? Did you have a nice time?"

Julie arranged crisp, drained slices of bacon

on a large blue-and-white platter and held it out while her mother spooned the eggs onto it.

"Yes, I did," she replied, attempting to sound matter-of-fact. "And I met—I mean, I really got to know—this cute new guy at school. His name's Quinn McNeal."

Mollie flashed her a discreet thumbs-up.

Julie could feel her cheeks redden and a dopey grin spread across her face at the mention of Quinn's name.

Fortunately, her father was buried behind the editorial pages of the paper and her mother's back was to her, or they would have picked up on both the blush and the grin. No one could ever accuse Mr. and Mrs. Hagan of being unconcerned parents. They were always a little *too* concerned in Julie's and Mollie's opinions.

"New boy?" her mother said vaguely, pouring the orange juice and setting the glasses on the table. "I don't recall you mentioning a new boy at school. McNeal, you say? I don't think I've ever met his parents."

Julie tried to smother her annoyance. Why did Mom always have to think in terms of Who's Who in Braxton Falls?

"He doesn't have any parents," she said shortly. "He's an orphan."

Her father put down his paper at that. "An orphan? Does he live with relatives, or what?"

"No, he lives alone in a basement apartment in town. He expects to get a small inheritance from the sale of his father's house, but in the meantime he supports himself by . . ." She paused and drew a deep breath. Her mother wasn't going to like this one. ". . . by delivering pizzas."

Her mother sat down quickly in her chair and eyed Julie shrewdly. "Do you think there's a chance that you and this . . . this McNeal person will be seeing each other socially? Dating, I mean?"

Julie returned her stare. "Yes, Mom, I'd say we're going to be seeing a lot of each other. He's really special. And he seems to think I am, too."

"He's incredibly good-looking," Mollie put in, trying to be helpful. "All the girls are crazy about him. They'll be furious when they find out Julie's got him."

"*Got* him?" her mother said. "You've got a pizza-delivery boy?"

Help came from an unexpected quarter.

"Don't be such a snob, Vivian," Mr. Hagan said, laying his newspaper aside and picking up his fork. "He sounds like a nice kid. And for the record, I was hustling hamburgers in a greasy-spoon diner when you got me, remember?"

Telling Tara wasn't as bad as Julie had expected.

Tara didn't appear at all surprised or angry at the news that Julie and Quinn were now a couple. She actually seemed pleasant, almost sisterly, about it.

"I've noticed the way he looks at you, Julie," she said affably. "He's got it bad for you. When I saw him leave the party right behind you, I figured he was up to something."

She laughed her trademark melodious laugh and wagged her finger with its long scarlet nail before Julie's face. "Now, you better hang on to him and treat him right, or I'll move in on you, hear? That guy's a real hunk!"

Julie's relief turned sour when she saw Shelley and Jessica share a secret smile at Tara's words. Naturally they were on Tara's side. They always would be.

So what did that nasty little smile mean?

Tara moved off down the hall and Julie turned to Jess and Shelley.

"Look, I hope what's happened between Quinn and me isn't going to change things between us," she said.

Jessica looked uncomfortable and refused to meet Julie's eyes, but Shelley faced her squarely.

"Of course it's going to change things between us, Julie. Why shouldn't it? You didn't play fair with Tara, so why should we trust you? There's nothing lower than a boyfriend stealer. She told us right from the start that she wanted Quinn for herself, but you had to go and cut in on her, didn't you?"

Julie stared at her friend helplessly. "For the last time, Shelley, I didn't *steal* Quinn. You can't steal people. Besides, he never belonged to Tara in the first place. What made her think she owned him?"

"Come on, Jess," Shelley said. "We've got to catch up with Tara."

Julie watched bleakly as the two of them hurried away from her, not looking back.

It was over. Their friendship was over. Julie was sure of it now. Tara would never forgive her as long as she was going with Quinn, and Jess and Shelley would always stick with Tara, no matter what. Shelley was a blind follower, and Jess was too weak to take a stand on anything.

Julie had been critical of them these past few months, but she would still miss them. Miss the things they did together. Miss being part of a charmed circle of four.

She sighed, grasped her books tightly, and headed down the hall to her next class. But just then she saw Quinn coming toward her, shouldering his way through clumps of giggling, chattering teens, and smiling a special smile, just for her.

We're a couple now, she thought, smiling back and moving toward him, forgetting Tara and the others. *I have Quinn and that's all that matters.*

Quinn put his arm around her shoulder and gave her a quick kiss on the top of her head, almost as if he were staking a claim on her for all the world to see.

All around them were astonished eyes and surprised faces, and Julie was aware that everyone was staring at her, and that she probably looked silly and lovestruck.

Well, let them look, she thought happily, kissing him back. *By lunchtime it will be all over school about Quinn and me, anyway. So I might as well relax and let it all hang out.*

Brad Stafford had been one of those standing, watching. He smiled at Julie as she went past with Quinn. It wasn't his usual smile. This was a regretful, almost sad little smile, not at all like Brad.

Quinn was waiting for Julie in the hall outside every classroom that day.

"You don't have to do that, Quinn," she protested. "I don't want you to be late for your own classes."

"But I want to," he said. "I like carrying your books. It makes me feel like one of those old-fashioned boyfriends."

He was missing from his post only once, and that was when Julie came out of world history.

He wasn't far away, though. Boy-crazy Karen Slack had him pinned up against the wall a little way down the hall. She was saying something to him, posing a bit, shaking back her thick, heavily permed hair and smiling an arch, teasing smile.

She seemed to be asking—no, telling—him something. Julie couldn't see Quinn's face when he replied, but when he finally got away from Karen and came toward Julie, he looked annoyed.

"I'm not going to ask what you and Karen were up to," Julie told him, laughing. "I don't want you to accuse me of being jealous of her."

Quinn rolled his eyes. "She was asking me how things worked out between you and me. I mean, about that dent I told her you put in my car. She even volunteered to help me find a good automotive shop where I can get my car fixed."

"I guess she hasn't heard the latest about us, then," Julie said. "She must be the only one in school who hasn't. This place is a real gossip mill."

"There's always one clueless person," Quinn said cheerfully, linking his arm with hers. "And now, Miss Hagan, since I don't have to report for work until late tonight, how about letting me take you out for frozen yogurt after last class?"

CHAPTER THIRTEEN

What was it with these girls at Jefferson High? Why were they all trying to put the make on him? Hadn't he made it clear, right from the start, that the only girl he was interested in was Julie?

First it had been Tara. She'd been attracted to him, he could tell, and she'd tried to make him interested in her, too. Fat chance. She wasn't his kind of girl. He only hoped Tara wasn't going to try to make Julie miserable on his account. She was the kind of girl who'd do something like that. Well, let her try. Julie had *him*, now, and he wasn't about to let anybody hurt her.

And now Karen Slack was hitting on him.

Why did she have to come after him? Didn't

she know he and Julie were a pair, or was she just plain stupid?

The girl was trouble, and he was going to have to do something about her before she ruined his life. No sense trying to kid himself, she had the power to really mess him up.

She'd caught him in the hall today and, acting all cute and flirty, had said, "I know your secret, Quinn McNeal!"

At first he didn't know what she meant. He'd thought maybe she was talking about him and Julie. But then she'd said, "I know where you've been the last four years."

He'd tried to play it cool, to keep a friendly expression on his face. He didn't want anyone wondering what they were saying and listening in.

"What do you mean?" he asked, stalling for time.

"You've got a real interesting past," she said. "No wonder you look so . . . experienced."

Her voice had drifted off but her eyes were bold.

It was funny how some girls were turned on by guys who'd been in The Place. It happened all the time, though, according to a couple of guys who'd been in there before.

But how did Karen know about his past?

Then it hit him. Karen worked in the principal's office. She'd seen his records! How could she have seen them, though? Mr. Reed said he was keeping them locked up in his special safe. The one only he had the combination to.

Mr. Reed was a nice man, an okay guy. He wasn't the sort to betray a trust. You developed a sixth sense about people when you'd been in The Place for a while. You could always tell those you could trust from those you couldn't.

He'd talked to Quinn in his office the day Quinn registered.

"Look, son," he'd said, "what you did is in the past, and you've certainly paid enough for it. It's the future that matters now. So I'm going to put these records and the letters that accompanied them here in my private safe, where only I can have access to them."

Seeing that Quinn was still a little uncertain, Mr. Reed had continued, "Sometimes a high-school principal has to be like a doctor or a priest. There are some things we keep to ourselves."

"But the other teachers," Quinn said. "Won't they have to—"

"No. I'll personally compile your reports. The important thing here, Quinn, is to get you back on the right track, and the less others know about your past, the better."

And now Karen said she knew his secret. How did that happen?

"What is this, Karen?" he'd asked, trying to keep it low-key. "Are you pulling my leg or what?"

She'd smiled and run her hands through her hair. It was an annoying mannerism, Quinn noted, but she obviously thought she looked sexy doing it.

"Mr. Reed's gotten real absent-minded lately," she said. "Would you believe he went off this morning and left his safe wide open? Why, anyone could have gone in and read your records, Quinn."

She smiled again, but a threat lay beneath that smile.

"I closed it up real quick, though," she said. "Of course, I just *might* have glanced at some of the stuff Mr. Reed had in there about you. But don't worry, Quinn. Your secret is safe with me."

Well, at least she hadn't told anyone else . . . yet.

That figured—knowledge was power. And she had the knowledge about his past, so she had power over him. She probably wouldn't want to share it with anyone until she found out what it would buy.

He'd played it cool with her. He pretended he felt friendly toward her and that maybe they could get together and talk about it. Tonight, even. He said he'd call her. That way, even if she heard about him and Julie, she'd figure it was just gossip.

That pizza-delivery job sure made things easier. It gave him an alibi.

He'd call her after school and set up a meeting for tonight.

CHAPTER FOURTEEN

On Tuesday afternoon two policemen found the body of Karen Slack.

Her car was parked a few miles from town at a scenic overlook, a high bluff with a view of the Potomac River and the famous falls for which the town was named.

Her body was lying, spread-eagled, on the rocks below.

The police said she had either jumped, fallen, or been pushed from the overlook at approximately eleven o'clock on Monday night.

Murder, her shocked classmates agreed, was completely out of the question. Who would want to murder Karen Slack?

The police seemed to agree with the students of Jefferson High. They could find no motive for the possible murder of Karen Slack. And her body showed no signs of any injuries other than those caused by the impact of her fall.

That left accident and suicide.

Suicide seemed about as unlikely as murder. The police interviewed Karen's friends and classmates, and no one could remember her ever acting "down" or depressed, or saying anything about wishing she were dead.

"Just the opposite," her best friend, Cassie Latimore, told the police. "She was always disgustingly cheerful. But what I can't figure out is, why did she go up to the overlook? I mean, that's a big parking spot for kids who want to make out, and Karen didn't have anyone to make out with."

"Maybe she just wanted to go up there at night and pretend," suggested Ann Collins, another of Karen's friends. "And you know what a klutz Karen was. She probably leaned over the railing too far, lost her balance, and fell."

Accidental death, the police ruled it, and closed their books on the case.

"I feel so awful about Karen," Julie told Quinn at lunch the next day as they sat in a private, sunny spot down by the gym, sharing sandwiches and cookies.

The two of them were brown-bagging it these days at Quinn's suggestion. He said he didn't like cafeteria food. Julie suspected it was actually the cafeteria and the "in" crowd at the special table he disliked. She was relieved he didn't want to eat with them. It would be awkward to sit there now, considering how Tara, Jess, and Shelley felt about her.

Actually, Quinn acted as if he wanted to keep her away from *everybody*, not just her old friends.

"Why should you feel awful about Karen?" Quinn asked her, polishing an apple on the sleeve of his sweater.

"Well, you know. I feel guilty for not realizing how needy and insecure she must have been. Can you imagine going up to the overlook at night by yourself? I guess no guy ever took her there."

"Are you saying you've been up there, Julie?" Quinn asked. He was smiling, but his eyes were cold. "How many guys have taken you up there?"

"Oh, Quinn, it's not like that at all."

"Who'd you make out with up there? That Brad Stafford creep?"

He reached over and grasped Julie's wrist.

102

She tried to pull away, but his grip tightened. "I mean it, Julie. I really want to know."

"Let go of me, Quinn!" she gasped. "You're hurting me!"

He didn't seem to hear her. Didn't seem to realize she was in pain. His eyes had darkened. They looked almost black now.

"Who?" he repeated. "Answer me."

"Nobody," Julie said, close to tears. "I've never made out with anybody up on The Point. Now let go of my arm, Quinn."

He loosened his grip on her wrist but didn't remove his hand. "Are you telling me the truth? You've never been with somebody up there?"

Julie tore her arm free and rubbed her wrist. She could see the red imprint of his fingers on it.

"I didn't say I've never been up there," she snapped. "Sure, I've gone up to The Point, but it's always been with a bunch of kids, and we never did anything . . . like that."

She turned and faced him, tears of anger welling up in her eyes. "So listen to me good, Quinn, because I'm not going to say it again. I've never made out with a guy up there. I don't think I've ever actually 'made out'—I mean, well, you know—with anybody anywhere. You're looking at a real inexperienced girl here. So there. Are you satisfied now?"

He stared at her silently for several seconds. She could see his face softening and his eyes losing that wild black look.

"Oh, Julie," he finally said. "I'm sorry. I'm really sorry. I don't know what came over me."

He tried to put his arms around her, but she pulled away.

"No, don't touch me," she commanded. "I don't want you to touch me."

Obediently, he put his hands in his lap and stared bleakly down at them.

"Okay, I won't touch you. But can I say something?"

"What?"

"That I've been a real jerk and I was wrong to act the way I did. It's just that I'm so crazy about you, Julie, it makes me half-nuts sometimes. The thought of you kissing another guy— I mean, parking someplace and really making out with him—nearly drives me wild."

He looked up at her pleadingly. She didn't reply.

"I love you," he repeated. "I guess I'm not showing it the right way, but I do. And I'm sorry I grabbed you like that. Does it hurt?"

"No," Julie told him. "Not now."

"I'll never do anything like that again," he said. "That's a promise."

"Are you sure?"

"Am I sure? Does the sun rise in the east? Do you want me to prove it to you? Ask me to do anything, Julie, and I will. I'll walk on hot coals if you want, just say the word."

"Oh, stop it, dummy," Julie said, smiling in spite of herself. "I forgive you."

Quinn threw out his arms and looked heavenward. "Thank you! Thank you, Lord!"

Later that night, as she lay in bed, Julie thought about what had happened. How jealous Quinn had been. Wild with jealousy.

It was scary to be loved like that. Scary but thrilling. She couldn't believe he felt all that emotion for her. She didn't know any other girl whose boyfriend was that crazy in love with her.

She'd been angry with Quinn when he'd grabbed her wrist and acted so wild, but she couldn't stay mad at him long.

And he'd promised never to do anything like that again, hadn't he?

So everything was okay with them, now.

He had come by after supper and taken her

out to the movies. He'd really impressed her parents.

He'd called her mother "ma'am" and her father "sir." They'd simply eaten it up, her mother in particular. She was always going on about good manners, and how the kids today didn't act respectful around their elders.

Well, Quinn's manners had been perfect, absolutely perfect, and he'd looked like a real Prince Charming in that blue shirt that matched the color of his eyes.

And she could tell that her father was impressed by the fact that Quinn was on his own, earning his own living and going to school at the same time.

When she'd gone upstairs for her purse, Mollie had followed her and said, "Wow, Julie that guy's a walking sexpot. Tara's probably making a wax doll of you this very minute, so be ready for some strange, shooting pains when she starts sticking in the pins."

All in all it had been a very successful first meeting with the folks.

Forget that other stuff at lunch.

It would never happen again.

CHAPTER FIFTEEN

That was a close call at lunch.

He really blew it and nearly lost her for good.

But it wasn't his fault. It was just that he loved her so much.

She shouldn't have talked as if it were natural to go up to The Point. It wasn't. Decent girls didn't do things like that. He was looking for a good girl, someone special, who'd saved herself just for him.

That's why he'd flipped out when Julie started in about The Point. He suddenly got this mental picture of her up there, with some lousy little rich kid's dirty hands all over her.

He hoped she'd never find out just how angry he'd really been. Lucky for him he'd managed to explain it away and make her smile at him again.

He'd liked it when she'd told him she never "made out" with any guy anywhere. What an angel! If she ever changed, he didn't know what he'd do.

Well, he'd been lucky today, all right. Julie's folks really liked him. He could tell. And he had an idea that her father would probably want to take him into the family business if—*when*—he and Julie were married.

That Karen Slack thing had worked out okay, too.

He'd been lucky. The Point was deserted, as he'd hoped it would be, and the whole thing took only a few minutes.

He had no regrets for what he did. After all, it was entirely Karen's fault. She hadn't left him any choice. She should have realized it was dangerous to try to blackmail someone into being your boyfriend.

He'd made sure she hadn't told anyone about him—his records and his past—before he did what needed to be done. She hadn't.

She didn't have much of a chance, though, to realize her big mistake—that she shouldn't have messed with him. One shove and she was on her way down. And by the time she hit those rocks, she'd probably blacked out.

Grady hopped up on the bed and curled into a ball beside him. Good old Grady. Quinn stretched out one hand and rubbed Grady's ears.

"I really hurt Julie today," he told the cat, "so what can I do to make it up to her, old buddy?"

No reply from Grady.

"I know what I *do* owe her, although she'll never know I was the one who did it."

Those two bums. The muggers from Tara's driveway. It was high time he did something about them. Something permanent. They were probably starting to get over the aches and pains he'd given them. They were probably planning revenge.

He should have taken care of them before, but he'd had too many other things on his mind. Well, better late than never. He'd do it as soon as possible.

He rolled over on his side and immediately fell into a dreamless and untroubled sleep.

CHAPTER SIXTEEN

"Hey, Julie!" Mollie said the next morning, climbing into the car and snapping her seat belt. "I've got something interesting to tell you. I was dying to tell you last night, but you were too busy drooling over that gorgeous hunkerino."

"I was *not* drooling, Mollie. Salivating a little, maybe, but not drooling."

Julie released the hand brake and backed out of the driveway. Her mother was letting her take one of the family cars anytime she wanted now. *One of the benefits of my new maturity,* she thought with a smile. *There's nothing like a big romance to throw you into a whole new league.*

"It's about Tara," Mollie said.

"Tara? She barely even speaks to me these days."

"Then this should dull the pain," Mollie said. "Tommy and I just uncovered the juiciest dirt on sweet little Tara's fancy ancestors."

"How? You don't usually listen to gossip, Mollie."

"No, but this is high-tech snooping, sister dear. It's that new program I got for my computer, the one that allows me to access newspaper files. I found a couple of really neat stories in some old 1920's issues of one of the Richmond papers that said—"

"You can actually do that? Tap into old newspaper files?"

"Yeah. It's great," Mollie said with a grin. "Anyway, it seems that back in the twenties, Tara's family owned Maywood, which was a broken-down wreck, and not much else. They'd lost just about everything in the Civil War and—"

"You mean they were poor?"

"Poor as church mice. Stop interrupting or we'll be at school before I get to all the good stuff."

"Sorry."

"Well, evidently Tara's great-grandaddy decided to do something about the family finances, so he became—get this, Julie—a bootlegger."

"You're kidding me," Julie said. "You're talking about Tara's honored and genteel ancestors?"

"That's right. Prohibition was in full swing, so the Braxtons became big-time bootleggers, just like the gangsters in all those movies."

"The newspapers said all that?"

"Well," Mollie went on, "the paper ran this big story because the government was trying to get the goods on them, but the witnesses kept backing out or changing their stories. The Braxtons were poor, but they sure must have known people in the right places. So they eventually got filthy rich via illegal booze. Old Great-Granddaddy Braxton really knew how to recoup his losses."

"The Braxtons, bootleggers," Julie said wonderingly. "Can you imagine? No wonder they could afford all the remodeling and restoration they did on Maywood, not to mention the heated pool and billiard room, *and* that party-sized hot tub Tara goes skinny-dipping in. Well, I'm glad I don't have any secret crimes I'm trying to hide, with the two of you snooping around.

Tara was definitely up to something.

Julie could tell by the way she, Shelley, and

Jessica abruptly stopped talking when Julie came up, unexpectedly, behind them in the hall.

It wasn't the first time something like this had happened lately. The three of them always seemed to have their heads together, plotting.

It was pretty clear to everyone in the school now that Julie was no longer a part of what used to be a close-knit foursome. The three of them had excluded her from all their activities. Not that she minded; she was too busy these days with Quinn to take much notice. It was amazing how he filled her life.

Sometimes, though, she missed their big shopping trips to the mall. That always used to be fun, trying things on and giggling. Tara was a shopoholic and practically lived at the mall. She knew every department of every store and had a sixth sense about when things would be going on sale.

My wardrobe will never be that good again, Julie thought with a sigh. *We did have some good times together.*

But now the other three were up to something.

Well, it can't be too bad, Julie reassured herself. *If Tara thinks she can break up Quinn and me, she's wrong. And that's all that matters now—Quinn, and what we have going for us.*

She went over to her locker and took out the books she would need for first period.

"Something wrong, gorgeous?" said a voice behind her.

"Oh, Brad," Julie said, turning. "You scared me. I was a million miles away."

"So I noticed," he said. "I wish it was me you were with, a million miles away."

He didn't appear to be joking. Brad had changed recently, Julie thought. He'd grown more serious.

"Is that a line or what?" she said lightly.

"It's an 'or what.' It definitely isn't a line," Brad told her.

"If I didn't know you better, I'd think you were for real." Julie tried to cover her growing uneasiness with a laugh.

"It is for real," he said.

People had begun to drift off down the halls to their classes. Julie and Brad were alone in front of her locker. He didn't seem to want to leave her.

She really didn't feel like getting into a big discussion right now with Brad. And where was Quinn? He usually met her before first period.

"Don't you know how I feel about you, Julie?" Brad persisted.

"No. No, I don't," she replied, fiddling with her books, her eyes lowered. This was getting downright embarrassing. "You're such a kidder, Brad. I never know how to take you."

"Take me any way you want, I'm yours! There I go again, acting smart-mouthed. But I do mean it, Julie."

"Since when?"

"Since always. Well, since the big swim party last summer, anyway. You looked so cute in that polka-dot bikini, with the matching freckles popping out across your nose. I thought to myself, 'Hey, what's happening here?'"

"But you never said anything to me until now," Julie said. "Why? If you really felt that way, why didn't you say something instead of acting like a clown?"

Brad shrugged. "Because I was . . . *am* . . . a dumb jerk, that's why. I thought I'd impress you with my wit and charm, but I guess you were looking for a Greek god, not a clown."

"You mean Quinn."

"Yeah, Quinn, God's gift to Braxton Falls. And speaking of Quinn, Julie . . ." Brad's voice trailed off, and he looked uncomfortable.

"What about him?"

"I don't know, exactly. It's just a feeling I have. He's too . . . something. Intense. Brooding. I don't know. I wish you weren't so crazy about him."

Julie opened her mouth to protest, but Brad held his hand up to silence her. "You're a real sensible girl, Julie, but Quinn could be the original Jack the Ripper and you probably wouldn't even notice."

"What a terrible thing to say!" Julie snapped. "Has it ever crossed your mind, Brad, that maybe you're just a little bit jealous of him?"

"Sure I'm jealous of him," Brad said. "Who wouldn't be? He's got you, hasn't he? But that's not why I'm telling you this. If I thought he was right for you, I wouldn't say a word. But I swear, Julie, there's something wrong with that guy. I can feel it in my bones."

"There's absolutely nothing wrong with Quinn! And if that's all you wanted to tell me, I've got to get to class now."

"Okay, okay, if that's how you feel," Brad said. "Uh-oh, here comes your Greek god right now. Talk about jealous. Look at that face! He doesn't want you to be around anyone but him, haven't you noticed? That's not healthy, Julie."

Quinn was walking quickly down the hall toward them. *He must have overslept*, Julie thought. *That's why he's late.* But Brad was right about the expression on Quinn's face. He didn't like her talking to Brad, that was clear.

"I hope you aren't expecting me to duke it out with that guy over you," Brad said. "I don't have a chance against all those muscles. Besides, I faint at the sight of blood. My blood, anyway."

The bell for first period rang.

"Ah, saved—literally—by the bell! I'm out of here," Brad called over his shoulder as he trotted down the hall.

Brad was wrong, Julie thought defensively. Quinn was perfect, just perfect. Maybe he was a little jealous, but he was getting over that. Hadn't they talked all that out yesterday, and hadn't he apologized? It's just that he cared so much for her that he wanted her all to himself now, until they got to know each other better.

So why, then, did she tell him Brad was only getting a history assignment from her? Why was it important to convince him that her conversation with Brad was strictly business? Why did she feel she needed to tell a lie like that?

And why had the look on Quinn's face frightened her so?

CHAPTER SEVENTEEN

BRAXTON FALLS—The bodies of two young men were found late yesterday afternoon in the woods south of town. They were the victims of apparent foul play.

The bodies, lying in the backseat of a 1989 gray Ford Escort, were discovered by a family hiking in that area.

Each of the victims, who appeared to be in their early twenties, had been dealt a blow to the head. Police found a crowbar next to the bodies. It is estimated the deaths occurred sometime between 10 P.M. and midnight on Saturday.

Traces of drugs and drug paraphernalia have been found in the car, leading police investigators to suspect that the murders were drug related.

Although neither victim carried identification, the car was registered to a Norman Clayborn of Custisville, Virginia. Clayborn was subsequently identified as one of the victims. The other has been identified as Frank E. Soames, also of Custisville. . . .

Norman and Frank.

Norm and Frankie! A gray Ford Escort!

Julie suddenly felt dizzy and nauseated. Those were the two men in Tara's driveway. The ones who'd threatened her. The ones that Quinn had beaten up. It had to be them!

"Are you finished with the front page, Julie?" asked her mother. "There's absolutely nothing in the feature pages this morning. Julie? Are you feeling all right? You look so pale."

"No . . . no, Mom. I'm fine. It's just that I didn't get to bed until late last night."

"I told you so," scolded her mother. "You were out with Quinn until all hours Friday night. And then again last night. Thank goodness the boy had to work Saturday night, or I'd hate to think how exhausted you'd be this morning!"

Julie wasn't listening to her mother.

Those men. Murdered!

Julie could hardly wait to be alone with Quinn at school, in a spot where they couldn't be overheard.

She waited in the school parking lot for him and ran over to his car as he opened the door and unfolded his long legs. She couldn't help admiring Quinn as he smiled at her. But this was not the time for thoughts like that. Hadn't he seen the article in this morning's paper? How could he be so cheerful when *this* had happened?

"Quinn, did you see this morning's paper?"

He nodded. "About those two guys?"

"Yes. Oh, Quinn—they were murdered. With a crowbar! It's so awful!"

Quinn put his arms around Julie and pulled her to him. She could feel his heart beating fast, the way it always did when he held her close.

"I'd say they got what they deserved, Julie," he said gently.

"To be murdered? Nobody deserves that."

"They did. They were going to hurt you." Quinn's voice was grim. Unforgiving.

"Maybe we should have reported what happened to the police," Julie said. "Can we be in any trouble? I mean, can they connect us with those two in any way? What if they find out about what happened in Tara's driveway and think *we* had something to do with their deaths?"

Quinn put his cheek on her hair and rocked her back and forth, the way a mother would soothe an overexcited child.

"Listen to what you're saying, honey," he told her. "You're not making any sense. Why should they think we had something to do with the murders? No one knows anything about what those two tried to do to us. No one except you and me, and neither of us is going to tell the police about *that*, are we?"

"Maybe we should, Quinn."

Quinn stopped rocking and pressed Julie closer to him, resting his cheek on her hair. "Why? Why get involved in something like that? We'd only be asking for trouble, Julie."

"But if—"

"Look, you don't want to go down to the police station and answer all sorts of questions about your relationship with Norm and Frankie, do you?"

"Of course not," Julie said.

"Then leave it alone. You had nothing to do

with their deaths. Besides, think about all the publicity you and your family would get if you—we—got mixed up in this thing."

Julie pictured her mother's reaction and shuddered. "I . . . I guess I just panicked. You're right, of course, Quinn. I haven't told a soul about what happened, not even my sister."

"Good." He released her, putting his hands on her shoulders and stooping down to look into her eyes.

"Those two were bad, Julie. Really bad."

As they walked together toward the school building, Julie could only think how lucky she was to have found someone like Quinn.

Someone strong and dependable.

Someone good.

Someone she could always count on, no matter what.

Quinn's jealousy was growing worse, and Julie didn't know what to do about it. Why was he getting more and more possessive of her every day? Why didn't he want her to talk to or be around anyone but him?

At first Julie thought it was her fault, that she was doing something wrong, or not being understanding enough in some way.

Then at times, in a burst of resentment, she was sure it had nothing to do with her. It was Quinn's fault. His problem, not hers. There was something in him, not her, that made him behave this way. Made him turn sullen and angry whenever any of the guys at school talked to her or paid her compliments, even in fun.

And then she'd remember what he'd told her about his childhood and his alcoholic, abusive father.

"He's the one who broke my nose," Quinn said one night. "I was never anything to him but a punching bag when he had too many. I look a little like my mother, so I guess I reminded him of her. He never forgave her for running off and leaving him, so he took it out on me."

They were alone in Julie's kitchen when he told her this. It was almost midnight and they were having milk and cake, not because they were hungry, but because they always managed to find some way of prolonging their time together.

Julie would never forget the expression on Quinn's face when he flattened the cake with the back of his fork, pressing it into pulp, and said, "And I'll tell you this, Julie. When that guy died, it was the happiest day of my life."

Thinking about his unhappy childhood made Julie love Quinn even more. It made her feel guilty for not being patient enough with him, for not taking into account the fact that, growing up, he'd been starved for love and attention.

And so the cycle would start all over again.

And each new incident made it worse. His jealousy was like a snowball rolling downhill, growing larger and more menacing as it went.

Even a casual conversation outside a classroom now, if Quinn saw it, brought on questions: "What were you talking about with him, Julie?" "Have you two ever dated?" And worst of all, when she *had* dated the boy, "Did you ever kiss him?"

Julie always lied when she answered this last one.

"No, Quinn. He was just a casual date. You know . . ."

"Are you *sure*, Julie?"

Julie would always try to look innocent. But the truthful answer was yes, and she hated having to lie like this all the time. Yes, if she'd dated the guy in question, she probably *had* kissed him.

There had never been anything serious, though, between her and any of those guys. Just a few kisses at parties or at her front door, but nothing hot and heavy.

Julie lied because she wasn't sure what Quinn would do if she *did* admit kissing, however casually, any guy other than him. He would, she knew, consider it a kind of betrayal of him, even though it had happened long before he came into her life.

He hadn't gotten into a fight with any of her old boyfriends over her . . . so far. The word was getting out about him, though, and guys were starting to leave Julie alone.

She resented this. She'd always liked people and enjoyed school, but now she felt as if she had an invisible wall around her.

Well, Quinn would get over this phase. He'd settle in and make friends. It was always hard to start a new school.

Face it, Julie, she thought. *You're making excuses for Quinn and you know it.*

Yes, but what else can I do? The alternative is to break up with him and I could never, never *do that.*

Even Mollie seemed to be looking at Quinn differently now.

"Don't you and Quinn ever double-date or go to parties, Julie?" she asked. "When I see you in the halls or at lunchtime, the two of you are always off together in some corner. Is that right? I mean, is this *really* what you want?"

Mollie must have mentioned this to her mother, because Mrs. Hagan had been coming on strong lately about how the teen years were the time for fun and friendship and lots of school activities.

Even Brad had something to say about it. He took Julie aside one day when Quinn was nowhere in sight.

"Are you and Quinn okay?" he asked. "I mean, does he lock you up in a dark closet if you try to leave your ivory tower or something?"

Julie smiled. "I'm not Rapunzel, Brad. My hair's not long enough."

He didn't smile back. "I mean it, Julie. I know you don't like me to criticize him, but I don't like what Quinn's doing to you. You've still got two years of high school to get through, and he's making a hermit out of you."

Julie sighed. "Don't you start in on me, too, Brad."

"I figured I wasn't the first. Just about everyone has noticed it, Julie."

Julie bristled. "I don't know why everybody's suddenly so concerned about my personal affairs."

"Because there are a lot of people here at Jefferson High who like you. Really like you," Brad said. "Oh, I know you thought Tara and her buddies were your closest friends, but that's a laugh. I'm talking about the kids in your classes. Maybe you don't pal around with them socially, but they admire you and hate to see you get messed up the way you are now."

"Messed up?" Julie shook her head in amazement. "Brad—I've never been as happy in my entire life as I am with Quinn. He's everything I ever wanted in a guy. I'll always feel this way about him."

"Yeah, well." Brad's face fell and his shoulders slumped. Then he gave himself a little shake and said, "I just hope he gets over this jealous stuff, Julie. It's not normal."

"He's not *that* jealous," Julie protested.

Another lie. That was all she seemed to do these days. Nobody had ever told her that love involved a lot of lying.

"Not that jealous?" Brad repeated. "You could've fooled me. One more thing," he said as he turned away from Julie. "Tara's still on your case. Be careful. That girl's a witch with a capital B."

Julie had just about written Tara off as a threat. All the plotting Tara, Jessica, and

Shelley seemed to be doing right after Julie and Quinn paired off had come to nothing.

True, Julie had found a dime-store rubber rat in her locker one morning, but that was all. She figured that's what they had been planning that day they'd been in the huddle. As dirty tricks went, it had been pretty mild.

To her surprise Julie discovered that Brad was right when he'd said a lot of kids at Jefferson High liked her. Now that she'd broken with Tara, Jess, and Shelley, Julie found herself being included in other groups, and receiving invitations to join extracurricular activities that she never would have considered before.

Of course, Quinn objected to anything that would take her away from him.

"What about me, Julie?" he'd ask plaintively. "What am I supposed to be doing when you're running around up to your pretty little ears in rah-rah stuff?"

And then he'd play with her hair or kiss her until she was breathless and she'd forget what it was she'd been saying.

But lately Julie had been giving a lot of thought to what Brad and Mollie had said, and what her mother had implied with her lectures about the necessity for friends and activities in the teen years.

"I've let a lot of activities slide this semester," she told Quinn one night when they'd returned home from a date. "Working on the school newspaper, for example. I haven't pulled my weight on the staff for the past couple of weeks. I think they're about to delete my name from the masthead."

"So let them," he said. "Let somebody else write those stories."

"You don't understand," Julie said, evading his encircling arms. "I like writing, and I'm good at it. It's important to me, Quinn!"

So he'd grudgingly agreed to her working on the school paper.

And that's when things had taken a turn for the worse for her and Quinn.

CHAPTER EIGHTEEN

"This Nick Wells guy, the editor of the paper," Quinn began. Julie knew exactly what was coming next. "Have you ever gone out with him?"

"No," she said firmly, truthfully. "Nick has always had a big thing for Tara, but they only started dating heavily last summer. He's really crazy about her, Quinn."

That seemed to satisfy him for the moment. Then, predictably, he asked, "Are there a lot of guys on the staff of the paper?"

"Only a couple. It's mostly girls. At least during football season."

"What guys?"

"What?"

"What guys are on the staff?"

"Oh, you know, the real grinds."

Julie hated herself for this, for making the serious students sound unappealing, but otherwise Quinn would give her even more flack about working on the paper.

"Are you going to have to work every afternoon?" he asked. "Will it mean you won't have much time for me after school now, Julie?"

"Oh, no, not at all. I'll probably spend only half an hour in the newspaper office a couple of times a week. Most of the articles I'll write in study hall or at home."

It hadn't quite worked out that way, though. By the middle of the second week, Julie found she was working almost every afternoon in the newspaper office with Nick.

She tried to explain the situation to Quinn.

"Nick says he's been getting complaints about how dull the paper is this year, and we're trying to come up with some ideas for new features and columns."

"Just you and Nick?"

"No, there are others, too, usually"—she hoped he wouldn't ask how often she and Nick were alone, working—"but Nick has asked me if I'd consider being feature editor. I'd really like that, Quinn. I think I can do a good job on it."

Quinn reluctantly agreed, but insisted on

waiting for her after school every afternoon and driving her home.

Julie was pleased he wasn't putting up an argument about her new job as feature editor and her long hours. He was taking it well. Maybe they were working out their problems, after all. This jealousy thing of Quinn's would run its course. It had to.

She just wished, though, that Nick didn't always walk her out to the parking lot. She could tell Quinn didn't like that.

"It's just that Nick always thinks of something else he wants to talk to me about, so he follows me out rather than making me stay even later," she explained.

"Yeah, I bet," Quinn said. "If I were him, I'd want to stick around you for as long as I could, too."

One afternoon Nick made the mistake of putting his arm around Julie and giving her a quick hug when they parted.

It was all perfectly innocent. Even Tara and a couple of cheerleaders, who'd just come out of school after rehearsal, glanced over and didn't act as if Julie and Nick were doing anything out of the ordinary.

But Quinn came boiling out of his car, fists

clenched, and strode over to Nick.

"Hey, Nick," he said, "take your hands off my girl."

At first Nick must have thought Quinn was joking, because he laughed. But then Quinn said it again.

"You heard me, take your hands off Julie. Find somebody else to paw."

Nick's face went white, then red. "I wasn't pawing Julie," he snapped. "Why don't you grow up? You're starting to be a real drag with your jealousy bit, McNeal."

Quinn took a step forward, eyes narrowed and lips set in a tight line.

"Quinn, no!" Julie grabbed Quinn's arm and stepped between them. "Don't do this. Please! It was nothing. Nick wasn't doing anything."

Nick put his hands up placatingly. "Look, Quinn, I don't want any trouble with you. It isn't fair to Julie. And besides, I have a thing about not getting my nose broken. If I did something you didn't like, I apologize. So back off, okay?"

"Please, Quinn," Julie pleaded.

Quinn finally nodded, his eyes still narrowed and glaring, and allowed Julie to lead him to his car.

"Listen, Quinn—" Julie began.

"Forget it," he snapped. "I don't want to talk about it."

"I suppose this means you're going to give me a hard time now about working on the paper," Julie said, her voice sharp. "So I'm warning you right now, Quinn—don't. Don't try."

"Is it Nick? Is that why you're being so stubborn about this?" Quinn asked.

His anger had suddenly passed, and now he was looking at her sadly, pleadingly.

His battered-child look, Julie thought, fighting back the impulse to take his face in her hands and kiss him, make him well. *No, he does this to me all the time*, she told herself fiercely. *And, like a fool, I always fall for it.*

"No," she told him. "It isn't Nick. You know it isn't. So why do you do this, Quinn? You've got to stop."

"I'm sorry, Julie. I don't mean to. Something just comes over me and I can't help myself."

Julie knew what he would say next and prepared herself for it. She could almost say it by heart now.

"It's just that I love you so much, honey. . . ."

We can't go on like this, Julie thought. *Talking doesn't seem to help. Maybe if we went to the school counselor, she could help us or tell us where to go to get help.*

But this wasn't the time to bring it up. She'd wait until she and Quinn were alone, and he was feeling mellow. That would be tomorrow night. Friday. They had a big date planned. Dinner in a little restaurant on the edge of town. *That's the right time*, Julie thought. *Tomorrow night . . .*

What a shame he had to act this way today, when she'd thought he was getting better about this jealousy thing. And in front of an audience, too.

Julie remembered the expression on Tara's face as she'd stood watching the exchange between Quinn and Nick.

She'd been smiling.

Quinn stood Julie up for their Friday-night date.

She'd put a lot of thought into what she would wear and finally settled on a dark-gold dress with a flaring skirt and a wide, tight belt. With it she wore the amber earrings and pendant her aunt had brought home from a recent trip to Europe.

The color of the dress brought out the gold

flecks in Julie's eyes, and the amber jewelry suited her coloring. This would soften Quinn up and make him agree to a heart-to-heart talk. Something about her coloring turned Quinn on, and she was really playing it up for all it was worth tonight.

At eight-thirty Julie realized Quinn wasn't coming.

All dressed up and no place to go, she thought dismally. *Where is he?*

She tried calling his apartment, but there was no answer.

"Do you suppose something's happened to him?" she asked her parents. "I mean, like an accident or something? Should I call the police?"

"No," her mother said. "Something's probably come up. Maybe they called him in suddenly to work. You said they've done it before. He'll call and explain—just be patient."

But he didn't call. Finally, a little before midnight, Julie went to bed.

She was just falling asleep when she heard a gentle tapping at her window. Her bedroom was on the second floor, overlooking the backyard. At first she thought a branch of the huge old elm tree that grew beside the house was blowing against the window.

But then it came again. Tap, tap, tap. More insistent this time.

She climbed out of bed, shaking back her long hair, and went to the window.

Quinn's face peered in at her. He'd climbed the elm tree and was crouched on a limb outside her window.

"Quinn! What . . . ?" Julie pushed up the window, grabbing her robe from the back of her desk chair and slipping into it.

Quinn crawled through the window. "So you're home." He sounded relieved.

"Sssh!" she cautioned. "You'll wake the family. Of course I'm home. What did you think? And where on earth have you been? I've been worried sick."

Quinn took her in his arms. He was rough, almost hurtful, and Julie was painfully aware that he shouldn't be in her room at this hour, with her parents sleeping just down the hall. What would happen if her mother came in and found her here in Quinn's passionate embrace? She'd ground Julie forever.

"Then you weren't out with Nick Wells?" Quinn asked.

"What? I was supposed to have a date with

you, remember? Why would I go out with Nick Wells, anyway?"

"I've seen the way he looks at you, Julie. And I've seen you looking back at him. You like him, don't you?"

"Oh, no, Quinn! Not *that* again. No, I—"

He overrode her protest. "Why *wouldn't* you have a thing for Nick? He's a real big shot, and his folks are rich and all that."

"Are you out of your mind, Quinn? What's wrong with you? You stood me up and now you come crawling through my window at midnight because you have some crazy idea I've been out with Nick Wells. I don't feel that way about Nick. I never have!"

Quinn's hands tightened on her shoulders. "Do you really mean that, Julie? You aren't just saying that because you're afraid of what I might do to you?"

"*Do to me?* What are you talking about? What made you think I was out with Nick?"

"I saw the note."

"What note?"

"The note from Nick, telling you to meet him at eight at The Point. I went there and waited, but no one came. I thought maybe you two decided to meet someplace else, but I came

138

by the house anyway, just in case. That's when I thought I saw you moving around in your bedroom. So I waited in the car until all the lights went out and—"

Julie was aghast. "You actually thought I'd . . . and you've been watching the house all this time?"

Quinn pulled her more tightly to him, pinioning her arms. She couldn't move.

"Don't try to change the subject, Julie. What about that note?" His voice was quiet and menacing.

"I don't know anything about a note. Are you making this up or what? Let me go. You're hurting me."

Quinn loosened his hold slightly. "I found a note—*the* note—on top of my books this afternoon after school. You'd already left. It was from Nick to you, telling you where to meet him. Nick hates my guts now, after yesterday. I thought he put it there to show me he'd moved in on you."

"It doesn't even make sense," Julie said, shaking her head. "If the note was to *me*, I'd have it, wouldn't I, not him?"

"Yeah, I guess you're right. Maybe Nick was just yanking my chain," Quinn said, after thinking it over for a few moments. "I swear, Julie, I was so freaked out at the thought of him and you, I didn't know what I was doing. I just went crazy, I guess."

Julie struggled to free herself from his grasp. How many times had she heard *that?* How many more times would she hear it?

Quinn pulled her to him again and kissed her hard. As if he were punishing her, showing her who was boss.

There was a light tapping at the door.

"Julie?" Mollie whispered. "Are you all right in there?"

Frantic, Julie pushed Quinn toward the window. "Go. If my parents find out you're here, we're both in big trouble."

When she finally opened the door to Mollie, her sister regarded her suspiciously. "I heard someone talking in here. I didn't know what to think."

"It was the radio," Julie said.

Mollie looked unconvinced, but replied, "As long as you're okay, then. It's just that your voice sounded kind of . . ."

She took another look around the room. "Well, good night, Julie."

Is this a crazy dream? Julie asked herself after

Mollie left. *Did Quinn really crawl through my window and accuse me of secretly dating Nick Wells?*

She put her hand to her mouth. She could still feel Quinn's fierce kiss on her lips.

No, it wasn't a dream.

If only it had been.

CHAPTER NINETEEN

Quinn sat in his car, still staring at the house. He could see Julie's room from this angle. He watched it until the light went out.

His hands were trembling on the wheel. He'd been nearly out of his mind at the thought of Julie—his Julie—out with that stuck-up Nick creep.

He should have known better. Julie wouldn't do something like that. Julie would never betray him.

Betray.

He'd looked that word up in the dictionary once when he and Alison . . .

Well, he'd looked the word up, and it meant "be a traitor to, prove faithless, deliver up to an enemy."

If Julie had gone out with Nick, she'd have been doing all those things. She was his. He loved her and he wanted her to love him the same way. Completely. Totally. And for the rest of her life.

He'd loved Alison that way once. Yes, he could allow himself to think of her now that he was certain he and Julie would be together forever.

He'd fallen in love with Alison—or at least he'd thought it was love—the first time he saw her. Of course, that was four years ago, when he was only fourteen, so what had he known about love then? At the time, though, he'd thought it was the real thing.

How could I have been so dumb? So obsessed? he asked himself. He'd tried to make Alison notice him, even though he knew she was way above him. She was like a princess, and he was just a skinny kid from the crummiest part of town.

Maybe he shouldn't have followed her home from school all the time and hung around her neighborhood day and night, watching her house, but he couldn't help himself.

But Alison didn't like all that attention. Didn't like him trailing her in the halls at school and following her home afterward. She'd complain and tell him off, but her coldness only made him more enchanted, more in love with her.

And then he started watching her through her bedroom window. He found he could hide behind a bush and . . . But that was when her old man caught him and threatened to report him to the police.

He didn't report him, though, not out of kindness but because he didn't want a family scandal. The next day at school Alison had said, "You better leave me alone from now on, Quinn McNeal. Leave me alone or you'll be sorry. Really sorry."

But he couldn't leave her alone. He tried, and it just wouldn't work. He loved her too much.

So that's when Alison and her rich little girl friends and their dumb jock buddies did that terrible thing to him. . . .

Quinn realized he'd been biting his lip so furiously that he'd drawn blood.

I shouldn't let myself think about that night, he told himself. *The shrink at The Place said I have to let it go. It's all in the past now, and there's no reason to hang on to it anymore.*

CHAPTER TWENTY

On Monday morning Julie found Tara, Jessica, and Shelley waiting for her on the front steps of the school, the way they used to before she and Quinn became an item.

There was no sign of Quinn. His car wasn't in the parking lot, either.

I hope he isn't still angry, Julie thought fearfully, rubbing her arms where Quinn had grabbed her Friday night. Something had to be done about Quinn's crazy jealousy. And soon.

Tara came over to her, followed by Shelley and Jessica.

"How was your weekend, Julie?" she asked with a sly smile.

"Fine," Julie said uncertainly, wondering what Tara was up to. It was clear by the expression on Tara's face that it was something nasty.

Julie tried to act normal and casual. "I went—"

Tara interrupted, a look of fake girlish interest on her face. "How was your date with Quinn Friday night? Did you have a good time?"

Shelley and Jessica were exchanging furtive glances. As usual, they were transparently obvious. What were those three trying to pull now?

Julie suddenly realized what it was. *Of course,* she thought. *Why didn't I think of it right away? It was Tara who wrote that note and put it in Quinn's books.*

But why?

To make trouble between us, that's why.

"Why are you interested in my weekends all of a sudden, Tara?" Julie asked.

Tara widened her gray eyes innocently. "Why, Julie, I've always been interested in your love life. Remember when the four of us would tell each other everything?"

"That was then. This is now. And the three of you have been giving me the cold shoulder ever since I started going with Quinn."

Tara sputtered a little protest, but Julie cut her off.

"Obviously *you're* responsible for what

happened Friday night," she said, her anger building.

"You wrote that note, didn't you? And you put it on Quinn's books so he'd be sure to see it. And I know why. You were trying to make trouble between Quinn and me."

She went on, knowing even as she spoke that she was handling the situation badly. She was too angry now. She was losing her head. Her questioning was coming out all wrong, making her seem paranoid and unstable.

"So don't think you're pulling the wool over my eyes, Tara, with your chummy little best-friends act," she concluded. "And if you think you can break up Quinn and me, then guess again."

Tara was regarding her with a look of puzzled concern, one delicate eyebrow raised in ladylike astonishment. Her two hangers-on, Jessica and Shelley, were also playing their parts to perfection, looking at Julie as if she were a raving maniac.

Why are Jess and Shelley doing this? Julie wondered. Were they really *that* much under Tara's thumb? How could they let Tara dominate them the way she did?

Was I that easily led, once?

Not that much, maybe, but yes. Tara led me around by the nose, too. It's good to be free of her now.

"Honestly, Julie," Tara finally said with pretended concern. "I think you're losing it entirely. Why would I try to break up you and Quinn? It was probably just one of those macho male things, you know? We all know Nick and Quinn hate each other's guts after that big jealous act Quinn pulled in the parking lot last week."

The hostile, envious look Tara shot Julie when she said that told her Tara wouldn't mind having Quinn act jealous over *her*.

"So maybe Nick decided to play a little joke on Quinn," Tara went on, regaining her cool. "He knows Quinn would totally hit the roof if he thought you were dating somebody else." Then she said wistfully, sweetly, "I'm just hurt, Julie, terribly hurt, that you would ever think I'd do something like that to you."

I should have known, Julie thought as Tara turned and walked away. *I should have realized that Tara always wins.*

Quinn didn't show up at school until noon. Julie was headed toward the cafeteria when he caught up with her.

She didn't like the way he looked. His lips were set in a tight, thin line, and his eyes were dark and glaring.

He's probably been brooding all weekend about what he thinks Nick did to him, Julie thought with a shiver. *I've got to tell him what really happened before he sees Nick.*

Pulling him aside, she said, "Quinn, listen to me. I know who pulled that trick on us Friday night."

"So do I," he said grimly. "Nick Wells."

"No, it wasn't Nick. It was Tara."

Quinn looked at her in disbelief. "*Tara?* Why would she do something like that? What's she got to do with us?"

His eyes shifted from her face to the far end of the hall. He was still looking for Nick.

"Tara has a lot to do with us, can't you see?" Julie clutched his arm. "She's jealous of me—us—and wants to come between us, so—"

"That's crazy, Julie. You're imagining things. It was Nick, and I'm going to punch him out for it when I see him."

He started to leave, but Julie pulled him back.

"No, Quinn, don't do that! You'll only be making trouble for yourself. You'll be put on suspension for starting a fight. Mr. Reed really comes down hard on things like that."

"I can't help how I feel, Julie. I'd like to smash Nick's face in."

"You don't mean that. I know you, and you couldn't possibly feel that . . . that violent about somebody."

"Then you don't really know me, Julie. There's a lot about me you don't know."

"Promise me, Quinn. You've got to promise you won't hit Nick!"

Julie was trembling. "Please," she repeated. "For me. Please."

"All right," he said, almost as if he were humoring her. "I promise I won't hit Nick."

Was it her imagination, or did he stress the word "hit"?

Quinn's promise, if it really *was* a promise, lasted only until they were seated at a table in one corner of the cafeteria.

Suddenly, glancing across the table, Julie saw Quinn's face change. The dark look of anger came into his eyes. It was a look she was learning to recognize, and dread.

She turned around to see what he was staring at. It was Nick, headed toward his usual table with a loaded tray.

Before she could stop him, Quinn jumped to his feet.

"No, Quinn! You promised," she said, but it came out a whisper.

Quinn walked over to Nick. One corner of Julie's mind appreciatively recorded the fact that Quinn was as lithe and lean as a jungle cat.

And then, just like a cat, he moved. With one quick motion he flipped the tray up and into Nick's face.

Spaghetti and chocolate pudding dripped from Nick's startled face.

"Hey! What the—?" he sputtered. "Dammit, I'm going to get you for this one, McNeal!"

"Food fight!" someone in the cafeteria yelled, but it was quickly squelched.

One of the lunchroom monitors rushed over to investigate. Fortunately it was only Ms. Magnussen, a first-year teacher, so Nick and Quinn were able to pretend that what had happened was an accident and get away with it. Julie hoped Quinn would notice that Nick was no squealer.

As soon as Ms. Magnussen left, Quinn turned on his heel and left the cafeteria. Half sobbing, Julie followed him.

She found him in the parking lot, sitting in his car. She got in beside him.

"We need to talk," she said.

"You've been saying that a lot lately," he replied angrily.

Why did his mouth, that mouth she loved so, twist in a sneer when he said that?

"Yes, I know," she said, trying to sound reasonable and soothing. "But we never have. At least we've never gotten anywhere with it."

"So what do you want to tell me?"

"I don't want to *tell* you anything, Quinn. *Telling* isn't communicating. And we've got to communicate about this awful jealousy of yours."

"Jealousy? Jealousy has nothing to do with what that loser, Nick, did to us."

"That's what we have to talk about," Julie argued. "Nick had nothing to do with it. It was Tara. Tara's trying to break us up."

"What are you saying, Julie?"

"That it was Tara, not Nick, who wrote that note. But what really matters is the way you're acting. Can't you see? You're so jealous and possessive of me. It's gotten worse over the past couple of weeks, and I don't know what to do about it."

"I don't know what you've got to complain about," Quinn said sulkily. "I thought you'd like a guy who acts like he really cares about you."

"I do. Quinn, I love you, but—"

Quinn's sullen look disappeared. He smiled and tried to put his arms around her, but she moved away from him on the car seat.

"No. Please don't do that," she said quietly. "There's been too much of *that*. It only confuses the issue."

"Oh, come on, Julie. . . ."

"Listen to me, Quinn. It isn't good, this jealousy thing. We shouldn't let the fact that we're a couple cut us off from other activities and friendships at school."

Quinn's eyes flashed. "Are you telling me you want to go out with other guys?" he demanded hotly.

His face was wild. Crazy looking. Julie was frightened.

"No, of course not," she said hastily. "Why would I want to go out with someone else? You know how I feel about you. Why, you . . . you're . . . It's just that I think we have a problem we have to work out."

Quinn started the car. He revved the engine, his foot tromping heavily on the pedal.

"I'm out of here," he said curtly. "This conversation's crazy—and getting crazier. I need some space."

Julie got out of the car and went around to the driver's side. She put her head in the window for a good-bye kiss.

"I wish you'd stay and talk," she said.

Quinn didn't reply. He revved the motor again and suddenly the car shot forward. He sped out of the parking lot without a backward glance.

Julie was left standing, shocked. She'd barely had time to withdraw her head and shoulders from the window when he took off.

What if I hadn't? she asked herself, trembling. She pressed her hands to her cheekbones, imagining the crunch of bone if the side of the car had hit her.

I could have been hurt, she thought.

And what was that he shouted at her as he took off? It had been hard to hear him over the squealing of tires as he peeled away.

It sounded like, "Good-bye, Alison!"

The afternoon crept by slowly.

Julie wondered if she should go to the nurse's station and plead sick so she could go home.

She couldn't ever remember feeling this depressed. It almost hurt to draw a breath. She felt as if there were a tight band around her chest.

But if she did go home, there would be even more talk around school than there was now. No, she would make it through the day somehow, and hold her head high, too.

Brad came up to her after English lit and said, "Look, Julie, I was there in the cafeteria when Quinn did his fun-with-food thing."

Julie looked at him wearily. "So?"

"So I think you need a friend." He tapped his shoulder. "You're welcome to cry on this anytime you want, even if it means Quinn will come and rip my head off."

He spoke flippantly, the way he always did, but his blue eyes were gentle and concerned.

And to think I had him pegged for a conceited, stuck-up playboy, Julie thought sadly. *I guess he tried to be a friend all along, but I didn't see it that way.*

What a shame she wasn't in love with Brad, instead of Quinn. Wouldn't everything be easy then?

Brad seemed to read her thoughts. "You know, Julie, I wish I was able to act real cool and laid-back around you, the way Quinn does.

Then maybe it would be you and me, instead of you and him. But you're so pretty and sweet and totally lovable, that I get stupid whenever I'm around you. And so I just have to stand up and make a perfect fool of myself."

Julie laughed faintly, near tears. She leaned forward and kissed him lightly on his cheek. "Now, now, Brad. Nobody's perfect."

Brad smiled. But his voice was serious as he said, "Remember, Julie, if you ever want anybody to talk to, I'm here for you. And I'm good at keeping my mouth shut, too, about anything you say."

Julie resisted an urge to cry. Biting her lower lip to keep it from quivering, she said, "Thanks, Brad. You're a good friend. I might take you up on that sometime."

Julie waited all evening for Quinn to call, to apologize, to make things right between them, but the phone was silent.

She couldn't bear to think about how he'd revved his car and sped away like that, nearly ripping her head off.

She would have liked to talk to someone about it, but she was too ashamed. She almost felt as if it were her fault, as if she had done something to deserve the punishment Quinn had just given her.

How can I let some guy take advantage of me this way? she asked herself. Julie wanted no part of this. She didn't want to be anyone's victim.

By the time she reached school the next morning, she was seething with anger. How could she have let Quinn treat her like that?

To make matters worse, she overheard Nick telling everyone that this morning, when he went out to his car, he found his headlights bashed in. Julie didn't say anything, but she had a sickening feeling that Quinn was responsible.

She was at her locker when Quinn came up behind her, lifting her hair and kissing her on the nape of her neck. "Hi, sugar!"

He was behaving as if nothing had happened between them, an innocent smile on his face.

How could he? How dare he think he could treat her the way he had yesterday and then make everything all right with a kiss?

"Leave me alone, Quinn," Julie snapped. "I don't want to talk to you. You owe me an apology for what you did yesterday. And until you do, and until you're ready to sit down with me and talk out our problems, I'd prefer you leave me alone."

She slammed her locker shut, turned on her heel, and left.

Quinn stared after her, but she didn't look back.

CHAPTER TWENTY-ONE

Leave me alone.

Leave me alone, he thought. *Julie. My Julie, and she wants me to leave her alone.*

That was what Alison had said.

Is Julie going to betray me the way Alison did?

No. He refused to believe that. She'd just been a little upset, that was all. But what about? He couldn't remember. His mind was a blank. Yesterday—what happened yesterday— seemed fuzzy. He couldn't remember what he and Julie had done, and why she was angry with him.

He'd have to think about it, figure out what was wrong and what to do about it. No big thing. Julie loved him. Everything would be all right.

He couldn't think straight today, what with this pounding headache. . . .

Again he left school early and went home. Mr. Reed was sure to get him on this one.

Grady greeted him when he entered his apartment. What would he do without Grady?

He lay down on the bed, a cold cloth over his head and Grady nestled close beside him, and slept. His sleep was restless, marred by ugly, troubling dreams. Dreams of broken glass and screams. And blood. Lots of blood.

He awoke trembling and covered with sweat. Grady had wandered off somewhere. When he'd stopped shaking and got his breath under control again, Quinn got up, showered, and dressed. Then he left his apartment and drove over to Poco's Pizza, where he worked.

"Glad you could make it tonight, Quinn," his boss said. "We've got a lot of delivery orders."

One of his last deliveries was for a slumber party. *It must be a birthday*, Quinn thought, *being a weeknight and all*. Most slumber parties were on Friday or Saturday nights. And here it was, nearly midnight on a school night, and those kids were still up and bouncing around.

He pulled up before the house, a large, sprawling ranch style with a vast front picture

160

window. Suddenly he felt almost dizzy with a sense of déjà vu.

He remained in the car, staring through the window at the young girls in the living room, his pizzas growing cold on the seat beside him, the cheese hardening.

They were laughing, he noticed.

Alison and her friends were laughing at their slumber party that night, he thought. *Laughing at me. Laughing because they knew they'd made a real fool of me.*

"Leave me alone," Alison had said. But, of course, he couldn't do that. He'd loved her too much. And he'd been sure that some day soon she'd realize she loved him, too. That was the way with love, wasn't it?

So when he'd received that letter from Alison—and he'd been sure it was her handwriting—he was deliriously happy. Hadn't he known all along that things would turn out this way?

In her letter Alison said she was sorry for the mean things she'd said to him and promised she'd make it all up to him if he'd meet her after dark in the local park, in an isolated spot where the older kids went to make out.

His heart had been beating wildly when he arrived at the park. He could hardly wait to see

Alison. Could hardly wait to tell her how much he loved her.

And then, suddenly, he'd been seized from behind. Alison was nowhere in sight, nor were her silly girlfriends. He was being yanked and dragged around by some big, husky jock types. He knew who they were, even though they wore ski masks. They were three of those older guys Alison and her friends ran around with.

"We're not going to hurt you, kid," one said. "We only want to teach you a little lesson. And you know what that is, don't you?"

He couldn't answer. He was being held too tightly around the neck by a burly arm.

"Well," the voice went on, "since you don't know, I'll have to tell you. The lesson is that in the future, when a girl says to leave her alone, you leave her alone, okay?"

"We're talking about Alison," another said. "She's asked you nicely to bug off, but you won't do it."

Although Quinn put up a fight, he was thrown to the ground. Two of his captors pinned down his arms and shoulders while the third unhooked Quinn's belt and yanked his jeans off.

Then they ran away, carrying his jeans, leaving him there humiliated and half-naked, to make his way home as best he could without being seen.

When he finally reached his house, he was in a terrible state. Alison—his beautiful Alison—had been in on the terrible thing that had just happened to him. She'd written that letter. She'd schemed with that bunch to make a fool of him, and they were probably all together now, laughing at him.

He dressed quickly and got into his father's pickup truck. His father wasn't home. Probably out somewhere with his drinking buddies.

Quinn was too young to drive. Too young for a license, but he knew how to change gears, what pedals to push. He started the motor, and the truck lurched down the street.

He drove toward Alison's house.

All the lights in the house were burning brightly. He drove past slowly, looking in.

It was a sprawling, ranch-style house, with a huge picture window in the living room that looked out over a long, level lawn.

He could see right into the living room. Alison and three of her girlfriends were moving about the room. They were laughing. He was sure they were laughing at him, making fun of him, saying what a fool he was.

Then something came over him. Something he couldn't control.

A red haze swam before his eyes, and before he realized what he was doing, he'd backed the truck up the length of the street, floored the gas pedal, and came at Alison's house at top speed, driving across the lawn and hitting the picture window with a shattering force.

The truck came to a halt against an inner wall of the living room. He saw two of the girls cowering in the corner, screaming. The third was kneeling on the floor crying, and bleeding from the many wounds inflicted by the flying glass.

And Alison . . .

He looked for the girl he loved. He felt his heart wrench, twist, nearly push its way out of his body when he saw her.

She was lying on the floor, a terrible, bloodless shade of white. A large shard of glass, like a crystal dagger, was embedded in her throat.

The truck door was twisted and jammed, but he managed to wrench it open and make his way through the debris of the living room to Alison's side.

She was dead. Alison was dead. He'd killed her.

His lip was bleeding and his head hurt from the blow he'd received in the crash. He felt dizzy. Everything seemed unreal to him.

He was sobbing uncontrollably when the police arrived. . . .

Quinn found himself crying now as he remembered it, just as he had cried four years before.

But Alison did betray me, he thought. I didn't want to believe it at the time, but she did.

The guys in The Place told me that was always the way it was. Even the best ones could get tripped up by a girl. They said nobody believes it, though. Everybody thinks the one he's in love with is perfect. Can do no wrong.

So what about Julie? Will she be like Alison? No, Julie loves me. She'd not faking it. I know she loves me. And yet lately . . .

No. Julie's the real thing. She's my second chance at happiness. My chance to finally do it right. I hurt her somehow, can't remember how, but I have to make it up to her. Somehow.

He started his car and drove away, his pizza undelivered.

CHAPTER TWENTY-TWO

"I've got to see you, Julie. I'm about to go crazy thinking about you." Quinn's voice was low. Sincere. Repentant.

Julie sat up in bed and propped a pillow behind her back. "Quinn, do you know what time it is?" she whispered into the phone.

"I know, but I couldn't sleep. I wondered if maybe you were lying there thinking about me, too."

She had been, but she didn't want to admit that to him. She didn't want to give him any more power over her than he already had. She was still angry with him.

"So what do you want?" she asked coldly.

"I told you. I need to see you. I need to see you real bad."

"Why?"

Julie's voice was remote, hostile, but it was a growing struggle to keep it that way. The sound of his voice over the phone was giving her the usual fluttery, shivery feelings.

"Because I've got so much to tell you. Things have gone bad between us, but I love you, Julie. And I want everything to be the way it was before."

Julie didn't reply, so Quinn said, "I could come over right now, if you'd let me."

"No, not now," she told him quickly. "What would you do, crawl in my window again?"

"Well, maybe you could come out and we could drive somewhere," he suggested.

Julie pulled the covers over her head, so that she and the telephone were in a little tent, a soundproofed cocoon. She was sure Mollie was asleep, but didn't want to take any chances. What she had to say to Quinn was private. Very private.

"Look, Quinn," she said. "I don't think that's a good idea."

"You looked so beautiful that time I came in your window," Quinn said dreamily. "Your face was scrubbed and shiny, and your hair was hanging down your back. I couldn't keep my hands off you."

"That's why it isn't a good idea for us to see each other right now," Julie said sharply.

She took a deep breath and continued. "You know, Quinn, you and I don't do the usual things kids our age do on a date. We don't hang out with a crowd or go to parties. We're always alone, just you and me."

"I thought you liked it that way," he protested.

"I did. I do." she said. "I mean, I like being alone with you, and that's the problem. There's such a thing as too much aloneness."

"Not for two people like us," Quinn said.

"Especially for two people like us," Julie insisted. "What do we do on a date? We go someplace in your car and then we sit and park. And then you start kissing me and I sort of blank out about things—important things like the fact that we don't really know each other. Why can't we do things with other kids? And why can't we talk about it? Why *can't* we discuss your jealousy, Quinn? It's getting worse. It scares me. You acted like a crazy man yesterday."

"Wait a minute," Quinn said. "Let's talk about this kissing in the car stuff, Julie. You know I'd never do anything you didn't want."

"That's the trouble. I do want it. The kissing. The being close to you."

"So," he said, "then what are we doing wrong?"

Julie sighed. "We aren't doing anything wrong, Quinn. It's just that this physical attraction we have for each other is always the center of every date. And if I sneaked out tonight to be with you, we wouldn't talk. You know we wouldn't."

"So what are you saying we should do?"

"I'm saying let's make a date for tomorrow night. A real, old-fashioned date, none of this out-of-the-way parking stuff. Early dinner, maybe. Sixish. It's a school night, remember, and Mom's started cracking down on my curfew. The Calico Giraffe would be nice. It's quiet and cozy. We can sit in a back booth and talk. Only talk."

"Is that what you really want, Julie?"

"It's what *we* really *need*, Quinn."

When Quinn picked her up Wednesday night, Julie was surprised to see a large, fat old cat in the backseat.

"Is this Grady?" she asked. "The famous Grady? I thought I'd never have the honor of meeting him."

She felt so happy, so lighthearted. Grady, Quinn's beloved cat, was a good omen. She had a feeling in her bones that the old cat would bring them good luck. They'd work things out tonight, she and Quinn, she just knew it. They were special. Their love was special. They would talk out their problems and then live happily ever after.

Quinn looked over the back of his seat at Grady, who was gazing out the window, the very picture of injured dignity.

"I hope you don't mind me bringing Grady, but I hated leaving him at home," Quinn said. "I had to take him to the vet's this afternoon for his shots, and he's kind of mad at me. So I figured he'd feel better if I let him come in the car with us."

Julie liked the tenderhearted way Quinn cared for his cat. She deliberately closed her mind to the way he'd acted on Monday, when he'd driven off so abruptly.

The Calico Giraffe was on the same street as the popular local hamburger hangout, and Quinn, who obviously had never been to either before, seemed surprised, then upset at their proximity.

"What's going on, Julie?" he asked suspiciously. "How come you always have to have your buddies close by for backup?"

"Please don't do this," she pleaded. "Don't start in on your jealousy routine again." She reached over and took his hand. "This is the sort of thing we have to talk about, Quinn."

Where was my head when I picked this restaurant for our date? Julie asked herself. *I ought to know that the least little thing sets him off these days. I should have found a place in another part of town. Tara and some of the gang might be hanging out around here, and Quinn is bound to make a scene.*

She'd even overheard Tara and a couple of the others making plans to grab some fast food and then go over to Tara's house. How could she have forgotten? Mr. and Mrs. Braxton were out of town for a few days, so Tara had the place to herself.

Julie knew what that meant—a little party in Tara's famous hot tub. She'd been invited to those parties often enough and had always refused. She was afraid Tara was going to suggest skinny-dipping, and the thought filled her with horror.

As Quinn pulled into a parking spot right across the street from the Calico Giraffe, Julie

171

looked around anxiously for any familiar cars. Much to her relief, she saw none.

Quinn turned off the ignition. "Watch out for Grady," he warned as she opened the door on her side of the car. "He likes to run off to do his thing, and then he gets lost, dumb cat."

Too late. Before Julie could draw the door closed, Grady had slipped past her, his warm, soft fur grazing her ankles, and was now bounding down the middle of the street.

"Grady! Get back here!" Quinn called.

"Grady!" Julie echoed. Then, as she saw an all-too-familiar dark-green sportscar approaching, she called more urgently this time, "Grady!"

But Grady didn't stop.

The green car was traveling fast, and the driver evidently didn't see the cat loping toward it down the center of the street.

"Grady!" Quinn screamed.

There was a thump and a screech of brakes.

Then silence. A terrible silence.

Grady lay at the edge of the street where he'd been flung by the force of the impact. He wasn't moving. A thin line of blood trickled from his nose.

Julie and Quinn ran over to the cat. Quinn dropped to his knees beside it.

"He's dead," Quinn said, picking up the cat in his arms and cradling it, rocking it.

Then, his voice cold and menacing, he said, "They killed Grady."

He said it again, as if he couldn't believe it. "They killed Grady. Murdered him."

Julie knew who "they" were. Tara, for one. It was her little green sportscar that hit Grady, and she'd been behind the wheel.

In a dim recess of her mind, she watched Tara, Nick, Shelley, and Colin get out of the car and come toward them. They seemed to be walking in slow motion, every step taking an eternity.

Finally the four of them reached Quinn and Julie.

"It wasn't my fault," Tara burst out. "I didn't see that cat until it was too late. It just came out of nowhere."

Quinn turned his head and gave her a look of cold loathing. "He didn't come out of nowhere. He was in the middle of the street. You might have seen him in time if you hadn't been speeding. And if you'd had your stupid eyes on the road."

"Now look, Quinn," Colin said, putting his hand on Quinn's shoulder. "I know how you must be feeling right now, but—"

Quinn angrily shook him off. "No, you don't. You don't know how I'm feeling right now. If you did, you wouldn't be standing here. You'd be running like hell."

"Is that some kind of threat?" Tara demanded.

"It's not a threat," Quinn told her. The expression on his face made her take a step backward. "I ought to kill you for what you just did."

"Quinn, please!" Julie cried, pulling on his sleeve.

Quinn ignored her.

"Did you hear me?" he asked Tara. "I'd like to see you dead for this."

"He's gone nuts," Nick said. "Let's get out of here before he does something crazy!"

"But isn't there something we should do?" Shelley protested.

Colin took her arm and pulled her away, toward the car where Tara and Nick were already headed. "Maybe later, when Quinn's got a grip."

They drove off slowly, almost reverently, as if by doing so they could being Grady back from the dead.

A crowd had gathered. The shrieking of the brakes and the drama being played out roadside had attracted a lot of attention. Kids milled around staring, eavesdropping.

"Did you hear what he said?" someone asked. "He wanted to kill that girl."

Julie ignored them.

"It wasn't Tara's fault, Quinn," she said, her lips close to his ear. "It was an accident. Grady was in the middle of the street. Tara didn't see him."

It was like talking to a deaf man.

Finally, gently, she raised Quinn from the ground, her hand on his elbow.

He still clutched Grady to him, his shirt stained with patches of blood.

Julie led him to his car and put him in the backseat with Grady.

The keys were still in the ignition. "You'll have to tell me how to get to your place, Quinn," she said.

Absently, he directed her. She had to ask him at every corner, "Do I keep going, or is this where I turn?"

They finally reached his house. It was a large old Victorian, with gingerbread trim. Quinn indicated, with a nod of his head, his entrance at the side.

Julie opened the door with a key she located

on the ring with the car keys. She stepped back, letting Quinn enter first.

He snapped on a wall switch with his elbow. Then he walked across the room and laid Grady on the sofa.

The apartment, Julie noted, was small and dark, but she was surprised to see how comfortably and tastefully Quinn had arranged it. And it was tidy. Books—there were a lot of them—were lined up according to size in the floor-to-ceiling bookcase, the sofa pillows were plumped up in each corner of the sofa, and the table was waxed and shining.

Julie drifted around the room, not knowing what to do. Quinn was sitting on the sofa beside Grady, lost in a world of his own.

Julie's eyes fell on a color photo propped on the coffee table. At first she thought it was a picture of herself—the resemblance was that strong. But on closer inspection she realized it was someone else.

It was a school picture of a young girl, a girl of about fourteen, and she was smiling into the camera.

Her coloring was the same as Julie's. She had the same long golden-brown hair, and the delicately featured oval of her face closely resembled Julie's.

But what was most amazing were her eyes. They were large and slightly tilted and amber-brown, just like Julie's.

Julie felt as if she were looking at a picture of herself taken two years ago.

She turned to Quinn for an explanation of this mysterious look-alike. But the minute she saw his face, the question died on her lips.

Quinn had picked up Grady in his arms again and had moved to an armchair, one that rocked and swiveled, and was rocking Grady, crooning over him, the way a mother does over a sick baby. There was a wild light in his eyes.

"Quinn," Julie said softly. "We have to bury Grady. You can't keep him . . . like this."

There were spots of blood on the sofa. It was amazing, Julie thought, how such a little bit of blood coming from Grady's mouth had dripped so much on Quinn's shirt and the sofa.

"We could bury him in your backyard, maybe," Julie went on. "Under a bush. That would be nice, wouldn't it, Quinn?"

There was no reply. Quinn sat, rocking, his face distant and brooding.

Julie stayed with Quinn for another hour. Or maybe it was two hours. She had no way of judging time in this shadow world of grief. Quinn didn't look at her once.

Finally, realizing there was nothing she could do, no way of making contact with Quinn, she decided to leave.

Maybe he'll feel better if I leave him alone, she thought.

She called a taxi. When it arrived, she went over to Quinn and said, "I'm leaving now, but I'll come back first thing tomorrow. Call me if you need me."

Quinn gave no sign that he'd heard her.

CHAPTER TWENTY-THREE

Her hands were trembling when she paid the taxi driver.

"Have a nice evening," he said.

As she climbed the front steps, Julie realized that her legs were trembling, too.

She was frightened. Terrified. Something was wrong, terribly wrong with Quinn, and there was nothing she could do about it.

Julie couldn't stop thinking about that look on Quinn's face when he'd turned to Tara and said, "I ought to kill you for what you just did." She felt the hairs on her arms stand on end just remembering it. She wondered if she should call somebody—a doctor, maybe. But what would she say? That her friend was acting extremely grief-stricken because his cat had just been run over? No doctor would be willing to pay a house call for something like that. She let herself into the house and walked slowly up the stairs.

"Julie? Are you okay?"

Mollie stood on the landing, looking curiously at her sister.

"How come you're home so early?" she asked. "I thought you had a date with Quinn."

"Oh, Mollie," Julie began, then burst into tears. "It was awful. Just awful!"

The story came spilling out: the date that was supposed to be their chance to work out their problems. Then Tara running the cat down. And how Quinn had acted.

"And now," Julie concluded, blowing her nose, "he's just sitting there like a zombie, holding Grady."

They were in the kitchen now, sharing a pot of instant cocoa that Mollie had hastily prepared. Ever since they were little, this had been their standard cure for injury and heartbreak.

"He didn't want to talk to you?" Mollie asked.

"No. He acted like I wasn't even there."

"Then I don't know what more you can do, Julie. Maybe he just needs some time alone."

"What really worries me though, Mollie, is

the way he looked at Tara. He was so mad at her. I was afraid he was going to hit her or something."

Mollie was silent. Finally she said, "I heard about what Quinn did to Nick in the cafeteria Monday—the whole school did. I was afraid to ask you about it."

Julie raised her head and looked at Mollie. "Ask me *what* about it?"

Mollie shifted uneasily in her chair. "Well, I guess I wanted to know if he's that hot-tempered all the time."

"Oh, no. No," Julie said hastily. "He and Nick just have this feud going, that's all."

"Is that what you two were fighting about last weekend?"

Julie was stunned. "What do you know about that?"

"A lot more than you think, Julie. I know Quinn was in your room Friday night, for starters. And I know you were arguing about something. I could tell you didn't want anyone to know he was here, so I didn't say anything about it."

Julie took a deep breath and then let it out slowly. "You don't miss a thing, Mollie."

"No, and I've been worrying about you and

Quinn," Mollie said. "I mean, you don't know very much about him, do you?"

"Yes, of course I do," Julie said. "Maybe not *everything* . . ."

"I mean, about his family, and where he was before he came to Braxton Falls. Has he told you anything about that?"

"Well, he did tell me about his father's death, and that his father abused him when he was a child," Julie said. "His mother left him and his father when Quinn was just a baby. It was all so awful, Mollie. I hated to make him think about it. And where he lived before didn't seem that important to me. I figured he'd tell me about it someday."

"Do you know when his father died?" Mollie asked abruptly.

"Yeah. It was only a few days after Quinn came to Jefferson High. Why?"

"So that would make it when? The middle of September?"

"Yes. I think it was around the thirteenth. Why?"

"Well," Mollie said, "there would have to be an obituary for the father, wouldn't there?"

"I suppose so, but—"

"Obituaries usually tell something about the

person. You know, his past, his family. That sort of thing," Mollie said.

"Do you really think you can find out about Quinn and his family from his father's obituary?" Julie asked. "I don't know, Mollie. I don't want to invade Quinn's privacy."

Mollie leaned across the table, waving her cup.

"Look, Julie, if this guy's going to be my brother-in-law someday—and from the way you carry on about him, he just *might*—then I have a right to snoop a little into his family's past. What if he has a cousin with two heads or something?"

"That wouldn't make a bit of difference to me," Julie said.

"If *Quinn* had two heads, it probably wouldn't make any difference to you."

"Are you going to use that new computer program of yours?" Julie asked. "The one that gives you access to old newspaper files?"

"Sure. Tommy and I use it all the time."

"Quinn's father lived in Middledale, though, Mollie. It's a really small town—I don't think it even *has* a paper."

"That doesn't matter," Mollie explained. "The Richmond papers usually pick up obits and news items and things like that from the smaller towns."

Julie took her cup to the sink and rinsed it out, then set it carefully in the drying rack. "I'm still not sure about this—it seems like spying."

"Since when is reading a man's obituary spying?"

"Well, okay. But count me out—I don't think I want to help you with this."

"Suit yourself," Mollie said. "You'd probably only push the wrong key, anyway."

"Julie! Julie, wake up!"

Mollie was leaning over her, shaking her.

Julie didn't know what time it was. She'd lain down on her bed with a book but kept reading the same page over and over again until she'd fallen asleep.

"What's wrong? And what time is it?"

"It's only nine. You haven't been asleep long. I have to show you something." There was a note of urgency in Mollie's voice that immediately brought Julie out of her daze. She slipped off the bed and followed Mollie to her room.

"I was right about the Richmond papers carrying news items from the smaller towns,"

Mollie told her, seating herself in front of her computer.

"News? I thought you were looking up an obituary."

"I was," Mollie said grimly. "But it led to more."

She shoved a computer printout into Julie's hand. "Here's an article about Mr. McNeal's death."

Julie obediently took the paper and began to read aloud.

"R. J. McNeal of Middledale, Virginia, was found dead yesterday, presumably of a fall down a flight of stairs in his home—"

Julie paused and looked up. "This is nothing new, Mollie. Quinn told me this."

"Keep reading," Mollie commanded.

"In order to rule out the possibility of foul play, McNeal's eighteen-year-old son was called in for questioning by the local police—"

She stopped reading again. "Quinn told me this, too. He said something about his father hitting his head so hard at the bottom of the stairs that the police thought maybe he'd been pushed. They ruled the death an accident, though."

"But there's more," Mollie said. "Things I don't think he's ever told you."

Julie picked up the paper again.

"Neighbors revealed that they were aware of several instances of loud quarreling between the two men, and that the son was known to have a violent temper. One neighbor confided that the son had recently been released from a juvenile correctional facility, where he had spent four years' confinement in connection with the manslaughter death of a young girl named Alison Barry. . . ."

Julie slumped down onto Mollie's bed. Her head was spinning and she was afraid she was going to faint.

Mollie dashed into the bathroom and reappeared with a wet washcloth. Julie laid it against her forehead.

"Thanks, Mollie. I'm okay now. It was just the shock."

"I couldn't believe it, either, Julie. Quinn, guilty of manslaughter!"

"There has to be a mistake," Julie said. "Quinn couldn't possibly do something like that!"

But even as she said this, Julie again had an unwelcome image. *"I ought to kill you for what you just did,"* Quinn had told Tara. *And the expression on his face when he said it!*

"I can't understand it," Mollie said. "He must have been only fourteen years old when he killed . . . when it happened. Her name was Alison. . . ." Mollie's voice trailed away.

Alison. The girl's name was Alison. What did Quinn call me that day in the parking lot when he gunned the car and roared away? Alison? Was that it? "Good-bye, Alison." Yes, that's what he shouted at me. But I didn't think either of us knew a girl named Alison.

"Is there any way we can find the newspaper article about the death?" Julie asked.

"I already did," Mollie said. "I'm not sure you should see it, though."

Julie silently held out her hand for the printout.

"Quinn's name wasn't used, of course," Mollie said. "He was legally a minor, and they never release the name of any minor who commits a crime."

"I know," Julie said. She smoothed the paper nervously on her knee, working up the courage to look at it.

Alison had been killed by a flying shard of glass, the article said.

"A male classmate," Julie read, "who had been stalking her and pressing unwanted attentions on her, in a fit of rage and jealousy, drove a pickup truck through the large picture window of the girl's home, killing her and seriously wounding her three companions. . . ." Julie's voice trailed off, and she looked at Mollie in horror.

Quinn, a killer? The thought made her feel sick.

Julie tried to imagine him at fourteen, angry and embittered enough to drive a car through the window of someone's house. But he hadn't meant to kill Alison. That was something Julie was sure of. He'd been angry, out of control, but not a cold-blooded killer. And he'd been so young.

He must have loved Alison very much. But to get that angry—mad enough to kill—wasn't normal. She couldn't believe that of Quinn. Julie looked up at her sister, her face deathly pale. Mollie eyed her anxiously.

"What time does the library close tonight?" Julie asked.

"It stays open until eleven. Why?"

"They must have all the back issues of the local papers," Julie answered, getting to her feet. "I want—I *have* to read all the local coverage of the killing. I have to see the pictures. Everything."

"Then I'm going with you," Mollie told her.

*   *   *

It didn't take the librarian long to find the issues of the small local papers that Julie had requested. The details were the same in all the issues.

And the pictures of Alison, the dead girl, were all the same—a school photograph of a smiling young girl.

Julie recognized it immediately. It was the one Quinn had on the table in his apartment.

Again she had that sensation of spinning, of faintness.

Mollie was peering over her shoulder.

"My god, Julie, she looks just like you!"

The faintness passed, and suddenly Julie could see everything very clearly. Why Quinn had stared at her so intently that first day. And why he'd fallen in love with her so quickly. Why he'd followed her at school, stalked her, always there, always watching her.

Those long, brooding looks. The way he touched her. All because she reminded him of Alison, the girl he'd killed.

He's not in love with me, Julie realized with a feeling of aching betrayal.

Quinn is in love with the ghost of Alison Barry.

CHAPTER TWENTY-FOUR

He knew now what he had to do.

Gently, he laid Grady on the bed and left his apartment, closing the door softly behind him.

She was evil. Tara was evil.

Why hadn't he seen it before?

She'd been masterminding a conspiracy to hurt Julie and him, the way Alison's girlfriends had four years ago.

Yes, Tara had been plotting secretly with the others, telling those rich guys with their sneaky eyes to come on to Julie, so that they could make a fool of him and set him up for some kind of cruel trick, like those jocks did in the park that time.

And then get him to kill Julie, just as he'd killed Alison!

Julie had tried to warn him about Tara, but he hadn't listened. He'd been too jealous, too stirred up to see that these so-called friends of Julie's were playing the same sort of murderous games as Alison's had.

But Tara overplayed her hand when she deliberately ran down Grady. She'd thought she could scare Quinn McNeal, push him around. But she hadn't succeeded. He didn't scare anymore, and all these hours sitting here, holding Grady in his arms, had given him time to think, and he'd figured everything out.

If only he didn't have this headache. This pounding and pounding in his head, as if somebody were in there, beating on his skull. Maybe that was one of Tara's tricks, too. She was evil. Yes, that must be it. Well, it would stop, then, the minute he did what needed to be done.

He laughed softly as he climbed into his car and started the engine. It would be easy, so easy. He knew where they were, Tara and her bunch, the ones who'd killed Grady and were plotting to destroy Julie and him. He'd heard them at school, planning their intimate little party at Tara's house. He'd even heard Tara say with a suggestive giggle that her parents wouldn't be home.

He drove up Tara's long, winding driveway and parked boldly in front of the house. Why hide? He was doing the right thing, after all, protecting Julie from danger.

The front door was open, so he didn't have to jimmy the lock the way one of the guys at The Place had shown him.

He walked through the vast, palatial rooms, listening for *their* voices. Maybe downstairs. Yeah, down where she had her party that night.

He hated them for what they had done and for what they were planning to do. He could feel his rage building, building, as he went down the stairs.

When he reached the bottom, his hands were trembling with fury.

They will pay for this, he vowed silently. *Pay dearly*.

He could hear laughing. He followed the sound down a hall and into the games room with its antique pool table and overhead Tiffany-style light.

On the far side of the room, French doors opened out upon a partially enclosed deck.

They were out there. He could hear high-pitched giggles and the splashing of water.

They were in the hot tub, all four of them, and their backs were toward him.

He stood in the shadows for a moment, deciding what to do next.

The water in the hot tub was warm and bubbling. Steam rose from it, but it was chilly on the deck itself.

He glanced over and saw a portable electric heater, glowing red. Nearby, a pile of clothing was scattered about.

His lip curled with disgust.

What trash, he thought.

He looked again at the electric heater on its long, coiled cord.

He walked quietly over to the heater, picked it up, and called to the group in the tub, "Hey! Remember me?"

He laughed aloud when he saw them turn, startled. Saw the expression of fear that came over each stupid, gawking face.

It was Nick, though, who was the first to realize what Quinn was about to do.

"No, Quinn! Put that heater down. Please, man!"

Then Tara started to whimper. She tried to get to her feet but slipped and fell back into the water.

"This one's for Julie," he called out, and hurled the heater into the hot tub.

There was a sizzling, popping noise. Then sparks and a blue flame.

The four of them began to scream and throw themselves around in the water.

Dancing, he thought, watching them with a satisfied smile. *They look like they're dancing. Hey, they're good. Really good.*

Finally they fell back, unmoving, into the water.

He jerked the heater cord unplugged, ignoring the shock that ran through his arm. Then he circled the tub, pushing their heads under the water for good measure. *Just to make sure*, he told himself. *Better safe than sorry. Anything worth doing is worth doing well.*

He took one long, last look from the doorway as he left.

It was quiet now on the deck, except for the gurgling of the hot tub. It continued to swirl festive little bubbles over the dead limbs of the four bodies bobbing facedown in the moving water.

CHAPTER TWENTY-FIVE

TEEN HOT-TUB SLAYINGS
PRIME SUSPECT STILL AT LARGE

BRAXTON FALLS—The body of their daughter, Tara, and three of her friends, identified as Nick Wells, Colin King, and Shelley Molino, all of this city, were discovered by Mr. and Mrs. Prescott Braxton late Thursday afternoon, upon their return from an out-of-town trip.

The victims, all in their teens, had been electrocuted in the family hot tub.

Although the possibility of accident has not been ruled out, it is, according to local police, highly unlikely.

"A large electric heater was present in the tub and apparently caused the deaths," stated Sheriff James "Dusty" Rhoades, who was first on the scene following a call from the distraught parents. "There is every indication of foul play."

Being sought in connection with the deaths is Quinn McNeal, also of this city and a schoolmate of the victims at Jefferson High School.

According to witnesses, McNeal directed forceful death threats toward the victims, following an incident in which Tara Braxton accidentally ran over and killed McNeal's cat.

"It was terrible, the way he looked at her and said, 'I ought to kill you for what you did,' and, 'I'll see you dead for this,'" stated eyewitness Violet Purdy, who was at the scene at the time. "He had such an awful expression on his face, too, when he said it."

McNeal's fingerprints were found on the Braxtons' front door and on the French doors that lead to the deck and hot tub.

McNeal was recently released from the Juvenile Correctional Facility at Mayfield, Virginia, where he spent four years' confinement in connection with the manslaughter death of a young girl.

McNeal was also questioned recently concerning the death of his father, R. J. McNeal of Middledale, Virginia. He was, however, released when the death was judged to be the result of an accident. The elder McNeal had fallen down the stairs of his home. Death was caused by a head injury and was instantaneous.

Although a massive manhunt has been launched, McNeal cannot be located. His car, a white 1987 Plymouth coupe, is missing. When police searched his apartment, they found the dead body of a large cat lying on the suspect's bed. The cat has been subsequently identified as the one accidentally run over by the car driven by Tara Braxton.

CHAPTER TWENTY-SIX

Ten days had passed since Braxton Falls was rocked by what was now being called "The Hot-Tub Massacre."

It was Halloween. Darkness had fallen. The small children of Braxton Falls, carefully chaperoned by watchful parents, had finished their trick-or-treating during daylight hours and were now home, happily gorging themselves on candy.

It had been a rough ten days.

Julie thought of herself as dead. Her past life, her old friends, the way she'd loved Quinn, were things that should be carved on her tombstone.

The only problem was that, at least technically, she was still alive.

Every morning she'd awaken with a feeling

of despair, knowing she had yet another sad, purposeless day to drag herself through.

On Thursday, the morning after Grady's death, Julie had tried to phone Quinn. She wanted to talk to him before she told her parents what had happened. Before they found out about his past.

There was a question she needed to ask him that couldn't wait. Only one question—the only one that mattered. Had he really loved her? All those times when he'd held her in his arms and told her so, had he meant it, or was he thinking only of Alison?

Julie had felt like a fool as she dialed his number, remembering the way she'd opened herself up to him. The times she'd told him of her intense feelings for him.

She was almost glad when the phone rang and rang and no one answered. She'd looked for him at school, but he wasn't there. And then, that night, she'd heard about the murders. Quinn, a prime suspect, had disappeared.

It was on the six o'clock news. The Braxtons had called the police immediately upon discovery of the bodies.

Julie spent that night and all the next day under sedation. Her mother had called in the family doctor, who'd prescribed something that made her feel sleepy and woozy.

She roused herself from bed only once, to talk to the police, but wasn't able to tell them anything they didn't already know.

Then Julie went back to bed and let Mollie give her a pill that allowed her to float off to a land where everything was pink and beautiful.

The only trouble with pills like that, she soon discovered, is that they make waking up even harder.

She would open her eyes and remember Quinn, and then her heart would start pounding again.

Her mother would appear, fleetingly, at her bedside every now and then, talking about how Julie could have been killed by this maniac. How he'd fooled them all with his perfect manners while, underneath it all, he was a cold-blooded killer!

In a small town like Braxton Falls, any unusual occurrence was a big event. The brutal deaths of four teenagers nearly turned the town upside down.

Grief counseling was available at the high school. Funeral services, attended by hundreds, were held for the four teenagers.

For the first few days people walked in fear, locking doors and not going out at night in case the murderer might be lurking about, ready to kill them, too.

And then the news broke, to everyone's relief, that Quinn had been sighted in southern Virginia, in the mountains just across the border from North Carolina. The net, the police assured everyone, was closing on him. They'd have him soon.

Julie hoped Quinn would escape capture. She knew she'd never see him again, that he wouldn't dare show his face in Braxton Falls for fear of being caught. What he had done was loathsome and unforgivable, but still she hoped he wouldn't be caught.

I can't help it, she thought. *I can't bear the thought of Quinn in prison again. It would be for life this time.* He'd been locked up for four years, and she didn't know how he'd been able to survive even that.

Why, Quinn? she asked herself over and over again. *Why did it have to be this way?*

That Halloween night the neighborhood was quiet, except for the older kids.

Julie was well enough now, the doctor had said, to return to school. She'd been dreading it, dreading the curious stares and whispers. But on Halloween, her first day back, it wasn't like that at all. The other kids were sympathetic and helpful. As Brad said, "You have more friends than you think you do, Julie. At least, they're willing to be your friends if you'll let them."

Because of the deaths, the annual Halloween dance at the high school was canceled, and since many of the students had already had costumes made, groups of them were going from door to door, overgrown trick-or-treaters.

Julie was alone in the house, to her relief. Much as she loved them, she needed a break from her family. Both her parents and Mollie kept telling her she ought to "talk it out," get it out of her system. But Julie wasn't ready for that yet. She hadn't even been able to cry about it. Everyone always said that tears were healing. Well, she wasn't healed yet. Maybe she never would be.

A couple of kids from school, boys, came to the door, and Julie tried to talk and even laugh a little with them. She knew she at least had to *act* normal, even if she didn't feel that way.

Her parents were next door at a party, and Mollie was out with her friend, Tommy. Julie hoped none of them felt they had to rush home just to be with her. They cared about her, and she was grateful for that, but right now she simply wanted to be alone, not with others hovering over her, wanting progress reports on the hoped-for lessening of her grief.

She went to the window and looked out at the dark street, playing with the cord that pulled the drapes.

Across the street someone in a skeleton costume was loitering under a tree. She could see him by the light of the streetlamp. She wondered idly which of her schoolmates he was and who he was waiting for. She hoped he wouldn't come over here. Maybe she should turn off the porch and foyer lights. He might think no one was home and pass her house by.

Before she could, though, the phone rang.

It was Brad. Sweet, thoughtful Brad.

He'd stuck close to her at school, meeting her between classes and taking her off campus to lunch.

"Why are you doing this, Brad?" she'd asked him.

"Don't you know?" he replied.

"Look, I appreciate what you're doing, but I'm not ready for someone else right now," she'd said apologetically. "I might never feel that way about someone again. I'm sorry, Brad, but it's only fair to tell you that, so you won't waste any more time on me."

And then Brad had looked at her, his blue eyes bright and hard. "No time spent with you, Julie, is wasted. You'll get through this someday, and when you do, I'll be ready and waiting. And even if you don't, I'll still be here for you."

That had made her cry, and he'd patted her awkwardly.

Funny how she could cry over little things, like a sudden, unexpected kindness, when she had no tears for the thing that gnawed away at her night and day.

"Do you have a lot of trick-or-treaters?" Brad was asking now.

"We did earlier. Now I'm getting the high-school kids. I guess they want to get some wear out of the costumes they made for the dance."

"Maybe canceling the dance was a bad idea," Brad said. "This whole town needs to get back to normal as soon as possible. But then, it's only been ten days."

Ten days, ten years. Some of us will never get back to normal, Julie thought hopelessly.

"I'd love to come over, if you'd let me," Brad said.

"Thanks, but no. I'm kind of tired. I was just about to go to bed when you called."

There was a slight hesitation on the other end of the line.

"You're sure you're okay?" Brad asked.

"I'm fine. Really. But thanks."

The doorbell rang. Then again, impatiently.

"Uh-oh, the door. Gotta go now, Brad.

"Okay. Sleep tight."

If I only could.

"Who's there?" Julie asked before opening the door.

"Death," said a muffled voice.

What a bore these Halloweeners are, she thought with a resigned sigh.

She opened the door and the figure in the skeleton costume pushed her aside, came into the foyer, and closed the door behind him.

He removed his mask.

Julie gasped and had to put her hand against the wall to support herself. Her knees buckled, and her heart was beating at twice its normal rate.

"Quinn!" she whispered. "But they said you were miles away . . . down by the state border!"

He smiled. The thin white scar that bisected his upper lip gave him the fierce, dashing look of a pirate when he smiled like that. How she'd loved kissing that scar, that pirate's smile . . . once.

"Yeah, I fooled them, the jerks. They must have seen someone who looked like me. No, I've been living out in the woods, waiting for things to cool down so I could come back for you."

"Come . . . come back for me?" Julie echoed faintly.

"Of course. Didn't you think I would?" He tried to pull her to him, but she struggled free.

"No, wait a minute, Quinn. Tara and the rest. Did you . . . are you really the . . ."

Her lips were stiff. She could barely move them. She couldn't say the word "murderer."

"Yes," he said calmly. "I killed them. I had to. I did it for you. For us."

"For *us*? How can you say that? You didn't do it for me, or for us. How could you do something like that? It's so awful. I've been sick for days, thinking about it and hoping—*praying*—that something would happen and we would find out it hadn't been you, after all."

Quinn seemed surprised. "But they had to die. They were evil and they had to die. They were as bad as my father."

206

"Your father? What's he got to do with it?"

"You mean you haven't guessed? You really didn't know I killed my father?"

Julie pressed her knuckles to her lips to keep them from trembling. Her voice was faint. "No. I didn't know that, Quinn."

"The police were right all along," Quinn said. "I really *did* push him down the stairs. I should have done it years ago. It was so easy. And it left me free to come to you, Alison. To find you again."

Alison?

Julie looked deep into Quinn's eyes. They were glazed, unfocused. Mad looking.

Oh God, Julie thought. *Where are my parents? No! I don't want them to come in right now. He won't hurt me, I'm sure of that, but he might try to do something to them. Maybe he has a knife. Or . . .*

Or a crowbar! Norm and Frankie were killed with a crowbar.

Julie tried to keep her voice level and calm. "And Norm and Frankie. Did you kill them, too, Quinn?"

"Of course, Alison. I wanted to take care of you. They tried to hurt you, so I fixed them. They'll never try to hurt you again. It was my first gift to you—"

He broke off and frowned.

"No. That was my *second* gift to you. Do you remember what my first one was?"

Julie shook her head, her eyes wide with fear.

"Karen Slack," he said proudly.

"Wh-what?"

"I killed Karen Slack. I pushed her off the cliff at The Point."

"Karen?" Julie's voice had become high-pitched, almost a shriek. *Calm,* she told herself. *I have to act calm. Keep everything under control.*

"But Karen didn't do anything to hurt us, Quinn.

His eyes narrowed. "She would have, though. She saw my records. The ones that Mr. Reed kept locked up. And she was going to tell everyone about how I'd been in that prison for juveniles."

He paused and smiled triumphantly. "So I killed her. She deserved it, Alison."

Julie shuddered. Those hands. She almost expected to see blood, the blood of his victims, on them.

He moved toward her and took her in his arms.

She felt a terrible repugnance for him now.

He drew her closer, and she suddenly felt sick

208

to her stomach. The very scent of him, once so exciting, was making her ill. All the attraction she'd felt toward him in the past had turned to repulsion. Nausea.

Gently, she pulled away from him, swallowing a spasm of nausea as he tried to cling to her.

"So what are you going to do now?" she asked him softly. "The police are looking for you, you know. You can't stay here or they'll find you. You took a real chance coming here to see me."

Quinn laughed. He picked up his mask and put it back on.

Julie could see only his eyes, those wild, mad eyes, glittering behind the mask.

"I have a plan. The perfect plan." He took her arm. "I didn't come here just to *see* you. Like I said, I came here to *get* you. I'm taking you with me. We have to be together, don't we? Always and forever. That's what you want, too, isn't it, my darling Alison?"

CHAPTER TWENTY-SEVEN

Quinn gripped Julie's arm with a heavy hand. There was no way she could wrench it from his grasp, and even if she could, she would never be able to outrun him. She was unable to put up any resistance as Quinn propelled her down the walk to a dark-gray sedan parked a few yards away. It was a very average, inconspicuous-looking car, not likely to draw anyone's attention.

That's why he chose it, she thought.

The street was deserted. Any hope she had of calling for help from passersby vanished.

He helped her into the car.

"This isn't your old one," she said, as if they were on a date. Normal. She had to act normal. "Where did you get it?"

"Let's just say I borrowed it for the occasion,"

Quinn replied, laughing. It was a strange laugh. High-pitched. Giggly.

He was still laughing when they headed out of town. This new mood terrified Julie.

"Where are we going, Quinn?" She tried to sound cool, relaxed.

Quinn wagged a finger before her face.

"It's a surprise," he said. "You'll love it, Alison. It's the perfect way for us to be together forever."

She could see now where they were going. They were on the road to The Point.

The Point. The bluff overlooking the Potomac River and the falls.

The place Quinn had been so afraid Julie had gone on dates.

The place where he'd killed Karen Slack. Julie felt another wave of nausea.

When they reached the turnoff to The Point, Quinn stopped the car, his arms, crossed at the wrist, resting lightly on the wheel.

"Have you guessed my surprise yet, Alison?"

A *surprise like Karen Slack got?* Julie thought. "No, Quinn, please. Take me home. Oh, please, Quinn!" Julie was sobbing now, too terrified to speak clearly.

Quinn backed up the car, looking over his

shoulder. He seemed to be aligning the vehicle with the observation platform.

A wave of relief swept over Julie. "Where are we going? Back to town?"

"Back? No, Alison, we can never go back. Only forward. The two of us, together forever."

He gazed at her tenderly, lovingly. "Can't you see how perfect it is? Just one moment of flying, and then an eternity of happiness together."

He put the car in overdrive.

Julie knew now what he planned to do. Drive them over the cliff. Kill them both.

"No! No!" she sobbed. "I don't want to die!"

"But we'll be famous, Alison." Quinn sounded surprised and faintly reproving. "Lovers will come up here and be inspired by our love and the beautiful gift we gave each other. Poets will write poems about us. You'd like that, wouldn't you, sweetheart? To have people remember our love forever?"

He reached over and took her hand.

Julie tried to pull her hand from his, but he wouldn't let go.

She went crazy, caught in a frenzy of fear and frustration. Wildly, she yanked on his hand. His grip tightened.

With her other hand she frantically tried to open the car door on her side.

"What are you doing?" he demanded. "Are you trying to get away? Why do you want to spoil things, Alison?"

"Quinn!" Julie cried. "Look at me! I'm not Alison. I'm Julie. Julie! And I don't want to die. I don't want to go over the cliff with you. I don't want to be famous. I just want to live. *Live*, Quinn!" She sobbed uncontrollably. "Please! Please, Quinn!"

He looked at her as if he hadn't recognized her until now.

Through the holes in the death's-head mask, Julie could see his eyes losing their wild look. It was almost as if the old Quinn, the boy she'd loved, was looking out at her again.

"Julie? Julie, is that you?"

"Yes. It's always been me."

"I've been so mixed up. It's like another person comes in and out of my body sometimes."

Quinn released her hand and took off his mask.

His thick, dark hair tumbled over his forehead. For an instant Julie remembered the way he looked the first time she saw him.

"I think I've done some terrible things, Julie."

Julie nodded. "Yes, but we can get help for you. You need help, Quinn."

He smiled a little, that scarred, pirate smile.

Then he ran his hand gently over her hair, caressing every strand lovingly, the way he used to. "I love you, Julie. I'd never hurt you. You know that, don't you?"

He reached across her and opened her door. "Get out of the car."

For a moment she couldn't move. She sat staring at him, her eyes wide.

He leaned over and kissed her gently, his lips warm and smooth. "Get out, Julie."

She crawled out, her legs trembling.

Then Quinn revved the car and floored the gas pedal. The car threw up gravel as it streaked forward toward the observation platform.

Julie had just begun to scream when the car smashed through the railing and went over the cliff.

It seemed to hang in midair for a moment. Then it tipped crazily and fell. She heard a crash and a shuddering echo. She knew the car had fallen among the sharp, jagged rocks that lay, partially submerged, in the river just below the falls.

By the time Julie could make her legs carry her to the edge of the cliff to look down, the car was on fire.

It teetered on the edge of a large, flat rock. The current of the river was making it move back and forth. Soon it would be swept away.

Quinn—was he in that car, burning?

Julie hoped he was already dead. She couldn't bear the thought of him feeling that fire, feeling it consuming his flesh, burning him alive.

But he wasn't in the car. The flames revealed a dark figure, sprawled on a nearby rock. The impact of the crash must have flung him from the car when it hit.

He wasn't moving. He was lying on his back, and his head was twisted at an unnatural angle. His arms and legs were flung out, bent, and Julie saw that they were bent the wrong way.

No one's legs, she thought, with rising hysteria, *bend that way*.

He was dead. She knew, then, that he was dead.

The car tipped back and forth again and then slipped into the river. It was borne, still blazing, downstream.

Julie stood a moment, head bowed, looking down at the broken body on the rocks, feeling a deep, aching pity for Quinn.

She also felt a spasm of loss that would get worse, she knew, before it got better. It would never go away. She knew that. But maybe it would get better.

Julie sat down weakly on the edge of the wooden platform and put her head in her hands.

And then, at last, she cried.

Great, racking sobs nearly wrenched her apart. Tears flowed down her cheeks and she wiped them away with the palms of her hands.

Then she folded her arms on her knees, rested her head on them, and cried some more.

When she was finally done, her eyes were so swollen she could barely see, but she felt better. Cleansed, somehow. At peace.

And then, to her great surprise, she realized she was hungry.

Yes, she was hungry and her stomach was growling. Julie couldn't remember the last time she'd been hungry. Food hadn't mattered to her these past ten days.

And then she thought about Brad. How kind he'd been to her. And she had always thought of him as conceited and silly.

What's the matter with me? she wondered. *What kind of person am I, to be thinking about food and Brad Stafford right now, after what I've been through? After what's happened to Quinn?*

A survivor, that's what.

Maybe there really were such things as survivors. And maybe she was one.

I'll just rest here for a few more minutes, Julie thought. *And then I'll start walking.*

It was a long way back to town.

DEADLY STRANGER

There was a loud thump from the front of the car. Startled, Kelly dropped the map and saw Lauren leaning against the hood of the car. She was facing the gas station, holding herself up with a hand on the hood of the Mustang. Her normally tan skin was grey as stone. Beyond her, the door to the gas station swung slowly closed on its spring hinges.

Kelly pushed open her door. "Lauren? Lauren, are you okay?"

There was a crash from the gas station as the front door flew open. Marshall stepped out into the sunlight. His face was as calm as ever, but his blue eyes were blazing. "What are you two doing back here?" he said in a cold voice.

NIGHTMARES

DEADLY STRANGER

M.C. Sumner

For my wife, who put up with me quitting my day job; the members of the Alternate Historians, without whom I never would have sold a thing; and for Sherwood, who gave me a boost when I needed it.

ONE

Kelly Tallon came awake at the first note of music from the clock radio. She smiled to herself. Her parents had been convinced that she wouldn't get up this early on the first day of spring break. But her parents had never understood Kelly's obsession with skiing. For a week of spring skiing in Colorado, she would have gotten up at four in the morning every day for a year.

Fumbling in the dark, she found the switch and managed to shut off the alarm. Across the room, her younger sister Amanda muttered something in her sleep, and the springs of her bed squeaked as she rolled over.

Kelly climbed out of bed. The hardwood floor was cool under her bare feet. She navigated

1

through the darkness until her hands found the clothes she had left on a chair. She peeled her nightshirt over her head and tossed it onto the bed, slid into her jeans, and pulled on a cotton sweatshirt.

She stepped carefully across the room toward the dresser. Her searching fingers picked out a brush in the pile of objects that covered the dresser's top. Squinting at the mirror above the dresser, Kelly ran the brush through her chin-length auburn hair. She wished she could turn on the lights.

One more summer, she thought. *I just have to get through this summer and I'll be out on my own.* College was only months away, and Kelly was anxious to get out of her house, out of high school—on with her life. She smiled, and she could just see the reflection of her white teeth in the darkened mirror.

She found her soft-sided suitcase where she'd left it by the door and hefted it with her left hand. The bag was heavy, filled with a week's worth of clothes. Kelly leaned far to the right as she opened the door and staggered into the hallway.

Her skis and ski poles were waiting at the top of the stairs. The skis were several inches longer than Kelly was tall. Getting them balanced across her right shoulder was quite a trick. The combination of heavy bag and lengthy skis made her wobble as she walked down the hallway, the tips of her skis drawing figure eights in the air.

As she turned to go down the stairs, the skis cracked loudly against the wall. Kelly cringed. She stopped, waiting to see if there was any reaction. When no one stirred, she started down again. Two steps later, the skis hit the wall a second time. After that, Kelly took the steps very, very slowly.

She had to put her bag down to get the front door open. Stepping out into the cool morning air, she pulled her bag through and carefully eased the door shut behind her. Stars still shone overhead, but the sky in the east was turning gray-pink. A quarter moon floated between wispy clouds and reflected silver light from a yard covered in dew. Kelly walked across the grass, leaving dark footprints behind her. She sat her suitcase down by the curb and waited.

She didn't have to wait long. There was a screech of tires from the corner, and headlights spilled down the empty street. A blue Mustang, looking black in the moonlight, came sliding around the corner, sped down the street, and stopped in front of Kelly's house with a final squeal of burning rubber. Lauren Miki threw her door open and stepped onto the road.

"Morning," Kelly said cheerfully.

"It's not morning—the sun's not even up," Lauren replied. She arched her back and stretched. "Come on, Kel. Let's get your skis loaded."

Kelly had not taken two steps toward Lauren before her mouth dropped open in surprise. "Lauren! What happened to your hair?"

Lauren reached a hand up to the nape of her neck and ran a finger across the bare skin. Her black hair was cut short in the back and on the sides, with thick bangs left to tumble across her forehead. "What do you think?" she asked.

Kelly tilted her head to one side and studied her friend for a moment. "It suits you," she said at last. "It really shows off your face. But it's a bit of a shock. You've had long hair since the second grade."

"Yeah, well, it's time to make some changes."

Lauren stepped onto the grass and took the skis from Kelly. Almost a foot taller than Kelly, Lauren handled the long skis with ease. She slid them under an arrangement of cords and straps that crisscrossed the Mustang's roof.

"Are you sure that rig is going to work?" Kelly asked skeptically.

"Absolutely. I've got my skis in it too."

"All right. Just as long as my skis don't end up on the interstate somewhere in Kansas."

Lauren popped the hatch open and tossed in

Kelly's bag. Packed together with Lauren's luggage, it made for a tight fit, and it took Lauren two tries to get the cover closed. As it finally clicked shut, a light came on in the upper floor of Kelly's house.

"Let's get going," Lauren said softly.

Kelly opened her door and started to get in, but another light came on in the house. She climbed back out of the car.

Lauren was fumbling for her keys. "Where are you going?" she asked, and Kelly was surprised at the tension in her voice.

"It's probably just my dad. I'm sure he just—"

"Get in," Lauren hissed.

"But . . ."

"Get in!"

She said it with such authority that Kelly didn't even think about arguing. She dropped into her seat and slammed the door. A moment later Lauren found the right key and ground the Mustang's motor to life. They shot off down the street just as the outside light of Kelly's house snapped on.

Looking back, Kelly could see a figure coming out her front door. "What was that all about?"

"What was what all about?" Lauren asked. She had a habit of evading questions by repeating them—a habit that always drove Kelly nuts.

5

"Why were you in such a hurry to leave?" Kelly said. "I'm sure my dad just wanted to give me his 'Be careful' speech."

"Maybe," Lauren said. She shifted the Mustang through its gears and made the turn at the corner so fast that Kelly was thrown up against her door. The back tires lost their grip on the blacktop, and the car began to spin wildly. Then Lauren fought it under control.

"Are you trying to get us killed, Lauren?" Kelly asked, her fingers tightly gripping her seat. "What's going on?"

"I didn't want you to talk to your dad, because your dad probably got a call from my dad," Lauren said. A traffic light turned red ahead of them, and Kelly was grateful that Lauren brought the car to a stop.

"So what was your dad going to say?"

Lauren looked over at her. Even in the dim light, her dark-brown eyes were bright. "That I don't have permission to go on this trip."

For the second time that morning, Kelly felt her mouth drop open. "Lauren! Why would he say that? I was there when he gave you permission. We've been planning this for months."

A car honked behind them, and they both looked up to see that the light had turned green. Lauren accelerated into the intersection. "It's my grades," she said.

"You've got great grades. When's the last time you made below a B?"

"Not my regular grades, my grades on the SATs."

Kelly frowned. "But I thought you did fine on those."

"Fine is not fine enough, my dear," Lauren replied, putting on a snooty accent. "Not if one expects to attend college within the selective ranks of the Ivy League."

"Now I'm really confused. I thought you were going to UCLA."

"Yeah, that's where I want to go. But of course, where I want to go doesn't count for anything." Lauren steered the car across the highway and onto the access ramp to the interstate. Even this early on a Saturday, the interstate was half choked with trucks and cars. Behind them the sun peeked over the horizon, and orange light shone across the highway, flashing from glass and chrome.

Kelly watched Lauren as she moved the car from lane to lane. She had always envied Lauren's beauty and maturity. Her height and figure had let Lauren pass for a college student before she was old enough to drive. Kelly hadn't grown an inch since she was twelve, and even at eighteen people still mistook her for an eighth grader.

Where Lauren had never had any shortage of boyfriends, Kelly's dates had been few and far between. While Kelly went through high school almost unnoticed, Lauren had been on several sports teams, a class officer almost every year, and a leader in more clubs than Kelly could count.

And then there was the money. Kelly's family wasn't exactly poor; they had a nice house and all the standard stuff. But Lauren's family had a huge house, and Lauren always had a new car and fancy clothes. Lauren was rich.

It was easy to be jealous of Lauren, but there was one thing that Kelly had never envied: Lauren's father. In all the times she'd met Mr. Miki, Kelly didn't think she'd ever seen him smile. No matter what Lauren did, it never seemed good enough for him. When Lauren got an A, he wanted it to be an A plus. When Lauren made cheerleader, he wanted her to be head cheerleader. When Lauren was on the volleyball team, he wanted her to be the star of the team.

"What are we going to do now?" Kelly asked.

"What do you mean?"

"Well, we can't go all the way to Colorado without permission."

"Why not?" Lauren said. There was a tone in her voice that made Kelly nervous.

"For one thing, we'll get killed when we get home."

Lauren gave a choked laugh. "My dad's already as mad as he's going to get."

"Yeah, but my dad's not that mad yet," Kelly said.

"Don't tell him."

Kelly frowned. "Don't tell him what?"

"Don't tell him you knew I wasn't supposed to go." Lauren paused to slide the car across two lanes and slammed on the gas to get around a line of slower-moving traffic. "He can't get mad at you if you didn't know you were doing anything wrong."

Kelly thought about it for a moment, then shook her head. "Won't work. As soon as we get there, I'm supposed to call in. And as soon as I do, my dad will tell me to beat it back home."

"What if you don't call?" Lauren suggested.

"If I don't, he'll probably have the National Guard after us. He made me promise to call every day."

"We could tell him the phone wasn't working."

"That might work for the first night," Kelly said. "But then what?"

Lauren slapped her hands against the steering wheel. "I don't know!" She closed her eyes, and Kelly fought the temptation to grab the wheel. But the car stayed straight until Lauren opened her eyes again. "I don't know," she repeated more softly, "but I'll figure out something by the time we get there."

Kelly put a hand on her friend's arm. "I think this is a bad idea, Lauren. You know how much I wanted to go on this trip, but I think the best thing we can do is go home. Maybe if we talk to your dad, he'll change his mind."

"He won't change his mind," Lauren insisted. Her dark eyes were fixed on the road ahead. "I'm going."

"Lauren . . ."

"No. If you want me to take you back home, I will. But I'm going."

Kelly bit her lip and tried to figure out the right thing to do. If she went home, she wouldn't be in trouble, but there was no telling what Lauren would do. In the mood she was in, Kelly didn't doubt that she might go on the trip by herself. And she wasn't sure that Lauren would come back.

"All right," Kelly said at last. "I'll go. I still think it's the wrong thing, but I'll go."

"Thanks, Kel. We'll have fun, just wait and see."

"Yeah, well, I hope so. But I still don't see how we're going to keep from being shipped straight home as soon as we get there."

A smile came to Lauren's lips. "I can think of some pretty twisted ways to get there. If we don't have to check in with your dad until we get to Colorado, we might have longer than you think."

"Just as long as you don't try to drive to Colorado by way of California," Kelly said. "That might be kind of hard to explain."

"We could still go to Florida, like I wanted to do in the first place." Lauren's face brightened, and she seemed to shake off her anger. "Anyway, at least we'll have the trip. I love to drive."

"I'm glad you do, because I sure don't." Kelly looked out the window at the shopping strips and gas stations that clustered around each exit of the highway. "How long is this going to take—assuming no detours through L.A.?"

"St. Louis to Denver is about twenty hours each way, I guess," Lauren said. "And we better figure on another couple of hours to get to the resort. If we drive hard, we should make it there sometime tomorrow."

Kelly sighed. Twenty-something hours each way, plus whatever time they took to eat or sleep. It was a long way to go just to get yelled at. "Promise me one thing, okay?"

"What's that?"

"Promise me that no matter what else happens, I get to make at least one run down the slopes."

Lauren raised her right hand like someone being sworn in for court. "I solemnly swear that Kelly Tallon will not end this spring break without getting a chance to ski."

"Good," Kelly said. "Now no matter what happens, it'll be worth it."

TWO

Kelly jerked awake from a dream of falling. A radio was playing loudly, and she fumbled to her right, trying to find the switch to shut off the alarm. Her hand hit smooth glass. She blinked and pushed her hair back from her eyes. Then she remembered that she was in Lauren's car on the way to Colorado.

"You okay?" Lauren asked.

"Yeah. I've just never been very good at sleeping in cars."

Kelly sat up and looked through her window. They were passing fields where the brilliant green of spring wheat was just starting to poke through the brown earth. The sky overhead was a very dark gray and looked even darker ahead.

"Where are we?" she asked.

13

Lauren pulled a map from the space between the seats and passed it to Kelly. "I think we're about thirty miles from Kansas City. There's an exit coming up. See if you can find it on the map."

Kelly read the green sign on the road and ran her finger down the line of the interstate on the map until she found the small town she was looking for. "I don't think we've gone as far as you think. It looks more like fifty or sixty miles."

The dark sky caught Kelly's attention. Among the knots of gray cloud, there were streaks of greenish yellow that looked like bruises in the air. "Radio say anything about a storm?" she asked.

"Uh-uh."

"Looks like a big one up there. I'm surprised they haven't been saying anything."

"Nope," Lauren said. "But I've been listening to music stations."

Seconds later scattered drops of rain began to smash against the Mustang's windshield. Kelly leaned her face against the side window and looked up at the sky. The blackened clouds were heaving up and down. "Wow," she said. "It really looks bad."

Over the next few minutes the rain grew harder and the wind stronger. The sky got so dark that it was hard to believe that the sun hadn't set. Lauren barely slowed, even when they began to pass other cars that had pulled over to wait out the storm.

"You sure you can see okay?" Kelly asked.

"I can see," Lauren said. "As long as it doesn't get any worse." She had barely finished speaking when there was a sudden bang from the hood of the car. "What was that?"

There was another bang, and a sharp crack as something struck the windshield. Kelly saw a white lump glance off the fender of the car, and another bounce along the dark shoulder of the road.

"It's hail!" she shouted. "Big hail."

"It's going to beat my car to death," Lauren cried. There was another bang of hail against the roof, and another against the hood.

Kelly squinted through the gray sheets of wind-driven rain and hail. "It looks like there's a bridge over the road up ahead. If we can get under that . . ."

"You got it!" Lauren leaned far forward as she steered along a road that neither of them could clearly see. The sound of impacting hail increased until Kelly felt like she was inside a popcorn machine. The racket was deafening.

Just ahead the shadow of the bridge became visible. The second they slipped under it, the deafening sound cut off as though someone had thrown a switch.

Lauren steered the car to the side of the road. For a second the girls just sat there, catching their breath. Kelly was breathing so hard, she felt as if she had pushed the car those last hundred yards down the highway.

"Look at the hood," Lauren said.

Kelly looked, and saw dozens of small circular dents in the sheet metal of the car's hood. She opened her door and stepped out, and Lauren did the same. "It's not too bad," Kelly said.

"Not bad? It's got more dents than a waffle!"

"When the sun comes out, it'll probably pop out most of them."

Lightning struck somewhere close by, and thunder boomed under the bridge like a bomb blast. Lauren and Kelly jumped. Kelly saw Lauren's eyes round and white against her tan skin. Lauren stared back for a moment, and then she surprised Kelly by bursting into laughter.

"What is wrong with you?" Kelly asked.

Lauren waved her hand and fought to hold down her laughter. "It's just . . . it's just that you looked so funny! With your eyes popping out and everything."

Kelly shook her head. "You're nuts."

"I know," Lauren said. She managed to strangle the last bit of her laughter just as another clap of thunder shook the ground under their feet. Somewhere in the distance, a high-pitched siren began to blow. "What's that? Fire engine? Something started by the lightning?"

"I don't think so," Kelly said after a moment. "I think it's a tornado warning."

Lauren tilted her head back and looked upward. "Great. What is this, some kind of sign? Well, it's not going to work. I'm going on this trip, and that's that." Lightning flashed close by and they both jumped again.

"At least I don't see any tornado coming," Kelly said. They leaned against the car and watched as the hail pounded on the roadway beyond the bridge. Every now and then a gust of wind brought some of the rain almost to their feet, and the girls flinched every time the thunder crashed. A single car went zipping past them so quickly that they barely saw it before it had vanished behind the wall of rain and hail.

"There's somebody in a hurry," Kelly said.

"And somebody that doesn't care about their car," Lauren added.

A few minutes later the lightning began to lessen and the distant wail of the siren went away. The hail vanished, and the rain settled down to a steady drizzle. Most of the storm seemed to have passed to the east, leaving a gray, overcast sky in the west that promised days of rain.

"Think we should go now?" Kelly asked.

"I guess so." Lauren opened the driver's door and started to get in.

"Lauren," Kelly said softly.

Lauren leaned back out. "What?"

"Maybe we should go home. I mean, this isn't exactly the best way to start a trip. And with your dad and everything. Maybe it *is* some kind of sign."

Lauren ran a hand through her short hair. Kelly could see that the resolve she had shown that morning had been eroded by the storm. But finally she shook her head. "No, let's go on."

"Do you really think we should?" Kelly asked.

"Of course I do. Just wait," Lauren replied. "Good things are going to start to happen soon."

The storm had filled the ditches at the side of the road with rivers of surging water and turned the green fields into dark-brown mud. Kelly saw some trees down beside a distant white house and a truck mired in the water-choked ruts of a dirt road.

They had gone only a few miles when they

18

passed a green sedan on the side of the road. It was an old car, and its squared-off sides showed the dents of the hailstorm. The hood was up, and as they went past, a figure waved at them from the driver's window.

Lauren slowed and turned her head to look back at the car. "Is that the car that passed us while we were waiting?"

Kelly thought for a moment. "I'm not sure. It could be."

Lauren pulled over to the side of the road, stopped, and shifted the Mustang into reverse. "Let's see what his trouble is."

"Why don't we just go on to the next exit and tell somebody to come back for him?" Kelly asked. "It might not be such a great idea to stop out here in the middle of nowhere."

"Come on, Kel. If we want good things to happen, we have to do good things, right?"

"Sounds right," Kelly agreed. "But let's do good things someplace else, okay?"

Lauren kept backing up. The green sedan appeared through the haze of the drizzle, and the driver got out and started jogging toward the Mustang. Lauren rolled down the window as he approached.

"Thanks for stopping," the guy said. "I was afraid I would be stuck here for hours."

From the passenger seat Kelly couldn't see

the man very well. A strong chin, slightly curly dark hair, a flash of white teeth between smiling lips—that was all. But she didn't have to see him to know what he looked like; Lauren's response told her everything.

Lauren tilted her head slightly and put on a knowing smile. "I'm just glad we could help," she said. Her voice was half an octave lower than normal and it oozed sophistication. "Do you want us to send someone back for you?" She paused for a moment, and her smile widened. "Or maybe you'd like a ride to the next gas station?"

"I wouldn't want to cause you any trouble. . . ."

"It's no problem," Lauren said. "Climb in."

"Thanks," the man said. "Let me go lock up the car and get a couple of things, and I'll be right back." He trotted back down the rainy highway.

"I still think this is a bad idea," Kelly said.

Lauren turned to her and raised an eyebrow. "Did you get a good look at him?"

"Not really."

"Just wait till you do."

"Look," Kelly said. "I'm sure he's cute, but shouldn't we just send someone for him? I mean, it's not safe to pick people up off the side of the road."

"Relax. It's only until the next exit."

Kelly started to make one last protest, but she was interrupted by a rapping against her window. She turned to see the guy looking in at her.

At first she thought Lauren was wrong—there was nothing special about him. He was average. He was young, maybe no older than they were, maybe college age. His faded letter jacket fit loosely over a trim build. *Okay*, she thought, *he is pretty good-looking, but nothing to get all that worked up about*. Then Kelly saw his eyes.

His eyes were blue. Not blue like most blue eyes, but an incredibly deep blue like sapphires. Those eyes transformed his face.

Without thinking about it, Kelly pushed her door open and climbed out into the drizzle. She felt nervous, as if the guy was going to ask her out instead of bumming a ride in Lauren's car. "Uh, the backseat's pretty cramped," she said. "Maybe I better ride back there."

"No," he said. "It's enough that you're giving me a ride. I'm not going to kick you out of your seat. I'll be fine in the back."

Kelly stood aside as he pulled her seat forward and slid into the small rear seat of the Mustang. "You're sure you fit okay?" she asked as she climbed back into the front.

"I'm fine," he said. Kelly got another flash of his very white teeth as he gave her a quick smile. Then he turned toward Lauren. "I really appreciate you ladies rescuing me like this."

"We're happy to help," Lauren said. "You have everything you need out of your car?"

He held up a small leather satchel in his right hand. "Right here."

"Then let's get going." Lauren hit the gas and shifted the gears as the Mustang sped up. The rain had dropped off enough to crank the wipers down to intermittent. In the distance a dull orange glow at the base of the clouds showed that the sun had almost set.

"My name's Marshall," the man said as they left the green sedan behind. Kelly thought there was something unusual in his voice. Maybe it was a trace of a southern accent, maybe it was just his relaxed, slow way of talking. Whatever it was, it made her feel comfortable.

Lauren spoke up. "Hi, Marshall, I'm Lauren." She took one hand off the wheel and stretched her arm toward the backseat to exchange a quick shake.

Kelly turned in her seat. "Kelly." She reached out her hand, and Marshall took it. He held it for a long moment between fingers that were strong and had the slight roughness that came from hard work.

"You girls on vacation?" he asked.

"How'd you guess?" Lauren asked.

"Spring break?"

"Yeah," Lauren said. "You too?"

"You got it. Let me guess, you two are . . . juniors?"

"Seniors," Lauren told him.

"Wow, seniors. What college?"

"Oh, we're still in high school," Kelly said.

Lauren glanced over at her with a look that could have cut glass, and Kelly realized that she had just stomped on the image Lauren had been constructing. "But only for one more month," she finished weakly.

"I never would have guessed you were still in high school," Marshall said. "You look older."

Kelly could feel the blood rise in her face and hoped her blush wasn't obvious in the dim light. She knew he was talking only about Lauren. No one had ever thought Kelly looked older than she was. Younger all the time, but never older.

"What about you?" Lauren asked. "Are you in college?"

"I just finished up a premed program," Marshall said. "I guess I'll start med school in the fall, but I'm still trying to decide where."

Kelly was surprised. She wouldn't have thought Marshall was old enough to be out of college already, and his clothes, car, and rough hands didn't match her idea of a medical student. But maybe he had gotten through school on a scholarship. And if he was as young as he looked, maybe he had been one of those genius kids that started college years early. Or maybe, like Kelly, he just looked younger than he was.

"Have you made college plans yet, Lauren?" Marshall asked.

"Well, if it were up to me, I'd be heading for the West Coast. But my dad wants me back east somewhere."

"Well, if you'll excuse me for giving advice, I don't think you should listen to your dad. The West Coast is a great place to be in college."

"My dad thinks that the Ivy League schools are the only place to get a good education," Lauren said.

"Maybe fifty years ago," Marshall said, "but not today. Go where you want to go. You're only in college once. Why spend four years in a place you don't want to be?"

"I wish my dad could hear you say that! He won't listen to me, but a med student that's been to those schools . . . Maybe he'd listen to you."

"Hey, if you think it would help, I'll be happy to give him a call."

Lauren began to talk about her father and all the things he'd put her through. For the most part Marshall listened quietly, interjecting a comment every now and then or asking a few questions. He gave the impression that he was hanging on her every word.

Kelly felt left out. She looked for a chance to get back in the conversation, but Lauren was on a roll, and Kelly couldn't get a word in edgewise. She leaned her head against the cool glass of the window and watched the darkening countryside roll past.

A few minutes later the car sped over a gentle rise. A mile up the road was an exit ramp, and just a few hundred yards from the intersection was a sprawling truck stop.

"Look," Kelly said. "There's a place we can see about getting a tow."

Lauren stopped her story about her father in midsentence and turned to look at the approaching truck stop. "I don't know. That place doesn't look like they'd notice anything that had less than a dozen wheels. They might not even have a tow truck."

"We'd better check," Kelly said. "We're probably twenty miles from Marshall's car already. If we go any farther, it'll cost him a fortune to tow it."

"Kelly's right," Marshall said. "We'd better stop."

Lauren pursed her lips, but she nodded and guided the car onto the exit ramp. There were a dozen semis clustered around the pumps and washing bays of the truck stop. Lauren steered through the giant metal tractor trailers toward the service station. At the entrance Lauren spotted a small restaurant.

"Why don't we get something to eat first?" she suggested. "We haven't stopped in hours."

Kelly didn't want to eat at this place. The white brick walls of the building had been splashed with mud from the passing trucks, and the inside didn't look much cleaner. But she realized that what Lauren wanted was not a chance to eat but an excuse to spend a few more minutes with Marshall. "Okay," she said. "Sounds good."

They climbed out of the car and Kelly stretched, trying to work the stiffness of the long ride out of her arms and legs. The door opened and one of the truckers inside the restaurant came out. He was a potbellied man with arms as big as hams and dark hair that was streaked with gray. He had his arm tight around the waist of a pretty girl that looked to be high-school age or younger.

"Are you sure you're going all the way to L.A.?" the girl asked.

"Sure, honey," said the tall man. "Don't you want to get to California?"

"I guess," the girl said. She followed the man to one of the parked trucks and he boosted her up into the cab. Kelly couldn't hear the rest of their conversation, but she could hear the man laughing as he climbed in. She thought the girl was pretty stupid—or pretty desperate—to get in that truck, and she wondered if the girl would ever see L.A.

"Let's get inside," Lauren said.

Kelly nodded and followed Marshall and Lauren into the small restaurant. There was a sign over the largest part of the room that said TRUCK DRIVERS ONLY. What was left was a pair of booths crammed into the space beside the kitchen door.

"I think we better sit over there," Marshall said. "No one is going to mistake you two for truck drivers."

Kelly thought about the girl in the parking lot. No one would have taken her for a truck driver either.

Marshall waited while the two girls slipped into a booth, then took a seat next to Lauren. "Cheer up," he said to Kelly. "The food in these places is usually pretty good."

Kelly took a plastic menu from the rack at the back of the table and looked over the options. It was the expected collection of sandwiches and dinner plates.

The waitress, a middle-aged woman in a faded blue uniform, came over to the table. "You ready to order?" she asked.

"Burger and fries," Lauren said without looking at the menu.

"Sounds good," Marshall said. "I'll have the same."

Kelly scanned the menu, trying to find something that wasn't drenched in grease. "Can I just get a green salad?"

"Sure," the waitress said. She scribbled their order on her pad. "Be up in just a minute."

As she walked away, Marshall stood. "While we're waiting for our food, I think I'll go check on getting my car towed. Okay?"

"Okay," Lauren said. "Want me to come with you?"

"You better wait," he said. "I'll be right back." He went to the front of the restaurant and shoved the glass door open. He waited a moment, holding the door while a man in a green T-shirt came in and walked into the truck drivers' section of the little restaurant. As he slipped out the door, Marshall turned to flash one last smile.

"What do you think?" Lauren said as soon as the door had closed.

"About what?" Kelly asked.

"You know. About Marshall."

Kelly picked up a saltshaker shaped like a tiny truck and turned it around in her hand. "I don't know. He's cute."

28

"He's more than cute," Lauren said. "Way more. And he's a med student."

"Yeah, he's really nice, but what does it matter? We're going to Colorado, and he's going . . . wherever it is he's going."

Lauren frowned for a moment. "You know, I don't think we ever talked about that. I wonder where he is going?"

"Good evenin'," said a voice.

Kelly looked up and saw the trucker in the green shirt standing above them. He was well over six feet tall, and his shoulders were thick with muscle. A baseball cap was pulled low over his dark-blond hair. His gray eyes were fixed on Lauren. "You need a ride tonight, little lady?" he asked.

Lauren looked up at him in confusion. "Ride?"

"We don't need a ride," Kelly said. "Thanks anyway."

The trucker's eyes shifted over to Kelly and scanned her as if he were seeing her for the first time. "I wasn't asking you, kid." He turned back to Lauren. "Come on, sugar. Let's go for a ride in a big rig." He reached down a large hand to Lauren.

She leaned away from him. "I've . . . I've got a car," she sputtered.

"A car's only a car," he said. His beefy fingers

29

closed on her shoulder and he let his hand drift across the soft material of her sweater.

Kelly reached across the table and grabbed his arm. "We're just waiting for a friend."

The trucker didn't bother to look at her this time. "Don't worry. I can be friendly."

Lauren looked over at Kelly. Her dark eyes, usually so confident, seemed lost.

Kelly looked around for the waitress, for some other customers, for anybody. But the room was empty. She started to push herself up from her seat. She wasn't sure what she could do against this guy, but she had to do something.

Kelly had just stood up, when the glass door of the restaurant swung open and Marshall came striding in. His deep-blue eyes locked on the trucker. "What's the problem here?" he asked.

The trucker looked up. "There's no problem here, sonny. I was just taking this lady for a ride."

Marshall took two slow steps toward the table. "Maybe the lady doesn't want a ride."

"Butt out," the trucker said, but he took his hand off of Lauren and straightened up to face Marshall. "This is none of your business, boy."

Marshall took another step. He was no more than three feet from the trucker. Kelly could see the muscles in the trucker's arms knotting as he clinched his hands into fists.

30

"Lauren," Marshall said softly. "Did this man hurt you?"

"No," Lauren said.

"Not yet," Kelly added.

"Then everything's okay." Marshall nodded his head toward the empty trucker's side of the restaurant. "If you could just go back to your seat, we can go on with our dinner."

"Sure," the trucker said. "As soon as the lady tells me herself. I'm going to—" started the trucker.

Marshall's hand pistoned out as fast as a striking snake and hit the bigger man in the chest. The trucker's gray eyes bugged out and he staggered backward. A honking noise came from his mouth as he fought to pull in a breath.

Marshall turned to Kelly. "Why don't you take Lauren out to the car," he said. His voice was still so very calm, completely unhurried, but there was something in his eyes—a light that hadn't been there before. "I'll find the waitress and see if I can get our food to go."

The trucker managed to pull in a long whistling breath. He coughed. "You son of a—"

Marshall hit him again. This time the big man didn't just stagger—he fell like a puppet with its strings cut.

"Is he okay?" Kelly asked.

31

"He'll be fine in a few minutes," Marshall said. "I just hit him in the solar maxus. Come on, there's no tow truck here. Let's just forget the waitress and get something at another place." He held out a hand to Lauren, and she took it quickly.

She climbed to her feet and followed him toward the door. They were almost out before she turned back to Kelly. "You coming, Kel?" she asked.

"Sure. I'll be right there." Kelly watched them go out the door, then took a look at the man on the floor. She was relieved when he finally groaned and turned over on his side.

At the front door, she paused and watched Marshall guiding Lauren across the wet parking lot. Kelly might have had only high-school biology, but she knew that the place where Marshall had punched the guy was called the solar plexus, not the solar maxus.

Would a guy that had graduated premed make a mistake like that? Kelly didn't know. She pushed open the door and walked out.

THREE

"Sorry to keep you running around like this," Marshall said.

"Are you kidding?" Lauren said. "After the way you took care of that jerk at the truck stop, you deserve a medal or something."

"It's really unfortunate that this had to happen. You know, most truckers are really decent guys. Don't let this give you a bad impression of them."

"You think this next place will have a towing service?" Kelly asked.

"That's what they said at the last place," Marshall replied.

Since leaving the truck stop, they had been to three other places along the interstate. One even had a tow truck parked in front, but Marshall had come back out saying that the truck was broken. By now they were getting close to Kansas City, and Marshall's old green sedan was thirty or forty miles back down the road. Kelly was beginning to wonder if they would ever find a place to go back for it.

"Where are you going, anyway, Marshall?" Kelly asked.

"Just on my way to visit some friends out west," he replied.

Kelly waited for him to go on, but that seemed to be all he was going to say. "Sounds nice. Where at?"

"Oh, some different places," he said. "Hey, there's our exit."

At this exit the road was lined with fast-food places and a couple of cheap motels. There were two gas stations, but neither of them had a garage or any sign of a towing service.

"You sure this is the place?" Kelly asked.

"Just following directions," Marshall said.

"They probably told you the wrong thing back at that last place," Lauren added. "Should we go on to the next exit?"

Kelly groaned to herself. She didn't care how cute this guy was or how much Lauren liked him. There was something strange about him, and she wanted him out of the car.

34

"Wait," Marshall said. "I just thought of something. Pull in at that gas station."

"Which one?"

"That one, the one with the minimart."

Lauren slid into the parking lot and pulled up next to the gas pumps. "As long as we're here, we might as well fill up. What did you think of?" she asked.

"The auto club," Marshall said. "I've got their card right here in my pocket. All I have to do is give them a call and they'll send someone to get my car. I don't know why I didn't think of it before."

"That's great!" Lauren said. "Will you need a ride someplace else?"

"I'll let you know as soon as I call," Marshall said. "And don't worry about the gas. I'll take care of it."

Kelly climbed out of the car so Marshall could get free of the backseat. She watched as he walked across the parking lot to a bank of pay phones on one side of the building. He pulled a wallet from the pocket of his jeans, glanced at something inside, and started dialing.

"Maybe we can finally get on with our trip," she said.

Lauren looked up from sticking the nozzle of the gas pump into the Mustang. "Why are

35

you in such a hurry? I like Marshall. Don't you?"

"Sure. He's fine."

Lauren squinted her dark eyes. "What's wrong, Kel? You've been acting like Marshall has three heads ever since we picked him up."

"I don't know," Kelly said. She shrugged her shoulders and tried to shake off her dark mood. She wanted to get back the excitement she had felt when the day started. "Let's just get on with our trip. You can get his phone number and get back to him later, but right now it's skiing time."

Lauren laughed. "I should have known," she said. "You and your skiing. Don't worry. I promised to get you on skis, didn't I?" She topped off the gas and hung up the hose. "You want anything to eat?"

"No, thanks. They never have anything but junk at these places. I'll wait."

"Well, I'm going to go grab a soda. Back in a sec."

Kelly checked on Lauren's makeshift ski rack. So far it seemed to be holding up fine. She leaned against the front of the car. It was chilly and the air was still damp from the storm. Despite the cool weather, a flurry of moths skittered around the fluorescent lighting at the edges of the lot. Standing there by herself, Kelly came closer to relaxing than she had in hours.

She heard footsteps and turned to see Marshall walking toward her from the phones. "Everything's taken care of," he said.

"They're going back for your car?" Kelly asked.

"They promised to get to it in about an hour, and they'll take it to a garage where it can be fixed."

"Sounds good, but don't you have to go with them? I mean, how will they get into your car?"

Marshall smiled. "It's an auto club. I'm sure they know what they're doing."

"I guess so," Kelly said. Whatever was going on, she was glad it was over.

Lauren came walking up with a can of soda. "Are they coming to get your car?" she asked Marshall.

"You bet," he said. "Everything's settled." He reached out and took Lauren's hand in his. "I really want to thank you for helping me out like this. I don't know what I would have done without you."

"Is there anything else we can do? Anywhere else you need to go?"

Marshall released her hand and sighed. "No, I guess not. It's just too bad I'm going to miss seeing my friends."

"Why's that?"

"Well, I was going to meet them in a couple of days, out in Denver. But by the time my car is fixed, they'll be gone."

Lauren's face brightened. "We're going through Denver! We could take you to meet your friends."

"I couldn't ask you to do that," Marshall said.

"Besides," Kelly added, "he wouldn't have any way to get back."

"Oh, getting back isn't a problem," Marshall said, "but I couldn't put you out like that."

"Sure you could," Lauren said with enthusiasm. "We don't mind at all."

"No, really. This is your vacation," Marshall said.

"Don't be silly! We don't mind, do we, Kelly?"

Yes, thought Kelly, *I mind a lot*. But what she said was: "No, you can ride with us."

Marshall gave a smile that seemed to reflect most of the light in the area. "Great! Really, you don't know how important this is to me."

Kelly closed her eyes and tried to convince herself it would be okay. After all, it was only one more day riding in a car. What could go wrong?

"If you're going to ride with us that far," she said, "you better get in front." This time Marshall didn't argue.

Kelly climbed into the back and folded herself into the small seat. Even as short as she was, it was cramped. When Marshall pushed the passenger seat back into place, Kelly felt like there was a wall between her and the others. The radio that had been just right in the front seat was so loud in the back that Kelly could barely hear Lauren and Marshall talking.

They were about a mile down the road before Kelly remembered something. "Lauren, did you pay for the gas?"

"What?"

"The gas!" Lauren leaned forward into the gap between the front seats. "Did you pay for the gas?"

"No," Lauren said. "Marshall took care of it."

Marshall nodded.

"No he didn't."

"What?"

"No he didn't!" Kelly almost shouted. "Marshall didn't even go inside the store." Marshall said something that Kelly didn't understand. "What?" she called. "Lauren, can you turn down the radio? I can't hear what you're saying."

Lauren turned down the radio. "Marshall says it's okay," she said.

Kelly looked back and forth between them.

"Okay? Lauren, he didn't pay for the gas. We have to go back and pay for it."

"Don't worry about it," Marshall said. "People forget all the time. Places like that expect to lose a few. They just add it to their prices."

Kelly tried to ignore him and talk to Lauren. "It's stealing, Lauren. We've got to go back and pay."

Lauren started to answer, but Marshall spoke first. "Stealing? Do you know how much profit oil companies make off of stations like that? Do you really think their prices are fair?"

"What does that have to do with it?"

"These people make billions. They don't care about a tank of gas. They have the prices so jacked up that half the people in the place could leave without paying and they'd still make money." Marshall gave a little chuckle. "Don't cry for the oil companies. If anybody is stealing anything, it's them stealing money from all their customers."

Kelly tried to stay calm. "I'm not crying for any oil company, or even for the gas station. I just want to do what's right."

"Look," Marshall said. His calm voice was really starting to get on Kelly's nerves. "It's probably ten miles to the next exit. And by then, you're going to be in the city, and it'll probably take you an hour just to get turned around." He glanced at the watch on his wrist. "It's getting close to ten now. By the time you get back here, it'll be midnight."

Kelly had to admit that spending two hours backtracking didn't sound like a lot of fun. When she and Lauren had planned the trip, they had thought they'd make it almost to Denver on the first day. But the storm and all the running around with Marshall had put them hours behind schedule.

"I don't want to waste time, but we should go back and pay for the gas," she said.

Marshall leaned over to Lauren and said something. Lauren nodded.

"What?" Kelly said. "What's he saying?"

"Marshall's right," Lauren said. "It's too big of a waste of time to go back."

"Lauren!"

"Come on, Kel. I thought you wanted to get to the slopes, right? I don't see any snow around here." She turned the radio back up, and Kelly was again cut off from the conversation.

Kelly fell back in her seat and gritted her teeth. *This was supposed to be our spring break,* she thought. *If Lauren just wanted to pick up guys, she could have done that without leaving home or dragging me along. This is turning out to be one great vacation.*

Traffic increased as they rolled into the city. Lauren guided the Mustang between rows of trucks and cars, using the car's big engine to blast past knots of slow-moving traffic. Lauren and Marshall kept up a conversation all the time. Kelly could see Marshall waving his hands as he explained some point, and several times she heard Lauren laughing at something he had said.

Kelly leaned her face against the side of the car and watched the lights sweep past. From the elevated interstate, the neighborhoods were laid out in neat rows. Lines of street lamps gleamed green or amber or white. When they passed the downtown area, the tall buildings were topped with flashing lights. Kelly spotted several night-clubs where people milled by the door and strobe lights beat against the windows.

She stopped trying to hear what Lauren and Marshall were talking about and just watched things go by. She liked traveling at night. In the day everything looked so normal, so ordinary. But at night it was easy for Kelly to imagine that she was crossing some foreign country and the lights out there might have been London or Paris, not Kansas City.

FOUR

The lights grew sparser as they moved west.
Instead of the sparkling clusters of the city, Kelly
saw only the isolated lights of an occasional
farm. The farmhouses all looked ghostly white,
and the clumps of trees that surrounded each
house seemed old and evil. The clouds were beginning to break up, and a yellow moon hung
low in the west, casting dim shadows across the
flat land.

Kelly didn't realize she was dozing off until
Marshall shook her awake. "We need to stop
somewhere," he said. He had to say it again before Kelly's head cleared enough to understand
him. Her half-formed dreams evaporated, and
she became aware of the cramped confines of
the backseat.

"Stop?" she said.

"It's getting pretty late," Marshall explained. "We need to find a place to sleep for the night."

Kelly was disapointed to be stopping this far from their goal, but she didn't want Lauren driving if she was getting tired. "Sure. Whenever Lauren wants to pull over."

For long miles, the dark fields rolled by and the highway went on without any sign of an exit. And when an exit did come up, there was no motel. By the time they reached an exit that did have a motel, Kelly was half dozing again.

The motel was new, one of those buildings built from modules that could be assembled in a matter of days. Its square white sides looked alien against the dark Kansas fields. A red sign at the front flashed VACANCY.

"We could get one room," Marshall said. "It's cheaper that way."

"Sounds okay to me," Lauren said.

Kelly tried to shake the cobwebs out of her head. "I'd rather not."

Lauren stopped the car by the office door and cut the engine. "Come on, Kel. We'd have two beds."

"Sorry. I just wouldn't be comfortable."

Lauren's forehead creased in irritation. "First

the gas and now this. You're starting to sound like my mother."

Marshall held up his hands. "It's okay," he said. "We'll get two rooms. I don't want to cause any trouble."

Lauren shot Kelly another dark look, but she didn't argue. It took only a few minutes to get their rooms from a sleepy clerk. Kelly dragged her heavy suitcase from Lauren's car and wrestled it across the parking lot. Lauren handled her case with more ease.

Marshall waited there for them at the door to their room. He jerked his thumb at a restaurant on the other side of the parking lot. "That chain usually has a pretty good breakfast. You want to meet there in the morning?"

Lauren smiled at him. "Sounds good. About eight?"

"See you then," he said. He took two steps away, then turned back. "I'll be in room one fourteen if you need me."

"Do you have everything you need?" Lauren asked. "I think I've got some spare shampoo and stuff like that."

Marshall held up his small brown bag. "Nope. I've got everything I need right here."

"Good night!" Lauren called.

She opened the door and held it while Kelly pulled her bag inside. As soon as the door was shut, Lauren turned on Kelly. "What is your problem?"

"Come on, Lauren," Kelly said. "Let's not do this now. I'm tired."

The motel room looked like any of a million others: twin beds, a small table, some cabinets, and a television on a metal stand. The paintings on the wall were abstract jumbles of red and blue.

"I'm tired too," Lauren said. "I'm the one that's been driving all day." She tossed her suitcase onto one of the beds. "What have you got against Marshall?"

"I don't have anything against Marshall," Kelly replied. She sat on the edge of the bed. More than anything, she just wanted to go to sleep and get this day over with.

"Then why are you always arguing with him?"

"I'm not arguing with him. It's just that I don't think it's a good idea to steal things."

"We didn't steal anything! It was just an accident."

"Whatever," Kelly said. "Please, can we just go to bed?"

"What about the room?" Lauren insisted. "Why didn't you let him share a room with us?"

"We just met the guy this afternoon. Why

46

should we share a motel room with him?"

"There you go again! You treat him like he's a mass murderer or something. Marshall's a great guy."

Kelly opened her suitcase and searched through the folded clothes for her nightshirt. "What makes him so great? You don't know anything about him."

"Are you kidding? We've been talking for hours. I probably know him better than any of the guys in our class. He's . . . he's . . ." Lauren waved her hands, searching for the right words. "He's so different from all those high-school guys." She opened her suitcase, took out a smaller bag, and headed for the bathroom.

"He's different all right," Kelly said.

Lauren stopped and looked back at her. "And what is that supposed to mean?"

"Nothing."

"All I meant was, he listens to me. When I talk, I feel like he's really paying attention. High-school guys never listen." Lauren walked into the bathroom.

"Your dad never listens either," Kelly said, but she said it too softly for Lauren to hear. She raised her voice. "I just don't know what difference this makes. Even if he does ride with us to Denver, we're only going to see him for another day. Then he'll be gone."

"Right," Lauren called. "Can't you be nice to him for one day?"

"I have been nice to him."

"Oh, yeah. Don't think he hasn't noticed how you're treating him." Kelly heard Lauren unzip her small case. A moment later the sound of running water came from the bathroom.

Kelly bit back a sharp remark. Irritation was starting to outweigh her sleepiness. "Did he say something about me?"

"He just wants you to like him, Kel. He can't figure out why you don't. I mean, look what he did for us at the truck stop."

"What he did for us? What he did was beat up a guy and almost kill him. I don't know why that makes you think Marshall's some kind of hero."

Lauren stuck her head out of the bathroom. "Now I know you're crazy. That guy he hit could have done anything. Didn't you see how he was looking at me?"

"That guy didn't do anything but put a hand on your shoulder," Kelly said. "Marshall hit him first."

"He was only trying to protect me." Lauren stepped out of the bathroom with her toothbrush in one hand. "Would you be happier if he'd let that guy take me away? Or let himself get killed?"

"You know I don't want that."

48

"No, Kel. I don't know what you want."

Kelly closed her eyes and fell back on the bed. "I want things to be okay. I want us to get on with our trip. I want to go skiing."

"That's your problem," Lauren said. "All you ever think of is yourself."

"Oh, absolutely," Kelly said. "That's why I haven't called home like I was supposed to tonight." She opened one eye and looked over toward Lauren. "Please, we only have to get along with Marshall for one day, but you and I have been friends for years. Can't we get along?"

Lauren was silent for a moment. "We can talk about it again in the morning." She stomped back into the bathroom, making no effort to hide her anger.

Kelly sighed and forced herself to get up from the bed. She kicked off her shoes and sat down to peel off her socks. Once she had pulled off her clothes and slipped into her nightshirt, she felt better. She pulled the covers from the bed and slid into the cool sheets.

The shower kicked on in the bathroom. Kelly lay for a few minutes, replaying the events of the day. After a while she decided that maybe she was overreacting. As soon as Lauren came out of the shower, Kelly would apologize. After all, what could it hurt? But long before the shower stopped, Kelly was asleep.

*　　*　　*

Kelly woke and sat up in bed. Her breath was coming fast, and sweat glinted on her forehead. As soon as she had fallen asleep, the nightmares had started. They were a jumble of Lauren's face, the blue Mustang, and Marshall. But they made no sense. They were only dark, confusing images from which Kelly understood nothing but overwhelming fear.

There was a moment of confusion before she remembered where she was. The room was dark. The only light was what little filtered through the blinds from the parking lot outside. She looked over at Lauren's bed, saw the dark form lying there, and relaxed a little.

"Everything's okay," she whispered to herself. "Go back to sleep." She started to lie down. Then she took a better look at Lauren's bed.

Lauren wasn't in it.

The dark form she had seen was only Lauren's suitcase, her pillow, and the rumpled blankets. Not trusting her own eyes, Kelly got up and leaned over the vacant bed where Lauren should have been. She ran a hand over the empty sheets.

"Lauren?" Kelly said quietly. She crept around the corner toward the bathroom. The door was open and the inside of the room was dark. "Lauren?" she said more loudly. There was no reply.

Kelly walked quickly to the front of the room and flipped on the lights. Lauren was definitely not in the room, and it didn't take much thought to figure out where she was. The only question was what Kelly should do about it.

She opened the front door a crack and peeked outside. A cold draft came through the opening. The parking lot was only about half full, and fresh puddles showed that it had rained while Kelly slept. It was very quiet. The restaurant across the parking lot was dark, and even the highway seemed empty.

Kelly looked down the side of the motel toward room one fourteen. Marshall's room was only a few doors away. It would be easy to go there and knock on the door.

"Yeah," she whispered to herself. "And no matter what's going on in there, I'll end up looking like an even bigger jerk than I already do."

Kelly stepped back and shut the door on the cold Kansas night. Going to Marshall's room was definitely a bad idea. If Lauren was there, she'd be furious with her. If she wasn't there, then Kelly would have to explain herself to Marshall.

She dropped onto her bed. She wasn't sure what had made Lauren so attracted to Marshall. Lauren never had trouble getting dates, and she wasn't the type to jump at the first guy that came along. But it had been a very long, very strange day. And with the problems Lauren had been having with her dad, it wasn't surprising that she wasn't acting normal.

She's not an idiot. Lauren knows what she's doing and she can take care of herself. Kelly wondered how many times she'd have to think that before she believed it.

She got back in bed and pulled the sheets up. The motel room suddenly felt very cold and empty. She could hear a truck going past out on the highway. Somehow the sound only made the silence of the room seem thicker.

Lauren was right about one thing: Kelly did not trust Marshall. He was just too smooth, too quick with an answer to everything. Over and over Kelly kept coming back to the fight with the trucker and the mistake Marshall had made in describing where he hit the man. Solar maxus. Solar plexus. It was a very small difference. And Marshall had been under stress. Everyone makes mistakes. But would a student going into medical school make a mistake like that?

52

The other thing that stuck in Kelly's mind was the strange light in Marshall's eyes when he actually hit the trucker.

"This is one great spring break." Kelly punched a fist into her pillow, turned over, and tried to sleep.

FIVE

The nightmares didn't end when Kelly went back to bed. Her sleep came in troubled snatches that were darkened by wild images. Then, sometime after the window had begun to show the pearly light of approaching dawn, she turned over to see that Lauren was back in her bed. After that, sleep came easier.

"Kelly! Get up."

Kelly blinked her eyes against the light. Lauren was standing over her. She was already dressed in jeans and a violet turtleneck, and she looked agitated.

"What's wrong?" Kelly asked.

"We forgot to ask for a wake-up call," Lauren said. "It's already after eight. We need to meet Marshall and get on the road."

55

"Okay, but I need to take a shower."

Lauren frowned. "Why couldn't you have done that last night?"

"I was tired last night," Kelly said. "Look, I'm not hungry for breakfast. Why don't you go eat with Marshall, and you can come get me when you're done."

Kelly had expected Lauren to be happy to get a chance to be alone with Marshall, but instead she looked nervous. "Oh, okay," Lauren said. "I guess we can do that."

"What's wrong?"

"Nothing. It's just that . . ." Lauren stopped and shook herself. "I'm sure it'll be okay. I'll be back in a few minutes." She grabbed her purse from the table and hurried out the door.

Kelly wondered what had gone wrong the night before. She didn't think it could be too bad. Surely Lauren would have said something. But she was sure that the evening hadn't gone as Lauren had planned.

Kelly went to the window and peered around the edge of the blinds. The sky showed only a few clouds, but the trees were swaying from a strong breeze. People going into the restaurant were wearing sweaters or jackets. Kelly went back to her suitcase and searched for some warm clothing. She hadn't thought about it being that cold before they got to Colorado, so most of her heavy clothing was designed for the slopes, but she managed to find a light sweater to go with her jeans.

Kelly padded back across the carpet to the counter outside the bathroom and laid down her clothes. She slipped into the bathroom, stripped off her nightshirt, and stepped into the shower. The warm water sluiced over her and the soap smelled fresh and clean. By the time she'd washed her hair and rinsed herself, Kelly felt much better. With a good shower behind her, she was ready to get along with anybody.

She shut off the water and stepped out. As she did, she heard the door to the hotel room open, and a gust of cold air blew into the bathroom. She hugged her towel to her to ward off the chill.

"I'm just finishing my shower," she called. "I'll be out in a sec, Lauren." She toweled herself dry quickly and stepped over to the counter. With her hand reaching toward her clothes, she froze.

Marshall stood at the corner of the room, watching her. He had a wide smile on his face—the same gentle expression he had worn when they agreed to give him a lift. But his eyes were filled with the strange savage light Kelly had seen when he fought with the trucker.

It took Kelly a few moments to find her

voice. "Get out of here," she managed in a half-strangled whisper.

Marshall didn't get out, and he didn't reply. Instead he took a step closer. The smile stayed frozen on his face.

Kelly took a half step backward. She reached behind her with one hand, trying to find the bathroom door. With her other hand she held the towel tight against her. She was afraid to look down and see what it didn't cover.

"Get out," she said again. This time, despite all the fear tightening her stomach, Kelly was relieved to hear how firm her voice sounded. But Marshall didn't move.

Her fingers found the edge of the door. Kelly took two more steps backward and slammed the door. She went to lock it, then discovered that it didn't lock. She let the towel drop and pressed against the door with both hands. With the metal panel between them, much of her fear of Marshall was turned into anger. "Get out of my room!" she shouted.

There was the sound of movement. At first Kelly thought Marshall had decided to listen to her—that he was going away. Then his voice, his maddeningly calm voice, came from right outside the door. "I thought you were just a child, Kelly, but I was wrong. You're as much a woman as Lauren is."

Kelly shivered. "Please go away." There was only silence on the other side of the door.

It was several minutes before Kelly dared open the door again. When she did, there was no sign of Marshall. She tiptoed to the corner and looked around. The motel room was empty. Kelly ran across the room and locked every lock. Then she ran back to the bathroom and quickly pulled on her clothes.

She glanced at herself in the mirror. The sprinkling of freckles on her nose stood out against skin that had gone very pale. Her auburn hair was wet and tangled. She closed her eyes and took several deep breaths. She walked back to her suitcase and took out her comb and blow dryer.

The next time Kelly looked in the mirror, she liked what she saw a lot better. Her hair was dry and combed, her skin looked healthier, and her eyes had lost that scared-rabbit look. She nodded to herself and started to gather up her clothes to leave.

Then the door rattled. At once Kelly's heart leaped into overdrive. She walked toward the locked door. "Go away!" she shouted.

"Come on, Kel. We need to get going."

"Lauren!" Kelly quickly fumbled the locks open. Lauren was waiting outside the door with an amused smile on her face. Kelly stuck her head out and looked around. "Where's Marshall?" she asked.

"He's already waiting in the car," said Lauren. "Are you ready to go?"

"Lauren, Marshall, he . . . he . . ."

"He walked in on you while you were getting dressed. Yeah, I know."

Kelly looked at her in amazement. "He told you?"

Lauren nodded. "He's really sorry, Kel. He thought you were ready."

"He's sorry? If he was sorry, then why didn't he leave when I told him to?"

A shadow of concern passed over Lauren's face and her smile faded. "I don't know. I guess he was as shocked as you were."

"Lauren, he wasn't shocked; he was staring."

"I'm sure he'll apologize. Come on, let's get going." She turned toward the car and started walking away.

Kelly jammed her hands into the pockets of her jeans. "No," she said.

Lauren stopped and looked back over her shoulder. "What do you mean, no?"

"I mean no," Kelly said. "I'm not riding in a car with that guy."

"What are you going to do, stay here?"

"If I have to. I'll take a bus home or call my dad, but I'm not going anywhere with Marshall."

Lauren took two steps back toward Kelly. "Yeah, well, you'll be happy to hear that Marshall's only going with us for a couple of miles. He's made some kind of plans to get where he's going another way."

"Really? Did he tell you that last night?"

"No, he told me this . . ." Lauren's dark eyes narrowed. "How could he have told me anything last night?"

"I meant in the car," Kelly said quickly. It wouldn't do any good to confront Lauren about being absent from her bed—especially if Marshall had already dumped her. "It's hard to hear in the backseat," she added.

"Oh," Lauren said. "Well, are you going with us? Or are you going to stay here in middle of Nowhere, U.S.A.?"

"As long as it's only for a few miles."

Lauren turned without another word and stomped off toward the car. Kelly went back inside and grabbed her suitcase. She took a look around the room to make sure they hadn't forgotten anything, then shut the door for the last time.

Both Marshall and Lauren were waiting beside the car when Kelly walked up. Marshall stepped forward to help with her suitcase. Kelly held on to it for a second, but she let Marshall take it and heave it into the trunk of the Mustang.

"I'm sorry about walking in on you," he said.

Kelly stared into Marshall's sapphire eyes. He seemed so embarrassed and sincere, but she knew how he had acted in the room. "You're not riding all the way to Denver with us?" she asked.

Marshall shook his head sadly. "I'm sorry about that, too. But plans change."

Lauren wrapped her arms around herself and shivered. "You mind if we get going? It's freezing out here."

Kelly squeezed into the backseat and Marshall took his place in the front. Lauren cranked up the car and turned on the heat. They rolled around to the front of the motel, and Lauren got out to turn in the keys. Kelly waited for Marshall to say something while Lauren was out of the car, but he stayed facing the front of the car and didn't say a word until she came back.

"I just need to go back to the last exit," Marshall said. "My friend is going to pick me up there."

"Why not this exit?" Kelly asked.

"I'm afraid I gave him the wrong place when we were on the phone. But it's only a couple of miles back; it won't take long."

"Let's get it over with," Lauren said.

Amen, Kelly thought.

The wind was getting very gusty. Kelly could

feel it pushing against the car as they got out on the interstate and headed east. They passed a line of cars that had streamers of crepe paper dangling from their bumpers and hand-lettered signs in the windows. SPRING BREAK said one sign. FLORIDA! read another.

"Maybe they've got the right idea," Kelly said as they passed the last of the Florida-bound cars. "Maybe we should have gone to the beach like everybody else."

"You can't blame me for that one, Kel. This spring-skiing business was your idea."

It was farther back to the exit than Marshall had said, and it took them about twenty minutes to get there. When they arrived, there was only a single gas station and a dusty sign pointing up a pothole-scarred state road.

"You sure this is the place?" Lauren asked.

"Yes," Marshall said. "Just drop me off over there at the station."

Lauren pulled in beside the pumps. "We're almost out of gas again. We better fill up, or we'll have to stop in ten minutes."

Everyone piled out of the car, and there was an awkward moment as they all stood around in the parking lot. It was Marshall who spoke up first. "I really can't thank you girls enough for helping me out. You've done so much more than you had to."

"Yeah, well. Take care of yourself," Lauren said.

"Here," Marshall said, "take this." He held out a slip of greenish paper that was topped by the logo of the motel where they'd spent the night.

"What's this?"

"I wrote my address and phone number on it. When you get back from vacation, give me a call. We'll get together."

Lauren's gloomy expression brightened a little. "Okay, I will."

Marshall extended his hand to Kelly. "And thanks for your help too."

Kelly took his hand and gave it a fast shake. "I hope your ride shows up soon."

"Don't worry," Marshall said. "I'll be out of here in no time." He turned toward the door of the gas station, then turned back. "And don't worry about the gas. I'll pay." Kelly already had her purse out and she started to protest, but Marshall held up a hand. "Really," he said. "I'll take care of it. You guys just get going and have a great spring break."

"Bye," Lauren called.

Marshall gave a final wave and disappeared into the station. Lauren flipped the lid from her gas tank, and Kelly helped her get the hose in place.

"You ready to get on with the trip?" Kelly asked as the pump registered the gallons flowing into the tank.

"Yeah," Lauren said softly. Then she looked up and smiled. "Yeah, I am. And I'm sorry if I was a jerk last night."

"You weren't a jerk," Kelly said. "I was. I shouldn't have made such a big deal about Marshall."

"No, you were right. There was no point getting so worked up about a guy I'll probably never see again."

"You've got his address. Maybe you will see each other again."

"Maybe," Lauren said. "Friends again?"

"We never stopped being friends," Kelly said. The gas pump snapped off and Kelly looked toward the station. "Think we should go inside and pay for it?"

"Marshall said he'd take care of it. Let's believe him this time."

They piled into the car and rolled out to the edge of the parking lot. Kelly stretched out her legs, relishing the space of the front seat. "Skiing, here we come! Uh-oh."

"What?" Lauren said.

"I left my purse back there on the gas pump."

"You're lucky we're out here in the boonies, or someone would have it by now." Lauren

65

shifted the car into reverse and eased back to the side of the pumps.

"There it is," Kelly said. "It's right where I left it." She opened her door to get her purse.

Lauren stepped out too. "I think I'll go get a soda before we go," Lauren said.

"I don't know how you can drink those things in the morning," Kelly said. "Cola before noon, bleh!"

"What is life without caffeine?" Lauren asked with a laugh. "I'll just run in and get a couple of cans. You want anything?"

"Nope. Like I said, all they have at these places is soda and junk food. I'll wait until lunch."

"Back in a second!"

Kelly hopped back in the car and pulled the highway map out of the glove box. She found their location on the map and frowned at the long gap between where they were and where they wanted to be. Maybe she could convince Lauren to let her do some driving. If they took turns and stayed on the road all night, they could still be at the slopes before dawn.

There was a loud thump from the front of the car. Startled, Kelly dropped the map and saw Lauren leaning against the hood of the car. She was facing the station, holding herself up with a hand on the hail-dented hood of the Mustang.

Her normally tan skin was gray as stone. Beyond her, the door to the station swung slowly closed on its hinges.

Kelly pushed open her door. "Lauren? Lauren, are you okay?"

Lauren turned toward Kelly. Her dark eyes were dull and unfocused. Her hand slipped over the blue hood of the car, and she began to fall. Kelly struggled to release her seat belt and get out, but before she could, Lauren had toppled to the ground.

Kelly ran around the car and knelt beside Lauren. "Lauren! What happened?"

There was a crash from the station as the front door flew open. Marshall stepped out into the sunlight. His face was as calm as ever, but his blue eyes were blazing. His brown satchel dangled from his left hand. "What are you two doing back here?" he said in a cold voice.

Anger swept through Kelly. She looked up at him. "What did you do to Lauren?"

Marshall took a long step closer. "Why did you come back?" he said.

Kelly started to stand. "Answer my question, you son of—"

Marshall moved much faster than Kelly had expected; faster than she would have believed. He crossed the parking lot in a flash, and his long fingers bit into Kelly's shoulder as he pulled her to her feet. She felt the blood drain from her face. He pulled again, and Kelly felt her tennis shoes leave the ground as he held her out like a rag doll.

"Be very careful what you say," Marshall said. He spoke quietly, and there was no emotion in his voice, but it was more frightening than any mad screaming that Kelly had ever heard. He dropped her and she fell to her knees.

Marshall looked down at them. "To answer your question, I did nothing to her." He took a few steps away and stared off at the highway.

Kelly's heart was beating so hard that it made her head ring. She lifted Lauren's head and saw that her eyes were open. Tears streamed down her cheeks. "Get up!" Kelly whispered urgently. "We've got to get out of here."

Lauren put her hand on the bumper of the Mustang, and Kelly helped her up. She had almost made it to the door of the car when Marshall turned back to them. "Put her in the back," he said. "I want you to drive." When Kelly didn't move, he grabbed her by the arm and shoved her against the car. "Do it now."

Kelly scrambled away. "No! I'm not doing anything for you." She backed away, looking around for anything to use as a weapon.

"Obviously," Marshall said, "I'm not making myself clear." He reached into his satchel and pulled out a pistol. But he didn't point it at Kelly. He went over to where Lauren still leaned against the car and spun her around to face Kelly. Then he put the muzzle of the gun into the short black hair at the back of Lauren's head.

"Get in and drive or I'll blow your sexy friend's brains out." He wrapped his other arm around Lauren's throat and pulled her tight against his chest. "There. Is that clear enough?"

Tears were still sliding down Lauren's face, and her body jerked as she sobbed silently. Kelly licked her dry lips. "All right," she said. "I'll drive. Just leave Lauren alone."

"Of course," Marshall said. He guided Lauren over to the Mustang and helped her into the backseat.

Marshall climbed into the passenger seat as Kelly walked around the car. She opened the driver's-side door and got in slowly, keeping her eyes on Marshall.

"Good girl," Marshall said. He flashed a smile that was just as bright as it had been the day before. "Now drive."

Kelly had to adjust the seat so her feet could reach the pedals. She started the car and made a slow turn through the parking lot. As they passed the door to the station, she saw something on the floor just inside.

She couldn't be sure what it was, but she thought it was a body.

Kelly pulled away from the station. She flipped on her signal and headed for the ramp back to the interstate.

"No," Marshall said. "Stay on this road."

Kelly looked at the road ahead. It stretched out into the distance, running straight as an arrow between fields of black dirt. "Where does this road go?" she asked.

"Does it matter?" Marshall asked.

SIX

They stayed on the road for hours. There were very few trees, and the road seemed to stretch on forever. After a few miles the patchy blacktop gave way to rutted gravel. Clouds of pale dust followed the car as Kelly drove past barns and farmhouses separated by miles of empty fields. In some places herds of cattle looked up as they passed, but in most there was only the black earth.

For the first hour of that long bumpy ride, very little was said. Lauren's soft crying turned to silence, and when Kelly glanced in the rearview mirror, it appeared that Lauren had fallen asleep. She couldn't tell if it was a normal sleep or something like shock.

Marshall spent a few minutes looking over

the map. After that, he just stared at the gravel road ahead with single-minded intensity.

Finally boredom overcame Kelly's fear. "Can I turn on the radio?" she asked.

"Go ahead," Marshall said.

Kelly twisted the knob and got only a burst of static. She searched through the FM channels and found nothing but distant whispers. The AM band wasn't much better, but she found a religious station near the bottom of the dial. The voice of a country preacher boomed through the car for a few seconds.

Then Marshall put his hand over Kelly's and turned it off. "I can't take that stuff," he said.

A smart response came quickly to Kelly's tongue, but fear pushed it back. "Where are we going?" she asked.

"You'll see when we get there."

"Well, wherever it is, we're going to have to find a gas station soon. This car drinks a lot of gas."

"You let me worry about that," Marshall said.

Kelly risked a look at him and was surprised to see that he looked pale and nervous. "What are you going to do with us?" she asked.

"That depends on you," he said. "As long as you do what I say, you'll be fine."

Kelly swallowed. She didn't know if it was

better to keep him talking or leave him alone—high school hadn't included a course in dealing with maniacs. But every mile that they traveled down this desolate road was another mile away from the route where they were supposed to be. Every minute decreased the chance that anyone looking for them would ever find them.

"You killed someone back there, didn't you?" she said. She was surprised by the strength in her own voice.

"What do you think happened?" Marshall asked.

"I think you shot the station attendant," Kelly said. She stopped to lick her dry lips before going on. "I guess you were going to steal his car, or maybe you wanted the money. Anyway, we came back and Lauren saw everything."

"You're a very smart girl, Kelly." He stretched out an arm and put his hand on the back of her seat. "I can't say I'm sorry you came back. You girls have been a big help to me."

Kelly leaned forward to keep from touching his hand. "Why did you pick us in the first place?"

"That was really a great piece of luck. If you hadn't come along when you did, well, I could have been in a very tight spot."

"You were running," Kelly guessed. "When

we picked you up, I mean. You were running away from some crime."

"Let's just say I was in quite a hurry to do some traveling." He laughed, not the gentle chuckle he had used when joking with Lauren, but a mean, hard-edged laugh.

In the backseat Lauren moaned and mumbled something in her sleep. Kelly glanced at her in the mirror. She knew there was something wrong about the way Lauren was reacting, but she didn't know if waking her or letting her sleep was better.

Kelly looked over at Marshall and saw that his blue eyes were again touched with that frightening inner fire. "When you don't need us anymore, you'll kill us. Won't you?" she asked.

"Like I said," Marshall replied, "that depends on you."

"They're going to catch you," Kelly said.

Marshall snatched his hand back from her chair. "They won't catch me."

"You were going to ride with us all the way to Denver, but then you changed your mind. Why did you change your mind, Marshall? Did the police know where you were going?"

"We've talked enough," he said.

"They probably found your car."

"Shut up."

"I wonder if they've found that gas-station attendant yet?"

"That's enough!" For the first time his voice rose with anger. "You girls are useful, but if you get in my way, I'll leave you lying in a ditch. You understand?"

Kelly nodded. That was the end of the conversation.

It was well after noon and the gas gauge was almost at E before the road intersected a larger highway. "Which way?" Kelly asked.

"Turn left," Marshall replied.

A few minutes later Kelly saw a water tower standing above the plains. And not long after that she saw a small town at its base. "Just in time," she said.

"Turn in over there," Marshall said. He pointed to a store at the edge of the town. It had a row of gas pumps and a glass front that showed shelves of groceries inside.

Kelly pulled up next to one of the pumps. "Now what?"

"Fill it up, and get a six-pack of soda. If it were your friend here," he jerked his thumb at Lauren, "I'd have her get me something stronger. But I don't think they'd sell it to you."

"What about something to eat?"

"Get whatever you want. You have cash?" Marshall asked.

"Yes."

"Good, use it. Don't use a credit card."

"Okay," Kelly said. She opened her door and started to get out.

Marshall put a hand on her arm. "And remember, I'm right out here watching. You do anything I don't like—anything—and I'll make sure that pretty Lauren never wakes up."

Kelly had thought that she had run out of fear, but at his words her stomach tightened. "All right," she said.

"One more thing," he said. "Buy some shoelaces, the kind for sneakers. Get at least four pairs."

"Shoelaces," Kelly repeated numbly.

"Don't forget." Marshall eased the gun from his satchel. "I'd hate to have to use this."

Kelly closed the door and walked around the car to pump the gas. She hadn't noticed how her hands were shaking until she tried to get the nozzle into the gas tank. It took her three tries, and she spilled a puddle of gas beside the car. She could feel Marshall's eyes on her all the time.

When the tank was full, she wrestled the hose back onto the pump. Her hands were burning from the spilled gas, and she wished she could go to the bathroom and wash them off, but she was sure that Marshall wouldn't allow it. She settled for wiping her hands on her jeans and walked toward the store.

A cowbell over the door clanked as Kelly walked in, and the woman behind the counter looked up with a smile. She was an older lady, with short gray hair and thick metal-rimmed glasses. "Good afternoon," she said.

Kelly opened her mouth to answer, then remembered that Marshall was watching. She turned away from the counter and walked back between the racks of food. She snatched a bag of nacho chips from one rack. It wasn't what she wanted—she hated food like that—but it would have to do. She walked back to the refrigerated cases. There didn't seem to be any six-packs, so Kelly pulled out individual cans. The heap of cans made a cold clumsy bundle in her arms, and she hurried toward the counter to put them down.

"Is this everything?" the woman asked.

"Yes," Kelly said. "Wait, I mean no." She looked out the window and saw Marshall looking in. "Just a minute."

She backed away from the counter and went to find the shoelaces. She found car supplies, magazines, and toiletries, but no shoelaces. She went back to the counter and asked for them, aware every moment that Marshall might think she was saying something about him.

The woman pursed her lips and craned her neck as she peered around the store. "I know we have some. Hmmm . . . oh yes! They're right back there in the corner, beside the fishing lures."

"Thank you," Kelly said. She fought back a wave of hysterical laughter. Beside the fishing lures. Of course!

The laces were on a rack that separated them by size and type, but almost all of the slots in the rack were empty. All that remained were short black laces and long leather bootlaces. There were no sneaker laces.

Kelly grabbed the bootlaces. How many had Marshall asked for? She couldn't remember. There were six pairs. She took them all. When she turned to go back to the counter, a policeman was standing at the entrance to the store.

Like the woman behind the counter, the policeman had a head of shining silver hair. A matching gray mustache hung over his mouth. His uniform was tan, with a bright silver star that peeked through the open front of a worn leather jacket. When she saw him, the relief that went through Kelly was so strong that she almost fell. One of the packages of bootlaces dropped from her hands and clicked on the wooden floor. She didn't notice.

Everything's going to be all right. The police are here, and they'll take care of everything.

Kelly felt an unstoppable smile come to her face.

The policeman was looking at her curiously as she walked toward him. "You need something, miss?" he asked.

"Yes," Kelly breathed.

She was almost to him, the big grin still frozen on her face, when she remembered that Marshall was watching. Marshall was sitting outside with the barrel of his pistol against Lauren's sleeping head.

"What's wrong?" the policeman asked.

"Nothing's wrong," Kelly said quickly. She cursed herself for being so stupid. If Marshall even thought she had said something, he could be angry enough to kill Lauren. "I just wanted to know how far it is to Kansas City."

The policeman exchanged a puzzled look with the woman at the counter. "Child, if you're going to Kansas City, you're going the wrong way."

"I probably got things mixed up," she said. She dropped the packs of bootlaces on the counter. "That's all I need."

The woman pushed her glasses up with one finger. "You got gas, didn't you?"

"That's right."

The woman slowly worked the keys on her cash register. All the while the policeman stood at the end of the counter. "You're sure you're all right?" he asked.

I'm being kidnapped, she thought. But what she said was, "Yes, I'm fine." She added what she hoped was a reassuring smile.

The woman gave Kelly the total and put all her purchases in a paper sack. Kelly paid her and picked up the bag.

"Can I help you with that?" the policeman asked.

Kelly shook her head. She didn't trust herself to say another word without blurting out the whole story. She hurried out to the car and climbed in. Lauren was still asleep in the backseat.

Marshall took the sack from her and put it at his feet. "Drive," he demanded.

Kelly drove. In minutes only the water tower marked the location of the little town on the wide prairie behind them. The highway ended at a T intersection. Kelly stopped. The road in front of them was blacktopped and lined by telephone poles.

"Which way now?"

"What did you say to the policeman?" Marshall asked.

"Nothing," Kelly said. The pain was so sudden and intense that it took Kelly a moment to realize that he had slapped her.

80

"What did you say to the policeman?"

"He asked me if I needed anything."

"Yes?"

"And I told him no," she said.

"And that's all?" he asked mildly.

"That's all."

Marshall took her chin in his hand and turned her face toward him. "Kelly, Kelly. Don't lie to me. You said more than that, and so did he."

"I said yes." Her words were blurred by his hand on her face. "I asked him directions to Kansas City, and he told me I was going the wrong way."

"And then?"

"Nothing. I mean, that's all."

"You're sure?" he said.

"Yes."

Marshall released her chin. "Turn left again. And the next time I send you into someplace, don't talk to anyone. Is that clear?"

Kelly nodded, but his words hurt as much as the slap. *The next time*, he had said. How many times would she have to repeat this act? How long would this nightmare go on? There was a pain in her throat as sobs struggled to get out. It had been hours since she had eaten, but fear filled her like a lump of iron.

She drove the Mustang up onto the black-top. Gravel spun away from the tires as she accelerated. Driving on the smooth road seemed amazingly quiet after the hours they had spent rumbling across gravel.

There was a gentle rise ahead, and as they reached the top, a green sign went by on the right. WELCOME TO NEBRASKA, read the sign.

"Well, what do you know, Toto," Marshall said. "We're not in Kansas anymore." His laugh echoed in the car.

SEVEN

From the sun and the few highway signs she saw, Kelly figured they spent most of the afternoon going north. This road wasn't quite as desolate as the one they had followed across Kansas. They passed through several small towns, where there was more traffic. Lauren slept the entire time, and Kelly began to wonder if she would ever wake up. When sunset came, they were rolling though one of a series of small ranching communities.

"We'll have to stop soon," Marshall announced.

"Already?" Kelly asked.

"I don't want you to drive when you're tired," he said. "I can't afford an accident. And Lauren's in no condition to drive." Marshall pointed at a sign beside the road that advertised a motel some miles ahead. "We'll stay there tonight."

"Why don't you drive?" Kelly asked.

"Don't be stupid," Marshall replied. "It's too hard to drive and hold a gun at the same time."

"Oh." She glanced down at his rough hands on the knees of his jeans and the brown satchel resting in his lap. "I guess that's true."

The sunset was beautiful. A thousand shades of purple poured across the sky, and the western horizon glowed with crimson light for long minutes. It seemed wrong to Kelly that anything could look so nice when she was so terrified.

Then it was dark. There was no period of getting dark. It just was dark. And the black sky was filled with ten times the number of stars that Kelly could see from home.

A grayish form ran through the headlights and disappeared into the scrub at the side of the road. "What was that?" Kelly asked.

"Coyote," Marshall said. "There are lots of them around here."

Kelly glanced over at him. "Are you from around here, Marshall?"

"No," he said. "I'm not from anywhere."

"But you're not a medical student from Indiana, either. Are you?"

"As far as you're concerned, I am."

The motel turned out to be a small place where the rooms were little buildings set off by themselves. At one time it might have been charming. Now it looked run-down and shabby.

"Are you sure we should stay here?" Kelly asked.

"I've stayed in worse," Marshall said. He reached over and turned off the engine. "Go get us a room, and remember to pay with cash."

"What should I tell them?" she asked.

"About what?"

"About us. Who do I say we are?"

Marshall snorted. "Tell them anything you want. Tell them we're brother and sister. Tell them that we're married. Tell them that we're not married. I don't think the folks that run this place are going to care."

Marshall was right. The guy behind the motel counter wore a stained white T-shirt that was barely big enough to cover his bulging stomach. Kelly just asked for a room, and he gave it to her with no questions asked. For twenty-four dollars he handed over the keys to one of the little bungalows.

When she got back outside, Marshall was helping Lauren out of the car. Lauren still seemed half asleep, but Kelly was glad to see her standing up.

"Give me the keys," Marshall said. He took

the plastic key ring from Kelly and shoved it in his jeans. "Now help me get her to the room. She's still pretty out of it."

Kelly positioned herself on one side of Lauren, holding on to her right arm while her left was draped over Marshall's shoulders. Lauren stumbled forward with her head hanging down. Her eyes were open but unfocused.

"What's wrong with her?" Kelly asked. "Shouldn't she have snapped out of this by now?"

Marshall grunted as he took most of Lauren's weight. "How should I know?"

"Aren't you the medical student?"

"Shut up," he replied.

Marshall slipped as he tried to open the door to the room, and Lauren almost fell. Kelly strained to hold her up until Marshall could steady her again. Lauren's face lay on Kelly's shoulder, looking terribly slack and empty.

"She'd better be okay," Kelly said.

Marshall paused with his hand on the doorknob. "What was that?"

"Lauren better be okay, or I'll—"

"You'll what?" Marshall interrupted. At the sound of his voice, the anger that had been building in Kelly turned to fear. He leaned toward her, the limp form of Lauren the only thing between them. "Never threaten me," he said. He pushed open the door, and together they managed to get Lauren inside.

The heat wasn't on in the little cabin, and it was just as cold inside as out. The air smelled of old cigarettes and mildew. The two beds were narrow and covered with yellow blankets so faded they were almost white. There was a small round table with an ancient black phone at one end of the room and a green-painted dresser at the other. Only the television looked new.

"Charming," Marshall said. He eased Lauren onto one of the beds, and the old mattress squeaked and sagged.

He walked across the room and picked up the telephone. "They should charge extra for the antiques," he said. Then he gave the phone a savage yank. The cord came out of the wall with a little explosion of plaster dust. "Wouldn't want you to get tempted."

Kelly didn't mind. It had just occurred to her that Marshall meant to sleep. And if he slept, that would be their chance. All she had to do was hit him or maybe take the gun away. She was so caught up in this idea that she barely heard Marshall talking to her.

"What was that?"

"I asked you where the shoelaces were," he said.

"Oh, I left those in the car," she said.

"Go get them. I'll stay here and take care of your little friend." He ran a hand over Lauren's slack cheek. "Don't leave us alone too long."

Kelly hurried across the gravel to the car. The thought of what Marshall might do to the sleeping Lauren was enough to make her almost run. She knocked on the door and sweated every second until Marshall opened it.

"Here they are." She handed him the sack.

Marshall took out a package and looked at them. "I thought I said sneaker laces."

"They didn't have any."

"I suppose these will do." He looked up at Kelly. "If you need to do anything to get ready for bed, then do it now. You won't get another chance."

"I think I'll just keep my jeans on," Kelly said.

Marshall laughed. "Always a good idea. Okay then, lie down next to Lauren."

"Lie down? But there's not enough room on these beds."

"Fine. You can always sleep on the other bed with me."

Kelly sat down on the bed beside Lauren and took off her shoes. She watched as Marshall unwrapped the package and stretched the leather laces to their full length. And then she understood what she should have known since he first asked her to pick up the laces. Understood why Marshall wasn't worried about going to sleep. "You're going to use those to tie me up, right?"

"Yes," he said. "Put your feet together." He knelt in front of her with a pair of laces in his hand. "Don't get any bright ideas," he added.

Kelly shivered at the feel of his hands on her feet and the rough strands of leather sliding around her ankles. She tried to keep a small gap between her feet, to make some slack she might use to escape, but Marshall pushed her feet back together, binding them firmly.

"That's too tight," she said.

"It's your fault for getting leather laces," he replied. "They'll stretch, so I have to make them extra tight to begin with."

He stood up and held out another bootlace. "Now your hands."

Kelly was closer to crying than she had been since Lauren had come stumbling out of the gas station. It was hard to believe that it had only been that morning, that the whole long ordeal had lasted less than twenty-four hours. And two nights before, Kelly had gone to sleep in her own bed, dreaming of the great vacation to come. She closed her eyes to hold back the tears.

Marshall pulled Kelly's hands behind her back and lashed them together. He tugged the leather laces tight, and they bit into Kelly's wrist. "I could tie you to the bed," he said thoughtfully. "But I don't think that's necessary. You aren't going to go anywhere, are you?"

"No," she whispered.

Marshall leaned over her, and again his mask of charm slipped. The expression on his face wasn't a smile—it was a leer. "Seeing you like this is very tempting." He ran a hand through her hair and cradled her neck.

He lifted her from the bed until her face was only an inch from his. "You know, we could have a real good time together. I don't think Lauren will mind."

Kelly closed her eyes again. "Leave me alone," she choked out.

Marshall pulled his hand away and let her fall back to the bed. "Your friend is prettier anyway."

Kelly opened one eye and watched as Marshall started to tie up Lauren's feet. He looked up at her. "Maybe Lauren and me will have some fun before she even wakes up."

Lauren's foot came up and struck him in the face.

Marshall flew backward and fell across the dresser. Lauren surged to her feet and went toward him. Kelly strained against her bonds, but she could do nothing but watch.

Marshall rolled over and looked up with an emotion Kelly could have sworn was fear. Lauren was standing over him. The brown satchel that held his gun was on the other bed. She could surely beat him to it. Or she could kick him or . . . but it didn't matter, because Lauren wasn't really awake.

She was batting at the air in front of her; waving her arms as if she was fighting off cobwebs. Her eyes darted around the room, following things that Kelly couldn't see.

Marshall chuckled and stood up. Lauren's eyes danced across him unseeing. He grabbed her wrists. "It's all right, Lauren. Go back to bed." She struggled for a second longer; then she sagged against him. Marshall half carried her back to the bed and put her beside Kelly. She didn't stir again while he bound her feet and hands.

"Now," Marshall said, "if you'll be quiet, that's all it will take. If you start making any noise, I'll have to gag you. Understand?"

"Yes," Kelly said.

"Then I'm going to bed. You better hide your eyes if you don't want to see something, little girl." Marshall pulled off his shirt, revealing a body that was flat and hard. His hands went to the buckle of his jeans and Kelly looked away. A moment later she heard him slide into bed.

"When will you let us go?" she asked.

"When we get where we're going."

"Where are we going?"

"You don't need to know that," Marshall said. "Now go to sleep."

Kelly lay awake for a long time. Lauren seemed to be sleeping peacefully again, and after a while Kelly heard Marshall's breathing change to a slow, even rhythm. But Kelly was afraid to sleep. She was half afraid of what Marshall might do if he woke up first. And she was afraid of the dreams that might come. But when at last she did sleep, it was only darkness.

It was the shower that woke Kelly up. She rolled over and saw Lauren beside her, but Marshall's bed was empty. Kelly tried to sit up—a hard thing to do with her hands tied behind her back. Listening carefully to the sounds of the shower, she pushed herself off the end of the bed.

She felt like a human pogo stick as she hopped across the floor. Twice she fell to her knees and had to roll over before she could stand up again. But at last she reached her goal—the old green dresser. She knelt down, turned her back to the dresser, and worked the drawer open with her free fingers. Then she turned around and looked inside. There was only a thin blanket and a battered copy of the Gideon's Bible.

Kelly pushed the drawer closed with her legs and repeated the trick on the other three drawers in the dresser. They were all empty. Kelly slumped down. Her arms and legs ached from the effort of working against the knots Marshall had tied. She put her back against the wall and pushed her way to her feet. She was going to get back on the bed when she noticed there was a drawer in the small table that the phone sat on. She started hopping toward it.

The shower went off and Kelly froze. She looked at the bathroom door, then back at table. She bit her lip and kept going. She was almost there when she heard the shower curtain being pulled back. Kelly turned so she could open the drawer. Her fingers slid off the slick wood for a few frustrating seconds before she got a grip and it slipped open. She turned, sure that she was going to be disappointed again.

There was a pen, some stationery, and a stack of envelopes in the drawer. Kelly twisted around again and stretched her fingers down to grasp the pen. She couldn't get a grip on the stationery, but she managed a hold on one of the envelopes.

There was another noise from the bathroom. Kelly turned, knocked the drawer closed with her knee, and bounded toward the bed. The mattress was still bouncing from her impact when the bathroom door opened and Marshall came out.

He wore his jeans, and a ragged towel was over his shoulders. His dark hair was wet, and drops of water clung to his skin. "Good morning," he said.

Kelly worked her fingers behind her to slide the envelope and pen into her jeans. "I need to go to the bathroom," she said.

"Sure. I don't think you can get into any trouble in there." Marshall walked over and pulled her up. "Be good while I untie you, or you'll have to hop in there."

"Okay."

He set to work on the knots on her ankles. Kelly thought about trying to kick him like Lauren had, but she was sure that he was ready for that. Marshall had been right that the leather would stretch. The laces weren't nearly as painful as when he had first tied her. Still, she could feel blood rushing into her feet when he unraveled the last knot. She turned so he could get to her hands.

Kelly was afraid that he would spot the pen jutting from the back of her jeans, but he untied her hands without a word. "Thank you," she said as she massaged her aching hands.

"Just don't take too long in there," Marshall said.

She nodded and slipped past him. She shut the bathroom door, locked it, and leaned against it. Just having the barrier between herself and Marshall felt very good.

As soon as she slid the pen and envelope from her pocket, she had her doubts. The envelope was so old it had turned yellow. The pen looked just as ancient. It would be just perfect if she had done all of this only to find that the pen wouldn't write.

It wrote.

Kidnapped, Kelly wrote. *Kelly Tallon and Lauren Miki from St. Louis. Being held by a man with blue eyes and dark-brown hair who calls himself Marshall. Traveling north in a blue Mustang with Missouri plates.* She wished she could remember Lauren's license-plate number, or if Marshall had given a last name after they had picked him up. But she hoped what was on the note would be enough.

She looked around the bathroom for somewhere to hide the note. She wanted to put it someplace where Marshall wouldn't see it if he came back in the room, but where whoever came to clean up when they were gone would be bound to find it. Her first thought was the shower, but then she had a better idea.

Just above the sink was a light fixture that held a single bulb. Being careful not to make noise, Kelly removed the cover. The bulb was hot, but she managed to turn it enough to make it go out. With the light out it was pitch-black in the bathroom, but she managed to get the envelope into the lamp and the cover back on.

"You almost done in there?"

"Yes," Kelly called. "Just a minute."

When she came out, Kelly was startled to see Lauren sitting on the side of the bed talking with Marshall.

"Look who's up," Marshall said.

"Lauren, are you okay?"

"Sure, Kel, but . . . well, I just don't understand how we got here." Lauren smiled apologetically. "I don't know what's wrong with me."

Kelly walked over to Lauren. "What do you remember?"

"I remember getting to the motel, getting up to see . . . the rest of the night. But I just don't remember yesterday at all."

"I was telling her about the shortcut we were taking," Marshall said, "and how we got lost." He gave a little laugh. "I can understand why she doesn't want to remember that."

"But, Lauren, don't you remember the gas station?" Kelly asked.

"Gas station?" Lauren looked genuinely puzzled.

Marshall stepped between them. "Look, let

me get my stuff and we'll go find a place to eat. We can talk about it there." He walked around the corner into the bathroom.

Kelly heard him flip the light switch several times. "It's burned out," she called.

"What gas station?" Lauren repeated.

"Lauren!" Kelly whispered fiercely. "We didn't get lost, Marshall kidnapped us. Don't you remember anything?"

"Kidnapped?" Lauren said. "That's not funny, Kel."

Marshall came out of the bathroom. "Are we ready to go?"

"Yes," Lauren said. "I think so."

"Good. Then let's get out of this dump." Marshall held the door while Lauren went out. After she left, he turned to Kelly. "And you watch what you say."

She left the room and followed Lauren across the gravel parking lot.

EIGHT

Kelly wanted to scream. Not out of fear of Marshall, but out of pure frustration.

She had gone through the confusion and sudden terror of the gas station. Had suffered through the long drive filled with a mixture of fear and boredom. Had fought off panic back at the grocery store. Had submitted to being tied up with the leather strips while Marshall leered over her. And now, here was Lauren, talking and laughing with Marshall as if nothing had happened.

"I'm really sorry I'm acting so weird," Lauren said as Kelly walked up. "I don't know why I can't remember anything." She ran a hand over her short hair.

"It's all right," Marshall said. "It could be just some stress you're under."

"Or a shock," Kelly suggested.

Lauren turned to her. "What kind of shock?"

Behind Lauren's back Marshall was shaking his head and making suggestive gestures with the brown satchel that held his pistol. But Kelly was too upset to stop herself.

"Like being kidnapped and dragged across two states," she said.

Marshall laughed. "Sounds like Kelly must be having some trouble with her memory, too."

Lauren was looking at Kelly with a strange expression. She tilted her head to one side, and her forehead creased in confusion. "Why do you keep saying that, Kel?"

"Because it's true," Kelly said firmly.

Marshall sighed loudly. "Well, I guess I better explain what happened yesterday." He put his hands in his pockets and leaned back against the car. "You know that Kelly didn't want me riding along with you, right?"

Lauren nodded.

"Well," he continued, "she tried to get me to stay at that place we were at yesterday until a friend could come and get me."

"That's not true!" Kelly shouted, but she could see how much Marshall was enjoying this; how fooling Lauren had become another part of his game.

"You and Kelly fought," he said, and the expression on his face was a fine imitation of regret. "Believe me, I'm sorry about it. I never wanted to step between two friends like you."

"Liar," Kelly said.

Lauren hushed her. "Let him finish," she said.

"Anyway," Marshall said, "you told her you were going to help me, and we decided to get off the interstate and see some scenery along the way." He shrugged. "We got lost, and here we are."

"That's not the way it happened," Kelly said.

Lauren put both hands over her face and shook her head. "I just can't remember."

Marshall put a gentle hand on her shoulder. "It'll come back to you," he said. His voice was as kind as it had ever been, but over her lowered head, he was flashing Kelly a look of pure hate. "Do you feel up to driving?"

"Yes," Lauren said. She nodded her head and pulled her hands away. "Let's get on the road, okay?"

Marshall opened the door and helped Lauren into her seat. "Don't worry," he told her. "It'll be all right." He shut the door with a solid thump.

Kelly started to get in on the other side, but Marshall took her arm in a painfully tight grip. "You say one more word about what happened yesterday and I'll snap your little neck. We'll see how pretty Lauren reacts to that shock."

"You're sick," Kelly said. Her voice was trembling, but she hadn't cried yet, and she wasn't going to give Marshall that satisfaction now. "You're enjoying this."

"It helps to pass the time," Marshall said. He opened the door and pushed the front seat down so Kelly could get in the back.

A few miles up the road there was a town large enough to support a cluster of fast-food places. Marshall and Lauren picked a place and slid into the drive-thru lane. Kelly didn't want to ask for anything, didn't want to talk to either one of them. But she hadn't eaten much over the last two days, and she was getting very hungry. She gave her order as quickly as she could.

Marshall was keeping up the pretense that they had been lost the day before, and he consulted the map while they munched their food in the parking lot. "We could turn around and take this road back the way we came," he said, "but it'll take us all day and we'll still be a long way from where we need to go."

"Is there another way?"

Marshall pointed at the thin lines that wandered over the map. "If we stay on this road, it'll lead us to this other interstate. From there we can go west to Denver."

Kelly peered through the gap between the

front seats. "It looks to me like that interstate runs northwest."

"We'll have to turn south once we're in Wyoming, but it should be a lot faster than going back."

"All right," Lauren said. "Let's get going."

The landscape began to change from that of midwestern farms to the high plains. The plowed fields of dark earth gave way to gently rolling hills covered in sparse grass and brush. There were cows, but they were strung out in small clumps instead of tightly packed herds. Outside of the towns, the houses were even farther apart, and for miles they drove between hills where not a single building was visible.

Kelly was cold in the backseat. There had been frost on the car when they started out that morning, and if the heat was on in the front, none of it had worked its way back to Kelly. She curled into a ball, wishing she had never left home.

Marshall and Lauren carried on a conversation through most of the morning. Kelly didn't pay much attention to what they were saying. It seemed like the same conversation they had been having the night they picked up Marshall: Lauren's dad drove her too hard, the guys in high school never treated her like a person, why shouldn't she go to the school where she wanted to go? Marshall nodded and made agreeable noises to everything she said. Every now and then Marshall interjected some little story of his own that backed up what Lauren was saying.

Then Lauren suddenly stopped talking. She relaxed her foot on the gas pedal, and the car began to slow.

"What's wrong?" Marshall asked.

She looked over at him. "Didn't you say you weren't going to ride with us today?"

"No, I . . ."

Kelly leaned close. "It was yesterday. He said that about yesterday."

Lauren nodded. "You wanted us to take you somewhere. Then you were going to get a ride with someone else."

Marshall was shaking his head hard. "It never happened, Lauren. You must have dreamed it."

But Lauren didn't even seem to hear him. "We took you to—"

"A gas station!" Kelly shouted.

"Yes," Lauren said. "That's right, to a gas station."

"No," Marshall said. "It never happened."

"We dropped him off," Kelly prompted.

"And then I went back for a soda," Lauren said. She was nodding her head enthusiastically now. "I remember!"

"Lauren, stop this!" Marshall practically shouted.

"I went in for a soda, and I saw Marshall standing beside the counter and he had a . . ." She stumbled for a second, and Kelly saw her stiffen. "He had a gun in his hand and there was a—"

Lauren slammed on the brakes.

Kelly was thrown against the back of Lauren's seat. The force of the impact knocked the breath out of her, and she could see the landscape outside the car revolving like the view from a merry-go-round as the car went spinning down the highway.

The horn sounded as Lauren was pushed against the wheel, but she had her seat belt on. She fought with the car, trying to keep it from sliding into a ditch, but never letting the pressure off the brakes.

Marshall was not wearing his seat belt. His head struck the windshield hard enough to leave a star of cracks in the tinted glass. He bounced back, and Kelly got a glimpse of his dark-blue eyes rolling back as he slumped and slid down in his seat.

The Mustang slid around one last time, tottered on two wheels as if it might roll over, then fell back to the pavement and was still. For a few seconds Kelly was aware of nothing but her own painful effort to pull air into her bruised chest. Then the door opened, the seat in front of her flopped down, and Lauren was leaning over her.

"Are you okay, Kel?" she asked anxiously.

Kelly nodded. "Marshall," she choked out. "What about Marshall?"

Lauren looked over at the other seat and then back at Kelly. "He looks out of it. I think he hit his head."

Kelly nodded again, and she held her hands out. Lauren helped her climb out of the car. Standing up, Kelly felt better, and her labored breathing was easier.

Lauren was looking through the open door at Marshall's crumpled form. "You don't think he's dead, do you?"

"No," Kelly managed. "I don't think so."

"Oh, Kel. You were right, weren't you? He kidnapped us." She turned to Kelly and her eyes were very bright, brimming with tears. "I'm sorry I didn't listen to you."

Everything got blurry. It took Kelly a moment to realize it was because she was crying herself. "It's okay."

Lauren held out her arms, and for a long minute the two friends stood beside the road and hugged each other while a chill wind whistled around the stopped car.

"What do we do now?" Lauren said at last.

"We go to the police," Kelly said. "I think he killed more people than the one at the gas station."

"You think he'll stay out long enough for us to get somewhere with a police station?"

"I'm not taking a chance on that." Kelly walked around to the passenger side of the car and opened the door. "Come on, help me."

Lauren walked around to join her. "What are you going to do?"

"We'll leave him here. Then we don't have to worry about finding help before he wakes up."

Kelly reached in and grabbed one of Marshall's arms. She half expected him to suddenly spring up and grab her, but his arm was as limp as a rag doll's. It took all their strength to pull Marshall out of the car and into the lank grass at the side of the road. His forehead was swollen terrifically.

"Now what?" Lauren asked.

"Now we tie him up like he did to us."

"He tied us up?"

Kelly took Lauren's wrist and held it up to her face. "Look."

Lauren stared at the thin red lines where the tight leather strips had worked into her skin. "That jerk," she said fiercely.

Kelly spotted Marshall's brown satchel lying

on the floor of the car. She reached for it and pulled it out. "We need the shoelaces he used on us. Let's see if he's got them in here." She opened the satchel and started to look inside. She could see the dull metal gleam of the pistol, a roll of money, and what looked like several yellow plastic pill bottles.

Marshall groaned and rolled over.

"Kelly, come on, let's go."

"He's not tied up," Kelly said. "He might just get up and walk away."

Marshall moaned again. Lauren took several steps away from him. "Where can he go? It's been ten miles since we even saw a house. And at least we'll be away from him."

"Okay," Kelly said. She closed the satchel and tossed it back into the car. "Let's get out of here."

Lauren practically ran around the car and jumped into her seat. As Kelly was shutting her door, Marshall got his hands under him and pushed himself to his knees. By the time the car cleared the next hill, Marshall was on his feet and staggering after them.

"That was close," Lauren said. "Is the gun in the bag?"

"Yeah."

"We should have just shot him."

Kelly looked at her, trying to see if she was

serious. Lauren looked serious. "The police will get him," Kelly said.

A red pickup truck came toward them in the left lane. "Maybe we can get them to help us," Lauren suggested, pointing at the truck.

"It's probably just an old farmer or something. We better wait till we can find somebody that knows what they're doing." The truck rolled past on the left, and Kelly got a glimpse of a man in a cowboy hat. Kelly turned to watch the truck as it disappeared into the distance. Watching it pass out of sight, she suddenly felt very light-headed. "We made it," she said. "We got away from him."

They drove on for a few minutes before coming to a store on the side of the road. Even from a distance, it was obvious that the store had been closed for a very long time. But there was a bright blue sign at its side and a telephone booth that looked like it was still in business.

"Let's pull over there," Kelly said. "We can call the police before he has a chance to get away."

Lauren pulled off into the dirt parking lot. Both girls got out of the car and walked over to the booth. It was one of the old kind, a little metal-and-glass room with a folding door on one side. "Which one of us should call?" Lauren asked.

"I will." Kelly stepped into the booth. She picked up the phone and punched 911. Then she frowned.

"What's wrong?" Lauren asked.

"We're too far out in the country. There's no emergency system here."

"Call the operator. They'll know what to do."

It took a few minutes of question and answer for the operator to figure out which police department covered the area where they were calling from. Then Kelly had to insist that the call was a real emergency.

"What's going on?" Lauren asked.

"They're putting us through to a sheriff's office. It's ringing now." Over Lauren's shoulder Kelly saw a vehicle coming down the road in the same direction that they had come. It looked like a pickup.

"Sheriff's office," said a voice over the phone.

"Hello," Kelly said. "I want to report a murder and a kidnapping."

"Is this a joke?"

"No," Kelly said. "No joke."

"Can you hold on just minute while I get the sheriff on the line?"

"Sure." Kelly lowered the phone. "They're getting the sheriff now. It won't be long."

It was the noise that made her look up. The pickup had pulled off the road and was rumbling toward them across the parking lot.

"Miss? Are you there?" said a voice on the phone.

"Run!" Kelly shouted. She dropped the phone and ran. Lauren was just beside her as she rounded the corner of the deserted store. There was a huge crash behind them, and Kelly turned her head to see the truck—the same red pickup truck that had passed them on the road—plow through the phone both, shattering it into a thousand pieces.

"My car!" Lauren cried. "We've got to get to my car!" She turned away from the building and sprinted for the Mustang.

"No!" Kelly yelled.

But Lauren was running flat out. Brown dust puffed up around her tennis shoes as she ran. The pickup turned, and the engine roared as it started after Lauren.

Kelly ran after them, but there was nothing she could do. The truck was closing on Lauren. In a moment it would be on top of her. Then it did something that Kelly didn't expect. It swerved around Lauren, cut back in, and skidded to a stop next to the Mustang. The driver's door flew open.

Only a step away from the side of the truck,

Lauren screamed and stepped back. Kelly froze in midstep and almost fell.

Marshall stepped out of the truck.

The bump on his forehead had turned dark red. His blue eyes blazed like neon. Kelly expected him to threaten them, to strike Lauren, or to come for her. She expected to die. But none of those things happened.

Marshall stepped down out of the truck and immediately fell to his knees. He got a hand on the side of the truck and pulled himself back up. He looked at the two girls for a moment, his bright eyes sweeping over them as if he didn't recognize them. Then he walked around to the other side of the truck.

Kelly realized that she had been holding her breath since Marshall stepped out. She let her breath go in a ragged gasp and ran over to Lauren.

"Are you all right?"

Lauren shook her head. "How can I be?"

Then Kelly remembered that Marshall's satchel was in the car. "The gun!" She jumped to her feet.

Marshall came back in view around the rear of the truck. In his left hand was his small brown satchel. In his right was his gun.

"Get in the car," he said. He sounded more tired than angry. "Now." Neither girl moved.

The pistol shot was incredibly loud. The bullet kicked up a clod of hard earth from the parking lot. Kelly could feel some of it spray against the legs of her jeans. The echo of the shot bounced back and forth between the low hills.

"If I fire again," Marshall said. "It will be to kill you. Get in the car now."

Kelly gave Lauren a gentle push, and together they walked around the truck. Marshall followed close behind them with his pistol in his hand.

As she was getting in the car, Lauren stopped and looked at Kelly. "We'll never get away from him, will we?"

Kelly didn't have an answer.

NINE

"Thanks to that little stunt," Marshall said, "we're going to have to change directions again." He seemed to be gaining strength with every mile, returning to his usual state of frightening coldness. The swelling on his forehead was going down, leaving a multicolored bruise in its place.

"Where are you trying to get to?" Kelly asked.

"Wouldn't you like to know." He turned to Lauren. "There's a highway crossing coming up in a few miles. When we get there, turn left."

"What did you do back there?" Lauren asked.

"Back there?"

"How did you get the truck?"

"Oh, the truck." Marshall leaned back in his

seat and put his feet up on the dashboard. "The truck driver was a real Good Samaritan. He stopped to see what a poor fellow was doing staggering along the roadside out in the middle of nowhere." He stopped to put a hand on Lauren's shoulder. "This trip has been full of Good Samaritans."

"What did you do to him?" Kelly asked, but she already knew the answer.

Marshall tilted his head back to look at her over the high bucket seat. "Killed him," he said calmly. "Took a piece of metal fence post out of the back of his truck and split his head open with it."

Kelly shivered, and she heard Lauren say something under her breath.

"Well, I couldn't help it, could I?" Marshall said. "You girls were off causing who-knows-what kind of trouble, and I didn't have time to reason with the man. It's your fault, really, that he's dead. I certainly wouldn't have done anything like that if you hadn't forced my hand." He put on a look that imitated regret.

Kelly wondered if any of his expressions were real or if they were all just masks to cover his complete lack of normal emotion. She didn't think that Marshall ever felt regret, and she was sure that he didn't feel guilt. This little speech was just another part of his game. Kelly didn't even think he really expected them to feel guilty about the death of the man in the cowboy hat. He only wanted to see how they would react—something to pass the time.

They reached the highway cutoff that Marshall had mentioned, and Lauren made the left turn. The new road was in worse shape than the one they had been following. Lauren had to slow down to avoid numerous potholes and sections of broken pavement. The road took them past a few new and prosperous-looking ranch houses, but more often they passed houses with faded "For Sale" signs, or houses where the roof sagged down over broken empty rooms.

They had been traveling along the bumpy road for almost an hour when they came to another small town. Like the place they had passed through the day before, this one seemed to consist only of a gas station and a grocery store.

"Kelly's turn to get us some food again," Marshall said when they stopped at the store. He got out and let Kelly escape from the backseat, reminding her not to talk to anyone or do anything that he wouldn't like. He still had the gun in his hand, and he showed it to her now. "Remember your friend," he said.

This store was larger than the other one had been. It was an older building, with regular aisles instead of small racks, and its shelves held real groceries—bread, flour, meat—not the chips and candy bars of the usual roadside places.

Kelly walked along the shelves with a grocery basket dangling from her left hand, trying to pick items that they could use along the road. She wished they had a cooler to hold some luncheon meat, some sodas. If they had brought a cooler to start with, maybe Lauren wouldn't have gone back to the gas station where Marshall had shot the clerk. Then they wouldn't be in this mess.

Why not wish that Lauren never gave Marshall a ride in the first place? she asked herself. She went back to selecting groceries.

She had picked up some cookies, a bag of carrots, a small bunch of bananas, and a six-pack of soda when she noticed something odd about the store. The windows didn't go all the way across. The first three aisles of the store were lined up with plate-glass windows, and anyone outside could easily see into them. But the fourth aisle, the aisle where the meat and milk sat in refrigerated cases, was hidden from the outside by a section of bare wall. And standing at the end of the fourth aisle, in the spot that was hardest to see from outside, was a clerk stacking cans on one of the wooden shelves.

Kelly glanced outside and saw that Marshall

was keeping her under close inspection. She looked away, trying to appear unaware that he was watching. With her small collection of groceries swaying in their basket, she slowly walked around the corner into the fourth aisle, out of sight of Marshall.

Her heart was pounding in her ears as she walked down the stained tile floor toward the clerk. She had to stop several times to gather her courage. The short aisle stretched out in front of her until it seemed a mile long, but at last she was there standing right behind the clerk.

She couldn't do it. It was too big a chance. She started to turn away, to forget that she had ever thought about telling someone what was going on. Then the clerk turned first.

He was a middle-aged man whose black hair was sprinkled with early gray. His face was so tanned that Kelly thought he looked more like a cowboy than a grocery clerk. "Is there something I can do for you?" he asked.

Kelly opened her mouth to speak, but no words came out. She stopped, cleared her throat, and tried again. "There's this guy," she said. The clerk looked at her patiently. "He's out in the car, and—"

"Kelly! There you are," said a voice from behind her.

Kelly felt her heart stop, felt it freeze between beats and then stutter for a moment before it picked up its hammering beat. She turned to see Marshall walking quickly down the aisle with Lauren close beside him. With the bruise on his forehead and dirt on his jeans, he looked rather ragged, but the smile on his face was as broad as ever. Lauren was smiling too, but her smile was as brittle as glass.

"We were getting worried about you," Marshall said as he got closer.

"Just getting groceries," Kelly said. There was something strange about the way Lauren was walking—she wasn't just walking beside Marshall, she was almost walking on top of him. As Marshall came up to Kelly, he slid around Lauren. He threw his arm around Kelly, and she felt the hard barrel of his pistol digging into her ribs.

"You have everything?" he asked.

"Yes," she said. "I guess so."

"Come on, then. We need to hit the road." Marshall looked at the clerk. "We're burning daylight." He jammed the gun into Kelly and steered her away from the clerk.

Marshall stayed right behind her while Kelly took her collection of groceries to the front of the store and paid for them. He exchanged a bit of pleasant conversation with the woman at the checkout, asking her about the weather and complimenting her on how nice the area was. When they got out to the car, he flipped the door opened and shoved Kelly into the back.

"That was stupid," he said as Lauren started the car. "Very stupid."

"What?" Kelly asked.

Marshall laughed. "Oh, that's good. First you act stupid, then you play stupid." His hand lashed back.

It wasn't a slap, it was a punch. Marshall's knuckles pounded into Kelly's skull just over her ear and sent her head back against the car seat. Sparks ran across her vision, and her ears rang as if a flight of bees was loose in her head.

"I didn't say anything," she said. She could see Lauren looking at Marshall in shock.

"You didn't, huh? Then what were you doing with that guy in there?"

"I was asking him where something was."

"What something?"

"Ice," Kelly said. "I thought that if we had some ice, we could keep our soda cold."

Her lie seemed to cool Marshall down a few degrees. "Maybe," he said. He turned toward Lauren. "What are you waiting for? Drive!"

The punch seem to have stunned Lauren as much or more than it had Kelly. She almost stalled the car as she left the lot, and her foot slipped off the clutch as she shifted gears, causing the transmission to growl in protest.

Despite the chilly weather, Kelly was sweating. Drops of sweat trickled over her ribs. Her hands left damp prints on the vinyl of the Mustang's rear seat. She expected Marshall to turn back to her, to hit her again, or maybe even to pull out his gun. She almost wanted him to. Anything had to be better than just letting this thing go on and on. But Marshall didn't say another word to her.

Instead Marshall seemed to be intent on making Lauren change roads. They took so many turns that Kelly thought they had to be driving in circles.

The landscape grew even more desolate. The clumps of brown grass were separated by several feet of bare, stony ground, and the fences bordering the road were rusty and dilapidated. Tumbleweeds as big as barrels went skittering across the road like careless children. They passed fields that contained nothing but row after row of knee-high anthills, and other fields where prairie dogs stood sentry over cities of dusty holes.

It was still early when Marshall announced that they were going to stop for the night. "Why so soon?" Kelly asked.

Marshall turned to her with his warm, sincere smile—the smile Kelly had grown to hate the most. "Are you that anxious to keep traveling?"

"I just want this over with."

"It'll be over soon enough," he said. He ran his hand over the still-livid bruise on his forehead. "But I'm tired tonight, and for some reason I have a headache."

"There's nothing here," Lauren said. "Are we just going to sleep in the car?"

"Be patient," Marshall said. "You'll see."

Ten minutes later the narrow road they had been following reached the interstate. After two days of weeds and tiny towns, the clutter of burger places, gas stations, and motels around the interstate junction looked like a city.

There were three motels to choose from. Marshall picked the one that looked cheapest and had Lauren pull into the lot. Lauren climbed out and flipped the seat up so Kelly could get out, but Marshall shoved the seat back down before Kelly could move.

"Not this time," he said. "I still don't know if I believe little Kelly's story about what she was saying to that guy back there in the grocery." He looked at Lauren. "This time we'll let Lauren get us a room."

Lauren looked frightened at the idea. "What do I do?" she asked.

"Just go ask for a room for yourself and your two cousins," Marshall said. "And remember that Kelly's health depends on you keeping your cool."

"It'll be okay, Lauren," Kelly tried to reassure her.

Lauren nodded, but she still looked very nervous as she closed the door and walked toward the motel office. Marshall watched her go. "Your friend's got a great body," he said to Kelly. "Too bad I can't say the same thing about her mind."

"Are you kidding? Lauren's grades are great. She's probably going to be a doctor or something."

"She'll never be a doctor," he replied. "She's not tough enough."

"She's plenty tough," Kelly said. "She always has been."

Marshall reached over the seat and snared Kelly's wrist. He pulled her close. "She's not as tough as you, Kelly. She's never had to face real pressure before, and when she did, she couldn't take it." His arm left Kelly's wrist and went around her back. He pulled her even closer, so close that his lips almost brushed her cheek when he talked. "I'm really starting to like you."

"I'm sorry to hear that," Kelly said, "because I don't like you one bit."

Marshall smiled. "Oh, you will. Give yourself a few more days." Then he slammed her back in the seat with stunning force. "Where's Lauren?" he said.

"She's only been gone a couple of minutes."

"She's had plenty of time to get a room." He craned his neck to see through the window of the motel office. "She's still talking to that clerk. She's telling him everything." His voice was rising in tone and volume like a teapot about to boil.

"No she's not," Kelly said.

"Yes she is!" Marshall said, nearly shrieking. "She's got no guts! She's telling him everything!" Then his voice dropped to a somber whisper, and the blue light—the killing light, Kelly thought—came on in his eyes. "Your friend has just killed you," he said. He pulled out the pistol and pointed it straight at Kelly.

She wanted to run, wanted to dive for cover and scream for help. But she didn't. She didn't move a muscle, didn't even draw a breath. Fear had turned her into a statue. Somewhere in her head, a piece of Kelly flew free. She floated above her own body, drifted across the roof of the car, and began to fly far away. She didn't want to be anywhere near the trembling red-haired girl when the man with the pistol pulled the trigger.

Then Lauren opened the door of the Mustang and the two halves of Kelly's mind rushed back together.

"What's going on?" Lauren asked.

Marshall kept the pistol fixed on Kelly. "Did you get a room?"

"Yes."

He lowered the pistol and smiled. "Me and Kelly were just having a little fun, right, Kel?"

Kelly fumbled out the open door, fell on her knees, and was sick on the hard blacktop of the motel parking lot.

TEN

The leather bootlace bit into Kelly's wrist. "Ow! Do they have to be so tight this time?"

"They stretch," Marshall said. He rolled Kelly over to face the ceiling.

"I thought they'd already stretched."

"Be quiet," he said.

Lauren was beside her, also bound with the laces. Marshall hadn't stopped with tying their hands and feet. He'd also tied their legs at the knees and their arms at the elbows. He tied their hands again, wrapping the laces painfully tight.

"How long are you going to leave us like this?" Lauren asked.

"If I could trust you, I wouldn't have to do this." He leaned in close. "But I can't trust you, can I, Lauren?"

Marshall stood and walked across the room. Instead of getting ready for bed, as he'd done the night before, he pulled a comb from his little bag and stood in front of the mirror, combing back his dark hair. "Taking care of you girls is hard work. I think I deserve a night off."

"Night off?" Lauren said.

He nodded. "I'm feeling pretty thirsty. You girls won't mind if I step out and find a place to get my throat wet, will you?"

"I don't care if you drown yourself," Kelly said.

Marshall laughed. "You're so cute, Kelly. I can always count on you." He shoved the comb into the rear pocket of his jeans. "I'll be back in a while. And don't even think of trying anything."

"We'll be here," Kelly said bitterly.

He started toward the door, and then stepped back. "Oh, just one more thing." He walked across to Lauren's suitcase, which was lying on the table, and unzipped it.

"Stay out of there," Lauren said.

Marshall flipped through Lauren's clothes, throwing aside tops and flinging underwear onto the table. "I wouldn't want you two to lose your sexy voices yelling for help." He came out with two pair of rolled-up socks and walked to the bed.

"Don't do it," Kelly said. "We'll be quiet."

"I know you will."

"You don't have to—" Kelly started. Marshall shoved a pair of the socks into her mouth.

Immediately a cough shook her, but the wad of damp cotton in her mouth muffled everything but a thin squeak. She tried to open her jaws wider and push the socks out with her tongue, but every effort triggered a bout of choking that left her weak and struggling to breathe. Her eyes teared, and she could feel a blackness hovering over her as she fought to pull in air.

She barely heard Marshall struggling to get the socks into Lauren's mouth. He said something, but it came in the middle of a coughing fit, and Kelly only heard his mocking tone, not his words. Then she heard the door slam, and they were alone.

It took Kelly a few minutes to turn herself enough to see Lauren. When she did, she saw Lauren looking back at her. There was fury in Lauren's eyes, and her mouth was forced wide by a pair of socks.

It should have been frightening, or maddening, but the round circle of Lauren's red lips and the white tail of the socks sticking out made Kelly want to laugh. The idea that she must look just as foolish only made it seem funnier. The laughing fit triggered another bout of coughing, and again Kelly almost passed out before she could get her breathing under control.

Lauren wiggled closer. She tried to say something, but the socks made her words unintelligible. Her dark eyes bored into Kelly, trying to get the message across without words.

"What?" Kelly tried to say, but the word was only a muffled grunt.

Lauren rolled onto her side. Though her wrists were bound as tightly as Kelly's, her fingers were free. She grasped at the sleeve of Kelly's sweater and tugged hard. Then she looked back over her shoulder at Kelly.

Kelly understood what Lauren wanted. If they worked together they might be able to get free—probably could get free. But what if this was a trap?

Couldn't Marshall be testing them? He could be waiting right outside the door, listening for the sounds that would tell him they were trying to escape. And then he'd have another excuse to hit them and threaten them.

Lauren tugged at her sleeve again, more insistent this time. When she turned over, there was no mistaking the pleading in her eyes.

Kelly closed her eyes and pulled as deep a breath as she could around the mouthful of socks. Even if this wasn't a trap, was she up for it? Lauren had slept through a whole day, but

Kelly had spent that day in a pressure cooker. She wasn't sure that she had the energy to try anything. A few hours of sleep sounded almost as good as being free from Marshall.

But Lauren's fingers kept tugging, demanding attention. And at last Kelly rolled over onto her side and started worming her way down the bed.

With her legs tied together and her hands bound behind her back, it was an effort for Kelly to struggle along. Every move required her to bend and stretch like an inchworm. And with Lauren on the same bed, she had to be careful not to fall off.

The first thing she wanted out of the way was the socks in her mouth. They made it hard to communicate, and Kelly found even the thought of them disgusting.

Lauren seemed to understand what she was trying to do. As Kelly strained to slide down the bed, Lauren's fingers fumbled blindly over her face. Kelly tried to open her mouth even farther to give Lauren a better shot at the gag. She felt a tug, but the socks settled back. There was another pull, and Kelly strained her neck back. The socks slid over her teeth, and then they were out.

Kelly drew in a deep breath. "Thanks," she said. She paused for a second, relishing the ease of breathing without the gag. "What now?"

Lauren struggled to turn over and face Kelly. She jerked her chin upward.

Kelly frowned as she tried to puzzle out Lauren's meaning. "Come up there?"

Lauren jerked her chin upward again and made a muffled cry.

"Your gag? Take out the socks?"

Lauren nodded vigorously.

"Okay," Kelly said, "I'm coming."

It took more long minutes for Kelly to push herself back up the bed and for Lauren to get herself into position. Kelly rolled over and managed to snag the socks from Lauren's mouth—after poking her in the eye.

"I thought I was going to die," Lauren said as soon as the socks came out.

"We need to hurry," Kelly said. "Marshall could be back any minute."

"We don't need to get untied. We can just yell. Somebody's bound to hear us."

"Oh." Kelly felt uneasy about the idea, but Lauren had a point. "Hey!" she yelled. "Help!"

"In here!" Lauren cried.

They stopped for a second to listen, then yelled again. And again. And again. They yelled and screamed until their throats were raw. Lauren even twisted around so she could pound her feet against the wall. But every time they stopped, all they could hear was the sound of their own breathing.

"It's no use," Kelly said at last. "The parking lot only had a dozen cars in it. There probably isn't anybody in the rooms near us."

"So now what?" Lauren asked.

"Now we try and get our hands loose, I guess."

They went through the tedious process of getting themselves back to back and getting their hands together. For a while they both tried to work at the same time, but they got in each other's way.

"You hold still, and I'll untie you first," Kelly said. Lauren stopped moving and waited.

Kelly soon found that it wasn't as easy as she had expected. For one thing, her hands were tied squarely behind her back, and no matter how she twisted or craned her neck, she couldn't see what she was doing. For another, Marshall's knots were tight—every time Kelly tried to pull on the wrong end, Lauren gasped in pain.

After ten minutes of increasing frustration, Kelly was ready to give up. "Why don't you work on mine first?" she suggested. "I'm sure I can get you loose once my hands are untied."

But Lauren had no more luck than Kelly. By the time she stopped, Kelly's wrists were aching, and it felt as if the leather laces were buried deep in her skin.

They lay side by side on the bed, staring up at the water spots on the motel ceiling. "It's too bad we don't have a knife," Lauren said.

"Sure," Kelly said. "And we could also ask Marshall to leave his gun for us. I'm sure he wouldn't mind."

Lauren turned toward her, her eyes drawn into narrow slits. "Don't get sarcastic with me. If you hadn't wanted to go skiing, we wouldn't be in this mess."

"Me! Wait a minute. You're saying that this whole thing is my fault?"

"Well, you were the one who wanted to go west. I wanted to go to Florida for spring break, but—"

"Wait one minute," Kelly said. "You were the one that stopped to pick up Marshall."

"I was trying to do the right thing."

Just leave it alone, Kelly told herself. But her anger was building, and no matter how she wanted to hold it in, she couldn't. "Sure you were," she said. "His looks didn't have anything to do with it."

"What do you mean?" Lauren's voice was chilly.

"Come on, Lauren. You were going on and on about how great he was. I thought you were going to ask him to marry you."

"It wasn't like that. Besides, I didn't see you

134

saying anything bad about his looks."

"Yeah, but I didn't sleep with him."

As soon as the words left Kelly's mouth, Lauren stiffened. There was a painful silence, and Kelly was almost glad they were tied up. Otherwise Lauren might have slapped her.

Kelly's anger had vanished, and she wished she could take it back. But she knew that was impossible.

"I'm sorry," she said after the silence had stretched on for minutes. "I shouldn't have said that."

"How did you know?" Lauren asked softly.

"I woke up in the middle of the night and you were gone. I was worried about you."

Lauren made a strangled noise that could have been laughing or crying. Kelly could feel Lauren shaking with muffled sobs.

There was a click at the door, and both girls jerked.

"The socks," Kelly whispered. "Where are they?" Then the sound at the door turned into a rattle, and there was no time to do anything about the gags.

Marshall shoved the door open and staggered in. "Hey, how are my two babes?" Even from across the room, the smoky smell of whiskey was strong.

He slammed the door and walked over to the

bed. "I don't think I have ever seen such a good-looking pair as you two." His legs wobbled and he fell to the ground.

For a moment Kelly thought that he had passed out, but then his hands came over the edge of the bed and he pulled himself to his knees. His hair spilled down over his forehead, and his blue eyes were fuzzy and unfocused. There was a stupid smile on his lips, and for just a moment he looked like a harmless fool.

Then he reached for Kelly. He grabbed her ankle and pulled her to the edge of the bed. His face came down over hers and he kissed her with a mouth that reeked of whiskey.

Kelly twisted her face away. "Leave me alone!" she shouted.

He backed away, but the grin on his face no longer looked so harmless. "Why should I?" he said, his voice slurred by alcohol. "I've had to take care of you for days, and I'm not getting anything for it."

"Leave her alone!" Lauren said.

Marshall glanced at Lauren. "Don't be jealous, honey. I'll get back to you."

He leaned down and nuzzled his face against the base of Kelly's neck, his breath very warm on her skin. "Please stop," she cried.

"Can't stop now," he said. "Just starting to

136

have fun." Then he stopped and sat up halfway. "Didn't I gag you?"

"Please, just stop."

"Doesn't matter," Marshall said. "Better for kissing you this way."

He leaned in again, but before he could do anything else, he slumped against the side of the bed, asleep.

"It'll be okay," Lauren whispered. "We'll get away."

Kelly shook her head, sending a small shower of hot tears across the bed. For the first time since the nightmare had started, she gave herself over to her fear, and cried in long, aching sobs.

ELEVEN

Kelly lay awake, staring at the ceiling as gray morning light filtered through the closed blinds. She thought about the note she had left in the last motel room. She tried to imagine someone coming into the room to clean up. They would try the bathroom light, and when they went to replace it, they would find the note. And then the police would come looking and rescue them.

Children's voices echoed from the parking lot, followed by slamming car doors, as some vacationing family started their day. Kelly lost her train of thought and looked around the room.

Lauren was asleep beside her. She had talked for an hour after Marshall had passed out, helping Kelly as much as she could.

Marshall's sleep was more troubled. Sometime in the night he had woken up enough to stumble to his own bed. He lay on top of the blankets with his arms and legs sprawled out. Every now and then he muttered something in his sleep. In between mumbling he snored. Even now his breath still smelled of stale whiskey.

Kelly hadn't slept at all. But she didn't feel tired. She felt refreshed, like her mind was working better than it had in days.

Lauren coughed and rolled over. Her eyes fluttered open, and she squinted against the gray light. "Morning," she mumbled.

"Stay quiet," Kelly whispered. "He's still asleep."

Lauren nodded.

"I don't think we're going to have many more chances."

"What . . ." Lauren started, then remembered to whisper. "What do you mean?"

"He's been making us drive north ever since he killed that guy at the gas station. I think he's heading for Canada," Kelly whispered. "And I don't think he's going to want to take us past the border guards."

Fear tightened Lauren's face. "What will he do with us?"

"I doubt he'll leave us around to tell where

he went. He'll wait until we're out on one of those side roads, in a place where there's nobody around. Then he'll take care of us."

"How long?"

Kelly would have shrugged, but lying down with her hands tied, it wasn't possible. "I don't know. Probably no more than a day or two. He's taken a big chance by keeping us around this long. Look how many times we've almost given him away."

"Why?" Lauren said. "Why keep us around if he's just going to kill us?"

"He likes the power. Everybody else that knows what he did is dead. He took us along so he'd have someone to brag to, someone to scare, someone to push around."

They were silent for a long time.

Out on the highway a big truck honked its bass horn at some obstruction. Lauren laughed under her breath.

"What?" Kelly asked.

"I was just thinking," she said, "how much better it would have been if I'd gone with that trucker instead of Marshall." She looked toward Kelly again, and though her lips were still smiling, her eyes were bright with tears.

"No!" Kelly whispered fiercely. "We're not going to cry anymore. We can't give him that." She looked across the small gap that separated

Marshall's bed from theirs. "We've got to get him before he gets us."

"You mean kill him?" Lauren asked.

"If that's what it takes."

They waited a long time for Marshall to wake up. When he finally did, he sat on the edge of the bed with his face in his hands, then stumbled into the bathroom.

"Think he's still hurting from last night?" Lauren asked.

"Yeah," Kelly replied as the sound of the shower started up in the bathroom. "Keep a close watch on him today. If he's nursing a hangover, he may not pay as much attention to us."

Marshall emerged from the bathroom with wet hair and a damp towel over his shoulders. His walk seemed more steady, but his eyes were bloodshot and his shoulders sagged. "I should have gotten more clothes out of my car when I went with you," he said as he looked at his faded flannel shirt. "I think I ought to have one of you girls run into a store and pick me up a new one."

"I want to take a shower," Kelly said.

"What?"

"A shower. We haven't had one in two days."

"A little girl as sweet as you might melt in the shower," he said, but he walked back into the bathroom for a second, then returned. "All right, there's no window in there. As long as you don't start sending Morse code with the toilet, I don't see how you can get in trouble."

He walked over to the bed and pushed Kelly onto her stomach. The knots they had tried to open the night before parted under his fingers with maddening ease. He freed her legs just as casually.

"Go take your shower," he said. "But be quick about it. I want to get moving."

"I want a shower too," Lauren said.

Marshall frowned. "If your friend here can get finished fast enough, you can have a shower too. If she takes too long, you do without."

Kelly stood up and almost fell. The leather laces had left her feet numb. She made her way to the bathroom on feet full of pins and needles, staggering even worse than Marshall had. Once inside she slammed the white door. This motel had a lock on the bathroom, and Kelly quickly turned it.

After two long days on the road, her clothes felt plastered on. She peeled them off and stepped into the shower. For the next ten minutes, she didn't think about anything but how good hot water and soap could feel.

A pounding at the door interrupted her reverie.

"If your friend is going to get a shower, you better get out now."

143

Kelly didn't want to stop. If she didn't open the door, would he break it down? No, he'd just threaten to shoot Lauren. But he couldn't do that. Not here in the motel room.

She turned off the water and stepped out of the shower. She was willing to take some chances with Marshall, but that was one risk she wasn't ready to take.

She had no choice but to put her dirty clothes back on—Marshall had carried Lauren's suitcase in to get material for his gags, but Kelly's luggage was still out in the car. She pulled on the clothes, wincing at the smell of Marshall's whiskey, which lingered on the collar of the sweater. Reluctantly she opened the bathroom door and stepped out.

"Well, there she is," Marshall said. He turned to Lauren. "All right, your turn. And don't make me have to knock twice."

Lauren hurried past with some clothes in her arms. She slammed the bathroom door behind her, and Kelly heard her fumbling at the lock. *Enjoy it while you can*, she thought.

Kelly half expected Marshall to be all over her while Lauren was in the shower, but he sat on the bed and stared off into space with his bloodshot eyes. Kelly found a brush and blow dryer in Lauren's suitcase and took them over to the counter. She flipped on the dryer and ran the brush through her damp auburn hair. Even if she couldn't have clean clothes, it made her feel a little better to have clean hair.

A hard tug on the power cord pulled the dryer from her hand. Kelly turned to see Marshall jerk the cord from the wall and throw the dryer across the room. He gave her a dull glance, then walked back over to the bed.

"Why did you do that?"

"Too loud," he said. "Use a towel."

Kelly looked around the room. There was a chair beside the dresser. Could she move fast enough to hit him with it? Where was his gun? Could she get to it first? Kelly looked at the towel in her hands. If she could get it around his neck, could she strangle him? She took a step toward Marshall, not sure what she would do, knowing only that she had to do something.

Marshall raised his head slowly and looked up at her with his deep-blue eyes. "You have a problem?"

Kelly nodded. "You."

He threw his legs off the side of the bed and sat up. "You think you can do something about it, little girl?"

With her heart pounding in her ears, Kelly nodded again. "Whatever I have to." She took another step toward him.

She never saw where the gun came from, but

suddenly it was in his hand. He pointed the weapon at her casually. "I like you, Kelly. Don't make me use this."

"You're going to kill me soon, aren't you? In only a day or two you're going to kill me and Lauren."

He stood. The hand with the gun came slowly up until the black hole of the barrel was inches from Kelly's face. Marshall might be suffering from a hangover, but it didn't show in that steady hand.

"It could be now, Kelly." His voice was cold, every word carved in ice. "Even a couple of days are better than nothing, don't you think?"

Kelly looked at the gun.

"If you cooperate," Marshall said softly, "I won't have to kill you. Now calm down before you get hurt."

She didn't believe him. Deep down she knew he still meant to kill them both. But Marshall was right about one thing: Two days were better than nothing, even two days of torture.

Kelly stepped back and turned away from him.

"Good girl," Marshall said.

Lauren came out of the bathroom a few minutes later without prompting.

"Get everything," Marshall said. "We're leaving now."

Kelly helped Lauren get her things back into her suitcase. Once everything was in, Lauren hefted the heavy bag and headed for the door. Kelly picked up her purse from the table. Then she glanced around and saw that Marshall was looking away. Quickly, she dropped her purse to the carpeted floor and pushed it under the dresser with the toe of her sneaker.

With Marshall following, Kelly opened the door. She was amazed to see that several inches of snow blanketed the cars and blacktop. The air that rushed into the room was bitterly cold.

"You sure we can drive in this?" Kelly asked, shivering in the doorway.

Lauren looked over her shoulder. "I don't know. I haven't got snow tires or chains."

"You can drive," Marshall snarled. "Get moving."

The wet snow chilled Kelly's feet as they hurried across the parking lot. The wind cut through her sweater and raised goose bumps on her arms. She waited while Lauren heaved her suitcase into the back of the car before speaking.

"Uh-oh," she said. "I left my purse in the room."

Marshall looked at her across the snow-covered car. "Go get it," he said, his breath making clouds of steam. "And don't get distracted or try to run. One minute too long, and you and your friend will both regret it."

He tossed the key to her, and Kelly caught it out of the cold air. "Right."

She dashed back to the room and opened the door. Leaving the key dangling from the lock, she ran across the room and snatched up the phone.

Several billing options were listed on the phone. Kelly couldn't charge the call to the room, because Marshall might see the bill when they went to check out. And she couldn't take the time to ask information for the number of the local police. She quickly punched the button for the operator.

"I want to make a collect call," she said as soon as a voice came on the line. She told the operator her home phone number. "That's collect from Kelly to whoever answers."

While the phone was ringing, she plotted what she was going to say. It had to be fast—Marshall wouldn't wait for long before coming after her—and it had to contain as much information as possible: the location, Lauren's car, kidnapped, heading northwest, call the police. Whoever answered would call the police. Once they knew what had happened and where she was, Kelly was sure her parents would take care of things.

The phone clicked as someone on the other end picked up. "Hello," said Kelly's father.

"I have a collect call from Kelly," said the operator. "Will you pay—"

"There's no one available to take your call. If you'll leave your name and number at the beep, we'll get back to you as soon as possible."

"I'm sorry," the operator said. "You can try your call again later."

"Operator!" Kelly shouted. "Don't hang up."

"I can't complete the call unless someone accepts the charges."

The answering machine beeped.

"Dad! It's Kelly!"

There was a click as the connection was broken. "I am sorry," said the operator. "You can try the call later or use a convenient calling card to pay for the charges at your end."

"Sure," Kelly said. "Wait! This is an—"

There was a noise at the door. She dropped the phone back onto its cradle and walked across the room. She was just bending to get her purse when Marshall came in with his arm tight around Lauren's waist.

"Find your purse?" he asked.

"Yeah, just found it," she said. "Here it is."

Marshall threw something across the room. When it settled on one of the beds, Kelly realized that it was her ski jacket. "Lauren thought you might need this until the car warms up," he said.

Kelly took the nylon-shelled jacket and zipped it over her arms. The bulky padding made her feel clumsy, but it was deliciously warm.

"Thanks," she said.

"Don't I take good care of you?" Marshall said. He escorted the girls out of the room and back across the slushy snow of the parking lot. Only Marshall knew their destination.

TWELVE

The sky was gray in every direction. The road below was covered in a slush of half-melted snow. The wind whistled past the Mustang, pushing the car sideways and blowing streamers of snow through the sagebrush at the side of the highway.

Lauren had the heat on high, but very little made it to the backseat. Kelly huddled with her knees drawn up to her chest. It helped to keep her legs warm, but it did nothing for her freezing feet.

Lauren leaned over the steering wheel, staring intently at the treacherous road. Beside her Marshall slumped in his seat and nursed a soda Lauren had purchased when they stopped for gas that morning. He wouldn't let Lauren play the radio, not even for weather bulletins. It was obvious that he still hadn't worked off his hangover.

151

It had started to snow again soon after they had gotten on the road. At first it had been only scattered flakes, but by noon it was a steady fall, almost a blizzard. The flakes came in sheets, looking gray in the Mustang's headlights. Lauren had to keep the wipers on high just to keep the windows clear. And from the look of the overcast sky, it wasn't going to stop any time soon.

The traffic was thinner than it had been the evening before. Apparently many people had decided to sit out the storm where they were. The farther they went, the smarter that idea seemed. They passed several accidents—tractor trailers overturned in the median of the highway, cars almost buried in the drifts along the road, vehicles of all sorts that had smacked into each other or the railing.

Lauren asked to stop several times. The Mustang handled well in dry weather, but it was out of its element in the snow. The wide rear tires slipped constantly, and Lauren wrenched at the wheel to keep them in their lane.

"Please," she said after fighting the car through a drift that had started to grow out on the interstate. "It's getting worse. Can't we stop now?"

"Keep going," Marshall said.

"But I'm getting tired."

"Then Kelly can drive for a while."

"I'm not very good at driving in the snow," Kelly said.

"I guess you'd better hope it clears up soon," Marshall said. Then he slumped back in his seat. But the weather didn't improve. It got worse.

By two in the afternoon it was as dark as midnight, and the snow was falling so fast, the wipers couldn't handle it at any speed. The snowdrifts on the side of the road quickly spread across the highway, and soon the Mustang was up to its floorboards in snow. The car jumped and slipped. The snow underneath groaned as they plowed through.

If there were any other vehicles still traveling through the gloom, they were invisible behind the wall of snow. Kelly suspected that the only way they'd ever know if another car was near would be if they ran into it.

A green sign was visible for a moment through a gap in the snowstorm. "There's an exit just ahead," Kelly called, yelling to be heard over the howling wind and groaning snow. "We better take it."

"No," Marshall said. "We keep going."

The car bumped as they passed over a drift, and for a moment the engine raced as the wheels lost traction. "We can't keep going," Lauren protested. "We're going to get trapped soon."

"Keep going," Marshall said.

"Look," Kelly yelled, "you might be able to shoot us, but it won't keep you from freezing to death if the car gets stuck in this storm. We need to find a place to wait it out. Then we can go as far as you want."

"All right, pull over," he said. "But we go on as soon as it clears."

Lauren had a hard time getting up the exit ramp. It was covered in snow at least six inches deep, and the Mustang's tail swung back and forth like a pendulum as the tires sought some grip on the gentle slope. Kelly was afraid that someone would have to get out and push—and she knew that someone would not be Marshall—but Lauren worked the gas skillfully, and the car crested the exit ramp with enough momentum to slide out into the street.

The dark form of a motel was visible ahead. They couldn't see it all, but it was obviously a big place. Lauren missed the entrance to the parking lot and drove across the low median, smashing several small bushes on the way to the front office.

"Kelly," Marshall said. "You get the room this time."

"All right."

"And remember, pay cash. Do you have enough money?"

"I think so."

"Then get in there and be quick about it."

The wind was so strong that it almost knocked Kelly down when she stepped out of the car. Her legs sank to the knee in the fresh-fallen snow, and her already chilly feet became instantly numb. She struggled to the door of the motel, kicked off as much snow as she could, and stepped inside.

The motel was not only big, it was new and much fancier than the places where they had been staying. The lobby featured a huge fireplace that put out a welcome warmth, and long leather couches flanked by tall potted plants. The entrance to a restaurant was visible at the rear of the lobby. Signs pointed to a lounge, a health club, and an indoor pool.

The pool reminded Kelly that her swimsuit was packed in her suitcase. She had brought it along because the ski resort where they had been heading had hot tubs. Now the swimsuit was just as useless as her skis.

She walked across the tiled floor to the reception desk. Behind the desk was a young man with sandy hair and warm brown eyes.

"Good afternoon," he said pleasantly. "Checking in?"

"Yes," Kelly said. "I need a room for myself, and my . . . cousins. Three people, all together."

"Do you have a reservation?"

"No." She waved a hand toward the door. "The storm made us stop."

"I see." He sorted through some cards on his desk. "Well, we're really supposed to be full tonight, but half those people are probably stuck somewhere else. If you promise not to tell my boss, I'll forge a reservation for you."

"Thanks."

"What's your name?"

"Kelly Tallon."

He pulled a card out of a drawer and wrote down her name. "And your address?" As she gave it to him, he started shaking his head. "That's a shame," he said.

"What?"

"It's a shame that you live so far away," he said. He looked up at her and smiled. It was a quirky, off-center smile, but it was so obviously nice, so real, that Kelly wondered how she had ever been taken in by Marshall's imitation.

"Well, Kelly Tallon," he said. "Here's a card that says you called in a reservation two weeks ago, and here's the key to your room."

"Thanks again," she said. "I really appreciate it." She reached for the key and felt his fingers grip hers gently.

"If you want to show me how much you appreciate it," he said, "why not have dinner with me tonight? The restaurant here's not very intimate, but the food is good."

After everything she'd been through, Kelly was surprised to find that she could still blush. "I don't think I can," she said.

"If you change your mind, you'll know where to find me. My name's Bill, and I'll be out here until six."

"Okay, Bill." Kelly took the key and went back across the lobby. She paused at the door. It was hard to face the idea of going back out into the snow, where Marshall waited with his gun. It would be much easier to run back over to Bill and tell him everything that had happened. But Lauren was out there, and if Kelly believed one thing that Marshall had said, it was that he wouldn't hesitate to kill her.

Marshall didn't seem concerned with how long it had taken Kelly to get the room. He even agreed to let Kelly carry in her suitcase. She fell twice as she slogged across the snowbound parking lot. He didn't help her up.

Their room turned out to be on the first floor near the front of the motel. It was really two rooms: a suite with two phones and a huge bathroom whose tub could have held four people at once.

"Wow," Lauren said. "How much did this place cost?"

"I don't know," Kelly replied, looking around the room in wonder. "I didn't pay yet."

Marshall's fingers closed on her shoulder like a vise. "You didn't pay?"

Kelly tried to pull away. "Not yet. You have to pay when you leave."

Marshall shoved her, and she stumbled across the room. Her heavy suitcase thudded on the carpeted floor. "Next time follow instructions." He strolled across the room, running his fingers over a gleaming marble countertop. "I like this place."

Kelly bent to pick up her suitcase.

Lauren switched on the television, and the dramatic music of a soap opera filled the room. "We haven't even watched TV in days," she said. "It feels like we've been in some other country."

We have, thought Kelly.

The beds were wide, with ornate brass headboards. Instead of tying their hands behind their backs, Marshall put them on separate beds and lashed their wrists to the headboards.

"Where are you going to sleep?" Lauren asked.

"Don't worry about me, sweetheart," Marshall said. "When I get back, we'll have some fun." He went over to Kelly's suitcase and flipped open the latches. "Let's see what we can

158

find. You got those socks out of your mouths last night, so we'll have to find something better."

He pawed through Kelly's clothes, tossing them carelessly aside. Kelly had been looking forward to the chance to wear something clean, but now that Marshall had handled them, none of her clothes would seem clean. He stopped when he found a pair of knee socks. But this time, instead of pushing them into their mouths, he pulled them tight across their lips and tied the stretched socks at the back of their heads.

"Let's see you get that off," Marshall said. He paused by the mirror to give his hair a final inspection, then stepped out of the room.

Kelly tried to open her mouth, but the sock only peeled her lips back farther. At least when they were tied up this way, they were able to move their feet and look around. But they couldn't work together to get free. She turned her head to look at Lauren.

Lauren had pulled herself up the bed until she was sitting with her bound arms almost straight out at the side. Her gaze was fixed on the television screen, where beautiful actors spoke lines someone else had written and looked at each other with sparkling eyes.

For Kelly the soap opera didn't seem like something from another country; it seemed like something from another world. She couldn't imagine how Lauren could watch it. But tied up like they were, there was nothing else to do. She watched for a few minutes, letting the images pass without trying to understand them. Then she heard a soft noise from Lauren's bed.

It took Kelly a minute to figure out what Lauren was doing. She was leaning against the bed frame, swaying back and forth and moving her hands up and down as if she was listening to some music that Kelly couldn't hear. Kelly saw how frayed the leather laces had become, and realized what Lauren was up to: She was sawing through her bonds by rubbing them on the bedposts.

Kelly felt the back of the bed frame on her own bed. The front of the headboard was slick and polished, but it was unfinished and rough behind. Kelly began to imitate Lauren, scuffing the laces against the rough edge of metal. It wasn't long before she saw strands of leather peeling away.

There was a pop, and Kelly looked up to see one of Lauren's hands free. She reached up and pulled the sock over her head. "We're going to make it this time," Lauren said. "This time he was too smart for his own good." She tugged at the lace on her other wrist.

There was a knock at the door. Both girls froze, their eyes locked on the door.

"It's Marshall," Lauren whispered.

Kelly shook her head. Marshall wouldn't knock.

"Kelly?" called a voice at the door. "It's Bill."

Lauren frowned and looked at Kelly. "Who's Bill?"

Kelly nodded enthusiastically.

"Wait a second." Lauren leaned across the gap between the beds, stretching to her limits to snare the sock around Kelly's head and pull it free. "Now let's try it again. Who is Bill?"

Kelly didn't bother to reply. Instead she yelled toward the door. "Bill! We're in here! Help!"

Lauren followed Kelly's lead and started to yell herself. There was a rattling at the door, and a moment latter it sprang open. Bill flew into the room with a huge key chain held up like a club. He stumbled to a stop when he saw the two girls tied to the bed.

"What's going on here?" he asked.

"Get us loose!" Lauren cried.

"We've been kidnapped," Kelly said. "Get us out of here before the kidnapper comes back."

"Kidnapped?" Bill said. He looked around the room as if he expected someone to jump out from the corner.

"Hurry," Kelly urged. "We've got to get out of here before he comes back."

"He's a killer!" Lauren shouted.

161

Lauren's words made Bill's eyes widen, but he didn't run away. Instead he dropped to his knees beside Kelly's bed and fumbled at the laces. "Where's your other cousin?" he asked as he worked.

"Other cousin?"

"Didn't you check in with two cousins?"

"Oh," Kelly said. "The other one is the kidnapper."

Bill stopped and looked up at her with a puzzled expression. "You were kidnapped by your cousin?"

"No, no. He's not my cousin. He . . . oh, just hurry and get us out of here before he comes back."

It took only a minute to get Kelly loose. Then Bill turned his attention to Lauren's one remaining bond. In a few more seconds they were ready to go.

"Do you need anything out of here?" Bill asked.

"I don't think so," Kelly said. "If we do, we can get it after the police come."

Bill paused at the door on the way out and looked at Kelly with his crooked grin. "And to think, I just came to see if you'd changed your mind about dinner."

"Bill," Kelly said. "I'll be happy to have dinner with you."

He laughed.

The door flew open, spinning Bill around and driving him back into the room. He staggered back another step, as Kelly and Lauren stood paralyzed behind him.

For Kelly everything was happening in slow motion. She saw Marshall step into the room. She saw the gun in his hand and the gleam of his smile as he raised the barrel. The light in his blue eyes was like a neon sign.

Then the gun went off, and time snapped back to normal. Bill fell to the side, glancing off the wall. Marshall fired again, and Bill doubled over backward with his knees under him. His eyes stared sightlessly up at the ceiling. His mouth was open in an O of surprise.

"Sorry to spoil your dinner plans, Bill," Marshall said. "But that's the way it goes."

THIRTEEN

Kelly leaned over Bill and reached out a hand to his face. A single drop of blood ran down his cheek like a scarlet tear. At Kelly's touch he slumped to the side and crumpled to the floor.

Vaguely she could hear people shouting, doors slamming, feet running. Lauren was screaming. But all of that seemed far away. She felt sleepy. It seemed like the best idea in the world to just lie down here on the carpet and sleep for days and days.

A hand jerked her up from the floor. "Move now," Marshall said. "Or I'll kill you."

Kelly wasn't sure that sounded so bad, but she let Marshall push her out of the motel room and down the hallway. A woman in a robe and shower cap opened a door ahead of them, took one look, and then slammed the door again. Kelly found that terribly funny, and laughed all the rest of the way down the hall.

Marshall opened the door to the parking lot, and Kelly was suddenly aware that her coat and all the rest of her luggage was back in the motel room. That was funny too. Wind whipped her hair around her face. It was still snowing, and the cars outside were little more than white lumps in the snow. Fat flakes of snow blew over the cars, and there weren't even any tracks in the parking lot. Kelly thought that was hilarious.

"Be quiet," Marshall said.

That was the funniest thing of all, and Kelly laughed even harder.

"Shut up," Marshall said. He slapped her. Hard.

Kelly wanted to keep laughing, but she couldn't remember why everything had seemed so funny. She wanted to, because funny was something she could definitely use, but it was gone. She was standing in the snow-blanketed parking lot, shivering in her sweater.

"We can't go anywhere in this," Lauren said.

"Get in the car and drive," Marshall said.

"Look at it!" Lauren shouted. She waved a hand at the snow. "Even if we get out of the parking lot, we can't go anywhere."

166

Marshall fired a shot that missed Lauren by inches and crashed through the windshield of a car behind her. "Get in the car," he said.

Marshall shoved Kelly into the backseat and took his spot in the front. Lauren worked wonders in getting the Mustang out of its parking slot and nursing it onto the highway. By the time they went sliding away, quite a crowd had gathered at the door of the motel. Their faces looked red in the glow of the Mustang's taillights. Several of them were pointing toward the car. Kelly didn't mention that to Marshall.

There was no way to tell where the exit from the parking lot was. And the road beyond was a guess. The car bounced over buried obstacles, and Kelly struck her head against the roof. They went down the ramp to the interstate in one prolonged slide, but once they were back on the interstate, it wasn't as bad as Kelly had expected.

Snowplows had gone past while they were in the motel, and the new snow hadn't quite matched the previous depth. They bumped along with no sound but the grinding of the snow under the tires and the hiss of the flakes whipping past the car.

They hadn't been on the road ten minutes before Kelly was wondering if they had ever really stopped at a motel. She remembered checking in, and the brass beds, and Bill getting shot. But it all seemed so distant, like the soap-opera images she had glimpsed on the motel TV.

Blue lights came out of the gloom. As they drew closer, the form of three black-and-white police cars could be seen.

"Just keep driving," Marshall said. He watched the police cars go past on the other side of the interstate. "We've got to get off this road."

Kelly looked along the side of the highway. In some places the drifts were higher than the car, and the dirty snow thrown up by the plows made a formidable barrier. "You're sure you want to get off?" she asked.

"At the next exit," Marshall said. "We'll get off there."

The next exit was a long time in coming. Another police car went by in the opposite lane, followed by an ambulance with its red light flashing.

That ambulance is for Bill, Kelly thought. But it still didn't seem real. Marshall had killed Bill. There was no impact, none at all.

It was very cold in the backseat. The vinyl was stiff and the few gusts of heat that made it back to Kelly only reminded her of how cold she was.

An exit finally came up. There was nothing at this one, not even a gas station. According to the signs, there was a highway that ran across the interstate, but beyond the obvious trail of the overpass railings, it was impossible to pick the road out of the flat expanse of snow.

"What now?" Lauren asked.

"Turn south."

"Which way?"

"Left. Turn left."

There were no tracks to follow, and the Mustang plowed a wake as it rode down the slope away from the interstate. Without the plows and the traffic, the snow here had not been compacted. In many places that was good, because the wind had scoured the road clean. But in other places drifts the size of small houses edged the road and trailed waist-deep tails across the blacktop.

Headlights appeared behind them. Marshall stared back between the seats, looking at the lights through the rear window. "Funny, nobody on this road for hours, then somebody turns off right behind us." He turned to Lauren. "Drive faster."

"If I drive any faster, we'll have a wreck."

"Drive faster," he repeated.

Kelly watched the headlights behind them as they bounced and weaved around the drifts. The police are after us because Marshall killed Bill. This time the memory brought with it images of Bill's brown eyes and crooked grin. And it brought pain. Kelly was glad to feel even pain.

"The police are going to catch you," she said.

"You better hope not," Marshall said. "Because if they catch me, they catch you, too."

"We haven't done anything," Lauren said.

"Haven't done anything?" he said. "Haven't you sheltered a known criminal for days and driven him halfway across the country?"

"You forced us to do that," Kelly said.

"You want to ask the people at all the places we've stopped if you were forced?" Marshall snorted. "Why, the way I remember it, Lauren here was tired of being pushed around by her rich daddy and decided she wanted to play things a little fast and loose."

"They'll never believe that," Lauren said.

"I wouldn't be too sure, little girl. You spent two days telling me everything about yourself." He put on his best, most innocent smile. "I can be very convincing."

He killed Bill. He killed the gas station attendant. He killed the man in the pickup truck. And there's no doubt, none at all, that he's going to kill us both. Pain flooded in and brought with it a load of anger and fear. And this time Kelly didn't try to repress it.

She lunged out of her seat toward Marshall. He turned quickly and swung at her, but his arm glanced off the back of his car seat and the blow missed. She wasn't sure what she meant to do until she did it. What she did was reach past Marshall, grab the door handle, and push open the passenger door.

Lauren slammed on the brakes, but instead of skidding to a stop, the Mustang went into a spin.

Kelly was hurled from one side of the car to the other. She saw that Marshall had his gun in one hand and his satchel in the other. That left him with no hands to hold on. She screamed, and jumped at him.

The gun went off, and she felt the bullet passing close by her ear. The car seemed to be spinning faster, the headlights giving glimpses of road, drifts, snow-covered fields. Kelly was almost in the front seat with Marshall, and she was kicking, punching, doing everything to push him toward the open door.

She saw him leaning into the void, whirling the hand with the satchel like an acrobat trying to balance on a high wire.

Kelly screamed. She didn't scream any words; it was the scream itself that felt good. She put her feet on him and kicked. She punched with her hands. And she kept screaming.

Despite the pressure she put on him, Marshall managed to hook his elbows on the door frame and regain his balance. He started to shove himself back into his seat. The gun barrel came up again, and his lips moved in some threat, but Kelly couldn't hear it over the wind.

Lauren let go of the wheel and swung at him. Her hand missed Kelly by a fraction of an inch and hit Marshall just above the eye, and he slipped back several inches. She swung again, and her fist struck his straight nose.

There was a new look on Marshall's face, a mixture of surprise and fear.

Kelly kicked at his legs, and his feet went skidding over the wet floormat. He was almost completely out the door now, and the force of the spinning car pulled at him.

At the last second Marshall dropped his gun and grabbed at the car seat. Kelly stomped on his hand as hard as she could.

Marshall fell out the open door.

As the car spun, the headlights swept over him like a strobe. In one sweep of the lights Kelly saw him strike the pavement. In the next he was tumbling along the road, his arms and legs bent at impossible angles. One more flash and he seemed to be still—a dark shape fading in the distance. Then the Mustang slammed into a snowdrift.

The car rolled onto its side. Kelly almost fell out the door herself, and she saw snow-covered blacktop sliding by beneath her dangling feet before the car rolled again. Now it was skating along on its roof. Kelly heard Lauren's home-made ski rack crack loose and grind between the car and the road. The Mustang rolled almost to the other side, then settled back on its roof.

Kelly had time to look over and see Lauren dangling from the wheel. Her hands were still trying to steer, even though none of the wheels was on the ground. Then the Mustang struck a more substantial drift. Kelly fell forward, her head striking the windshield only inches from the place where Marshall's forehead had starred the glass. The car made one last roll, landing on its side with the open passenger door facing down.

The car stopped moving. The engine coughed and died. The snow continued to come down, and in only a few minutes the hole they had made in the snowbank healed.

Inside the Mustang everything was very, very quiet.

FOURTEEN

Kelly pushed at the door over her head. The hinges groaned, but it didn't open. She shifted her feet, hooking one foot on the steering wheel and planting the other on the parking brake, and tried again. This time the door opened with a grinding squeak. Snow and sunlight spilled down into the car. Kelly climbed onto the side of the driver's seat and stuck her head up into the day.

"Do you see anything?" Lauren called from where she sat at the bottom of the wreck.

"Yeah," Kelly said. "I see something."

"What?"

Kelly shook her head. "You aren't going to believe it."

The view outside was like nothing Kelly had

ever seen before. It wasn't the snow that covered everything in a gentle, undulating sheet—it was what she saw rising above the snow that shocked her. All around them great towers of jagged rock jutted hundreds of feet into the sky. Some stood alone and looked as sharp as knives; others were clumped together to form pale rock castles. The gray sides of the towers were stained with splashes of green and yellow and red.

Kelly eased herself back into the car and climbed down beside Lauren. "It looks like we've crashed on the moon," she said.

"Did you see any houses or other cars?" Lauren asked.

"Nothing. I didn't see anything but rock and snow."

"What about . . ." She hesitated and looked up at the open door. "What about Marshall?"

"No," Kelly said. "He must be buried under the snow."

Lauren closed her eyes and nodded. She put her right arm under her and tried to sit up. Kelly reached to help her. Lauren's other arm dangled limp at her side, broken in the crash.

"How does your side feel?" Kelly asked.

"Not too good. How about your head?"

Kelly touched the tender bump on her skull. A shock of pain that left her dizzy went through her. "It's better, I think. Listen, we're going to have to get out of here."

"And go where?"

"I don't know, but we can't wait here. There's not a single track in the snow out there. We're probably miles from where the police think we are. There might be nobody down this road for a week, and we'll freeze to death by then."

"I'm not sure I can get up," Lauren said.

"You have to," Kelly told her, "because I'm not leaving you here."

It took twenty terrible minutes to get Lauren out of the car. Her arm wasn't just broken—it was broken so badly that the jagged end of the bone pressed against her skin. And Kelly suspected that Lauren had broken several ribs as well. Her side was puffy, and the skin was slick and bruised. Kelly helped her climb down from the top of the wrecked car and into the soft drift.

"Wow," Lauren said as she looked around. "You weren't kidding. This is one weird place."

Once they were outside and away from the car, Kelly remembered just how cold it was. It had stopped snowing, but the sky showed only thin patches of blue and the air held the threat of more snow. The wind roared in from the north, cutting through their thin clothing.

"I'm going back into the car," Kelly told Lauren. "I'm going to get more of your clothes out of your suitcase. We'll need everything we have to keep warm."

Kelly burrowed into the car and dragged Lauren's suitcase from the back. She managed to get it to the top of the car and pitch it off into the snow. Then she climbed down and snapped it open. There was a jacket inside. She saved that for Lauren. For herself she pulled out two of Lauren's soft, expensive sweaters and slid them over the sweater she was already wearing.

Lauren was sitting in the snow, staring toward the open car door that jutted into the air. "Look at my Mustang," she said. "It's not even a year old. Just look at it."

Kelly did look, but except for the door and the few feet of the side they had exposed in climbing out, there was nothing to see but a lump in the snow. "Think of it this way," she said. "At least now you don't have to worry about the hail damage."

Lauren did not laugh.

Kelly got Lauren on her feet and helped her into the jacket. Lauren's face shone with sweat, and her lips were very pale. Kelly was beginning to suspect that Lauren might have not only broken ribs but some kind of internal injury.

178

"Come on," Kelly said gently. "Let's get moving."

"Which way?" Lauren asked.

Kelly opened her mouth to answer, then shut it again. It wasn't as easy a question as she'd thought.

The car had spun around so many times, there was no way to know if it was facing the way they had been traveling or back the way they'd come. Any tracks they had made had been erased by the wind. And the level stretch of snow that showed the location of the road looked the same in both directions.

"That way," Kelly said at last. She pointed down the road.

"Toward the biggest rocks?" Lauren asked.

Kelly nodded. "I think we'd have seen those things even in the dark. It's probably twenty miles back to the motel, and I don't remember a store, or even a house, between here and there. Let's take our chances going forward."

Walking through the snow was hard work. With every step Kelly sank past her knees. And though the layers of Lauren's sweaters were enough to keep her arms and chest warm, her feet were protected only by thin sneakers. They were numb before she had walked a hundred yards.

Kelly was suffering, but she knew it was

worse for Lauren. She held her broken arm tight across her side, but with every step, Kelly saw her wince in pain. Her normally tan skin looked very pasty.

The spires of rock never seemed to get any closer, but after only a few minutes of walking, Kelly looked back to see that the Mustang had been lost in the whiteness. Even their footsteps were being erased by the wind.

Lauren slipped and fell facedown in the snow. Kelly helped her up. A few minutes later she fell again. This time she didn't try to get up.

"Can we stop and rest?" she asked.

"I don't know," Kelly said. "I don't think it's such a good idea."

"Just a few minutes. I'm really feeling bad."

Kelly didn't like the idea of sitting in the snow—hypothermia was just around the corner even without giving it a hand—but one look at her friend's face was all it took to see just how serious things were getting. Lauren's lips weren't just pale—they were as white as the snow. And as cold as it was, fine beads of sweat ran down her forehead.

Kelly put a hand to her cheek. "Lauren! You're burning up."

"I know," she said. "World's fastest flu."

"It can't be the flu. I think you hurt yourself in the accident."

"I know I hurt myself in the wreck. Just look at my arm."

"It's not your arm I'm worried about," Kelly said. "It's that bruise on your side. I'm afraid you're bruised, or even bleeding, on the inside."

Lauren didn't seem too shocked by the idea. She just nodded her head. "I think you're right. I feel . . . funny. Like something in me is twisting when we walk. It doesn't hurt, but it feels really strange." She looked up at Kelly. "So what do we do about it?"

"We keep walking," Kelly said. "There's nothing else we can do." She helped Lauren up, and they struggled on down the road.

The rock towers finally seemed to be drawing nearer. Kelly could see crowns of snow clinging at the tops and ruffles of snow on ledges along the side. On a few of the ridges and crests, little clumps of dull-brown sage were visible. As pitiful as they were, Kelly was glad to see any sign of life.

Then Kelly fell in the snow. Her foot caught on some hidden obstacle, and she tumbled over, windmilling her arms and falling facedown in a drift. It took her a few seconds to realize that what had caught her foot was the top strand of a barbed-wire fence and a few seconds more to realize that they didn't put fences in the middle of the road.

181

"Are you okay?" Lauren asked.

"Yeah," Kelly replied, "but I'm not sure we're okay. We've gotten off the road." She looked at the flat plain around them. The snow formed gentle dunes, subtle hills with pale-blue shadows. But nothing gave a hint of where the road might run.

"Does it matter?"

"It does if we want to get somewhere. We'll have to go back until we find it."

Wearily Lauren turned and began to go back the way they'd come. Kelly followed her, stepping in her footprints and looking for anything that might mark the edge of the buried road.

Fortunately they had to backtrack only for a couple of minutes before Kelly saw what had happened. The road hadn't ended; it had intersected another highway in a T intersection.

"Another decision to make," she said. "Which way now?"

"Right," Lauren said immediately.

"Why?"

"Because I think you were right last time—we didn't come this way last night. And if I remember the turns we took last night, then right would be north. Back toward the interstate."

Kelly could barely remember any of the turns they'd taken during that wild ride. She hoped Lauren was remembering the course as well as she seemed to and not just imagining it out of her fever. The sun stubbornly hid behind the clouds, refusing to help indicate whether Lauren was correct about the direction.

"Right it is," Kelly said.

They trudged up the highway to the right, past the top two inches of a red stop sign sticking out of a drift, and on across the featureless plain. A few minutes later the ground began to slope upward, and the road curved back toward the towers of rock. Kelly was afraid they might lose the highway again if it didn't stay straight, but the snow wasn't as deep on the slope. The tops of rusty fences peeked out of the snow on both sides, conveniently bracketing the location of the road.

They were almost to the first of the stone pillars when Lauren found the sign. It was a wide green highway marker with an arrow pointing up the road in the direction they were traveling.

Kelly knelt to brush the snow away.

"What's it say?" Lauren asked.

"'Wall ten,'" Kelly said.

"What's Wall?"

Kelly shrugged. "A town maybe? And it must be ten miles away." ‑

"Ten miles doesn't seem so bad," Lauren said. "I've walked farther than that before. We hiked almost sixteen miles when we were camping in Washington Park. Remember?"

"Right. We can do ten miles! Let's get moving."

Lauren turned and headed up the road, moving a little faster than before. She had sounded better when she talked about the ten-mile distance. Almost cheerful.

Kelly had tried to sound cheerful too. They had hiked sixteen miles back home, but it had been in the summer. They hadn't been freezing. Or starving. And neither of them had been suffering from broken bones and who-knew-what kind of internal injuries.

The wind picked up again, blowing Kelly's hair around her face so violently that it stung. *We didn't have to face a wind like this in Washington Park*, she thought. *Or wade chest-deep in snow.*

She looked up at the sky and saw that there were several more patches of blue than there had been when they started walking. But those patches were getting darker. Kelly knew there was no way they could make it into the town of Wall before nightfall. If this nightmare place wasn't bad enough, they'd soon be walking through it in the dark.

At least it isn't snowing.

But the first flakes fell even before Kelly could finish the thought.

FIFTEEN

The snow came down, but it never seemed to hit the ground. The wind blew it so hard that it traveled along horizontally, stinging Kelly on her bare face and neck. It felt like needles against her cheeks. She hunched her shoulders and lowered her chin, but it wasn't much help.

The road sloped up, and the cliffs to the left and right of the road grew higher and steeper the farther they walked. The towers of stone pointed to the gray sky. The silence of the place was eerie. There were no car horns—no cars. Nothing but the passing wind and the hissing snow.

"How far?" Lauren said.

Kelly turned to her, squinting against the snow. "How far to what?"

"How far have we gone? Since we saw the sign, I mean."

"I think about a mile."

"Is that all?"

"Maybe more like two," Kelly said, but it was a lie. Lauren had started out with renewed energy after they'd seen the sign. For a short while she seemed almost well. But she wasn't well; she was very ill. And after a few minutes her pace had slowed to a crawl. Far from believing they'd gone two miles, Kelly doubted that they'd gone even one.

Kelly wasn't feeling too well herself. Her head pounded from its collision with the Mustang's windshield, and another dozen bruises she had picked up in the crash were starting to make themselves known. And she was cold: her head was cold, her hands were icy, and her feet had been numb so long, she worried that she had frostbite up to her knees. She stopped for a moment to fight off a bout of dizziness and nausea.

When she looked up again, she decided that she'd have to add optical illusions to her growing lists of problems. Stretching across this narrow winding road, in the middle of this desolate wilderness, were what looked like tollbooths.

"Kelly, what is that?" Lauren said.

"You see it too?"

"Of course. It looks like the booths on the highway."

"I know," Kelly said. "But it can't be. Come on, let's see what it really is."

They didn't have to go as far as she'd thought. The answer actually came a hundred yards before they reached the strange booths. Another sign stuck up out of the snow at the edge of the road. When Kelly brushed it clean with her frozen fingers, it showed words written in white on brown.

WELCOME TO
BADLANDS
NATIONAL PARK

"A national park?" Lauren said numbly as if she'd never heard of such a thing.

"Yep," Kelly said. *Badlands*, she thought. *We've been going through badlands ever since we left home.* Despite the name, the sign brought Kelly a feeling of hope, the first she'd felt in hours. It swept over her and warmed her.

"They made a national park out of this place?"

"All these rocks and cliffs are kind of spectacular. It's probably prettier and a lot easier to get around in the summer. Besides, a national park means park rangers." Kelly couldn't keep the smile off her face. "Rangers that are probably right up there at the entrance. Come on!"

Kelly charged into the snow like someone running through ocean waves. Lauren ran at her side, and though her breath hissed between her teeth as she fought back the pain of her arm and side, she didn't stumble or slow until they reached the entrance gate.

The two buildings guarding the entrance to the park were larger than tollbooths, but just barely. The one on the left was obviously closed—its smoked-glass windows were dark, and a barrier projected from its side to block the snow-choked road. But the other booth glowed with lights, and the door on its side gaped open.

"Hello!" Kelly called. "Can you help us?" She climbed over the compacted snow around the booth and stepped down into the almost-clear area by the door. "Hello?" she called again.

She pushed at the door, and it opened easily. There was a green plastic lawn chair in the center of the booth. A shelf in the back had stacks of brown leaflets that carried the name of the park in bright letters. Beside them was a white plastic case whose front carried a large red cross. A black telephone clung to the wall.

Lauren slid down the snow to stand beside Kelly. "Where's the ranger?" she asked.

"Not home," Kelly told her, "but he left us a phone."

It was an odd telephone. It didn't have a dial or buttons, but as soon as Kelly picked it up, it started to ring. It rang three times. Four. "Come on, come on," Kelly said softly. "Somebody answer." The phone continued to ring.

"What's wrong?" Lauren asked.

"Nobody's picking up." Kelly gave up after twenty rings. "It's just not my week for telephones. I wonder where it was ringing, anyway."

"Probably up there." Lauren wiped snow away from her eyes and pointed past the booths.

Kelly turned and saw a group of buildings through the driving snow. A small house was flanked by several gray metal buildings that could have been storage sheds, and the dark, round shape of a satellite dish. They were all huddled together on a small flat area at the edge of a cliff.

The snow between the entrance booths and the house had been shoveled recently to make an almost-clear path. Fresh snow had started to fill in the path, but patches of blacktop still showed through.

"That must be where the rangers live," Kelly said.

"Great. Then let's get over there."

"Wait a second." Kelly ducked into the

189

booth and grabbed the white first-aid kit. She opened it and dug through the contents. There were bandages and ointments, some of which would probably help with Lauren's arm, but Kelly didn't know enough about first aid to use them properly. There was a bottle of aspirin, and that was something she could use. The child-protector top was almost too much for her stiff, cold fingers, but eventually she got it open.

"Here," she said, handing a pair of the white tablets to Lauren. "This might help the pain, and it'll get your fever down."

Lauren took the pills from her and choked them down. "Can we go now?"

Kelly looked around. It was starting to get dark, and the colors of the rock spires had faded to shades of gray. Even the snow reflected the slatelike color of the darkening sky. Against this frozen, forbidding background, the little house was a beacon of warmth. Yellow light spilled out from curtained windows, and a bright-green welcome mat was visible through a dusting of snow on the porch.

"Yeah, let's go," she said. "Even if there's nobody home, we'll be okay."

"You sure?"

"Absolutely. We'll be warm, and we'll have food, and there's bound to be a real phone over there."

Lauren leaned against the entrance booth with her good arm. "I just want to go home."

"Then let's go home," Kelly said.

Lauren pushed herself away from the booth and started shuffling up the path. Kelly followed close behind.

Kelly was no wilderness scout, but from the many footprints, it was obvious that more than one person had gone up the path since the snow had started falling again. They climbed up onto the front step, and Lauren rapped on the door. "I hear someone," she said.

Kelly heard voices too, but they had the distinctive tinniness of a radio or television show. "Knock again."

Lauren pounded the door harder, and it creaked open. Light and the sound of canned laughter spilled out. "I don't like this," Lauren said.

"I'm sure it's okay," Kelly said. "The ranger is probably out . . . rangering." She stepped past Lauren into the house.

"Hello," she called. "Anyone home?" The front room was tiny. There was no furniture except a stained coffee table with a lamp and a threadbare recliner. The worn carpet was almost covered in knee-high stacks of books. As shabby as it was, the room was deliciously warm.

"Park rangers have to live in this place?"

Lauren said from the doorway. "Out here by themselves?"

"They're dedicated," Kelly said.

She walked around the stacks and through the doorway into the kitchen. The refrigerator was new, but the other appliances were old and dented. There was no dining table. Instead, a counter ran most of the way across the room. A neat stack of dishes rested on the counter. Beside the dishes a pile of silverware lay wrapped in a yellow towel.

There was a smell of hot metal in the air. Kelly stepped forward, sniffing.

There was a pan on the stove. The pan was empty, but the burner under it glowed cherry-red. Kelly took another half step toward the stove, reaching out to turn off the burner. Then she saw the boots.

The boots were scuffed brown leather with heavy rubber soles and long leather laces like the ones Marshall had used to tie Kelly and Lauren. Drops of water that must have come from melted snow still clung to the sides of the boots. They were sticking out from behind the breakfast counter.

With her hand still frozen in the air from reaching toward the stove, Kelly stepped around the counter. There were pants legs that ran into the boots. And a shirt above the pants. There was a long moment in which that was all Kelly could see—the boots, the pants, and the shirt. It took longer to see the body.

The park ranger had been a small woman with dark-blond hair pulled back in a ponytail. Her arms were stretched out across the floor. A glass lay on the tile beside her in the middle of a pool of milk. Her pale gray eyes looked up at the ceiling from a face that was surprisingly calm.

Kelly stumbled back a step. "Lauren! We've got to get out of here."

"Oh, I think it's too late for that, sweetheart," Marshall said.

Kelly whirled around and saw him standing beside the doorway with his arm locked around Lauren's throat. There was no doubt that it was Marshall, but the attractive guy that Lauren had stopped to help was gone. In his place was a monster.

His face was as puffy as an old melon, and his blue eyes peered from dark pits in the swollen flesh. His skin was torn. Dried blood caked his cheeks. The hand that was clamped over Lauren's mouth was dark and twisted. His jeans and his jacket were tattered.

He smiled. Dark gaps of broken teeth marred his perfect smile. His lips were swollen and split. "You can't imagine how happy I am to see you two girls."

Kelly stepped back into the kitchen and slid past the hot stove. She stretched her hand back across the counter, feeling for the silverware. "Let her go."

Marshall stepped through the kitchen door, forcing Lauren ahead of him. "I don't think so," he said. "I don't think so."

Kelly's hand felt the outlines of a knife. It wasn't huge, but it was a knife. She wrapped her fingers around it, whipped it from behind her, and held it with the point angled toward Marshall's battered face.

"Let her go now!"

Marshall smiled again. Blood trickled from the corner of his mouth. "I can break her neck before you take a step."

"I'll kill you," Kelly said. She was amazed at how calm her voice sounded, even though her heart was pounding like a bass drum in her ears.

"You'll try," Marshall said. "I know you'll try. But this is the end of the line, little Kelly." He took a half step back into the tiny front room. "I'm going to have to kill you both now. Sorry about that."

As injured as he was, he still managed to sound sincere.

SIXTEEN

Kelly didn't wait for Marshall to move first. She lunged toward him, slashing the air with her knife.

Marshall pivoted, putting Lauren between them like a shield. "Oh, a knife. You'd better be careful, little girl. You wouldn't want to scratch your friend," he said.

"Why not? You're going to kill her anyway." Kelly jumped again.

She missed, but this time Marshall released his grip on Lauren and shoved her away. Kelly stabbed at him again, and he caught her arm as it drove upward with the knife. He shoved her back against the stove and stepped in close. Slowly he began to turn her arm and force the knife back toward her.

Trembling as she fought to resist him, Kelly's fingers opened and she dropped the knife. It thudded on the kitchen floor. Still holding Kelly's arm, Marshall bent to pick up the knife. Kelly drove her knee into his swollen face.

Marshall grunted in surprise and pain. He released Kelly's arm and fell back. He lay on the floor for a second, and Kelly thought he might be unconscious, but then he jumped back onto his feet and swung at her.

Kelly didn't realize he was holding the knife until it sliced into the sweaters at her throat. It snagged in the many layers of cloth. She could feel the point against her skin. She was afraid to even breathe.

He pulled the knife free and grinned at her with the stumps of his bloody teeth. "Good-bye, Kelly," he said, then plunged the knife toward her chest.

There was a hollow thud, and the knife fell from his hand. Marshall staggered to the side, and Kelly saw Lauren standing behind him with a lamp in her good arm. "Are you okay?" she had time to say, and then Marshall was up again, shoving Lauren back into the front room.

Kelly jumped at him, pounding her fists into his back. He spun and caught her by the throat. He squeezed until his fingers cut off the air and blackness hovered at the edge of Kelly's vision.

He jerked his arm up until only the tips of her toes were still on the ground. Slowly he brought back his other hand and balled the fingers into a fist. His arm jabbed forward, and Marshall's fist struck Kelly on the chin.

This was no slap to get her attention; it was a crushing blow that sent her flying across the room. She smashed into the counter, and it collapsed onto the floor in a heap of wood and metal. She lay there in the wreckage of the counter while bells and sirens echoed in her skull. Distantly she heard yelling and fighting, and the front door banged shut twice.

Kelly wasn't sure how long she lay there. Eventually she climbed to her feet and stepped across the kitchen to the front room. The books that had been stacked so neatly were now scattered over the floor. The worn chair was overturned, and the table lay on its side beside the wall.

"Lauren?" Kelly called softly.

The front door opened again, and Marshall stepped back in.

"Where's Lauren? What have you done to her?"

"One down," he said, "and one to go."

He stepped into the room, and Kelly saw that his left leg was as stiff as deadwood. He advanced on her with his arms outstretched, blood running from fresh scratches on his face and his injured leg dragging behind him.

Kelly's mind suddenly flashed the image of the mummy in an old horror movie. In the midst of everything she almost laughed. She had been close to hysteria ever since she had first seen the gun in Marshall's hand back in Kansas, and now she was almost ready to give in to it.

She backed into the kitchen and pulled the empty pan from the still-glowing burner. "Stay back," she said as he took another dragging step. She swung the pan at his head.

He blocked her swing with his forearm, stopping the pan inches from his face. "There's no one to save you this time, Kelly," he said. Then he grabbed the side of the pan.

Marshall's fingers sizzled as they touched the hot metal. His blue eyes bulged in his damaged face. A whimper started down in his throat and grew into a noise that was not a scream or a shout, but simply a pure expression of pain.

He pulled his hand away, and the skin of his fingers was ashy white.

Kelly swung the pan at him again, and Marshall stumbled back. He looked at Kelly, then down at his smoking hand, then back at Kelly.

"Where's Lauren?" she shouted.

She swung a third time. He tried to duck

198

back, but the pan glanced off his cheek, causing him to cry out again. Marshall faced her for a moment longer, then turned and staggered out the front door with his injured leg dragging behind.

Trembling and holding the pan out in front of her, Kelly walked to the door. It was very dark, and snow streaked across the yellow rectangle of light that spilled out the door. There was a crumpled form draped across the edge of the step.

"Lauren!" Kelly dropped the pan and rushed outside.

Lauren was lying on her side. A frosting of snow covered her dark hair. When Kelly rolled her over, she saw that Lauren's eyes were rolled back to show only whites. Blood streamed from her nose. In the light from the house, the blood was amazingly bright. In the snow where Lauren lay, it made a startling pink stain.

"Oh, Lauren," Kelly whispered.

There was a blur of movement, and Kelly was thrown into the snow. She climbed to her knees, but before she could get to her feet, hands grabbed at her back and shoved her down again. Her hand searched for the ground in front of her and found only air. Dimly she realized that she was at the edge of the cliff on which the house was perched. She was shoved again and then flipped over to lie faceup in the snow.

Marshall stood over her, his breath puffing out in the cold air. "Now you're going to die," he hissed.

Kelly kicked his injured leg and he toppled into the snow. "You keep saying that," she screamed back at him. "But you're the one that's going to die." Before he could rise, she kicked him again and drew a satisfying gasp of pain.

She tried for a third kick, but Marshall's hand closed on her ankle and he flipped her away. Away and off the cliff.

Kelly found herself spinning through space. She brushed against hard stone. The cliff face was bare of snow, and her hands felt rocks and frozen earth sliding past. Then she was back in the air. She had time to wonder how far it was to the bottom. As the seconds passed, it seemed clear that it was more than far enough to kill her.

It was the snow that saved her.

The snow at the base of the cliff had drifted into a huge frozen wave that reared a dozen feet into the air. Kelly fell into it with a force that drove the air from her lungs and left her struggling for breath. But the cushioning of the snow kept her from being broken on the barren ground.

Kelly came up sputtering and gasping from

the snowdrift like a diver coming out of deep water. By the time she was able to draw a breath, she had tumbled to the base of the drift. She lay there gasping and staring up at the dark cliff face.

The line between the sky and the edge of the cliff was hard to make out, but Kelly thought she could see it high above her. For a moment she even imagined she could see someone moving around on the edge of the cliff, but she knew that had to be her imagination.

Looking up, she realized just how long the fall had been, and how lucky she had been to survive it. She felt a strange mixture of triumph and fear.

Then she remembered Lauren. Lauren was up there, either dead or dying, and there was no one with her but Marshall.

Kelly rolled out of the snowdrift and stood up. She wondered how long it would take her to climb the cliff. *Forever. That's how long*, she thought.

There was no way she could get back up the cliff. She tried to think back to what she had seen during the day. The ground had been almost level at the spot where the Mustang had crashed. It was only when they had started up the road that led to the park that the ground had begun to rise.

So if Kelly walked back along the cliff toward the Mustang, then the cliffs would be smaller. There was no way she could walk all the way back to the car—even if Lauren wasn't dead already, she'd be frozen by the time Kelly made such a long trip. And Kelly doubted she had the energy left to make the trip herself. She'd just have to follow the cliff back until she came to an easy place to climb. *There has to be a place like that*, she told herself. *Has to be*.

She had to get away from the cliff face to walk; the snowdrifts were too deep close to the wall. Away from the bluff, the wind had blown the snow into a series of dunes. The ground between the dunes was almost bare. Kelly walked through these bare patches, stepping over isolated sage bushes and chunks of ice-crusted rock.

Every hundred steps she pushed through the drifts to the side of the cliff, looking for a place to get back to the top. *If I can just get back to the top*, she thought, *everything will be okay*.

Suddenly Kelly realized that when she got back to the top, Marshall would be waiting for her.

No, he won't. He's got to think he killed me. Even if he's still up there, I'll surprise him. I'll save Lauren, find a telephone, and go home.

When she finally found a place where the

steep side of the cliff was sliced by a narrow gully, she didn't hesitate for a second but stepped right in and started climbing.

The gully was easy for the first few yards, but it quickly got steeper. Kelly had to get down on her hands and knees to push herself up. In the dark it was hard to find places to plant her hands and feet, and her frozen limbs made her clumsy. But none of that mattered to her now, because her tired mind was focused on going home.

She couldn't see the top of the cliff as she started to climb, but it soon became apparent to her that she had turned the wrong way in her confusion after the fall. She hadn't been walking back toward the car, but away from it. And all the time she had been walking, the cliff had been growing higher.

Kelly labored for what seemed like hours, and by the time she realized her mistake, she was at least a hundred feet above ground. Kelly knew that if she was ever going to go home, she would have to keep climbing, no matter how many hundreds of feet of wind-swept rock waited over her head. All of it would have to be climbed.

SEVENTEEN

Kelly had never been cold before. She remembered playing in the snow when she was little, and her first ski trip when she hadn't known what to wear. Those had been times when she had thought she was cold. But those had been slight chills. They couldn't compare with the painful, lung-tightening coldness that held her now.

Kelly had never been tired before, either. She had never reached the point where every muscle in her body—from the tips of her skinned and bleeding fingers to the tips of her frozen and battered toes—twitched in uncontrollable spasms.

The climb had taken hours. Hours of being buffeted by winds and blasted by snow. Kelly knew it was hours and not days only because the sun had not come up. It was coming up now, coming up red and strong in a deep-blue sky.

Kelly stood on a ledge of icy stone that was barely as wide as her feet. Her left hand held a tiny nubbin of rock above her, while her right hand scrambled over the wall, trying to feel out a new grip. Her cheek was pressed against the cold rock, and she watched the sunrise while she climbed.

For the first time she could see the valley floor beneath her. Fingers of rock jabbed upward, and the drifts of snow looked like a dusting of powdered sugar. Terrifying as it was, it wasn't the distance below her that scared Kelly; it was the distance above. She was so tired that she knew if it was very far, she'd never make it. She looked up, and saw that her long struggle had left her only twenty feet from the top of the cliff. Twenty feet was just barely possible.

Moving slowly, Kelly pulled her feet up and onto an even-smaller ledge. She put her weight on it only gradually, and when she was sure it would hold, she lifted her left hand and searched for another, higher hold. Her fingers found a crack in the rock, and she moved her right hand up. Then she lifted her feet onto the spot where her hands had been a few minutes before, and the whole process started again.

The climb went much faster in the daylight.

Soon there were only ten feet of cliff above her, then five. There was a ledge there, a wide ledge on which Kelly could stand and put her hands over the cliff rim onto the blessed flat ground above her.

For most of the climb Kelly hadn't thought about what Marshall might be doing. She wouldn't let herself think that Lauren was dead. She thought about nothing but the climb. Now, with the end in sight, all the anxiety came rushing back. Kelly took a good grip and began to pull herself up.

A hand grabbed her wrist and dragged her up the cliff. Another hand took her by the hair and jerked her head back.

"Hello, little girl," Marshall said. "I didn't expect to see you again." He pulled her face close to his. Blood vessels had popped in his eye, and the blue centers were surrounded by a sea of scarlet.

Kelly tried to spit at him, but the climb had left her mouth too dry. "How did you find me?" she choked out.

He jerked his head toward the cliff face. "Saw you climbing up. Never thought you would make it, but you were sure fun to watch." He leaned forward quickly and kissed her with his split and swollen lips.

Kelly pulled away, but Marshall tightened his

grip on her hair. She didn't ask him to stop or to let her go. She knew it wasn't going to happen. She reached out her tired arms and clawed at his face.

She was just too exhausted. After the long climb she could barely reach up, and her fingers didn't have the strength to do any damage.

Marshall threw her to the snow-covered ground and put a boot over her throat. "You flew once, little Kelly. How about I push you off and we see how you fly this time?"

He started to laugh, but Kelly wasn't looking at him. She was looking at the unlikely figure that was coming up behind him.

Lauren was approaching at a run. Her skin was pale as milk, but she had a long pole in her good arm and she raised it as she came.

Marshall drew his foot back to deliver a kick that would send Kelly back over the cliff. "Good-bye again, little Kelly," he said.

The pole whistled as it cut through the air. It rang off the back of his head, and Marshall staggered forward. His raised boot passed over Kelly and he tumbled over the side of the cliff. He vanished without a sound.

Lauren collapsed into the snow at Kelly's side. "Are you okay?" she gasped.

"Am I okay?" Kelly said. She sat up and

looked at Lauren in wonder. "I thought you were dead!"

"So did I," Lauren said. "Marshall knocked me cold and left me back at the house. When I woke up, you were gone and he was in the house digging around in the kitchen." Lauren stopped and closed her eyes.

Kelly put her hand on her friend's shoulder. "You're not okay. Where did you spend the night?"

"In one of the sheds beside the house. There was a lot of stuff in there, blankets and this." She shook the pole.

For the first time Kelly noticed the ring near the base of the pole. "A ski pole?"

"Yeah," Lauren said. "And there's—"

A hand came over the edge of the cliff and landed an inch away from Kelly. She shouted and rolled away as Marshall's other hand reached over the edge.

Lauren stood up and raised the ski pole. She swayed on her feet, winced, and crumbled into the snow. The pole bounced out of her hand and over the cliff.

Kelly took a half step toward Lauren; then Marshall dragged his face over the rim. In another few seconds he would be back on top.

Kelly felt a coldness drop over her. It wasn't the physical coldness she had felt climbing the

209

cliff. It was a mental coldness. She stepped toward Marshall and looked down at his bloody face. She could see the ledge where she had paused near the top of her climb—it must have saved Marshall. She raised her foot.

"You don't want to do that, Kelly," he said. "You let me up, and I won't hurt either one of you. Promise." His voice was as calm as ever.

"Good-bye, Marshall," Kelly said. She smashed her ice-crusted shoe into his face.

For just a second he held on. Then his hands slipped in the snow and his feet slid from the ledge. Slowly, but with increasing speed, he fell away. He began to scream as he fell, the pitch going up and up. There was a distant thud, and the screaming stopped. Still wrapped in her mental coldness, Kelly turned away.

She knelt next to Lauren. "Lauren?" Lauren's eyes were closed and her forehead was creased in pain. "Lauren? Lauren!" She put her head close to Lauren's face and listened to her breathing. It was fast and shallow.

Kelly looked back down the ridge. The ranger house wasn't far away. Being careful to touch her injured side and arm as little as possible, Kelly got her hands under Lauren's arms and began to drag her across the snow. "Don't worry," she whispered. "You'll be all right."

Lauren's only response was a moan.

The door to the house was open. Kelly dragged Lauren right up the icy steps and into the book-strewn front room. She wanted to collapse herself—about two weeks of solid sleep sounded right—but after all this, she couldn't let Lauren die.

She walked through the kitchen. The dead woman was gone. Kelly didn't know what Marshall had done with the body, and she didn't want to know. She went into the bedroom and pulled the blankets from the bed. Then she went back to the living room and covered Lauren.

Lauren's skin was cool and clammy. She cried out as Kelly wrapped the blanket over her, and her legs thrashed feebly. Her eyes snapped open and she looked around. "Is he gone?"

"Yes," Kelly said. "Gone for good."

Lauren shook her head. "He always comes back," she said.

"Not this time," Kelly told her. But Lauren's eyes were closed again, and Kelly wasn't sure that she'd heard.

Kelly listened to Lauren's breathing again, relieved to hear that it now sounded normal, like she was asleep.

It shouldn't be long now. I only have to find the phone, and the police and an ambulance will be on their way, Kelly thought. She looked around the small room and didn't see a phone. Her aching legs protested, but she got to her feet and went to look in the kitchen.

There was no phone in the kitchen, either. And no phone in the bedroom. Kelly shuffled through the house twice more, even opening drawers and closets to look inside. There was no phone in the house. Marshall must have gotten rid of it.

Kelly sat on the edge of the overturned chair and looked down at Lauren. She knew it would take hours to walk the eight or so miles that remained to reach Wall. As tired as she was, Kelly was sure she couldn't make it.

Lauren moaned in her sleep. Kelly saw sweat gleaming on her friend's forehead. Her fever was back. Kelly bit her lip and wondered what to do.

It was amazing that Lauren had made it through the night after the beating she had taken. When she had run out to help Kelly, she couldn't have been running on anything but pure adrenaline. Kelly didn't believe that Lauren could last another night without medical attention.

But there was no way to get help in time, Kelly knew. There was no phone, no car, nothing. Deliriously Kelly tried to figure out how to get to Wall. *I would settle for a snowmobile*, she thought, *or a dogsled, or . . .*

Kelly suddenly remembered what Lauren had used to hit Marshall, and just where she had gotten it from. She jumped up from the chair. "Wait here!" she told Lauren. "I'll be right back."

Lauren slept on.

It was blindingly bright outside. The brisk northern wind had swept the clouds away, and the sun reflected back from the blanket of snow. It took Kelly only a few minutes to find which of the several sheds Lauren had used for shelter. The metal door opened with a creak, and Kelly stepped into the darkness inside.

As Lauren had said, there was a stack of blankets. Beside them were boxes that contained what looked like old clothes. Leaning against the wall was another ski pole—the mate to the one Lauren had used on Marshall. There was another set of poles, and beside them were two sets of cross-country skis.

Kelly took down the skis and looked at the bindings. The skis were bright yellow, with stripes of orange across the tips. She ran her hand over the slick fiberglass surface. She couldn't remember when she'd seen anything more beautiful.

She was glad to see that they were the kind that didn't require special boots. She took a pair of skis out into the brilliant sun, then went back to get a pair of poles.

The poles were a bit long for her, and there was no way to adjust them. Kelly would have to make do. It took her several tries to get the bindings clamped on her snow-encrusted sneakers. Once they were on, she bent over carefully and picked up the poles.

One push and she was sliding across the surface of the snow. The skis hadn't been waxed, and Kelly could feel them sticking to the snow, but they were good enough—far better than walking. She coasted to a stop and looked off down the road. The impossible trip to town should take only a couple of hours on skis.

Kelly looked back at the house where Lauren was sleeping. She hated to leave her friend without letting her know what she was up to, but she wasn't sure that she could wake Lauren up if she tried. Besides, every minute that she spent in the house was a minute she could have been on her way to get help.

Kelly planted the poles and shoved hard. The undulating snow passed under her skis with a comforting hissing sound. She worked at getting the rhythm, pushing out and back with her skis, shoving with the poles. Kelly hadn't done as much cross-country skiing as she had downhill, but the movements were familiar and it came back to her as she went on.

Soon she was gliding over the sunlit snow,

pushing and pumping, the wind whipping through her auburn hair. Kelly's arms and legs still ached from all she had put them through. For the moment, she was able to ignore the pain.

She was several miles down the road before she realized that Lauren had kept the promise she'd made at the very start of the trip. Despite everything else that had happened, Kelly was getting to ski.

EIGHTEEN

The skis were talking to Kelly. Over and over, with every gliding step, they said, "Sleep."

She tried to remember when she had slept last. She had been knocked unconscious in the car wreck. That had been . . . yesterday? The day before? Before that? . . .

Kelly couldn't remember before that.

Since then she had walked, and fought, and climbed a cliff. She had dragged Lauren though the snow. And she had skied. She was more than tired—she was exhausted. Even if it was only another hour to the town of Wall, Kelly no longer thought she would make it. She just didn't have another hour of effort in her.

Three times she had realized that she was standing still, just leaning on her poles. Each time it took her longer to remember what she was doing, longer to coax her aching muscles into moving.

Kelly saw something at the edge of her vision and turned her head. She gasped and twisted around, almost falling off her skis. There was nothing there, but she had been sure that Marshall was standing beside the road. She shook her head and skied on.

A minute later she saw him again, crouching among a pile of boulders. But when she looked straight at him, he disappeared. In his place was only a dark patch on the rocks.

It's not enough I have to die out here, she thought. *Do I have to go crazy first?*

There was another figure waiting for her in the road ahead. Kelly skied straight for it, determined to rid herself of these phantoms. In the glare of the sun and snow, it was hard to make out anything but a dark form. But this time it didn't go away.

As she drew closer, she saw that it was bigger than a man. Another few steps and she saw that it was a man on horseback—and he was coming her way.

She stopped and waited for the illusion to come to her. It moved at a trot, sending up a spray of snow, and stopped twenty feet away. The horse was large and reddish brown. It pawed the ground nervously, snorting twin jets of steam in the cold air.

Kelly squinted up at the dark figure on the horse's back. It was a man in a blue quilted jacket and heavy boots. His face was shaded by a wide-brimmed hat accented with red feathers. He took off the hat to reveal strong features and coal-black hair.

An Indian on horseback, thought Kelly. *At least my hallucinations are showing some imagination.*

The man on horseback looked down at her and frowned. "What are you doing with Mary's skis?" he said.

Black spots swam in Kelly's vision, and there was a roaring in her ears. Her legs went limp, and she pitched forward onto the ground. The snow felt surprisingly warm against her face.

The last thing she heard was the beat of the horse's hoofs coming closer.

There was a sharp metal smell in the air. Kelly reached out her hand, trying to find the pan. She had to turn off the stove before the ranger's house burned down.

She opened her eyes.

There was no pan, and no stove. She was in a room with beige walls and a television held on a high shelf. There were shiny metal rails along the side of her bed. Crisp white

219

sheets were stretched over her body and legs.

Kelly tried to sit up. Every inch of her body ached, and there was a dull pain in her feet. When she tried to move her arm, she saw that an IV line connected it to a bottle of clear fluid in a rack by her bed.

She knew she was in a hospital. She didn't have any idea where the hospital was, but just knowing it was a hospital was something. She eased down on the soft pillows and relaxed.

She might not be home, but it was over. They had made it through everything, and now she and Lauren . . .

Kelly sat up and looked around the room. She found a cable dangling near the bed that had a large red button. Kelly pressed the button, and kept pressing it until a nurse came through the door.

"Well," the nurse said, "I'm glad to see you awake."

"I had a friend with me," Kelly said. "She was back at the house in the park."

"Your friend's okay. She's just down the hall."

Kelly sighed in relief. "That's good. I was afraid nobody would find her."

"Well, according to John Grass, you told him about your friend over and over."

"I don't remember telling anyone. Who's John Grass? Wait, is he an Indian?"

The nurse sat down in the chair beside Kelly's bed. "John's from the Sioux tribal council. He was on his way to visit one of the park rangers and found you skiing down the road in the middle of the Badlands." She stopped and shook her head. "When he called for help, John said you were almost dead. He was right. We've all been very worried about you."

"But is Lauren okay?" Kelly asked.

The door opened again and a balding man in a white lab jacket came in. "I understand our little hero's awake!" he said heartily.

"Hero?" Kelly said.

"Didn't you fight off a killer and save your friend?" he asked.

"Well . . . sort of."

"That's enough to make you a hero in my book."

The nurse patted Kelly on the arm. "Dr. Rimbach's very hard to impress," she said. "But you've managed to impress just about everyone. According to your friend, you're a hero ten times over. Oh, that reminds me." She looked up at Dr. Rimbach. "Doctor, she was just asking about her friend."

"Lauren," Kelly said, "and she saved me just as many times as I saved her."

"Right, Lauren," the nurse said. "Well, I had better get on with my rounds." She gave Kelly a warm smile as she left the room.

Dr. Rimbach looked down at the clipboard in his hands. "Lauren has a compound fracture in her arm and two broken ribs. There was some internal bleeding, but she's been up and around for a day, and it looks like she's going to be fine."

"A day? How long have we been here?"

"Three days," said Dr. Rimbach.

"Three days!"

"You were a very sick young woman," he said. "Your friend was injured, but you were suffering from exposure, a concussion, and numerous small injuries." He gestured toward her feet. "You've lost some skin and a bit of your toes to frostbite."

Kelly lifted the sheet and tried to look at her feet. "How much of my toes?"

"Not much," Dr. Rimbach said. "They should heal just fine. But you're lucky we didn't have to take your feet. If you'd been out there just a few more hours, you'd have been in real trouble. And you're suffering from something else."

"What?"

Dr. Rimbach settled into the chair where the nurse had been sitting. "You've heard of people doing incredible things in emergencies—little old ladies picking up cars, mothers lifting metal girders off their kids?"

Kelly nodded.

"What you did was something like that," he said. "In taking care of yourself and your friend, you did things that you would never have been able to do normally. You've pushed your body far beyonds its limits."

"What does that mean?" she asked.

Dr. Rimbach stood. "It means you're probably going to be very weak for a few days, and you're going to discover aches in places you never knew you had. You've probably strained half the muscles in your body. We're going to want to keep you here for a while, just to make sure there aren't any other adverse effects."

"What about my family?"

"They're on their way," he said. "Your parents should be here sometime this afternoon. They would have been here sooner, but we weren't able to identify you positively until Lauren woke up."

"I guess our purses are still in the car," Kelly said.

"Last I heard, the police still hadn't found the car. Well, I'll be back to check on you shortly, but now I'd better get on with my rounds." He slammed his clipboard shut and headed for the door.

Kelly didn't want to ask the next question, but she had to know. "Have they found Marshall?"

Dr. Rimbach stopped. "No," he said quietly. "No, they haven't." He took a step back toward the bed. "But don't worry. There's a lot of ground out there, and Lauren wasn't able to tell them exactly where to look."

Kelly licked at her lips and tried to smile. "You're probably right. Can I talk to Lauren?"

"I don't see why not," he said. "But you stay here. I don't want you walking on those feet until they have more of a chance to heal. You got it?"

"Yes, Doctor."

"Fine. I'll send your friend right down." He gave her a nod and left the room.

Lauren came in a few minutes later. Her arm was supported by an enormous cast that made it stick out and forward. "Hi, Kel," she said. "I was starting to think you'd never wake up."

"So was I," Kelly said. She tried to sit up straighter. "How are you feeling?"

Lauren rolled her eyes and tapped the hard cast with her free hand. "The mummy strikes again," she said. She walked over to the chair next to Kelly's bed, tugging at the hospital gown as she sat. "You'd think they'd make these things a few inches longer."

"Gives the doctors a thrill," Kelly said. She smiled and discovered that even the muscles in her face were sore.

Lauren's eyes narrowed and she leaned close to the bed. "Kel, did you really get rid of Marshall? I figured he went over the cliff, but I wasn't sure."

"He's gone, Lauren. He took a fast trip a long, long way down."

Lauren nodded. "Remind me not to pick up any hitchhikers next time, okay?"

"I reminded you this time," Kelly said.

"Don't rub it in," Lauren said, but her eyes were bright, and for the first time in days Kelly thought that Lauren might actually laugh.

"Well, we won't have to worry about Marshall or anybody else."

"Why not?"

"Because," Kelly said, "as soon as our parents get here, they're going to kill us."

"You got that right," Lauren replied. "You should have heard my dad on the phone. He was ready to bite my head off from a thousand miles away."

"The phone!" Kelly would have slapped her forehead, but her arms seemed to weigh two tons each. "I didn't even ask to call home."

Lauren did laugh this time. "Don't worry. I think your whole family is going to be here in a couple of hours. My family's coming too. Even if you called home, there wouldn't be anybody there." She brushed her free hand across her dark hair. "You should hear everyone talking about us! I think every policeman in the country has been looking for us."

"Because of the killings?"

"Because of your note," Lauren said. "I didn't even know you left one, but somebody found the note you left back at that motel and called the FBI. There's been a big search on for us. The police must have just missed us a hundred times. They all seem kind of disappointed that we got away without them, and they all wanted to be the one that caught Evan."

"Who's Evan?" Kelly asked.

"That's Marshall's real name. Evan Bailey." Lauren shivered. "You wouldn't believe how many people he's supposed to have killed."

I'd believe it, Kelly thought.

"Anyway, there's supposed to be an FBI agent here to talk to us sometime today."

"Where is 'here,' anyway? I forgot to ask that, too."

"Rapid City, South Dakota. We're about thirty or forty miles from the park, I guess."

For a long moment they were both quiet; then they both started to talk at once.

"I want—"

"You—"

They stopped and laughed. "You first," Kelly said.

"What you did back there, everything you did." Lauren's voice was tight, and she had to stop to clear her throat. "I just wanted to thank you."

Kelly found the strength to lean out of the bed and hug Lauren. "You saved me," she said.

"Not like you did."

"We saved each other," Kelly said.

The door opened and the nurse leaned back in. "Sorry to break this up," she said, "but you're both going to be too tired to visit with your families if you don't get some rest."

"Okay," Lauren said. She pulled away and stood, tugging again at the thigh-length gown. "I'll see you in a little while."

"Sure," Kelly said. "And, Lauren?"

"Yeah?"

"If we take a trip next year, let's go to Florida."

Lauren's laughter echoed up the hall as she walked to her room.

Kelly leaned back and pulled the sheets up to her chin. It felt good to be clean and to sleep without having her arms tied. Even the hard hospital bed felt as soft as a feather bed. She closed her eyes and listened to the sounds of movement in the hallway.

"Hello, little girl."

Marshall leaned over her. His face was a

wreck that revealed bloody bones and the jagged stumps of teeth. His blue eyes shone out of dark sockets sunk into black, rotting flesh.

Kelly swung at him, and her hand struck the wall over her head. She blinked.

There was no Marshall. There was no one in the room at all. Everything was quiet except for the IV bottle swinging in its rack. And her heart pounding in her ears.

Kelly worked to control her breathing and slow her racing heart. *Marshall's gone. He's dead, and you never have to worry about him again.*

A few minutes later she got out of bed. Pulling the IV rack behind her and wincing at each step on her injured feet, Kelly pushed the chair across the room with her knees. She got it to the door and shoved it firmly under the doorknob. Then she limped back to bed.

If the nurses want in, they can knock.

Kelly climbed under the sheets and fell into a sound sleep.

Lions Tracks

The Outsiders by S. E. Hinton
£2.99
This is the chillingly realistic story of the Socs and the Greasers, rival teenage gangs, whose hatred for each other leads to the mindless violence of gang warfare.

Rumble Fish by S. E. Hinton
£2.99
Rusty-James has a reputation for toughness: he runs his own gang, and attends school only when he has nothing better to do. But his blind ambition to be just like his glamourous older brother, the Motor-cycle Boy, leads to an explosive and tragic climax.

That was Then, This is Now
by S. E. Hinton
£2.99
Caught in the violent and frustrating atmosphere of an American city slum, Mark and Bryon, who had always been like brothers, now find they are drifting apart. And then one day Bryon discovers the awful truth about Mark...

Taming the Star Runner by S. E. Hinton
£2.75
Travis's life in the country with his uncle after the bright lights of New York is pretty dull, but the choice is that or reform school. The only thing to liven it up is the girl with the horse called the Star Runner – and he's never thought much of girls.

Lions Tracks

After the First Death by Robert Cormier
£3.50

A busload of young children is hijacked by terrorists whose motive is to render useless one of the major secret service units. The general heading the unit is forced to employ his sixteen-year-old son Ben as a go-between, exposing him to appalling danger.

Eight Plus One by Robert Cormier
£3.50

These nine stories probe the feelings and reactions of people in life's most trying situations: a first love, leaving for college, a boy's discovery that his father is all too human. The stories are warm, touching and intensely personal.

Fade by Robert Cormier
£3.99

Paul inherits a strange gift: the power to become invisible. At first he thinks this is a thrilling trick, but when he finds out more, he gets scared. Is the fade a gift or a curse?

Tex by S. E. Hinton
£2.99

Life is fine for Tex until he comes home one day to find his horse has been sold to pay the mounting bills. From then on things get uglier – his father seems unconcerned about the trouble Tex is in at school, and his brother is determined to force matters to a head. For Tex, the truths revealed are devastating.

Lions Tracks

The Bumblebee Flies Anyway
by Robert Cormier
£3.50

Barney has volunteered for treatment in an experimental hospital. Then he comes across the Bumblebee – a glowing red MG, shiny and apparently perfect – and gradually evolves a crazy, daring plan to fulfil his companion's one remaining dream.

The Chocolate War by Robert Cormier
£2.99

Enthusiasm is weak in the school's annual fund-raising sale of chocolates, so Brother Leon, the organiser, turns to the Vigils, a secret society among the pupils, for help. They choose a new boy as their victim: the surest way to win the Chocolate War.

Beyond the Chocolate War
by Robert Cormier
£3.50

Although months have passed since the Chocolate War, the school still festers with the memory of it. The Vigils are more powerful than ever, but the cruelty of their leader, Archie, has made him many enemies, and now they are seeking their revenge.

Order Form

To order direct from the publishers, just make a list of the titles you want and fill in the form below:

Name ....

Address ....

....

....

Send to: Dept 6, HarperCollins Publishers Ltd, Westerhill Road, Bishopbriggs, Glasgow G64 2QT.

Please enclose a cheque or postal order to the value of the cover price, plus:

UK & BFPO: Add £1.00 for the first book, and 25p per copy for each addition book ordered.

Overseas and Eire: Add £2.95 service charge. Books will be sent by surface mail but quotes for airmail despatch will be given on request.

A 24-hour telephone ordering service is avail-able to Visa and Access card holders: 041-772 2281